BOOK THREE RAVEN

ODIN'S WOLVES

A NOVEL

GILES KRISTIAN

D1450259

BANTAM BOOKS
NEW YORK

A Bantam Books Mass Market Original

Copyright © 2011 by Giles Kristian

Published in the United States by Bantam Books, an imprint of The Random House Publishing Group, a division of Random House, Inc., New York.

BANTAM BOOKS and the rooster colophon are registered trademarks of Random House, Inc.

Originally published in hardcover in Great Britain in 2011 by Bantam Press, an imprint of Transworld Publishers.

ISBN 978-0-345-53509-2
eBook ISBN 978-0-345-53572-6

Front-cover images: Larry Rostant (top), Jae Song (bottom)
Cover design: Jae Song

Printed in the United States of America

www.bantamdell.com

Bantam Books mass market edition: October 2012

ÓDIN'S WOLVES *is for my sister, Jackie,
who has always been a golden thread
in the weave of my life.*

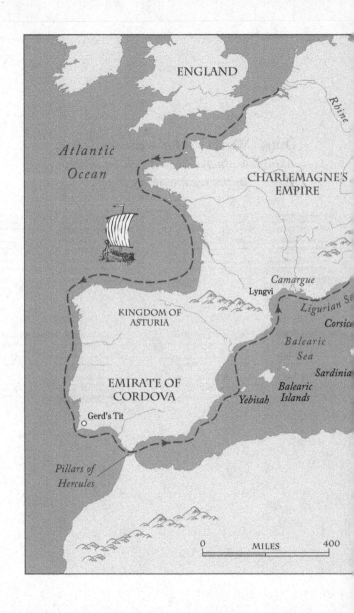

THE WOLFPACK'S VOYAGE TO MIKLAGARD

THE MEDITERRANEAN IN THE EARLY 9TH CENTURY

SLAVONIC
TRIBES

KINGDOM OF
THE AVARS

KINGDOM OF
THE BULGARIANS

VENETIAN
REPUBLIC

THE CROATIAN
PROVINCES

Pisa

Rome

Adriatic Sea

SERBIA

Constantinople
(Miklagard)

Sea of Marmara

Hellespont

Elaea

*Tyrrhenian
Sea*

BYZANTINE EMPIRE

*Aegean
Sea*

Ephesus

Sicily

*Ionian
Sea*

Crete

Mediterranean Sea

List of characters

NORSEMEN
Osric (Raven)
Sigurd the Lucky
Olaf (Uncle), shipmaster of *Serpent*
Knut, steersman of *Serpent*
Bragi the Egg, shipmaster of *Fjord-Elk*
Kjar, steersman of *Fjord-Elk*
Asgot, a godi
Svein the Red
Black Floki
Bjarni
Bram the Bear
Bothvar
Arnvid
Aslak
Gunnar
Halfdan
Halldor
Hastein
Hedin
Gap-Toothed Ingolf
Kalf
Kveldulf
Bag-Eyed Orm
Osk
Osten

Ulf
Yrsa Pig-Nose

WESSEXMEN
Penda
Baldred
Gytha
Ulfbert
Wiglaf
Cynethryth
Father Egfrith

DANES
Rolf
Agnar
Arngrim
Beiner
Boe
Bork
Byrnjolf
Egill Ketilsson (Burlufótr)
Geitir
Gorm
Kolfinn
Ogn
Ottar
Skap
Tufi
Yngvar

BLAUMEN
Amina
Völund

GREEKS
Nikephoros, Emperor of the Romans/Basileus
  Romaiôn
Staurakios, his son and coemperor
General Bardanes Tourkos
Arsaber
Karbeas
Theophilos

GODS
Ódin, the All-Father. God of warriors and war,
  wisdom and poetry
Frigg, wife of Ódin
Thór, slayer of giants and god of thunder. Son of Ódin
Baldr, the beautiful. Son of Ódin
Týr, Lord of Battle
Loki, the Mischiefmonger. Father of lies
Rán, Mother of the Waves
Njörd, Lord of the Sea and god of wind and flame
Frey, god of fertility, marriage, and growing things
Freyja, goddess of love and sex
Hel, goddess of the underworld and the place of the
  dead, specifically those who perish of sickness or
  old age
Völund, god of the forge and of experience
Eir, a healing goddess and handmaiden of Frigg
Heimdall, warden of the gods

MYTHOLOGY
Aesir, the Norse gods
Asgard, home of the gods
Valhöll, Odin's hall of the slain
Yggdrasil, the World-Tree, a holy place for the gods
Bifröst, the Rainbow-Bridge connecting the worlds
  of the gods and men

Ragnarök, doom of the gods

Valkyries, Choosers of the Slain

Norns, the three weavers who determine the fates of men

Fenrir, the mighty wolf

Jörmungand, the Midgard-Serpent

Hugin (Thought), one of the two ravens belonging to Ódin

Munin (Memory), one of the two ravens belonging to Ódin

Mjöllnir, the magic hammer of Thór

Fimbulvetr, "Terrible winter," heralding the beginning of Ragnarök

Fáfnir, "Embracer," a dragon that guards a great treasure hoard

Gleipnir, the magic fetter forged of a mountain's roots and birds' spittle, which restrained the wolf Fenrir

Garm, the greatest of dogs

Sköll, the wolf that pursues the sun

Gerd, a giantess

Svartálfar, dark elves that live underground in Svartálfheim

Gymir, a giant

Sæhrímnir, a boar that is cooked and consumed every night in Valhöll

Úlfhédnar, frenzied warriors who fight in animal skins

Máni, the personified moon and brother of Sól

Jötunheim, the realm of the giants

It is a dark thing now
To see empty benches at the oars
The southern sky stained red
With the hot blood of men.
The Valkyries came hunting
For heroes of the sword
Still they sing their battle song
Now just as then . . .

—*Raven's Saga*

RAVEN: ODIN'S WOLVES

pROLogUE

Y OU HAVE come again. Some new faces, too, by
my reckoning. Tramped through that thick pelt
of snow out there to hear more of an old man's memories. That's because none of you has ever done anything worth remembering. You live like the goats and
horses that even now tremble with fear by your
hearths while this ball-cracking blizzard frenzies out
there in the dark. Fimbulvetr has begun, mark me.
This is the first of three terrible winters that presage
the end of days and the gods' doom. Yet you have
soaked your shoes and left your warm furs. You are
tugging the ice lumps from your beards and rubbing
your hands like greedy Greek merchants, and here
you are in this drafty old hall. You have come for the
blood; do not deny it. You are here for the battles and
the death, because you think there is glory in such
tales. That is my fault, I suppose, because even though
I despise skalds and their lies, yet I still twist too
much golden thread into my stories and not enough
of the cold truth. A man rotting to death, stinking
and leaking rancid pus—that is the truth. Watching a
blood-slathered oarmate fumbling at his own gut
rope, trying to push it back into his belly—that is the
truth. Maybe I should talk more of those things so

that you might taste it for what it truly is. Less honey in the gruel.

Yet I still say this: if a jarl comes in the spring looking for men to pull his oars, you striplings and new-beards get yourselves down to the jetty. Puff up your chests and put a little brawn on those unscarred arms. Lads like you are not meant to carry slops to pigs and work the plow all day. That's a waste of good shoulders— rowing shoulders. You pack your sea chests! Kiss your mothers tenderly and tell your fathers you'll bring them back enough silver so that they no longer have to break their backs in shit with the thralls. Take the whale's road and see something of the world. Stand at the prow and feel the salt spray on your faces. I am telling you, it is the best feeling you will ever have.

Learn to fight, too. A man who fears other men because he does not know how to stand up for himself is a nithing. And the gods love courage. Not that they will spare you a horrible death if that is your wyrd. But I have lived long enough to learn something of men's fate. Wyrd is like a great heavy pile of logs stacked against a man's house. At the bottom of the pile you have the layers that were stacked and left to season years ago. These you cannot get to easily without trapping your fingers or bringing the whole lot down. Neither can you shift the whole pile at once from one place to another. If you have lived with no regard for the saga-tale you will leave behind, you will find your wyrd grown too big and heavy to move. You will likely die a straw death or fall from a cliff or see your flesh eaten by some foulness. But if you are a man who wants to leave a great blaze behind you when you cross the Rainbow-Bridge, you can, by great deeds or some act of courage, shift the newer layers and thus defy those bitches the Norns who love to spin men a poor end. Still, some men's destinies are entwined with others, and this sort of wyrd can be much too heavy, so that all you can do is fight hard, tooth and nail, whenever a bad death is stalking you.

I have moved my own log pile more times than I can recall. I have been unpicking the threads of my wyrd all my life and see no reason to stop now. That is why the well-worn hinges of my sea chest have been squeaking like a caught mouse recently, as well you all know. I have sent several of your sons and striplings out into the world, as well as five of my own thralls, who happen to be near to useless anyway and better kept out of my way for their own good. For I did not live so long and survive so many fights so that I could die in my sleep. I have too many friends and oarmates waiting for me in the All-Father's hall for that. Though I sometimes fear they will not recognize me after so long and with this white hair and frail body. For years I have kept burning the hope that some of my enemies still live. Gods, I made enough of them! *Surely there are some still out there to whom I owe a blood price.* I have so often whispered that into the dark. And your sons will earn good silver searching for them, even more if they spit my challenge into those whoresons' ears.

Now there are rumors in the village—shivering here and there like moths—that one or even more are coming. Hard men who know that my death will swell their reputation like a corpse's bloated belly. And I thank old One Eye for that, for it is He who pumps the bellows, fanning the fame-lust in men's chests.

"They are coming for Raven," men whisper into their mead horns, their eyes as shifting as the gray sea road.

Well, let them come.

chapter
ONE

WE WERE seventy-one warriors and as odd a crew as ever plowed the whale's road. Norse, Dane, and English—men who would normally face each other from behind the shieldwall—sat beside each other on sea chests, shared deck space beneath the stars, and pulled the spruce oars together so that they beat like eagles' wings, our bows slicing the sea. We even had a monk and a woman thrown in for good measure, though a monk aboard a longship is about as useful as a hole in a shield. Even so, Father Egfrith was a good man for all his fool's hope of sluicing the old gods from our black souls. As for the woman, she was Cynethryth, beautiful Cynethryth, and that was enough.

For seven weeks Jörmungand, *Serpent*'s dragon prow, had forged into the unknown, following the Frankish coast. Then, after a long passage south, we had sailed the Dark Sea west, along the margin of a barren, rockbound land from which jagged, treeless, boulder-strewn mountains surged into the sky. That desolate shoreline was cut with rocky beaches, most of which were trapped by steep cliffs that plunged into the white-tossed breakers, and we had rarely made landfall for fear of tearing open our hulls.

Now we were plowing south again. On our steerboard side the black water stretched away to the west
as far as the eye could see, and who knew what lay
that way? But we were staying as close to land as we
dared, for we had escaped the wrath of an empire
and were lucky to still have the skins on our backs
and the blood in our veins. Three other dragons followed in our wake: Sigurd's second ship, *Fjord-Elk*,
and the two remaining Dane ships, sleek fast snek-
kjas named *Wave-Steed* and *Sea-Arrow*. We had escaped the Franks, and so we had escaped death, but
in doing so we had lost our silver hoard, which had
glittered and shone so brightly that perhaps the gods
in Asgard had grown envious and decided to piss on
our glory. I have learned that that is the gods' way.
They are capricious and cruel, inspiriting you to
deeds worthy of a skald song and then knocking you
onto your arse for all to see. Perhaps they have no
love for us at all but merely watch the weave and weft
of our small lives—cutting or braiding a thread once
in a while—to help pass the great eternity of their
own. The gods may not love us, but they do love
chaos. And where there is chaos, there are warriors
and swords, spears and shields. There is blood and
pain and death.

And now we were sailing south to Miklagard, the
Great City, because although we had lost our Fáfnir's
hoard, we were warriors still and they said that in
Miklagard the buildings were made of gold. Besides
which, we lusted for an even greater prize. I could see
that hunger in men's eyes, reflected in the luster of
their well-polished war gear: helms, shield bosses,
and ax heads. That prize is fame. It is the meat of the

skald's song, which men and women feast on around the hearth while the wind batters the hall door. It is the one prize that can never be lost or stolen or burned.

And we would find fame in Miklagard.

"It's no way to go," Penda said with a slight shake of his head. The sail was up and bellying, taking advantage of a decent following wind, and most of us had thrown furs around our shoulders because that wind had fingers of ice in it and we were not rowing. "It must hurt like the Devil's own fire," the Wessexman muttered through a grimace.

"There's no hope, then?" I asked, knowing the answer but asking anyway.

"There might have been," Penda said, "if they'd opened it up again and washed the muck away in time. Now . . . ?" He shook his head again. "Poor bastard's got a few days, perhaps. Hard days, too."

Halldor was standing at *Serpent*'s prow, looking out rather than in, which I suspected was because he felt ashamed. A Frankish spear had sliced off half of his face, and although our godi, Asgot, had stitched it together, the wound rot had come, and now the Norseman's face was puffed up like a skin full of bad milk so that you couldn't even see his right eye. Reeking yellow pus oozed through the stitches, which seemed about to rip apart at any moment, and I could not imagine the pain of it. The previous day I had noticed a green tinge to the angry stretched skin. We all knew Halldor was a dead man.

"I wouldn't wait much longer if it was me," Penda said, drawing his knife from its sheath and testing the edge against his thumbnail. "There's always a length of rope and a rock," he suggested matter-of-factly, pointing his knife at *Serpent*'s ballast.

"And shiver in Hel until Ragnarök?" I shook my head. "No Norseman would choose drowning," I said, shivering at the thought. For a drowned man there is no Valhöll, just ice and the stiff black corpses of those who have died of old age or sickness. And there is a giant dog called Garm who will gnaw on your frozen bones to get to the marrow. "Black Floki will do it," I said. "When the time comes." A whining gust whipped cold spray across the deck and hit the sail's leeward side, making it snap angrily.

"Sooner rather than later, then," Penda gnarred, sheathing his blade with a satisfied nod. At sea you have to be careful not to oversharpen your blades for want of something to do.

"I think he's gathering memories to take with him," I said, taking a lungful of the cold sea air that was ever sweetened by the pitch-soaked twisted horsehair stuffed between *Serpent*'s strakes. "Wherever he is going, he'll want to remember what it felt like to ride the whale's road," I said, watching Halldor put a mead skin to the grimace that was his mouth to dull the pain.

"Have you finished your deep thinking yet, lad?" Bram the Bear growled, galumphing over to *Serpent*'s side, where he pulled down his breeks and began pissing over the sheer strake. "I want to know how you're going to pay me what you owe, you son of a goat. And I'm not the only one."

I sighed, knowing this was one matter that would keep coming back to me, like waves returning to the shore. For I had cast our silver adrift to tempt the

Franks, and they had chosen to scoop up that treasure rather than pursue us, which was just as well because they had outnumbered us five to one and we were as exhausted as a Norseman in a nunnery.

"It's you who owes me, Bear," I said, "for saving that hairy hide of yours. It would be nailed to some Frank's door if not for me."

"Pah!" He batted my words away like gnats. "It would take more than a few farting Franks to finish me, boy." Then he nodded toward Halldor and tugged his beard thoughtfully, his piss scattering downwind. "If he'd have kept his shield up . . . or his head down, he wouldn't be packing his sea chest for the dark journey." He shuddered, pulled up his breeks, and turned, pointing a thick finger at me. "No, you owe me, Raven, and I don't like being silver-light." I saw that Penda was grinning, meaning that he was beginning to piece together scraps of Norse, which would save me having to translate everything for him.

"What do you need silver for, Bear?" I asked. "You can't drink silver. And I can't see many taverns around here to spend it in." I scratched my chin and frowned. "I am wondering if you will even make it all the way to Miklagard, seeing as you are already older than the stars and the Great City is still far away." Some of the Norsemen chuckled at that, but Bram glowered at me like a man dragged from his death barrow.

"Wind in that tongue of yours, whelp," he rumbled, "or Bram'll trim it down to size for you." He patted the knife sheathed at his waist. "Older than the stars? You mouthy runt! Hey, Svein, can you hear this?"

"Raven has hit the rivet square, Bram," Svein said, studying his friend with a frown. "You *are* looking old these days."

"Son of a she troll!" Bram rumbled. "I'm going to shit in your beard when you're asleep tonight, Red," he threatened, at which Svein grinned. "As for you, runt," he warned me, "you'll be lucky to reach next summer if you don't learn to respect your betters." His beard bristled in the gathering wind. "Just remember the silver you owe us, Raven," he called out, stirring a few "aye"s and disgruntled murmurs, his eyes glinting. "No man likes to be silver-light." Even Svein nodded agreement with that.

And I sighed again.

But before long we were poking fun at Yrsa Pig-Nose for the great red boil that had bloomed on the side of his snout, and after Yrsa it was the Wessexman Baldred's turn to endure a good tongue-lashing because he had the shits and had grabbed the nearest bucket, which had happened to be one of our freshwater pails.

We were chaffing because we were nervous. Even I had been at sea long enough to smell a storm in the air, and this one was coming our way, its fingers already grasping at us. I had seen it first as swaths of dark rippling water contrasting against a lighter blue where current and wind fought over the direction in which the waves should move. Then the wind had whipped flecks of spume from those waves, and *Serpent*'s bowline had begun to swing and the reefing ropes began beating the sail. Now we were talking too much, trying to make out that it was nothing more than a sniff of a breeze that would sputter itself out before long, when the truth was we were afraid. I think the only man aboard who was not afraid was Halldor, because he was already a dead man, but then again, not even Halldor wanted a drowning death.

Ulfbert cursed when a gust swiped the bear-fur hat off his head, carrying it half a stone's throw away before ditching it among the wave furrows.

"What do you think, Uncle?" Sigurd called from the stern, where he stood beside Knut at the tiller. Olaf had ordered Osk and Hedin to check that our cargo was roped down securely, and now he and Bothvar were lowering the yard in preparation to reef the sail.

"I think that coast looks dangerous," Olaf replied, working the rope with practiced ease. "I think these waters have swallowed men and boats since before the All-Father could boast a beard. I also think my grandfather was right when he said it is always cleverer to reef too early than reef too late."

Sigurd nodded, eyeing the bruise-colored cloud that was swelling in the northeast and bearing down on us with unnatural haste. I fancied it was the Emperor Karolus's black rage coming to smite us. "Even so, Uncle, if we stay out here, Rán is going to have her fun with us."

"Aye, she's in a black mood," Olaf acknowledged, looking up at the rake as he lowered it a man's height from the masthead.

Sigurd spoke to Knut beside him, who, with his free hand, pulled his long beard through his fist and replied, frowning. Then Sigurd nodded, his mind made up. "We will make our way in and look for a mooring," he called, to which Olaf nodded unenthu-

siastically. Then Sigurd nodded to Osten, who took
the horn from his belt and blew three long deep notes:
the signal to the other ships that we were heading to
shore. I saw the men of *Fjord-Elk*, *Wave-Steed*, and
Sea-Arrow make their own preparations, some going
to the bows with fathom ropes and others peering
over the sides into the depths, looking out for rocks
or sandbanks. One of the Danes was even shimmying
up *Sea-Arrow*'s mast to get a better look at what was
below the waves, which was a brave thing to do in
that swell.

Knut worked the tiller, calling to Olaf, who barked at
those working the sail, and I was glad my life was in
their hands because there were few men with such sea-
craft. The steersman turned Jörmungand, our prow
beast, into an upsurging wave and we rode it well, but
I knew that swell was just a taste of what was coming
and I instinctively touched the Ódin amulet at my neck.
Old Asgot was ferreting around beneath the skins that
covered *Serpent*'s hold, and after a while he emerged
with a magnificent drinking horn, shaved and polished
to gleaming perfection and bound with silver bands. It
was a jarl's horn, and perhaps that was why Sigurd grimaced when the old godi dropped it over the side as an
offering to Njörd. But even Sigurd knew it was wise to
give the gods something precious, and he took a handful of silver coins from his own scrip and scattered
them into the billowing black water so that Rán,
Mother of the Waves, might be placated and not seek
to drown us all for the glittering things in our sea
chests.

Then it seemed we hit an invisible wall, for *Serpent*
lurched and skewed, her sail caught in a crosswind,

so that the sheet was ripped from Ulf and Arnvid's hands and the bottom of the sail flapped savagely and it seemed that the whole sail would collapse around the mast. But Olaf and Bothvar and some others were able to grip its thick edge, using themselves as weights to anchor it until sheet and block could be married again. Rain lashed into my face, which was a bad sign seeing as I was looking at the shore and it meant the wind had changed and was now against us.

"Christ on His cross, this isn't looking good!" Ulfbert said, wincing from the stinging deluge, looking at the shrouds, which were creaking under the strain of holding the mast steady. *Serpent* had been built to ride the punch of the sea rather than fight back against it, and she was as brave and worthy a craft as was ever hewn, but even she seemed to shudder as the waves slammed into her and the current swirled below her and the wind determined to screw into her sail and twist her mast from its keelson. "Where did this bastard come from?" Ulfbert asked, his eyes alert with fear. His friend Gytha was bailing with Father Egfrith, but it seemed to me that they were losing as more sheets of water slapped onto the deck.

"We'll get to shore before it can sink us," I said, though I had no such confidence. I could not even see the shore now because it had vanished behind a gray shroud and the rain was hammering into my eyes. Ulfbert kissed the wooden cross that he wore under his tunic, and I didn't mind seeing him do it, because I thought it could not hurt to have his god on our side in case mine was ale-addled and feasting in Asgard, unable to hear our petitions and the plaintive creaks of *Serpent*'s timbers. He stumbled over to join me, gripping the sheer strake, then offered the cross to me on its leather thong, a grim smile touching his lips.

"One kiss won't hurt a brave young heathen like you," he suggested, water sliding down the thick twists of his sodden hair.

"Get that thing out of my face before I throw it overboard and you with it," I said, and Ulfbert grinned, tucking the cross back into his tunic. I thought it said much about Sigurd that he had taken this handful of Christians into his Fellowship. They were good men despite their love for the nailed god, and I was glad we had not killed them.

"Hey! To your oars!" Sigurd bellowed against the wind's roar, the waves' crash, and the sail's snap. "*Serpent* has asked for our help and we owe her, so get to your benches and work! Three reefs, Uncle!"

The yard slid down the mast bit by bit as smoothly as Olaf and his men could manage, and others reefed the sail as it came, and all of us kept our feet as best we could now that *Serpent* belonged to the storm. But it felt good to get my oar into that black sea. What was a slender spruce oar against that enormous fury? And yet with those blades in the water we were stating our challenge, bellowing our refusal to yield, and that is what the gods love: when mortal men bloom with the arrogance of believing themselves a match for giants.

"Row!" Sigurd yelled, his drenched golden hair swept back from his scarred forehead. "Row, you wolves!" He was standing on the raised fighting platform at *Serpent*'s stern, facing the fury of the driving rain and the waves that kept thumping into my back as I bent to the oar. The jarl could do nothing for his other ships now—they were on their own—but he *could* help *Serpent,* and so he stood where we all could see him and roared defiantly as though we were going into battle.

So we rowed. And *Serpent* turned so that her prow was skewed against the wind, which meant that the swells were hitting us side on, rocking the ship violently, and only a finger's length of freeboard kept the Dark Sea from swamping us. By now Olaf had reefed the sail three times, reducing its area drastically; what was left he could control, though we could not sail any closer to the wind.

"Good to see her up and about," Penda said from the bench behind me, and I saw Cynethryth bailing with the others, her clothes, once fine but now tatty and torn, clinging soppingly to her frail-looking body. For weeks I had barely laid eyes on her, for she had been recovering in a makeshift tent at *Serpent*'s stern from the harm done her in the Frankish convent from which we had rescued her. Before, back in Wessex, she had warned us of her father's betrayal, and that had saved men's lives, and now she was as much a part of the Fellowship as anyone. Besides which, men thought she was my woman. I had thought so too for a time. Now I knew I had been a fool. Perhaps Cynethryth had loved me once or at least been fond enough. But perhaps she had bewitched me so that I would do her bidding, which I had done by saving her father. Though Ealdred was dead now, and by Cynethryth's hand too, and that might have been too much for her to take. Or maybe the nuns in Frankia, who had thought the girl possessed by Satan, had cracked Cynethryth's mind with their cruelty, for they had beaten and starved her half to death. Whatever the truth, Cynethryth had not come near me for weeks.

"She hates me, Penda," I said gloomily, pulling the oar and watching Cynethryth through stinging eyes. She was on her knees in the frothing water, gripping the sheer as *Serpent* rolled. Olaf, Bothvar, Ulfbert, and Wiglaf were still fighting with the reefed sail, which was soaking wet and heavy, and I knew that the ropes would be tearing the skin from the Wessexmen's fingers, for they were unused to the work.

"She was always too good for you, lad," Penda said. "But my guess is her hate isn't sitting square on you. The girl's been through rougher seas than this. She needs time." *Serpent* skewed again and surfed down an enormous wave, and I turned to see that her steering oar was completely clear of the water; then we cut up the face of another wave, and I heard Bjarni howl with the terrified joy of it. "And we need a wave to wash that old bastard overboard," Penda added, and I knew he was talking about Asgot, who was helping Cynethryth to her feet, his lank, bone-plaited hair stuck to his wolfish face. Somehow the old godi had sunk his claws into Cynethryth, which was the strangest thing because she was a Christian, or at least she had been.

"Land!" someone yelled, and whoever it was had better eyes than I, for when I turned, I could see nothing but murk. But my job was to row until Sigurd or Olaf told me to stop, and so I rowed and *Serpent* proved herself against that storm, so that we came to a narrow estuary, one of many inlets that looked to grow increasingly shallow from the breaking plunge of its mouth toward its head among the rocky hills.

"Steady now!" Olaf called from the stern. The yard was lying lengthways along the deck now that we needed the control that only oars can give, and Olaf and Asgot were on either side of Jörmungand with fathom ropes, clinging to the sheer strake and continually testing the depth as we neared the shore; that was no easy thing in an angry sea. Even above the wind's wailing and the men's shouts I could hear the furious suck and plunge of the breakers among the rocks, and that is a cold-terror sound when you are in a boat. Somewhere above, gulls were crying. I caught the tang of slick green weed. So close now. I half expected to hear the splintering of wood at any moment, but I bent my back and pulled the oar, and then Sigurd roared, "Whoa! Oars up!" and I pushed down on the stave to lift the blade clear of the water, and suddenly the tumult died.

We looked out, puffing and blowing snot, our breath clouding in the pelting rain and our knuckles white with cold. Rock rose from the frothing water on either side of us and we winced as *Serpent*'s hull scraped against a shelf, but then she was free and we were out of the storm's reach. I heard the calls of *Fjord-Elk*'s crew, and it was not long before her proud prow pushed into that sanctuary, her captain, Bragi the Egg, bent over the sheer strake, his bald head almost touching the water as he worked the fathom rope.

We had tied bow and stern to the rocks, dropped our anchor, and slaked our salty thirst by the time *Wave-Steed* and *Sea-Arrow* nosed into the channel. The Danes looked as though they had been chased out of Hel, cold fear etched in white faces. We cheered them, and when they heard us, they grinned their salt-crusted beards off for they knew they had done well to come through that in their small boats.

"They're good seamen," Aslak said grudgingly.

"Or lucky," Orm suggested.

"Or both," Olaf said, "which is the best recipe, if you ask me."

Black Floki spit over the sheer strake. "Are they good fighters? That is what we need to know. Before we stand shield to shield with them." That was greeted with murmurs of agreement, for it is not a good thing if in a fight you do not know whether the man beside you has a twist of steel in his spine.

We rowed deeper into that fjordlike ria, the rock walls reaching into the gray sky, their inaccessible heights crowned with dark forest, and the Norsemen looked up appreciatively because they said we had at last found a place that could be compared with Norway. We passed countless other branching estuaries that looked dangerously shallow until our channel became so narrow that when all four ships were berthed hull against hull, prows facing the sea, there was little water on either side. But the currents were weaker here, and the rocks sheltered us from the wind. We bailed the ships well so that we would know if they had sprung any new leaks, and when we were satisfied, we hunkered under wool blankets and greased skins to escape the rain.

The last to seek cover, Sigurd walked among us, slapping men's shoulders and laughing and saying he was proud to sail with such a motley crew as us, his voice loud within those rock walls. And we found our bluster again now that we were safe, boasting that it had been barely a storm at all.

"I have felt stronger winds blow from Svein's backside," Bram the Bear announced, raising a horn to Bjarni, who grinned and raised his in return.

"And I have seen higher waves in my ale cup," redfaced Hastein said, tugging a comb through his stiff yellow hair, and this stirred a few "hey"s.

Men were set to their watch while others gave themselves to sleep. And beyond that safe harbor the storm raged.

chapter
TWO

A T LAST the rain spent itself, but in its place came a thick fog that shrouded that bay and tumbled slowly from the great rock walls like unspun wool. Cold shadow clung to the ria because the sun had yet to surmount the high mountainous land to the east, and we puffed into cupped hands and beat our arms, and the warm breath of four crews rose, adding to the haze.

"Who wants to go for a sniff around, then, lads?" Olaf called as men slurped steaming oats from spoons and bowls. The water was so calm in that bay that we had hung cauldrons above the ballast and made a thin gruel with the rainwater we had collected the previous day.

Black Floki nodded, but no one else seemed excited by the prospect of clambering up the jagged rocks to better understand this coast.

"There'll be nothing worth taking around here, Uncle," Svein the Red said, giving a great belch and eyeing the wild, rugged cliffs around us. Men were moving from ship to ship, talking to friends and enjoying getting a feel for the other dragons.

"You think we're the first crews to run in here with our tails between our legs, Red?" Olaf said, putting on his helmet and tying the chin strap. "That's a mean old sea out there. I'll wager she's been ill tempered longer than Bram's Borghild."

"Aye, I'd rather cross the Dark Sea a hundred times than cross Borghild," Bram muttered into his beard.

"And some of those who sheltered in here might not have been as lazy as you whoresons," Olaf went on, "and they might have had the fire in their bellies to have a look around. And some of them might have decided to stay." He bent to pick up his spear. "Frigg's tits! For all we know, there might be a village full of whores the other side of that rock, all sitting there growing cobwebs for the want of customers."

Some of the men picked up helmets and spears. Black Floki rolled his eyes.

"You coming, Sigurd?" Olaf asked. The jarl was braiding his beard into a thick rope, which he tied with a leather thong clasped with a silver wolf's head.

"It will be good to work the knots out of my legs, Uncle," Sigurd said through a half smile. "Today I feel as old as you look."

I did not hear Olaf's answer to that because it was drowned by a great splash off *Serpent*'s bow.

"Njörd, what was that?" Bram rumbled. We had turned to the sound, but there was nothing to see.

"A sea monster?" Svein the Red offered as we went to the bow and looked out. The other crews did the same. Then a man yelled in pain, and suddenly arrows were thudding into the deck and splashing into the water around us. Another crash, and this time a gout of water soaked some of the men on *Fjord-Elk*. An arrow thwacked into Jörmungand's head behind the prow beast's faded red eyes.

"They must be angry whores," Bram growled to Olaf, bending to fetch his helmet.

"Shields!" Sigurd yelled, staring up at the jagged heights, searching for this invisible enemy. I saw the next rock in flight and followed its descent until it struck the water with a mighty *ka-splosh*.

"One of those bastards will go right through the hull!" Penda said, wide-eyed.

Looking up was not a good idea—never is when arrows are flying—but look up we did from behind our shields, and I could see men up on the ridge. Lots of men.

"They're on this side, too!" a man yelled from the port side. Arrows were clattering across all four ships, and men were roaring in anger and pain. Fearing for Cynethryth, I pushed my way through to the stern and found her sheltering under Kalf's shield. The Norseman nodded to me and stepped aside as I raised my shield above her.

"We need to find you a helmet, Cynethryth," I said, wincing because an arrow had thunked into the deck a finger's length from my right foot. Cynethryth laughed, which was a strange thing to do in those circumstances. I took off my helmet and put it on her head. It all but covered her eyes. "Do up the strap," I said. She laughed again, and it was a cold sound. Most of my shield was above her, meaning that most of me was uncovered, and I was not wearing my brynja. Would she still laugh if an arrow went through my neck? "I'll get you your own helmet," I said, "one that fits."

"I cannot be killed, Raven," she said lightly. Gods, she was beautiful. In spite of the ice that sheathed her these days.

"Even the gods can be killed," I muttered, watching the crews scramble for their war gear, many of them clambering from ship to ship.

"Are those whoresons going to come and fight us?" Bram bellowed. "Or are they just happy to drop things on us from the sky?" I would have preferred the first one, I thought.

"Asgot has taught me a charm," Cynethryth said conspiratorially, like a child sharing a secret. And those words made me feel sick. Cynethryth was unwell, and the godi had sunk his claws into her. He had murdered my foster father Ealhstan, and now he was taking Cynethryth from me. "Why do you think he has survived so long?" she said, seemingly unaware of the chaos around us. I knew then that if I walked away, taking my shield with me, Cynethryth would just stand where she was with that strange smile on her lips.

"I thought you were a Christian," I gnarred. An arrow tonked off my shield's boss and rolled across the wood, falling harmlessly to the deck.

Cynethryth spit then, her eyes filling with malice, and I was tempted to walk out into the arrow storm.

"You were not born to think, Raven," she said. "You are a killer. So go and kill."

A boulder crashed into the oars lying across *Fjord-Elk*'s oar trees, snapping several before shearing a splintered chunk off the mast step.

"I think I'll stay here if it's all the same to you," I said.

"Get the anchor up!" Sigurd roared. "We can't fight men who won't face us." Black Floki and Aslak were keeping close to the jarl, protecting him with their shields as he strode the deck giving orders. The only thing to our advantage was the sea fog that slowly snaked in damp billows through that gorge and must have partly veiled us.

"Come and fight us, cowards!" Svein bawled, his voice booming up the rock walls. He stood looking up at the cliff top, his arms outstretched invitingly. "What kind of men are you? Come and fight us, goat turds!" An arrow thudded into the bearskin on his shoulder. He grunted, pulled the shaft out, spit on its bloody head, and tossed it overboard. "My sister has bigger balls than you!" he rumbled like a rockfall.

"Can you hold the shield?" I asked Cynethryth. Men were taking to their benches, and I was torn. Cynethryth was staring at Father Egfrith, who stood by the mast, wearing nothing more for proof against boulders and arrows than his woolen habit, raising his wooden cross to the cliff tops as though the sight of it would turn our enemy to dust.

"He's a brave little bastard, isn't he?" Penda said, gesturing toward the monk from behind his shield.

"He's a bloody fool," I spit. "Can you hold it?" I asked Cynethryth, and this time she nodded vaguely and slid down against a rib, the shield raised above her head. And so I left her there, took my oar from the trees, and went to my bench. Penda came with me because Sigurd had ordered that half should row and half should shield themselves and the oarsmen. Though Halldor did neither. He stood by Jörmungand wearing no helmet and not carrying a shield. He stood there looking up, his jaw clenched in his hideous swollen, pus-filled face and his sword in a white-knuckle grip. Floki's cousin was hoping for a violent death, to be crushed by a rock or pierced by an arrow. That way, with his sword in his hand, he would be taken into Valhöll as a stout warrior rather than slowly rotting from an old wound. But for all that he made a sorry sight standing there waiting for death. It would still be a bad end for such a man.

The other dragons bristled with men as crews made ready to get under way, and all the time arrows and rocks and even pebbles rained down on us from the cliffs and we cursed the underhanded sons of trolls who would not fight like men.

I looked across at *Wave-Steed* and saw a Dane struck on the helmet by a rock. He stood staring for three heartbeats; then blood streamed down his face, and he pitched forward.

"This is not going into any skald's song," Bjarni called from his bench as we pulled away, our anchor ropes coiled untidily and clothes, weapons, and bowls of half-eaten food scattered around. "Remind me not to remember this day."

I looked across at Svein, who was now at his bench. He was a scowling mountain of thunder. I could just imagine Black Floki's face, too. But what could we do? If we stayed in that bay, we eventually would see our dragons sunk, but neither was there anything to gain by clambering up those steep rocks, cumbered with shields and swords, into the unknown. Sigurd knew that there was no glory to be won in that ria, and so we fled, just as we had fled from the Franks along that snaking river. But this time men must have felt knots of ice in their guts because we were rowing, where it was wide enough, back to the open sea that had mauled us and that might still be raging beyond the estuary.

For a while our craven enemies scrambled along the cliff tops, loosing arrows with fair skill as they moved. They even had the nerve to jeer us as though we were the cowards and not they, which was a hard thing to endure. Then, after some hard pulling by too few oarsmen, we were in deeper water beyond their reach and nearing the mouth. Which still seethed.

"At least the tide is with us, hey!" Bjarni called. I grimaced at my oar. The way things had gone for us, I suspected the gods were playing with us like a cat with a mouse, and we all know how that ends.

"Thór's balls, this is an ill thing," Bag-Eyed Orm said, not sharing Bjarni's optimism. He had been holding his shield over Arnvid at the oar, but now he had moved to *Serpent*'s side and was looking beyond her bow.

"From the pot to the fire," Halfdan agreed, laying his Thór's hammer pendant on the outside of his tunic so that the Thunderer would see it and know to watch over him.

We led now, with the other dragons following in our wake, and Olaf and Sigurd oversaw the reefing and raising of the sail, having been able to rob benches of oarsmen because the ebb tide was pulling us inexorably out to sea. Three reefs left only a small sail, which would make *Serpent* easier to handle in a storm, but there was still every chance that a mighty gust would lean into that sail and capsize us or a wave would wrench the steerboard from its block and leave us helpless, subject to Njörd's will. I could hear those waves now—Rán's white-haired daughters hurling themselves against the coast, smashing in spumy gouts. Then the estuary vomited us out into the maelstrom, and *Serpent*'s bow rose into the breakers and waves buffeted her hull, flinging themselves over the sheer strake to soak us again and sting our eyes and freeze our hands on the staves. Some of those waves were three times the height of a man, and *Serpent* moaned because we had returned her to that violence. Spent arrows, cups, and bowls sloshed around our feet as we grimly pulled the oars, trusting in Olaf's sail-craft and Knut's skill as a helmsman. All that the rest of us could give was muscle against the storm and muttered pleas to our gods to spare us from a bad end.

We rowed out into the open-water swells, and when Sigurd was satisfied that we were far enough away from the coastal rocks, he gave the order to stow oars. Now that we were past the headland on our steerboard side, a fierce northerly hammered across the sail, and Olaf caught that blast and harnessed it so that we rode the waves rather than plowing through them. It was a dangerous game to play, but it was also a thrilling one because *Serpent* flew and her rigging thrummed and her belly trembled with the madness of it.

Aboard *Fjord-Elk*, Bragi followed his jarl's lead; the Danes did likewise, and in this way all four dragons ran south before the wind. We worked the sail in shifts, forever tightening the stays and reefing or lengthening the sail according to Olaf and Sigurd's reckoning of the risks, and above us the gray cloud swirled in eerie likeness of the wind-tossed sea. We surfed past fog-shrouded green cliffs and inlets and lonely sharp rocks that seemed to burst up through the white breakwaters, and the rain lashed into us so

that men looked half drowned despite their best ef-
forts with greased skins and hats. That northerly
wind wanted to hurl us against the coast. It wailed
and whined, but Knut fought it, hauling on the tiller
so that *Serpent*'s steerboard drove against the Dark
Sea to hold our course. There was no sun to be seen,
just the faintest blush in the east behind the black
clouds and above the fog-veiled land.

"I will miss this, Sigurd!" Halldor yelled. He stood
on the foreship, gripping the bowline, square on to
the bow breakers and freezing spray, his dark yellow
hair daubed against his head and face. "This is what
we dream of, hey!"

"Men will talk of Halldor who laughs at storms!"
Sigurd yelled back, smiling. "We will carve it on your
runestone." A grin twisted Halldor's grotesquely
bloated face; the pain of it must have been terrible,
but the warrior clearly felt warm pride swell in his
heart at his jarl's words despite the icy spray, because
not every man could expect a runestone to be raised
in his honor. Halldor glanced at Bjarni, who nodded
as though assuring him that he would do a good job
of carving Halldor's rune story. Then Halldor turned
back into the spray, his head held high in challenge to
the leaden sky.

Later that day we came to a wide, flat wind-scoured
beach. It was exposed to the storm, a forsaken strand
above which gulls swirled like leaves in the wind, but
there were no rock walls from whose summits men
could drop boulders or rain arrows on us. Knowing it
was low tide and fearing we might not come across
another such place before nightfall, we turned our
prows landward, hoping that that sandy beach ex-

tended beyond the breakers. The wind filling our reefed sails, we rode the dragons right in, their keels slicing through the soft seabed and up into the green-brown cloak of weed that lay beyond the waterline. Then, the gusts howling in our ears and drowning our voices, we sank mooring posts deep into the sand and lashed the ships securely. We cowered onboard, for that stretch of coast was desolate and there was more shelter to be found in our ships than ashore, which was not saying a lot and was probably why there were no folk there to attack us or from whom we might steal.

Serpent rocked in the wind as though she were still at sea, the gusts keening through her oar ports as men tried to sleep. I lay in furs and skins, watching the pale moon slip in and out of the swollen black clouds, when movement at the foreship drew me from a mire of thoughts of which Cynethryth was the center. By the moon's pallid light I saw Olaf and Halldor each gripping the other's arm. Halldor's cousin Black Floki was there, too, as were Svein the Red and Bram Bear.

"It's time," a low voice said, and a hand gripped my shoulder. Sigurd's face was all shadow but for his eyes, which glinted. "Find me something shiny, Raven. Something for a warrior." His teeth glinted, but it was no smile. "Seeing as you are awake, you may as well join us."

"Yes, my lord," I said gruff-voiced as he moved off. I climbed out of my nest and with a shiver picked my way past the shrouded bodies of men so still that they could have been corpses, huffing into cold hands as I knelt by the hold. "Something for a warrior," I murmured to myself, lifting off the loose planks and skins that protected the cargo in *Serpent*'s belly; then I raised the lid of an oak chest to reveal its dully gleaming treasures to that ill night. There were brooches and silver cloak pins and coins and hacksilver. There were torcs, rings, and silver chains, and I tried to burrow quietly down to the bottom of that chest so that nothing would escape me in the darkness. Then my hand closed around something warm among those cold prizes, something smooth. Bringing it into the weak light, I saw a figure of a warrior carved from cream-colored bone, thumb-worn and of little worth compared with the other things in that chest. Yet it was a thing of power all the same, for it was a fine carving of Týr, Lord of Battle, one hand gripping the sword hilt at his waist, the other arm ending handless, having been mauled by Fenrir Wolf. His helmet's nose guard ended in a point between small eyes that were battle-wide because Týr is the god of victory. The figure was the size of my closed fist and would stand on a flat surface on boots that the carver had given the appearance of being made of fur.

"Throwing our hoard over the side one day and robbing us the next, hey," Osten growled, one eye gleaming from a swath of shadow between *Serpent*'s ribs.

"Go back to your dreams of wanton sheep, Osten," I said, to which he grinned, and clutching the carving, I made my way cautiously between snoring men to the foreship, then over the sheer strake and down the gangplank onto the wind-whipped sand. An arrow shot downwind, just beyond the reach of the white-flecked waves, a flame quivered violently against the night. I headed toward it, feeling my bones tremble with a sense of some dark seidr, and though I did not know why those men had left warm skins to gather on that wild shore, I was not surprised to see old Asgot there. I had not thought to see Cynethryth, though, and for some reason the sight of her froze my guts.

They turned at my approach, some nodding at my joining that strange party, and Halldor watched me from the corner of his left eye, which was just visible behind the grotesque, oozing swelling. You could not see his right eye at all. He looked like some troll horror from a child's nightmare, yet he half grinned at me before turning back to Asgot, who was talking to him in a low voice. Halldor was dressed for battle, his brynja polished to a gleam and his blades sheathed and belted. He wore no helmet, and I suspected that was because it would no longer fit on his misshapen head, but other than that he looked ready to take on the Midgard-Serpent. Then I noticed Black Floki cloaked in Halldor's shadow, his sword drawn and his face clenched in a grim frown, and I suddenly understood what Sigurd had meant when he said it was time.

"Raven, here, lad," Sigurd said, and so I stepped up, the wind whistling across the dark beach, lashing sand against my cheeks. I turned to spit out a wad of salty grit, then held out the bone Týr carving to my jarl. Sigurd took it and turned it over in his hand, *hmm*ing in the back of his throat. "I have seen shinier turds, Raven," he said disapprovingly.

"That the best you could find?" Olaf gnarred behind his hand. I shrugged, suddenly wishing I had brought a torc or a silver arm ring or at the least some hacksilver.

"It will have to do," Sigurd said, creasing his brow.

Then he nodded to Floki, who took a step forward, his sword raised slightly as though that honed, hungry blade could scent blood.

"No straw death for us, Cousin," Halldor said, a nervous edge to his voice. His face twisted with a sour smile. Svein and Bram shared a bleak look, their loose wild hair and beards tousling from the gusts, and Asgot stepped back from Halldor, nodding solemnly at Sigurd. *It will happen now,* I thought, glancing at Cynethryth. But she was staring at Halldor as though the man were already a haugbui buried in his death mound, and she was mumbling words that I could not hear.

"Wait for me in Valhöll, Cousin," Black Floki said, his eyes stony and his jaw clenched tight. "I will come soon enough." A blast of cold breath whined up the beach from the foam-flecked sea. I resisted the urge to pull my cloak tight at my throat.

"You better not drink all the good mead before I get there, you greedy whoreson," Bram warned, pointing a finger at Halldor. "And I'll want a swan-breasted wench or two to warm my bed, too," he added, "so you make sure old Bram is not left wanting when he crosses Bifröst and comes knocking."

Halldor nodded in Bram's direction, but his eyes were on Black Floki, who gestured at him to draw his sword, which he did, the blade rasping up the scabbard's throat.

"I have something for you, Halldor son of Oleg, something to take on your journey," Sigurd said, stepping forward with the Týr carving. "It is not silver," he added almost apologetically, "but maybe you can show it to the Aesir to test its likeness." He pursed his lips. "It is skilled work, I'm thinking." Sigurd held the figure up to the ashen moonlight for all to see, and far from seeming disappointed, Halldor appeared moved. The significance of his jarl giving him a carving of Týr, the bravest of all the gods, was not lost on him there under the cold shadow of Black Floki's sword.

Sigurd stepped forward and handed the thing to Halldor, and it seemed the two warriors would embrace. But there was a flash of steel and a low grunt from Halldor as Sigurd pulled the man in to him, and Halldor's one visible eye bulged horribly. Black Floki flew forward, but Olaf stopped him with an arm and a glower as Sigurd closed his hand around Halldor's so that the man could not drop his sword. Sigurd whispered something to Halldor then, and I swear that a smile skimmed over the dying man's lips like a flat stone across water. He gave a long gasping sigh, and his head lolled onto Sigurd's shoulder, and his knees buckled though his jarl held him up until the last whisper of life had flown from his corpse. And then it was over and the rest of us were left standing there, and I do not mind admitting that there was a lump in my throat the size of a hen's egg.

Slowly, Sigurd lowered the warrior's still body to the swirling sand, and we turned to Floki, who had shrugged free of Olaf and was glaring at Sigurd.

"That was for me to do, Sigurd!" he spit. "He was my kinsman. He expected me to do it." His sword was still raised, and for a moment I sensed it still hungered for carnage.

"I am his jarl, Floki," Sigurd replied, a snarl curling his lips. "He was oath-tied to me." Sigurd held up the blade he had sunk into Halldor's heart. Its bone handle, like the jarl's hand, was slick with blood, and I could see fog rising from it, vanishing into the night. "This was my right. Halldor had faced his own death for long enough and as straight-backed as any man could hope to. He did not need to stand there all night, eyeballing the sword that would bite his flesh. It is over." Sigurd looked to the rest of us. "We will meet Halldor at the high end of the All-Father's hall, each in our own time." He glanced down at the body, at the puffed-up dead face of one of his Fellowship. "It is over," he repeated tiredly, the words granite-heavy.

Floki loosened the cords in his neck and nodded shallowly, sheathing his sword. Then he went over to his cousin's lifeless body. Svein offered to help him carry it, but Floki would not take any help, lifting Halldor alone and hauling him over his shoulder before taking him off to prepare the corpse for the pyre.

"Back to your beds, ladies," Olaf said, hawking and spitting as an end to the whole rancid thing. "We'll be rowing tomorrow if Njörd keeps farting in this direction."

"And while we're rowing, that whoreson Halldor will already be rinsing his beard with Ódin's sweetest mead," Bram moaned to Svein, who conceded that to be a fair point as they started back up the beach behind Asgot, Olaf, and Cynethryth. Sigurd came over to me, his eyes gleaming dully in the half-light.

"Next time I ask you to find something shiny, bring me an arm ring or a handful of silver," he said, "not an old lump of bone."

"Yes, lord," I said, scratching my beard, but Sigurd was already walking down to the frothing sea to wash away the blood.

chapter
Three

AT DAWN Sigurd stood at *Serpent*'s sternpost and said some words about Halldor. Mainly he spoke of his bravery and how well he had died, albeit after suffering the way he had.

"The Norns spun a dark skein for our brother Halldor," Sigurd said, to which many murmured agreement, "but in the end he died as we all hunger to die, among our brothers, with a good sword in our hands. Even the Spinners cannot always cheat us of this right."

We made a pyre for Halldor and laid him on it with the things he would need on the other side of Bifröst, the Rainbow-Bridge, and in one hand the corpse gripped his sword and in the other it grasped the Týr carving Sigurd had given him at the end. But even in death poor Halldor could not shrug off his ill wyrd, for as soon as we had lit the sea-smoothed white driftwood beneath the corpse, the pitch-black clouds overhead began to spill stinging rain, with streaks of lightning and cracks of thunder loud enough to flay the skin from a man's bones. For a long time the wood just steamed, and even when a flame defied the deluge, it did nothing more than singe the corpse above it. For all of us gathered around, huddled pathetically in furs and skins, it was a sorry scene, and there must have been many warriors there who shivered with the fear that they might one day suffer such a pitiful rite.

Eventually, though, Bothvar remembered that we still had a couple of pails of seal's fat somewhere, and when they were found, we slathered handfuls over the wood and smeared it onto Halldor's cloak and even into his beard. Olaf added some old dry lumps of pine resin to the flames, and eventually the wood caught, at which we were all relieved, as much for the warmth of it as anything. A dirty column of smoke rose to meet the low-slung clouds, and the water that had puddled in the sand hissed and steamed where it met the fire's edge, and we watched from that blaze's shadow, talking in low voices when the thunder would let us be heard, as the wood crackled and hissed and popped and Halldor's corpse blistered and burned.

"If I'm killed, you're to make Father Egfrith say some words over me," Penda said, staring into the flames, water dripping from his woolen cloak, "and make sure they bury me properly. Nice and deep." He grimaced. "You can help them with the digging. I don't want some dog digging me up and chewing on me, but leave the rest of it to Egfrith."

I looked at the scar that ran the length of Penda's face, a wound that easily could have seen him as dead as Halldor.

"I'll dig you a hole deep enough to bury Svein standing up," I said, "and screw Egfrith. I'll speak for you, Penda. It would be an honor." He looked at me dubiously. "I'll say, 'Today we bury Penda. He was a bastard.'"

He spit into the rain. "That'll do," he said through

a half grin, turning back to watch as Halldor's beard burst into bright orange flame.

We waited another two days on that miserable beach for the wind to die down a little, and when eventually it did, we dug the ships free of the sand we had piled around them to stop them from rocking and prepared to sail. We had managed to catch plenty of fish, mackerel mainly but also some hooked from the sea-grass beds in the shallows that were flat and shaped like giant's eyes but that tasted better than any fish I had ever eaten. We hung soaking furs over the sheer strakes to dry in the wind and took to our benches, eager to put more of that treacherous, storm-lashed coast behind us and find smoother waters. We rowed for a while until we were out in the depths and clear of the winds that swirled within the shadow of that rocky shore. Then all four ships hoisted their sails, and we rested and worked in shifts, bailing or hauling the sheets, or else played tafl or watched wind-jumbled seabirds and the endless coast slip by.

In the next days we made good progress, mooring in the mouths of sheltered inlets at night and continuing on at dawn or when the wind allowed, thus decreasing the risk of being attacked by rock-hurling locals. At last the weather turned kinder. The gray sea, which had heaved and surged as though the rolling coils of Jörmungand stirred beneath, settled to an ill-tempered swell. The rain that had seemed sharp enough to pierce the skin on your face weakened to a steady drizzle that you hardly noticed, and men began to throw insults around again, which is a sure sign that they are happy. But the end of the storm gave Sigurd time to worry about another problem, and that problem was the Danes.

"They need war gear," Sigurd said to Olaf one dusk, watching the sun slip out of reach of Sköll's jaws behind the rim of the world. We were moored in the shelter of a rocky cove where the water was calm and the fishing good.

"Aye, they do," Olaf said, chewing meat from one of the few remaining smoked pig legs. "Because at the moment they're as useful to us as tits on a bull."

Sigurd glanced across at the Danish ships, whose crews seemed in good spirits despite what we'd been through. I guessed that to men who had thought they would rot to stinking mush in Frankia, a faceful of storm was an improvement. "They'll stand in the shieldwall if it comes to it," Sigurd said with a nod.

"Then they'll stand in the last bloody row," Olaf moaned, "and I'll have their guts for twine if they stick any of us with their rusty bloody spears!"

For we had seen smoke palling in the sky beyond a promontory swathed in holm oak, yew, and willow, and there was enough of it to suggest a large settlement. Sigurd was aware that his men needed something to get their blood pumping hot again, and there was nothing that could do that better than a fight and the chance for plunder. But he knew nothing of the land here or its people, and without decent war gear the Danes would be vulnerable if we ran into proper fighting men.

Olaf's teeth dragged his beard across his bottom lip. "I haven't seen them in a scrap yet, Sigurd," he said dubiously. "Even if they had good gear, we don't know if they know how to use it. Thór's hairy arse!

I've seen more meat on a sparrow's kneecap than on most of those Danes. A stiff breeze would carry them off."

"They'll stand, Uncle," Sigurd said. "But I won't ask them to fight without swords and helmets. Not until we know what sort of men those hearths belong to."

"So what's your plan, Loki?" Olaf baited, looking back to the Danes berthed on the other side of *Fjord-Elk*. "You want to send Floki to sniff it out?"

Sigurd pursed his lips but said nothing, and so Olaf turned to Yrsa. "Get off your arse, lad, and fetch that miserable whoreson Floki," he said, taking a comb from his belt and dragging it through his beard with a grimace. "And fetch us something to wet our throats." Yrsa nodded.

"Floki is not aboard, Uncle," Bag-Eyed Orm said. He was pissing over the side, and the hot fluid was fogging the evening air. "He was ashore before the anchor thumped the seabed. Haven't seen him since."

The comb went still in Olaf's hand as his brows arched. And Sigurd grinned.

Floki returned when a thin crimson was all that remained in the western sky. He was announced by the squawks of the black-faced gulls that bustled on the rocks we had moored up to, and I knew he would have hated that, for Floki was a warrior who thrived on stealth. He was the kind of man who believed he could steal Odin's beard without the All-Father feeling the breeze on his cheeks. Now he climbed aboard, naked but for his breeks, and shook the salt water from his long crow-black hair. The only weapon he had taken ashore was the long knife he now wiped dry with a linen strip before doing anything else. But even with a knife Floki was someone you would be a fool to take on. He was like the Wessexman Penda in that way: as dangerous as thin ice on a lake. A born killer.

"You greedy snot hogs better have saved me something to eat," he said to no one in particular, scrubbing his face with the linen. Arnvid blanched, suddenly realizing he had already shared out the last of the smoked meat and cheese. He would now have to tell Floki that all that was left was dried fish and some stale mead. That was another reason the pall of smoke had tempted Sigurd into that cove—we needed food.

"You rancid goat turd, Arnvid!" Floki said, fathoming the dread in the man's face. "I'm freezing my balls off out there while you're tucked up tighter than a hedgehog's arsehole, and when I get back, some putrid prick has eaten my share." The scars crisscrossing Floki's torso and arms were puckered and white from the cold water, and he shivered, grimacing at Arnvid before turning to bring his report to Sigurd, who was waiting, arms folded, his beard hanging in a single thick braid and his golden hair loose.

"You can send someone else next time, Sigurd," Floki moaned as he leaned against the hull to pull on his boots.

"If I sent someone else, you would whine even more," Sigurd said, sharing a knowing look with Olaf.

Floki accepted that with a grunt. "Well, you can at least save me something to eat for the love of Eir. My belly thinks my throat's been cut."

"A wise man does not overfeed his best hunting dog," Sigurd said, winking at Olaf, who stifled a grin. "But if you have good news for me, we shall all have full bellies soon enough."

Now it was Floki's turn to grin, his head appearing from a new dry tunic.

"We'll soon be as fat as you, Uncle," he said.

Twenty Danes would be the bait, and I suppose that made the others the hook. Sigurd had not used that word *bait*—he had said "anvil." The Danes were the anvil, and the rest of the Fellowship was to be the hammer. But I saw them as bait, which was probably because I was among them and that is what it felt like to me as we rowed *Sea-Arrow* out of the gathering dark right up to the jetty, thumping her hull against it. At least Penda was with me, for he relished the chance to wet his sword and had asked to come, and I was glad to have him. We and the twenty Danes had sailed *Sea-Arrow* around the promontory, leaving the Wolfpack in the quiet cove, and it had not been long before we had come to a wide bay in which a dozen or so fishing skiffs bobbed peacefully. The low shore threw out several wharves along which more boats were berthed, betraying a decent-size settlement beyond the barren low rise.

"It's not good fishing around here by the look of it," Penda had said with a wicked grin as the fishing skiffs scattered from us like fleas from a flame, and now we climbed onto the jetty with what poor weapons we had: spears mostly, though there were some axes and a couple of hunting bows. None wore brynjas, but Penda and I had insisted on bringing our swords at least, though our helmets were still aboard *Serpent*.

"What sort of men are they?" a Dane named Agnar asked, touching the amulet at his neck and spitting. The locals, who had been waiting to see who we might be, were now pounding away up the wharves, and they were like no men we had ever seen. Their skin was bluish black like that of a man who has been a week in his grave. Their beards were black or gray, and they wore what appeared to be piles of linen on their heads.

"I have never seen their like before," Rolf, the Danes' leader, said, hurling a spear after one of them and missing. "They look like dead men!"

"Draugar!" another Dane agreed, "risen from the grave."

"They run well for dead men," I said, breaking into a run myself, and we pounded up the wharf after those strange blue men—blaumen—leaving four of the Danes to guard *Sea-Arrow* under the command of a man named Ogn.

"Bloody legs feel like they belong to someone else!" Penda shouted as we ran, but he was grinning like me because we were loosed to the hunt and our prey was terrified and we felt the thrill of it coursing in our veins. We were fast, too, even on sand and sea legs. Without brynjas and shields we ate up the ground, and I surged with a rare joy from the freedom of not being aboard *Serpent*.

A Dane howled in delight as he dragged an old graybeard to the white sand, and I saw a bloom of red among undyed robes. We ran on through the deepening night, past discarded fishing nets and baskets of catch and upturned skiffs, up onto a hard-baked scrubland of stunted trees. The ululating cries of the dark men carried into the growing darkness, and it was a strange animal sound. But like hunted animals they were making the fatal mistake of leading us to their lair, which was a great clutter of white stone houses and brushwood lean-tos, patchily lit by torches and bowls of flame.

An arrow streaked toward us from an unseen archer. Then another shaft whipped through the air an arm's length from my right cheek, and I was tempted to yell "Shieldwall" and seek the safety of cohesion. But we were a raiding party, not a war band, and we had come without our heavy shields. If we made the skjaldborg, we would just present a large soft target for arrows and spears.

In a narrow torch-lit alley a Dane crouched over a dead man, unwinding the linen from his victim's head and cawing in bewilderment as the shroud kept coming, seemingly endless. The Danes were now among the dwellings, their stuttering, misshapen shadows playing monstrously on the white walls as they kicked down doors and dragged dark-skinned women—blauvifs—out into the night.

"Raven!" Penda yelled, pointing his spear at the northeast. "Looks like we might have a fight!" The Wessexman's eyes glinted, and the scar on his face glistened white in the glow of an enormous moon.

"Here they come!" I roared, and some of the Danes let go of the women they had caught and ran to me, eager for a real fight, which was just as well because among the dark-skinned men gathering some held shields that must have been covered in metal, for I could see flame reflected in them. There were already seven or eight, but more were coming and some of them were stringing bows to join the two archers already loosing shafts.

"How can a man be that color and still breathing?" one of the Danes asked, shaking his head.

"They want us to come to them," Penda said.

"Makes sense," I said, for their number was growing and the blaumen must have known that the longer we waited, the more of them we would have to fight. "We'll have to go to them," I said in Norse to Rolf, "and the sooner the better."

Rolf pursed his thin lips and scratched a hollow bearded cheek.

"Makes me wonder what's inside Gerd's Tit," he said, nodding toward a strange building. Some chuckled at that because Gerd is a beautiful giantess whom Frey the god of rain and sunshine humped at the cost of his self-wielding sword. It was a good name, I thought, given the building's shape.

"That's what they're protecting," he went on, "not their women." And Rolf was right, for the robed men seemed reluctant to stray from this stone building that was the size of three or four dwellings put together and whose roof was as round and smooth as Bragi's head. A wooden walkway encircled the swell of the roof and was lit by torches so that you could see the place from far and wide, even at night.

"I'll wager there's silver in there, lad. Maybe even gold."

"Call your men, Rolf," I said, eyeing the enemy, trying to weigh their willingness to take us on. Some of them had decent war gear by the look of it, but we still outnumbered them overall. "We need every Danish spear we've got," I said. "If we don't strike now, they will grow brave."

"We've got to hit the whoresons now," Penda hissed, "before they find their balls."

"I know," I growled, but a handful of the Danes were still looting the dwellings, and from the sound of the screams, some of them were getting to know the local women. One of the dark men was encouraging the others, waving his arms toward us and screaming like a madman. *It's got to be now*, I thought. So I gnarred at Ódin Spear-Shaker to flood me with the battle frenzy, and then I turned to Penda. "Are you coming or not, you Christ-loving sheep swiver?" I said, a spear in one hand, my sword in the other, and then I yelled as though I wanted to wake the dead and ran toward my enemies.

There is a joy in battle: a voracious, reckless, savage joy that strips us of dignity and care and all the things that raise us above beasts. There is fear, too, but when the blood starts flying, that fear is swallowed by the hunger to kill, because whatever you kill cannot kill you.

My spear clattered against a metal-skinned shield, but a Danish ax hooked that shield's rim. The Dane yanked it down, and I swung my sword into a dark-bearded face, cleaving the skull with a wet *crack*. That corpse crumpled, and I roared and barged through, knocking it aside and opening the enemy's shieldwall before it could close up. I spun and thrust the spear into a man's back between his shoulder blades, and Penda went low, hacking into legs, and the Danes were as feral as a pack of starving dogs, slashing wildly and howling, with no care for their own skins. The dark-skins were yelling too, and it was a wild, rampageous fight in which men went from living to dead in the flash of a blade in the moonlight.

"Your Danes are wild bastards!" Penda yelled, hurling his spear and bringing down a dark-skin who had made a run for it. I feinted with my spear, but my enemy read the bluff and knocked the shaft from my grip with his heavy curved sword. I bent my arm and stepped up, cracking my elbow into his chin, then threw a leg back and scythed my blade into his neck. His eyes rolled in his head and his knees buckled, and I yanked my blade out so that dark blood sprayed up the white moon-washed wall beside me. Then a Dane leaped on the man, growling and plunging a knife into his face and chest, and I put my back against the wall, gulping breath and watching the last of the killing.

"Didn't get them all," Penda said, pointing at three fleeing dark-skins who had dropped their weapons and bolted, leaving their brothers to be butchered.

"Good," I said, kneeling to wipe my blade clean on a dead man's robes. The Danes were laughing as they stripped the gore-slathered dead, looking for loot. Two of their own lay among the corpses and several others were hurt, but they had done well and they knew it as they reveled in the joy that comes when you see that you are still alive when others are not.

"They don't fight like Sigurd's lads," Penda said, sheathing his sword. He had barely broken a sweat, whereas I was slick with it and my limbs trembled with the battle thrill. "There's not much skill in them, though I don't suppose it makes much difference to this lot," he said, nodding at the white-robed carrion. "Dead is dead however it comes along."

"Dead is dead," I agreed, sheathing my blade and turning to piss up the blood-spattered wall. When I swung back around, Rolf was standing there, a grin etched on his crimson-smeared face.

"Now you know how Danemen can fight," he said proudly, "even with a few poor spears and axes." He glanced down at the bodies, which to the Danes' disappointment were not giving up much in the way of loot. "These blaumen have never faced Danes before."

"They never will again," a man named Byrnjolf added, revealing rotten teeth in his grin. Nearby, a Dane was straddling a bleating goat, slitting its neck.

"The others will hear of your men's bravery, Rolf," I said. "Sigurd will be pleased to know that the Danes are fierce fighters." Rolf nodded at that, satisfied with the night's work. "Now we might as well see what we can find around here," I said, turning and looking up at the impressive building before us, suddenly hoping there were not more men up there on the wooden walkway readying to drop something heavy on us.

"There must be something here that those men thought was worth dying for," I said, peering up into the flame-licked darkness. "Have you ever seen anything like this place?"

Penda scratched his head, saying that he hadn't and eyeing the iron-studded dark oak door, which was almost twice my height. The planks of that door could have come from a longship's deck, could even have been hull strakes, it seemed to me, though I did not say it. They were speckled with sea-worm holes, and there were even some worn scratchings that looked to me like runework.

"That's going to take some kicking in by its looks," Penda said.

The door needed no kicking at all because it was not locked. We were looking around us for something to use as a ram, when Rolf simply turned the iron ring and the door yawned open, exhaling sweet smoke.

Rolf's brows hitched up in surprise, and Penda rolled his eyes at our boneheadedness. We might well have smashed that door to splinters without ever trying it.

Some of the Danes stood watch, peering north into the night for signs of more blaumen, while the rest of us entered the strange stone building, our eyes hungry for silver.

"What is this place?" Penda asked, grimacing at the potent smell as he turned, trying to take in that hollow candlelit chamber. "No benches. No beds. Not even a bucket to piss in! Looks like the poor bastards have been pilfered already. There's more in big Svein's head than in this piss-poor place."

"Is it a church, Raven?" Rolf asked, for he had heard that I had lived for a time in Wessex among Christ worshippers.

"If it is, it's not like any church I've seen," I said, pressing a palm against the smooth wall, which was made of countless blue stones each not much larger than a brynja ring. Some were dark like the sea, and others were the blue of a summer sky. Still others, on the east wall, where they lined a doorway, were the bright yellow of cowslips. Only there was no door, just the outline of one, and it led nowhere but was instead an alcove two feet deep on which strange, sharp symbols twisted and twined with no sense of a pattern so far as I could see. "There would be a Christ cross somewhere if it were a church," I said, moving over to a stone trough of running water and splashing some on my face to wash off the drying blood.

"This damn smoke is making me dizzy," Penda said, pointing to the northeast corner, where stone steps twisted upward, stopping just below the bulging beamless roof. "Up you go then, lad," he said. "Maybe they hide their treasures in the clouds."

So I drew my sword again, just in case, and started up the narrow stairwell, wondering how long it must have taken to carve each step and hoping there were no blades waiting for me at the top. I pushed open another door and, with Penda close behind me, gingerly stepped onto the wooden platform we had seen from below. I half expected the planks to snap and to fall to my death, but I soon realized the gangway, like the rest of the strange building, was well made. I would be safe so long as I didn't lean out over the balustrade.

"I've never been this high off the ground," I said to Penda, eyeing the surrounding dwellings and the shadowed alleys. A dog was barking incessantly, but otherwise the place was quiet. Too quiet. If you really concentrated and turned your ears to the south, you could just hear the low murmur of the sea, though you could not see it in the dark beyond the low hump of shadowed scrubland above the beach.

"I feel closer to God up here," Penda said seriously.

"Which god?" I asked, trying not to grin. I was not used to hearing Penda talk of such things.

"Fucking heathen," he growled. "Though I wouldn't want to be up here after a skinful of Bram's mead. My head is spinning as it is after breathing that weird stink down there." Up on the walkway the air was cool and clean after the pungent smoke inside. Penda gestured that I go one way around the platform while he went the other so that all being well, we would meet around the other side. I set off, peering into the night and thinking about what the Wessexman had said about feeling closer to his god.

"Maybe it *is* a church," I suggested when we met on the swollen roof's west side. "Maybe the folk here don't worship the Christ cross. Frigg knows, they don't look like other Christians. But it could still be a church. Do you really feel that your god is near?" I asked, a slight shiver crawling across my skin because Penda's god and mine were enemies.

The Wessexman scratched the long scar on his cheek as we walked together to the northeast side, and when we were back where we had started from, he shook his head and turned to me. "A church would have something in it. Something worth protecting," he said. "This place is something else. For one thing it is a good place to watch out for raiders," he admitted, thumping the wooden balustrade appreciatively.

"They didn't see us coming," I said, sheathing my sword again.

"Aye, but we shall see them," he said, and now it was his turn to grin.

We set three of the Danes to watch from the platform while the rest of us paired up and went from house to house, kicking down doors and looking for anything of worth. The people of the place had fled while their warriors had fought us in the shadow of the great building, and Penda suggested that perhaps those warriors had wanted us to think they were protecting something inside so that their folk could escape. This seemed likely to me, and in truth I was glad of it because I knew what the Danes would do to anyone they found.

"Do you expect these godless bastards to lay out their loot for all to see?" Penda asked, pulling a clinking leather pouch from a small box beneath a child's crib. He pulled the string and poured a stream of silver coin into his palm. "That bony slash of piss Rolf and his bunch of berserkers will be stuffing coins into their arse cracks to keep them from Sigurd, you mark me, lad. They'll be rattling like an old whore's teeth."

"Are you going to share *that* little hoard, Penda?" I asked, nodding at the dully gleaming pile in his hands.

Penda scowled. "You can wipe that grin off your face, lad," he said, tipping the coins back into the pouch. "This is mine by rights for being the bait in the trap." He stuffed the purse into his belt and rolled his shoulders with a *crack*. "Well, lad, let's not stand here getting old." He tapped the pouch affectionately. "There's more where this came from, and I'll be damned if I'm going to let the bloody Danes get their filthy hands on it."

Rolf suddenly appeared in the doorway, and I did not miss how his eyes flicked down to the purse in Penda's belt. "Gorm has found something you should see," he said, turning back into the night.

"I hope it's something we can eat," Penda grumbled. "A pig would go down well. Anything with legs would be good. I've eaten enough dried fish to last till Judgment Day."

But what Gorm had found was not something even a mangy dog would chew on.

"I thought it must be ale. Even wine," the Dane announced, hands on hips before a barrel whose lid he had prized off. Most of the others had gathered, eager to know what Gorm had found and each one moonstruck by the thought of swigging the rest of the night into oblivion. Gorm glanced at Rolf, who nodded, and Gorm grabbed the barrel's rim and threw the thing over onto its side so that liquid splashed across the hard ground. With it came heads. And stink. There were five of them, and but for their ashen color, all looked as fresh as if they had been lopped from their necks that very morning.

"Gods!" a Dane exclaimed. Penda made the sign of the cross over his chest as Byrnjolf prodded one of the heads with his spear.

"There must be some strange seidr in the water they were in," Rolf said, "for surely those men were not breathing the same air as us these last days." And I thought Rolf must be right because the wound beneath each head's chin was the same dull gray as the rest of the skin rather than being like butchered flesh.

"We found something else, too," a Dane called Tufi said, hefting a silver Christ cross and washing it in moonlight. Some of the Danes recoiled at this, but Tufi seemed to care not at all about the thing's power and if anything made a show of sweeping it through the air to unnerve his friends. "It was wrapped in a rotten skin and locked in a chest," he said. "It's heavy, too. Imagine how many jarl torcs or arm rings you could make from this." Many, I thought, for it was as long as my arm.

"And I'll wager it belongs to one of those sorry-looking bastards," Penda said, pointing at one of the severed heads whose brown beard looked neater than most of ours, which was an odd thing given the circumstances.

"So these blaumen have no love for the White Christ either," Byrnjolf said, twisting a braid around a thick finger. "Maybe we should have traded with them instead of killing them. We could have given them Sigurd's Christ men, and they could have given us their women."

The others laughed at this, and I chose not to tell Penda what Byrnjolf had said. "Just be glad your head is not drowning in a blauman's barrel, Byrnjolf," I said, to which he nodded solemnly. "Now get back to work. If our scheme is running straight, we don't have long. Gather what silver you can find and burn whatever will take a flame. Then rally by Gerd's Tit," I said, pointing at the strange empty building. "Bring cooking pots, too, and fill them with earth."

"In Denmark we eat meat, Raven, not dirt," a tall man with an ash-flecked black beard said, his brows woven together.

"The pots are for dropping, not eating," I said, "but we will need food, so bring anything you can find. Two or three goats too. And bring your heads, Gorm," I said, glancing at the Dane, who grinned until he realized that I was serious. "They're heavy, aren't they?" I said.

"As heavy as any other head, I suppose," Gorm admitted with a shrug.

"So bring them," I said, turning my back on him. Then I walked back to Gerd's Tit, aiming a kick at the still barking dog and almost getting my foot bitten off for my trouble.

A cook fire was already crackling and popping, and as the smell of roasting meat wafted over to slicken my mouth, I hoped we would have more luck than the Christians whose heads were now stuck on spears over Danish shoulders.

chapter
FOUR

THE BLAUMEN came out of the red glare of the east. The first arrived on tall, lissome horses and lined the scrubby ridge above the beach, which suggested they were no fools. They must have ridden along the coast trying to find our ship, which would give them an idea of how many we were. I was sure Ogn and the men aboard *Sea-Arrow* would have been keen-eyed enough to see the riders coming. They would have sailed out of the blaumen's reach and would be holding in the bay a short distance offshore. But we were now cut off from the sea, and so the blaumen thought they could finish us.

"Your eyes are younger than mine. How many do you see?" Penda asked. We were up on the lookout platform of Gerd's Tit, shielding our eyes against the rising sun. That dawn was dry and fine, and the sky was a bowl of blue stretching beyond imagining. High up, higher than the black specks of birds, a few thin clouds skated east across the roof of the world on winds that did not reach us far below.

"It's hard to count them when they keep moving like that," I said. "Twenty-five? Thirty?" The horses were tossing their heads and whinnying, excited perhaps by their riders' nerves and the prospect of a fight. Beasts are like that; they can smell blood before it's even spilled. *Perhaps those are ravens up there*, I thought, glancing up at the sky, *patiently waiting because they know there will be flesh to feast on soon enough.*

"There'll be more before long," Penda said. "The silver-light bastards who have to walk on their own two legs will turn up, and then we'll have a fight on our hands." He was right, for in the time it takes to put an edge on a sword, another war band had appeared from the north. Their spear blades, helmets, and buckles glinted in the sun as they checked their weapons, stretched their limbs, and practiced spear thrusts. They wore the same white robes and bundles of linen on their heads as the men we had killed the day before, and they had the same metal-skinned shields too. Some of them were probably the same men who had run from us when we attacked the place, but they were back now, and they wanted revenge as any man would.

Our men were milling around the base of the building, checking their poor weapons and nervous now in the cold light of day, their blood sluggish and their instincts telling them that they were outnumbered and in a poor position. I turned and saw Gorm carefully lining up a row of earth-filled pots along the balustrade.

"Did you bring the heads?" I asked, my stomach growling in complaint at the tough goat meat I had eaten the previous evening.

Gorm's wind- and salt-cracked lips spread into a thin smile. "I brought them," he said, understanding now why I had asked for anything heavy. "They're on the steps in there," he said, nodding toward the door that led back inside the building. "I thought it was best to keep them out of the sun. Don't know how long we're likely to be up here." He frowned. "I could let them warm up a little," he suggested mischievously.

"They'll do fine as they are," I said. I smiled, trying to smother the fear whose icy fingers were beginning to caress my guts. "Hard and cold or warm and stinking, it's all the same. No one likes an old severed head dropped on them from a height." Gorm grinned, and I thought him as ugly as Völund's hairy scrotum yet a good man to have with you when you were in a strange land and outnumbered by men coming to kill you.

Rolf came over and leaned on the rail, his jaw set and his eyes fixed on the mounted men, who had not moved from the ridge three bow shots away to the southeast. He spit over the side. "How bold do you want to play this?" he asked without turning his head. I had not known whether Rolf would look to me to lead, or Penda, or whether he might have his own ideas. My guts tightened like a fist gripping water.

"Say something, lad," Penda muttered, and I realized I had not answered Rolf. "Anything will do, but give him something," Penda growled.

"We are the anvil, Rolf," I said, remembering my jarl's words, "and the blaumen are the lump of iron that must be placed on the anvil."

Rolf nodded, still staring at the riders. "And Sigurd?" he asked.

"Sigurd? Sigurd is the hammer," I said.

"Even their damn banner is black," Penda said, jerking his chin toward the north, where the horseless warriors had planted their banner in the earth. Then a strange, plaintive sound carried to us, a keening voice rising and falling as quickly as water over pebbles, as nimble as a thin wind through a forest. As one, the dark men dropped to their knees and touched their foreheads to the ground. Then they climbed back to their feet before dropping again as the voice melted away to silence. They repeated this action, and the weird voice grew, twisting and writhing like a serpent made of smoke, and from the corner of my eye I saw Rolf touch the cheek of the short ax tucked into his belt to ward off evil.

"That is some seidr," he said. "I have never heard a man bawl like that." He scratched the crook of his elbow. "Makes my damn skin itch."

"The Christians are always singing," I said, "and it can tempt your ears to jump off your head. But this . . . this is different." I looked at Penda questioningly.

"Sounds like a couple of wolves chewing on a lamb," he said unhelpfully. "And Christ alone knows why they keep putting their faces in the dirt." He grinned. "Poor bastards must be hungry." But even Penda must have felt that sound worming up his spine, for he made the sign of the cross before drawing his long knife and checking its edge.

To the southeast the riders had dismounted and were performing the same strange rite, their horses waiting patiently, some of them dipping their heads like their masters as though the seidr filled them too.

"Stay up here, Gorm, with two others," I said, to

which he nodded, calling the names of two Danes. "And don't drop anything on us or you'll wake up to find your own head in a barrel of piss."

"It wouldn't be the first time," Gorm said, grimacing at Rolf. Then, while the blaumen greeted the dawn with their faces in the dirt, we descended into Gerd's Tit and readied for a fight.

There were thirteen of us waiting for the blaumen to attack, with three more above us on the lookout platform whose job it was to keep an eye on the enemy and call down to us with their movements.

"Let's hope they come," I muttered to Penda as we stood in a dog's leg line so that half faced the northeast and the foot soldiers and half faced the mounted men to the southeast. We were a good spear's throw from the open doors of Gerd's Tit, meaning we would have to retreat forty paces over that hard-baked ground, and so it would all be in the timing.

"They'll come, Raven," Penda said, taking his spear in great circles to loosen his arm muscles. "They'll come eager as crows to a hanging. We burned their village. Some of it, anyway."

Columns of gray rose lazily into the blue sky from smoldering piles of ash where lean-tos, cattle stalls, and simple shelters had stood the day before. Many of the surrounding stone houses were scorched, their doors burned where they stood, hacked to splintered ruins, or taken to feed our fires. Chickens scrabbled in the ashes, pecking for food. Penda was right. The blaumen would come because we had brought death and fire to their homes. But they would also come because we looked like a sorry bunch of raiders with barely five or six decent blades among us. I glanced up at my spear's blade, noting that it could use a good whetstone. Then again, I knew that even a blunt spear can gather enough speed in the air to pass through a man's body. Not that I intended throwing it, not unless I had to.

"Danemen!" Rolf yelled in a voice that was bigger than he was. "You will take your orders from Raven. Do as he says and soon we will be back aboard *Sea-Arrow* with a decent silver catch and another tale for the skalds."

"I was killing men when Raven was still clawing at his mother's tit!" a man named Beiner shouted. I glanced over at him and he glared at me and shrugged, and I had no doubt he was telling the truth. He was a big man and had held on to some of his muscle even chained like a mad dog in that Frankish Hel. "Why should I take orders from a whelp? My woman has more of a beard between her legs!" The other Danes laughed at that, and Rolf rounded his cheek and hoisted his brows as though to say it was up to me to convince Beiner and any of the others who needed convincing. But I knew that I was beginning to get a reputation as a killer. Even Beiner must have heard how I had slaughtered the giant Frankish warrior who had leaped aboard *Serpent*, but reputations are hungry things and you must feed them to keep them alive. So without telling Penda what was going on, I undid my belt and handed it with the scabbarded sword to the Wessexman. Then I stepped out of the line and walked toward the blaumen to the northeast. And after just ten paces I cursed under my breath, because to my right two riders had urged their mounts forward and were now coming toward me, and I would rather have faced men on foot.

"Get back here, you bloody heathen fool!" I heard Penda yell, but I kept going, thinking to myself how the gods love to watch us mortals abandon good sense and throw ourselves into the Spinners' web to see whether the strands will hold or snap. "Raven! Get your arse back here!" The spear suddenly felt light in my hand because the blood in my veins was beginning to tremble like water over coals, as it always has before a fight. And yet strangely, my legs felt heavy, so heavy that I feared that if my nerve failed and I turned and ran, I would make it barely halfway back to the Danes before the blaumen cut me down. But that was a good thing because it meant that even though I was tempted to turn and run, I would not.

"Thór's hairy whore," I muttered in relief. One of the riders had stopped, and the other was coming on alone, his shield held wide to show he came in peace. I glanced up at the birds, dark specks still, jostling against the blue at the edge of the eyes' range. I had noticed that the sky seemed to grow bigger the farther south we sailed, and not just bigger but higher too, so that I wondered how Yggdrasil the World-Tree could be so huge that I could watch birds among the beams of the world yet still not see its branches.

The breeze shifted, bringing the stink of horse sweat and leather to my nose as the distance between the rider and myself closed. I could see his face clearly now, which was as dark as pitch, and his eyes, which were proud verging on haughty. He rode with his chin high, studying me down the length of a strong flaring nose. His mustaches and beard were short, neatly trimmed, and glistening, and the white robes beneath a short mail brynja were dusty and mud-spattered, though the linen wrapped around his head was as clean as fresh snow. When he was three spear lengths away, his eyes narrowed and his thick lips gathered, the expression of arrogance melting to a deep, cold revulsion because he could now see my blood-filled eye.

"*Al-majus,*" he said, tossing his head and tugging the reins to halt his bay mare. The beast whinnied and pulled its lips back from its yellow teeth, not liking the look of me either as the blauman burbled on at me in a tongue that I doubted even he could unravel. So I smiled and nodded, and the blauman frowned, half turning back to his companion fifty paces behind. Then I took my spear in both hands and ran forward and plunged the blade straight through the mail and into his chest. The man yelled in shock and fury, and his mare swung its head into me, teeth gnashing, almost knocking me off my feet, so that I let go of the shaft and staggered backward, leaving seven feet of ash jutting from the rider's chest. Blood frothed at the blauman's mouth and hung in gobbets from his short beard, and he died in the saddle, feebly clutching the spear, his mouth forming a scream that never came.

I heard the thunder of hooves and men yelling, and I turned and ran. I would rather have walked in my own time, heedless of the armed riders bearing down on me, my jaw firm, eyes cold as a nun's tit. That is the way a skald would weave it, but the truth was that I ran as fast as I could, and no doubt my eyes were stretched wide as a whore's legs. It's likely I was yelling, too, in fear and with the sheer thrill of it, because I was unarmed and the hooves were striking the earth and my heart was banging as fiercely as Thór's hammer. The Danes held their line, constrained by Rolf's bawling, but they were howling and punching the air with spears and axes, spurring me on, willing me to make it back to the line before the blaumen rode me down. Then Penda was running toward me, which told me that the riders must be close, and I pumped my legs and hoped Odin Spear-Shaker was shaking Valhöll's oak beams with a belly laugh like thunder.

"Down!" Penda screamed, hurling my scabbarded sword to me and then launching his spear, and I threw myself into the dirt and rolled to my right just in time to see the Wessexman leap and wrap his left arm around a horseman's neck so that the man toppled backward off his mount, and Penda was flung through the air like a hare from a hound's jaws. I scrambled to my feet, grabbed my sword, and saw that the rest of the blaumen were almost upon us, their curved swords held wide, ready to scythe our heads from our necks.

I hauled Penda to his feet, tensing as I turned to face the riders, who hauled on their reins, their horses screaming with anger.

"To us, Raven!" Rolf yelled, and I spun around to see that the Danes had moved up, still in line and horribly exposed, but there had been enough spears in that poor defense to deter the blaumen, or perhaps their horses, from riding into it. We began to step backward under a thin rain of javelins, joining the Danes.

"Everyone back!" I roared, and the Danes kept their spear blades up as we retreated raggedly. Rolf knocked a javelin out of the air with his spear, saving another man from being belly pierced. "Faster!" I shouted, because Gorm was yelling from Gerd's Tit that the other band of blaumen was coming for us now, and the Danes knew as well as I did that if we did not move faster, we would be trapped.

"If they get behind us, we're dead!" Tufi said, cursing as an arrow whipped past his face.

"Then move faster, Tufi, you son of a three-legged dog," I yelled. Among the bristling knot of horsemen in front of us I saw a man gesture to the others that they should ride around our flanks and get behind us.

"We'll be the bloody lump on the anvil soon enough," Penda spit through a grimace, clutching his shoulder. The rider he had hurled himself at lay a distance off, his neck broken.

"Give them your spears!" I yelled. "Then break and get to the tit!" I knew they did not want to lose their spears, but we had to buy some time, and so with curses the Danes pulled back their arms and launched their shafts toward man and beast. "Now run!" I yelled, and we turned and legged it, and beside me a Dane went down but two others took an arm each and ran as if their arses were on fire. The first to reach Gerd's Tit held the doors open, and we piled inside, half the Danes continuing up the stone stairwell while the rest of us barred the door and bolstered it with timbers taken from the surviving lean-tos.

"Why didn't they ride us down? Why didn't they fight?" Byrnjolf said, doubled over and gasping for breath. Candles still burned peacefully, chasing shadows into the dark corners of that strange empty place.

"Why would they?" Rolf answered, scowling at a slice in the shoulder of his jerkin. Dark blood stained the leather. "Now that we're holed up in here like rats in a pot, all they need to do is wait for us to starve."

"Soot-faced sons of whores," Tufi gnarred, then kicked a chicken that had strayed from the others to peck the stone floor by his foot.

"I don't think they will wait for long," I said. "This place means something to them. It's important. They made a stand out there yesterday," I said, nodding toward the barricaded door, "and they will not be happy about us being in here." As if in answer, something pounded against the door. The nearest candles guttered, and a cloud of dust bloomed, making Beiner sneeze.

"They want to come in, Gorm!" I yelled up into the hollow space above us. "Show them some famous Danish hospitality!" I don't know whether Gorm up there on the platform heard me, but within a few hammering heartbeats a succession of loud cracks, thumps, and yelps told us that he and the others were dropping their stones and earth-filled pots.

"That's it," Beiner called through another enormous sneeze. "Flatten some heads!"

Outside, the shouts faded, meaning Gorm and the others had persuaded the blaumen to leave, at least for now.

"They'll be back," Byrnjolf said, testing the blade of a short knife against a strip of leather.

"Aye, and when they do, what have we got to give them? Tooth and nail?" Tufi said, throwing his arms wide. He had nothing on him more dangerous than his eating knife. "Whoresons will stick us with our own damn spears."

"Don't piss your breeches, Tufi," Beiner said, gripping the throat of his long two-handled ax and slapping its cheek. "I've still got something to show those

Svartálfar out there." Svartálfar are the dark elves
that live underground, and that word made some of
the Danes spit or touch the Thór's hammers at their
necks. Now, for the first time since he had challenged
me, I locked eyes with Beiner, unsure how things
stood between us.

"I saw that your legs are swifter than your sword
arm, Beiner," I said, eyeballing him as I looped my
belt with the scabbarded sword back around my
waist. "Stronger too, I think, as your spear fell far
short of any of the blaumen." In truth I had not even
seen the big Dane throw his spear, but I knew I had
to finish what I had started outside when I had killed
the horseman who had come to talk. "I admit you are
a fast runner for an old man," I said, feeling men's
eyes on me as the insult hung for a moment in that
musky air.

Beiner glanced at Rolf, who gave nothing but a
clenched jaw so far as I could see. Then the big warrior grinned, cutting his grizzled beard with teeth.

"You must be a Dane, boy!" he said, shaking his
head and drawing in his friends with a sweep of his
arm. "You've got bats in your skull," he added, flapping his big hands. "Only a Dane would take on a
swarm of Svartálfar—or draugar or whatever in
Hel's reeking cunny they are—on horseback, armed
only with a bent spear and his own crooked cock."

I smiled, mostly in relief that the big Dane didn't
seem about to use that big ax on me. "Does that mean
you'll do as I say, Beiner?" I asked.

The Dane scratched his cheek and hoisted his brows.
"Do you want us to go out there and ask for our
spears back?"

"I want you to take that ax of yours and kill some chickens," I said, pointing into the shadows where the birds clucked and scratched quietly. "I'm hungry."

"Fucking bats in his skull," Beiner muttered, swinging his ax from his shoulder into his right hand and shambling off, musky smoke billowing in his wake. Rolf looked at me, bewilderment on his face, and I shrugged, unable to hide the surprise in mine.

chapter
five

Our plan was playing out like good flax on a drop spindle. The blaumen were encamped an arrow shot southeast of us, foot soldiers and mounted men together now, sharing fires and food whose strange smells carried up to us on the balcony of Gerd's Tit. I watched from those heights as they performed their strange ritual again, the day's light rolling westward, relinquishing the dry land to the shadows, as the ululating song wove a braid of sound. I had two fears, one that they would vanish, choosing not to fight us at all, and the other that they would press their attack on the door and break through. For we would eventually run out of heavy things to drop from the balustrade, and few of us had decent weapons. But our lack of good war gear was all part of the plan and no doubt much of the reason why the blaumen were still there. We had baited the hook, and they had all but swallowed it, though I wanted to draw them in one last time.

A roar of pain filled the tit as two Danes put Penda's shoulder back in its place.

"We need them closer," I said to Rolf beside me. "If they decide we're not worth the spilled blood, it has all been for nothing."

"Attack them?" he suggested, though there was no heart in the words.

"No. Out there they would ride us down. Trample us to dust and horse piss." I shook my head, biting a succulent hunk of meat off a chicken's leg. "Just keep your eyes turned to the sea," I said, "and I will think of something."

Inside Gerd's Tit, candles illuminated the darkness and the taut faces of men who now looked to me to keep them alive. The one who had fallen to an arrow outside lay choking on his own blood. Bubbles frothed over his beard, and his friends sat with him, talking in low voices of all the swiving he would soon be doing in Valhöll. They were good men, those Danes, tough and loyal, if a little wild in a fight, and as I sat in that hollow stone place, watching them sharpen their poor blades and throw insults back and forth, my mind summoned the new oath we had forged on that wind-swept island off the Frankish coast.

Each man had begun by proclaiming his ancestors and boasting of their deeds, if any was worth mentioning. I had dreaded my turn, for I did not even know my father's name, let alone whether he had been a farmer or a warrior or had done any deed worthy of a hearth-side tale. Not that I believed half of what blew through the beards around me that day. Had Svein the Red's grandfather really slain a family of giants? Could we believe that with the giants' blood still wet on his sword he had plunged into the breaking waves to slaughter a great sea monster? To my nose that had more than a whiff of Beowulf about it, and I wasn't alone in smelling it. But when the man next to me had spent his words, filling the world with a silence heavier than a mountain, and all eyes turned to me, I had swallowed my fear and spoken as best I could.

I swear this oath before my sword-brothers. That I Raven, foster son of Ealhstan of Wessex, am Jarl Sigurd's man and that my sword is his. We had said the words with our right hands on the hilt of Sigurd's sword, which had belonged to his father before him. *I will not flee from any man who is my equal in bravery and arms. I will avenge any of my oath-bound brothers as though we are brothers by blood. I will not utter words of fear or be afraid of anything no matter how hard things look. I will bring all booty to my jarl, and he will reward me as a ring-giver should.* Men nodded and murmured, and I folded my fingers around the sword's grip to stop my hand from trembling, because an oath is the heaviest thing a man can give and an oath breaker is no better than a murderer or a man who steals from his friend. *I will slaughter my enemies, and they shall know the name of Raven of the Wolfpack, who fights for Jarl Sigurd.* I felt Sigurd's eyes boring into me and could not meet them, so I caught Olaf's eye instead. He grinned and winked at me as though he had just caught me sneaking from the warm furs of my first whore. *If I break this oath, I betray my jarl and my Fellowship and I am a pus-filled nithing and may the All-Father riddle my eyes with maggots though I yet live.* And then it was done, and I had barely taken my hand from Sigurd's sword when another man's hand was on it, his words ringing out among the rocks.

When it was all done and every man but Father Egfrith had sworn the oath, it was as though a sodden blanket weighed on our spirits. It is always said that a wise man gives few oaths and breaks none, and all of us knew then that we bore fetters stronger than those which had bound some of us in that rotting Frankish hall, stronger even than Gleipnir, which holds Fenrir Wolf. But soon I felt that burden lift and knew it was because there is also strength in an oath because you know you are a part of something enduring and true.

In Gerd's Tit a shout brought me back to the present. A man up on the balcony was seeing a thin twist of smoke rising from the southeast beyond the enemy camp and the hillocks that concealed the seashore. I nodded, satisfied with the company I kept. Each man was oath-bound, each warrior like a branch of Yggdrasil, the great World-Tree, and together we would stand tall enough that the gods in Asgard would see our great deeds, no matter if my real father had never done a brave thing in his life. The gods would see me. They would mark me as a man worthy to be taken into Valhöll in preparation for the last battle.

"How is your shoulder?" I asked Penda. He was grimacing as he rolled his elbow in cautious circles, testing the fit of bone and joint.

"It's not my sword arm," he said with a pained grin, "and I don't have a shield anyway." But the pain had sharpened his eyes to points, and so I looked to big Beiner instead, thinking he deserved some recognition after the word lashing he had gotten from me.

"I could use a man who is good with an ax," I said. "Know anyone, Beiner?"

He grinned through his matted black beard, which was streaked with silver thread. His face was broad and long, and his gray eyes narrowed as though his mind sought to unravel whatever knots I was throwing at him.

"As it happens, I know just the man," he announced, tossing a half-chewed chicken bone behind him, and some of his friends began to chant his name as he pursed his greasy lips and touched them to his ax's cheek. I would not have been surprised if Beiner had been married to that ax and had a brood of little axes causing havoc back home in Denmark.

"Come with me," I said, getting to my feet and loosening my muscles, "and drag a comb through that bear's arse beard of yours." I smiled. "You're our champion, Beiner. And you're going to challenge those blaumen out there to come and spill your guts across the ground."

Beiner's eyebrows arched like the Midgard-Serpent's back. "I'm beginning to think you don't much like me, lad," he said, following me to the barricaded door.

After checking with the men up on the lookout platform that there were no blaumen within a hundred strides of the door, we cleared away the obstacles and I stepped out with Beiner behind me. Dusk was approaching, the sun a red clot far away in the western sky. I could smell strange spices and horse sweat and the oiled leather of harnesses and bridles. In the distance the blaumen seemed at their ease, though they got to their feet when they saw us. Above, the rich blue of the sky was streaked red, as though the sun had bled on its retreat west, and I did not like the look of that but decided that as it was the blaumen's land, it was an omen for them and not us.

"Now what?" Beiner said, seeming a little anxious

now that it was just us and his friends were safely barricaded in Gerd's Tit.

"Now you start swinging that ax around like you mean it," I said, "and walk at the same time if you can manage that. And keep the bloody thing away from me." I did not turn around, but I knew the Dane was doing as I had asked, because I could hear the hard slap every time the weapon's wooden haft struck his palm at the end of each pattern the ax wove through the air. I also knew that before long Beiner's shoulders would be screaming in pain as the muscles burned, but I counted on the big man's having too much pride to stop until I told him to.

We were now a Svein the Red spear's throw from the building and out in the open, and I admit that my skin was clammy with cold sweat because I felt like a mouse leaving his hole when he knows the owls are watching from the trees. It was all I could do to leave my sword in its scabbard when my hand ached to clasp it the way I had seen Egfrith hold his cross before him as though the very sight of it would flay the skin from a heathen.

"You're slowing down, Beiner; I can hear it," I accused him, licking a drop of salty sweat from my top lip.

"Screw you, whelp," he growled, breathing like a pair of forge bellows.

"Not long now," I said. "We've got their attention. Now we need to keep it." The blaumen were coming. Those with horses had mounted and those without trudged toward us, and all of them seemed to be cheering one man who strode lightly at their front and center. "Looks like they have chosen their own champion, Beiner," I said, "but I don't think a big Dane like you needs to worry about him. I've seen more meat on a fart."

"Aye, the dark whoreson walks like a woman," Beiner said, still looping his big ax through the air.

"You'll cut that sheep's dick in half without even realizing it," I said, trying to bolster Beiner's spirits. In truth, I had not meant for this fight to happen. The smoke that the Danes up on the platform of Gerd's Tit had seen rising from the shore had been the sign from Sigurd that the others had moored and were in position. I had taken Beiner out into the open to tempt the blaumen closer, to draw them deeper into the trap and keep their eyes turned from the beach, but now they were so close that I could smell them, and it looked as if Beiner would have to use that ax he had been swinging.

"Thór's balls, you can stop now, Beiner!" I said, stepping out of his ax's reach. "You're making me dizzy."

"Am I going to fight him?" he asked. His face was sheened with sweat, which was dripping from his newly combed beard.

"What did you think was going to happen?" I asked. He shrugged, chewing his bottom lip, then put the head of his ax on the ground, leaning its shaft against his leg so that he could wipe his sweaty palms on his breeches.

"Just don't kill the scrawny whoreson too quickly," I said, "because if you do, we'll both be too dead to see Sigurd tear them apart." I eyed the blaumen's champion and did not like what I saw. He moved with considered poise, like a cat, and he was thin and lithe-looking. Champions are usually big as trolls, men like Svein the Red and the Frank who had jumped aboard *Serpent* when we had fled from Frankia, but this one was slight, which told me he was fast. A curved sword was scabbarded at his hip, and beneath long yellow robes that were embroidered with red flowers and drawn in at the waist with a red sash, I could see rows of small iron plates that looked like fish scales. Beneath those scales ring-mail protected his throat and the lower half of his face, and unlike most of the other blaumen, his head was not covered in white cloth; instead, he wore a pointed helmet.

"Skinny slash of piss is done up like a crab," Beiner muttered. "I'll have to crack the damn shell to get to the meat."

"Your ax will cut through that lot like a hot knife through honey," I said. "Tell me you put a good edge on it."

"Good enough," he said as the blaumen stopped before us, their horses neighing and pissing steaming nerves into the dusty ground.

My heart was thumping like a man buried alive in his coffin. I thought they would simply kill us both right there, and I clenched my jaw to keep the fear off my face. After what I had done to the last man who had come to talk, I could not have blamed them for slicing me up where I stood. But luckily for me if not for Beiner, it seemed they wanted us all to see their champion at work, and one of the mounted men, whose saddle was draped in purple silk and whose head cloth was ringed with a fine band of gold, nodded to me in acknowledgment of the challenge. I supposed he was the local lord who commanded these new men, and as such it was his job to see raiders like us killed. He had brought these men to fight us, and I was glad to see they owned decent war gear: strange curved swords and some single-edged straight ones, too; spears, some with blades as long as a man's forearm; brynjas made of iron or tough leather scales; short hand axes; maces; and bows that, unstrung as they were now, had ears that curved away from the archer. Any other day I would have cursed our luck in facing an enemy who was so well armed. Not today.

The warlord spoke, but it might as well have been the clucking of a hen for all the meaning I could get from it, though I did recognize the word *Al-majus* somewhere midstream, which was something the last man had said before I skewered him.

The dark-skinned lord was still talking when I turned to Beiner. "Are you ready?" He nodded, but there was doubt in his iron-gray eyes, because he knew as well as I did that a small champion was likely to be a fast champion.

"All that iron will slow him down," I said.

"I hope so," he said through a grimace. "I can't kill him if I can't catch him."

In contrast to the warrior before us, who was now half crouched in a stretch that would have split my groin had I tried it, Beiner had only a few scraps of mail, taken from old brynjas, that he had sewn onto a sweat-stained leather gambeson that had seen better days. He wore no helmet and he did not own a shield, but the ax that was his only weapon looked sharp enough to cut a shadow.

The blaumen's black banner snapped, caught by a sudden gust from the east, and the man holding its shaft looked up as if to check that the thing hadn't been carried off. Then the mounted leader shouted a command, and all fifty of them shuffled backward, so I did the same, leaving their champion and ours facing each other across two spear lengths of dry ground.

"Forget what I said about making it last, Beiner," I said, suddenly fearful for the Dane, for their man looked as arrogant as a cat with a vole beneath its paw. "If you get the chance, gut the greasy bastard."

Then the blauman's sword rasped up the scabbard's throat and snaked at Beiner fast as lightning, slicing the Dane's shoulder before he could even raise the ax.

Beiner stepped back without looking at the wound, for he knew it was nothing serious. "That was a low thing to do," he said, spitting on the ground between them. "I wasn't ready."

The dark warrior jumped high into the air, his knees almost striking his chest, then landed in a crouch and leaped back up, spinning around, his sword slicing the air, and I wondered how it was possible to move like that in mail. His friends cheered his skill, then looked to Beiner for his response. But Beiner just stood there rooted to the ground like an ash.

"Heimdall's hairy ball sack!" he said. "He's a giant flea." The man darted in again, this time cutting low and gashing Beiner's right leg just above the knee. Beiner swung his ax, but his enemy was already out of range. "I felt that one," Beiner muttered, and I was about to tell him to make his ax dance, but the big Dane had already thought of that and the ax began to carve great rings through the air above his head. And Beiner began to roar.

I looked beyond the warriors but could see no sign

of the Wolfpack. *What are you waiting for, Sigurd?*
"Just keep that ax dancing," I said.

"It's easy for you to say!" Beiner spit, puffing like
an ox at the yoke as our enemy's champion began to
circle him with neat sideways steps, each foot crossing over the other in deft turns. Beiner shuffled his
booted feet, his eyes wide as he sought to keep the
lethal, heavy ax head between him and his opponent.
And he was doing well. The man knew one end of an
ax from the other, and every warrior there, including
the Danes watching from Gerd's Tit, knew that all
Beiner had to do was hit the little man once and the
chances were that it would be over. But no one knew
that better than the blauman, who moved as nimbly
as a new bed slave and must have been much stronger
than he looked.

I heard the next strike slice into Beiner's flesh along
the ribs beneath his right arm. He yelled in pain and
fury, spittle flying from his beard, and strode toward
the smaller man, looping the ax as though his intent
was to sever the Midgard-Serpent's head from its
monstrous coiled body. The other man was grinning,
and I ached to see those white teeth fly through the
back of his skull, because he was going to slice Beiner
up piece by living piece and the Dane would die a
death of red agony, and it would be my fault. Then,
from Gerd's Tit, I heard men howling like wolves. The
door was open, and the Danes were running toward
us, yelping wildly.

"Beiner, to me!" I shouted, and the big Dane stopped
his ax in midswing and hitched backward as I drew my
sword. I thought the Danes had killed us all then, for
against fifty we stood no chance. But then some of the

blaumen turned their backs on us and others scrambled to mount their horses as Sigurd and the Wolfpack ran down the crest, their painted shields a chaos of color and their blades gleaming dully in the reddish dusk.

"I was just about to gut that whelp," Beiner gasped, his chest heaving and his breath rattling like a sword in an ill-fitting scabbard.

"I could see that," I said, planting my feet for the coming fight. Then the Danes were around me, and we made a wall even without shields, and a heartbeat later nearly fifty well-armed warriors beneath a wolf's head banner crashed into the panicked press of robed men.

"Hold!" I yelled. "Hold, you Danish dogs!" Not because we were poorly armed and without brynjas but because if the enemy had any sense at all, they would break through us and run for Gerd's Tit, which would then protect them as it had us.

"Wait!" Penda bawled, grabbing a blood-hungry young Dane by one thick braid and yanking him back, and that made me think of Griffin of Abbotsend and his dog Arsebiter. "Stay here, you witless bastard!" Penda snarled, and the Dane suddenly understood, though he did not look happy about it. Horses screamed as Sigurd's men hamstrung them while their riders tried desperately to kick their way clear. The iron stink of blood bloomed in the air, and swords rang against metal and chopped into wet meat. Black Floki rammed his spear straight through a man's head and had drawn his sword before the man even knew he was dead. Bram Bear hacked off a horse's foreleg with his short ax, and blood sprayed across the nearest men, so that

they all broke off for a moment to wipe it from their
eyes. Sigurd gripped a spear in each hand and launched
them both together, the first time I had seen that done,
and each one plunged into its mark, and Sigurd was
laughing at the battle joy of it all.

"Now!" I yelled, striding forward into the fray. My
first swing took a man's head clean off his shoulders as
Penda and the Danes howled, released to the slaughter.
Some of the dark men fought, and fought well too, but
others we killed easily because they were too blinded
by fear and their panic to escape the butchery.

"Kill the bloodless things!" Tufi yelled, throwing
an arm around a man's neck and plunging a short
blade into his spine. The man screamed like an icy
wind through Hel as Tufi twisted the knife, grinning
viciously and mocking his victim's wailing.

The fight eddied around the dark-skinned champion who was keeping Bram and Bjarni at bay, his
sword streaking at them to bite their shields. The two
Norsemen seemed unsure how to deal with the man,
reminding me of two bears trying to paw a fish from
a stream, when Beiner limped up behind the blauman, looping his big ax through the air, then hammered the blade down through the man's left shoulder
and out above his right hip, cutting him into two
halves. Beiner roared in savage triumph, and Bram
and Bjarni looked at each other's blood-spattered
faces, their eyes sharing an appreciation of Beiner's ax
work. That man's death bought the others their lives,
for when our enemy's lord saw his champion slaughtered, he threw his curved sword onto the ground.
Aslak would have hacked him down if Sigurd had not
bellowed for him to stay his hand.

"Enough!" the jarl yelled, and his men raised their shields and stepped backward into space, instinctively finding the shoulder of a comrade. The blaumen followed their lord's lead and cast their weapons down; though some of them must have thought that was a stupid thing to do, they did it anyway.

The Wessexman Ulfbert lay dead, a hand ax wedged into the gristle and bone of his neck. Baldred, Wiglaf, and Gytha stood around him, shaking their heads and scratching their beards. Nearby lay the bodies of Geitir and another Dane whose name I didn't know, and several other men were clasping gashes or bruised limbs, awaiting their jarl's orders.

The sun fell behind the western horizon, retreating from the enormous swath of shadow that swept from the east across the land and vanquished the warmth of the day so that the sweat on my back felt suddenly cold and clammy. Ignoring Aslak, the lord of the blaumen turned to the east and raised his hands to the sky, and his men did the same.

"*Allahu akbar!*" he called, and the other men repeated the same words, and then another man began the wailing we had heard from them before. Black Floki glanced at Sigurd, who nodded; then Floki strode over to the wailing man and cracked a fist into his mouth, dropping him like a rock. But that didn't stop his companions from raising their arms and bowing. We looked at one another in disbelief, and some of us touched amulets or sword hilts to ward off this ill seidr. Meanwhile, old Asgot muttered counterspells, invoking Ódin to shield us from the blaumen's sorcery.

"Should have just killed them," Bothvar moaned,

holding his spear out toward one of them, his shield raised as though it could protect him from their strange words.

"You all know what to do," Sigurd said. "If any of the dogs resists, kill him." Aslak was the first. Grinning, he yanked the gold ring from the dark-skinned warlord's cloth-covered helmet and tossed it to Sigurd. Then he grabbed the man's scaled brynja at his neck and tugged viciously so that the man understood what was required of him. We all did the same with the men nearest to us, and reluctantly the blaumen began to pull off their war gear bit by bit, and I suddenly realized why Sigurd had stopped the killing. For it is much easier if a man gives you his mail voluntarily than it is to strip him of it when his corpse is stinking of blood and piss and shit and starting to stiffen. When we had gathered everything worth taking, we left the blaumen shivering in their underclothes, and still they seemed more concerned with their strange rites, so that we were happy to leave them and be gone. Penda had believed they were praying to their god, and I for one hoped that was the truth of it. Rather that than they had been weaving some powerful seidr against us. But I wondered what kind of god made his followers fall on their knees and touch their faces to the filthy ground to show their fealty. Such a god as that was a hard and cruel god or else his followers were not proud men like the Norse.

We watched the defeated dark-skins shamble off into the night, taking their dead with them on the surviving horses, which we had left, having no use for them. We knew we would have time to load food and plunder onto our ships and sail off before they returned with more warriors. But even so it was generous of Sigurd to spare them.

Rolf had questioned the decision, his thin face creased in puzzlement.

"A fox will kill every chicken in the coop just because he can," the jarl said. He had put the lord of the blaumen's gold ring around his own helmet and was carrying the man's fine leather saddle as well as his curved sword and scaled brynja. The pitch-skinned lord's helmet was tied to the jarl's belt, stripped of its linen wrapping, which Sigurd had used to clean his sword. "But a wolf," he said to Rolf, who walked beside him equally cumbered, "a wolf takes one lamb at a time, and the sheep grow to fear him. Next time we meet the blaumen, there is a good chance that they will run and not fight." Sigurd smiled, obviously happy with the day's work. "I don't know about you, Rolf, but I find I can heft twice as much plunder when my arms are not tired out from fighting."

The Dane laughed, and so did the rest of us. For our scheme had worked and the blaumen had blundered into our trap like witless animals, and we had killed and robbed them of everything they had that was worth taking to our ships. We had lost a handful of good men, which always leaves a bad taste in the mouth. These men, five Danes and a Wessexman, we buried together inside a ring of stones laid out in the shape of a longship, which did them some honor, though Sigurd sent them on their way across Bifröst with only spears and some of the Danes moaned about that. But we still had need of good swords and could not spare them for the dead. At first the Wessexmen had wanted to bury Ulfbert separately and in the Christian way. In the end, though, when the stone longship was finished, they decided to lay him in it beside the others.

"He will surely find heaven eventually," Baldred had said, scratching his balding head, "but let him sail with the heathens one more time, for he did so love the sea."

Sigurd now had enough war gear to equip every wolf in his pack properly. On the jetty before *Serpent* and *Fjord-Elk*, *Wave-Steed* and *Sea-Arrow*, by the silver light of a waxing moon, the Danes who had borrowed gear from the Norsemen returned it with thanks, complimenting the owners on the sharpness of their blades, the toughness of their shields, and the comfort of their helmets. Then Sigurd doled out spears and mail, short axes, strange-looking helmets, and the blaumen's light single-edged but wickedly sharp curved swords. Every Dane was grateful for the weapons he was given, for surely some of them were worth a heavy silver price, and when it was all done, the oath words whispered in my head: *I will not flee from any man who is my equal in bravery and arms. I will avenge any of my oath-bound brothers as though we are brothers by blood.* The wolves had fought for their jarl and made a slaughter to feed the crows and the worms, and Sigurd had played the part of the ring-giver, rewarding his warriors with fine arms. *If I break this oath, I betray my jarl and my fellowship and I am a pus-filled nithing.*

"They might have decent blades, but that doesn't make me happy about standing next to them in the shieldwall," Black Floki said, his words dispersing my thoughts like a pebble thrown into a pool. "They fight like wild dogs."

"Aye, but they killed their share," Olaf said. "Old Uncle Olaf will just have to teach them a few things," he added, his teeth white in the moon's glow as he examined a blauman's sword more closely, catching the reflected light on the blade as he looked along its edge.

"I would not stand too close when you do, Uncle," Osk said, tramping along the wharf, a butchered goat's leg over each shoulder. He passed the legs down to Bram in *Fjord-Elk,* and Bram smacked his lips eagerly. It felt good to be stocking our holds with fresh meat, though we would wait until we were a little farther along the coast before eating it.

"They'll learn, Osk," Olaf said, slicing the air with the sword, which looked too small in his hands. "There was a time when you couldn't hit your head on a low beam, lad. I'd seen monks of the White Christ handle whores with more skill than you did a spear."

Osk swore.

"I remember those days too, Uncle." Bram snorted like a bull, passing the meat to another man, who hefted it to *Fjord-Elk*'s steerboard side and passed it over to a man in *Serpent*, which was moored alongside. "Young Osk couldn't piss on his own shoes!"

"Fuck you, Bram," Osk said, climbing down into *Fjord-Elk*. Then the crowing really started.

"He couldn't hit my wife's arse with an oar!" ugly Hedin called.

"They used to say Osk once jumped into the sea and missed," Svein bellowed.

"He was such a bad shot with a bow that for the first fifteen years of his life his parents thought he was blind!" another man called, and in the end even Osk could not hide the smile in his beard.

Laughter was coming from *Sea-Arrow*, too, blending with the soft crash of the surf as her crew boarded in the moon-silvered dark, lugging the booty they had taken. I hoped the shine of that well-earned plunder might hold the Danes' eyes so that they would not linger on the newly turned earth on the ridge above the beach in which their brothers lay beside an Englishman. I needn't have worried from the sound of it. As I took to my sea chest, a Dane began to sing:

> "We came to fight the blaumen,
> Their skin was dark as soot.
> We screwed their black-haired women,
> We filled our ships with loot."

I sometimes wonder if men's laughter is offensive to the gods' ears, just as the bawdy songs and laughter from Hrothgar's mead hall Heorot made the monster Grendal's ears ring with red-hot pain. For it often seems the way that the man who is cheerful and free of cares one moment is dead the next. It is as though the Spinners cruelly weave a golden thread into a man's wyrd just before they cut it.

"Come on, lads!" Rolf called from *Sea-Arrow*'s mast step. "We don't want to be left behind in this arsehole of a place now that there's nothing left to steal!" The last of his Danes were boarding and being none too hasty about it, boasting of their kills as they emptied their bladders on dry land one final time.

Tufi was the last man, shouldering the big silver Christ cross he had found in the village and swaggering along the jetty like a man who has just humped a pair of whores. He came to *Sea-Arrow* and offered the cross to Ogn so that he could climb aboard, but seeing the thing, Ogn recoiled, touching the crude carving of Thór's hammer, Mjöllnir, at his neck.

"You're not bringing that thing on!" Ogn sputtered, rattled by Tufi's indifference to the cross.

"Don't be an old woman, Ogn," Tufi said. "Take the fucking thing. It's solid silver!"

"Ogn is right, Tufi," a red-haired man called Bork said. "You should leave it here."

Tufi shook his head and spit onto the jetty. "Out of my way, pale livers," he said, putting a foot on *Sea-Arrow*'s sheer strake. He must have slipped, or perhaps a wave rocked the slender ship, for Tufi's right leg plunged down and he followed it between *Sea-Arrow*'s hull and the jetty, and a *thud* and *splash* was the last anyone ever heard from the man. The Danes scrambled to help, and they must have thought they'd just pull him back in, for the water was not deep there, and some of us even laughed at first.

"He's gone!" Ogn yelled, peering over the side into the dark water. Rolf was there too, his hands gripping the sheer strake as he stared in disbelief.

"Shall I jump after him?" Gorm asked in a voice edged with fear.

Rolf shook his head, his brows reaching for the moon. "He's drowned!" he said. "The boneheaded son of a bitch is drowned and that silver with him." We were all staring now, for it did not seem possible that a man could die in ten feet of water. But poor Tufi must have hit his head on the sheer strake. Ogn, who had been the closest when it happened, said he thought an arm of the Christ cross had caught in Tufi's baldric and that was some very ill luck. We all knew how heavy that cross was.

"The White Christ seidr killed him!" Beiner said, giving words to what many of us were already thinking, and maybe that was why no one talked of trying to recover the man's corpse—in case that ill luck fastened on to him.

Father Egfrith crossed himself and offered a prayer up to his god. Sigurd, who was watching from the platform at *Serpent*'s stern, looked as stunned as I felt. He was shaking his head in astonishment as Olaf beside him muttered words I could not hear. Old Asgot's face was a twisted grimace, as though he had eaten something foul-tasting, and he looked with hatred at Egfrith. I said to Penda that I thought it was astonishing that the monk had not woken up dead before now, his blood crusting on the godi's knife.

"Let us leave this place!" Sigurd bellowed, gesturing for his stupefied crew to take to their benches and row us out to sea. And so we did.

chapter
SIX

I T WAS raining, and we were sailing east. We had
come to the southernmost reach of the coast we
had been tracking and the wind had picked up, and
so we had not needed to row for several days. On our
steerboard side another landmass reached out, as
mountainous and barren as that to the north, and
Egfrith informed us that it must be the place the Romans called the Pillars of Hercules.

"Who by Baldr's hairy left ball is Hercules?" Bothvar asked when I had spun Egfrith's words into Norse.

"He was a great hero, Bothvar, so the monk says
anyway," I said. "He was the son of the Greeks' chief
god, Zeus, and was the strongest man in the world."
Bothvar scratched his chin and pursed his lips. Yrsa
Pig-Nose nodded in appreciation.

"Sounds like Thór," Olaf said suspiciously.

"Or Beowulf," Sigurd suggested.

Egfrith seemed to be enjoying the interest the
Norsemen were showing in his story. He would lean
forward, telling me in English, then lean back against
Serpent's rib and study the men's faces.

"He was a great champion. A warrior of rare skill,"
I went on, addressing the next part to Sigurd, "but he
was also cunning and full of tricks."

"Sounds like you, Sigurd!" Uncle roared, slapping his jarl's back and laughing.

"I agree, Uncle," Sigurd said, a serious frown on his face. "It seems to me that this Hercules was the kind of man that if he pissed into the wind, the wind would change direction." And then the jarl burst into laughter, and so did we, perhaps overwringing the cloth. For the men had been quiet since Tufi's death. There had even been talk that we had not shaken off the bad luck that had seen us lose that Frankish hoard. Most of that talk came, as usual, from Asgot, and so I think we were all relieved that day to caulk the strakes with laughter. But that night, anchored in a steep-sided bay, the men were sullen again. Some of this, I think, was because we had run out of mead and not even Bram's stash had survived. The trouble with not being drunk is that you think too much. Ideas fly into your head whether you want them to or not, and the more you try to ignore them, the louder they become.

I was thinking about Halldor, whose face had swollen with pus and whose corpse had slowly blistered on a rain-soaked pyre. It seemed to me that there was still some nettle between Black Floki and Sigurd because Sigurd had killed Halldor. That had hurt Black Floki's pride, for Halldor had been his cousin and the way Floki saw it, the burden of killing the man should have been his alone. There had been no hard words between Sigurd and Floki as far as I knew, but the sting was there all the same. And Halldor's miserable death had gnawed at me ever since.

"You'd be better off putting the girl out of your head, lad," Olaf said. Penda and I were fishing off the stern, but I was hardly playing my line and Penda and

I had said less than three words to each other while the low sun slipped behind the mountains to the west.

"I'm not thinking about Cynethryth, Uncle," I said, which was true for once. Cynethryth was somewhere up near the bow, probably learning Norse from Asgot, which Egfrith had warned me about, though I had told him I did not know what I could do about it. "It's Halldor that won't leave me alone," I admitted.

From the corner of my eye I saw Olaf roll his. We had three sacks of horsehair that we had taken from the blaumen's mounts, and Olaf was teasing apart the strands and then twisting them together to make new caulking.

"You'd be best to put that from your mind, too," Olaf said. "No good can come of lingering on a thing like that."

"I've never seen a man die like that before. That's all."

I looked at Olaf now, and he frowned. "Halldor died a good death," he said. "By a good blade and holding one too."

I shook my head. "He was already dead," I said, remembering Halldor's hideous, misshapen head. "I have never smelled anything so bad. The man was rotten. Týr knows how he bore the pain."

"I just had a bite," Penda said, tugging his line. Then he cursed, staring into the black water. "Bastard got away." We ignored him.

"Sigurd did right by him," Olaf said. "He did what had to be done, and Halldor would have thanked him for it too."

I shook my head. "It's still boring into Floki, though," I said. "Like a woodworm."

Olaf grunted. "Floki ought to just let it lie. Ought to thank Sigurd himself if you ask me. But you know Floki. He was born miserable."

"Why did Sigurd do it, Uncle? He knew Halldor had asked Floki to do it. We all did."

Olaf glanced around to check that no one else was close. Most of the others were in their furs, either asleep or getting there. "Sigurd's boy," he said eventually.

"He died young. Horse kicked," I said, wondering what that had to do with things.

"Aye. But the poor little swine didn't die quick as he should have." Olaf tilted his shaggy head as though trying to weigh whether to speak or chew the words back down. "The boy was as good as dead, it's true. I'd seen rocks with more life in them. But he wasn't dead. Still breathing, he was, though barely enough to call it breathing."

Penda turned to say something else, then saw Olaf's face and turned back to his fishing, muttering that our heathen language was scaring off the fish.

"And he stayed like that for two weeks, might have been three. The poor little sod." Olaf cuffed a tear from his eye, and I glanced away for a heartbeat.

"A slow death," I said.

Olaf shook his head. "One night, Sigurd carried the boy out into the pasture, leaving Gudrid weeping at the door. He finished the boy himself. His own bairn."

Our eyes were locked, and I felt the shards of ice in mine. "He had no choice, lad. The boy he knew was long gone. There was nothing else for it."

"The Norns are bitches," I said, setting my jaw.

"I'll not argue with that," Olaf said, twisting the

horsehair again. "But Sigurd knows how it feels to kill your own kin. It weighs a man down. Will drag him under, like that Christ cross dragged Tufi to his end. Sigurd took that burden from Black Floki. Why? Because he's the best son of a wolf jarl who has ever led a crew across the whale's road. And Floki knows it too. He's pride-stung, that's all."

"If I ever get the wound rot, I'll cross Bifröst before I begin to stink," I said.

Olaf nodded, tugging his beard thoughtfully. "Just don't ask Osk to open you up, lad. He'd bloody miss."

I smiled but felt the cold in it, watching Olaf's surprisingly nimble fingers working the horsehair into fine, neat ropes.

"The fish are sleeping." Penda broke the silence. I locked eyes with him, but my mind saw Sigurd killing a small boy. Penda nodded at the line still clamped between my finger and thumb. "We might as well sleep too," he said, winding his line around the block. Then, shrugging, he turned and walked off.

And I stayed there at *Serpent*'s stern, with snores, farts, and the low murmur of men's voices breaking the whisper and slosh of the sea against the nearby rocks, until a crimson wash stained the eastern sky.

Three days later Bragi the Egg spotted a white sail. The small craft was cutting northwest toward the mountainous coast, making slow progress against the same westerly that kept our oars up in their trees and our salt-stained sails stretched. It was not the first vessel we had seen in these waters—there had been many—but as we came closer, we knew that this one was a trader. She was broad in the beam like a knörr so that she could not have used more than four pairs of oars, and those only for docking or keeping her bows into the wind in rough weather. She sat low in the water too, meaning she had a full hold, and it was likely that there were no more than twelve crewmen.

Bragi was standing at *Fjord-Elk*'s bow, and I could see his predatory smile even from a distance.

"My mother always says you should never turn down an invitation," he called across to Sigurd. "That looks like an invitation to me, hey!"

"Bragi's mother also said I was the best lover she had ever had," Bram the Bear growled, stirring a smattering of laughter.

Sigurd was up on *Serpent*'s mast step, watching the white-sailed ship like a hawk, his golden hair loose but for two braids falling on either side of his face.

"Should be as easy as skinning a hare," Olaf suggested, leaning on the sheer strake and squinting against the glare off the water. Above us the sun had broken through a blanket of fish-scale cloud that was questing east in a golden likeness of the sea. "We'll barely need to change course," Olaf went on. "Just snap them up on the way by."

Like a wolf snatching a moth from the air, I thought.

Sigurd seemed to consider it a moment longer; then he nodded and slapped the smooth mast before jumping down. "Bragi! Rolf! Today we are sea eagles, and there is our mackerel! Let us see which of us has the wings to match our talons!" And with that men whooped and hollered, because their jarl had made a contest of it and we would now see which of us was the fastest. Squalls raged aboard all four ships as crews worked the lines to best catch the wind on their sails while others grabbed their helmets and spears and bows. A few put on their brynjas, but I was one of those who did not bother, because no one expected the trader to make a fight of it against four dragons.

"The poor bastards must be wishing they had not put to sea this morning," Penda said, shaking his head.

"Leave them be, Sigurd!" Father Egfrith implored, wringing his hands.

"Out of my way, monk," Sigurd growled, putting on his helmet with its new gold band.

"But my lord, those poor souls have done you no harm," Egfrith protested.

"But I will do you enough harm if you keep buzzing in my ear," Sigurd said as Black Floki grabbed Egfrith's shoulder and shoved him so that he tripped over a sea chest and struck his arm on the hull.

"I'm beginning to think we will never make a Norseman of him," Sigurd said, shaking his head sadly. "Come on, Uncle!" he yelled, pointing to *Fjord-Elk* on our port side. "Those whoresons are beating us!" I saw Cynethryth at the prow, one arm wrapped around Jörmungand's throat, her hair, once golden as summer wheat but now darker with filth, flying behind in the wind. I wondered what was going through her mind, for I felt as though I no longer knew her, as though the girl I had known was gone and in her place stood a bitter woman who was in thrall to dark and twisted thoughts.

"They're going to get there first!" Bjarni yelled. He was making lewd gestures at the men of *Fjord-Elk*, and they were gesturing back with equal energy as the *Elk* sliced through the sea almost a length ahead of us now. Off our steerboard side *Sea-Arrow* was coming on well, and a spear's throw off her port stern *Wave-Steed* glided lightly over the rushing furrows. "We'll never hear the end of it!" Bjarni groaned.

"Throw Svein overboard!" Bag-Eyed Orm suggested, pointing his spear at Svein. "We'll fly like a fart in the wind then."

"I can't help having a giant's cock," Svein the Red said, shrugging his great shoulders.

The trader had her oars in the water now, desperately trying to reach the northern shore. She had no chance of doing that before we caught her, for we were flying. Our sails strained against the yard; the sheets, timbers, and blocks creaked; and my blood seemed to bubble with the sheer joy of it. I slapped Penda's back, feeling the grin stretch my wind- and salt-dried skin.

"You can't do this in Wessex!" I said, and he shook his head as though that was a great shame, then hefted his spear to get a feel for its balance. We were nearly level with the jagged headland that carved into the sea on our port side and about which the sea churned and thrashed in white spumy gouts. There was no catching *Fjord-Elk* now, which was the price we had paid for having most of the heavier cargo in our hold, but at least we would beat both of the Dane ships, whose sails were only half the size of *Serpent*'s.

"Frigg's arse!" Olaf clamored from the bow, turning back to Sigurd. "It's a trap!"

I jumped up onto my sea chest, clutching a shroud for balance, and saw two ships nosing from behind the headland, their oar banks beating like wings.

"They're fighters!" Olaf called.

Having seen the ships, Bragi was already leaking some of the wind out of his sail, waiting for us to catch up so that he could seek Sigurd's orders.

"You see what happens when you live by the sword!" Egfrith yelled, his eyes wide with fear.

"You still want to accept the invitation, Bragi?" Sigurd roared, but the words were lost in the wind.

"Do we fight them?" Olaf asked, tugging his beard, his face screwed up. As things stood, we would meet the enemy ships in the time it takes a hungry man to eat his breakfast.

"We are four and they are just two, Uncle," the jarl called back, sending Orm to fetch his brynja. "Now we will see how sea-bold they are." Olaf grimaced, not happy with his jarl's decision, but began barking orders and preparing for a fight.

When Bragi saw that we were not slowing, he caught the wind again and *Fjord-Elk* lurched into life. Then, as we scrambled into our brynjas, Bram blew the signal horn, the long note sounding like a bull's bellow, which told all the crews that they were to attack.

"Blaumen!" Olaf yelled from the bow, and Sigurd nodded, throwing his arms up through the sleeves of his brynja and slipping it over his head.

"These blaumen are proving to be worthy enemies," he said, bouncing his broad shoulders to let all the rings fall into place. "Their gods must be warriors, hey! We should catch one and take him back home to show our kinfolk." He turned to me. "Will we beat them, Raven?" he asked, pulling his belt tight around his waist, then fastening it.

"These blaumen are brave fighters, lord," I admitted, "and their gods might be warriors like ours. But we'll beat them." I had chosen a short ax because a sword can be cumbersome in a deck fight, and I slipped my left arm through the strap and made a fist around the leather-bound grip. Any men with bows were at the ship's bows now, choosing the first arrows they would send. Some of them touched the points against amulets of Ódin or Thór or Thór's hammer, Mjöllnir, for luck. Many of us lined the port side, for that was where we would board them from if Knut could get us alongside.

"It's a useful thing having four ships, Uncle," Sigurd said appreciatively. Olaf was beside him now, grimly staring out from beneath his helmet's rim.

"Only if the Danes know what they're about," Olaf said through gritted teeth.

Sea-Arrow would attack the first of the blaumen ships with us, getting in behind so that the blaumen would have to defend both bulwarks. *Wave-Steed* and *Fjord-Elk* would prey on the second ship in the same way. It was a good plan, and we were feeling confident.

That was, until we got a better look at the enemy.

"Christ and his angels, they're huge!" Baldred said, scratching his dense black beard, and the Wessexman was right. The blaumen's ships were big. Their hulls were long and slender, longer than *Serpent*, with freeboards perhaps two spear lengths from the waterline. We had fought a Frankish ship with high sides, but these two were longer and each had a fortress at its bow upon which up to a dozen blaumen bristled with bows and spears.

"These nuts are going to be hard to crack," Bram

Bear said, brows raised in wonder at the strange vessels.

"How many oars?" a man asked.

"Too many to count the bloody things," Olaf replied. "Must be over a hundred."

"One hundred and fifty," another man said. Those oars plunged and rose, plunged and rose, with incredible speed, bringing the ships on against the wind.

"They're bold bastards!" Gytha said.

"They'll use those to board us," Osk said, indicating the enemy prows, which pointed forward like birds' beaks and were wide enough for five men to stand shoulder to shoulder on.

"They'd break their damned necks," Olaf said, and I thought he was right, for though those beaks would be useful for boarding other high-sided ships, they would not be much use against us. Still, they could stand on them and shoot arrows into us, which was not a good thought.

"Furs!" Sigurd yelled. "Get your furs and put them over your shoulders! A good fur will stop an arrow." Then he whistled across to Bragi and made a series of gestures that *Fjord-Elk*'s captain must have understood, because he nodded and began barking orders at his crew. Then, as we fetched our furs and did as Sigurd had told us, using long-pinned brooches or piercing the furs and threading leather or twine through them that we could tie across our chests, the jarl strode aft and told his plan to Knut.

"We're still going to attack them, then?" Baldred said uneasily, dragging his teeth across his bottom lip.

Penda gripped the man's fur-clad shoulder and smiled. "What else were you going to do today, Baldred?" He nodded in my direction. "But I would keep my distance from Raven. I've seen him practicing with that ax." I swore at him.

Sigurd yelled to the Danes and threw his hand forward repeatedly, the gesture telling them to turn their prows southeast and keep going without engaging the enemy. Rolf, standing on *Sea-Arrow*'s sheer strake, waved back that he understood, then jumped down. We were close enough now to see the dark faces of the men on the enormous fighting platforms at the bows, though we could not see the rest of the crews, who were hidden in the bellies of those great wooden beasts.

"Shields!" a man roared, and we raised our shields and braced as the air shivered with the hiss of a large flock of arrows. A heartbeat later those shafts clattered among us, tonking off shield bosses, thudding into wood, and splashing into the sea.

"Anyone hit?" Sigurd yelled as men shuffled aside to let him through. No one was. I glanced up and saw several arrows hanging in *Serpent*'s sail and some holes where they had plunged through the thick wool. I looked back and saw Cynethryth crouching behind a sea chest, holding a shield over her head. She was wearing a toughened leather skullcap and a leather scaled brynja taken in the last raid. I hardly recognized her. Behind her Knut was at the tiller, protected by Bjarni, who had a shield in each hand.

"You don't need to see what's going on, lads," Olaf called, perhaps for my benefit. "Uncle Olaf will tell you what you need to know. Just keep your ugly arse faces behind those shields until me or your jarl tells you otherwise. We're going to show these draugar sons of whores that you don't lay a trap for wolves unless you have the balls to jump into the pit to finish them off!"

Another storm of arrows ripped into us, and this time there were a few yells of pain where the points had found their way past shields and between fur and mail into soft flesh. Again I looked back at Cynethryth and silently thanked the All-Father that she was not hurt. I could hear the blaumen shouting now. I saw Bram Bear and Bothvar and Yrsa Pig-Nose readying grappling hooks, and I heard the *twang* as some of our men loosed arrows. I wished I had a small pebble to suck because my mouth was so dry, and I gave myself over to fear because I knew that that fear would grow into the battle joy that helps a man butcher other men. The trembling was in the muscles above my knees. Soon it would spread upward, turning my bowels to water, and eventually it would reach my hands and even my jaw, putting a bitter taste in my mouth.

"They're trying to keep their bows toward us." Olaf was looking over his shield. "They must think we're going to roll over and let them scratch our bellies."

"Bragi is going to hit the first ship!" Sigurd yelled, which was a surprise to me. But risking a look myself, I saw that the second blaumen ship had turned southwest to cut off the two Dane snekkjes, leaving its sister ship to deal with us. *They're bold enough*, I thought. "You're going to need a bigger ax, Raven," Sigurd said, grinning at me. But it was too late to grab a two-hander from the hold, and before I could say as much, there was a great roar from the men of *Fjord-Elk* as her steersman, Kjar, with the help of the men working the sail, turned her steerboard on to the enemy ship and the others hurled spears and loosed arrows at the blaumen in the bow fortress. The oars on the blaumen ship's steerboard side thrashed the sea as her captain sought to turn her bow northward and keep that long beak between us and *Fjord-Elk*. There was enough wind across our sail to take us straight past her stern and into the open channel beyond, and if that happened, I doubted the blaumen could catch us even with two hundred oars. Bragi then dropped *Fjord-Elk*'s sail, and without oars in the water she was helpless. That was a daring move, for the blaumen captain was trying to maneuver his ship's beak over *Fjord-Elk* so that her men could use their height advantage. For a moment it seemed Sigurd was going to let the westerly carry us by, but then he roared at Knut, and Jörmungand bucked and snarled at our enemy. The sail snapped as the wind hit its leeward side, but that would not be enough to slow us now. The blaumen did not have time to pull in their oars, and *Serpent*'s prow smashed into their port-side oar bank, filling the world with the splintering crack as ten or more staves snapped like kindling. Rowers were screaming, their chests crushed by their oar grips, and then there were men above us, their dark faces twisted with hatred and fury.

"Carve them up, lads!" Sigurd yelled, his shield raised above his left shoulder as he hacked into an enemy oar amidships with his great sword. Svein the Red had already destroyed two oars and was roaring as he swung the two-handed battle-ax into another oar, cutting it clean in half. There were two arrows sticking in the brown bear fur across the giant's shoulders, but he paid them no heed. I hacked into an oar with my short ax, but the blade stuck and the ships moved, and so I had to leave it half buried in that stave and draw my sword instead.

"Bragi's men must have boarded them," Penda said, catching a spear on his shield and deflecting it into the sea. One of Hedin's arrows took a man on the ship's bow fortress in the throat, and he staggered against the bulwark and fell out of sight. We could not see *Fjord-Elk* on the blaumen ship's steerboard side, but the enemy ship was ringing with the sound of battle; somehow Bragi's crew must have climbed aboard. I glanced eastward and saw that the other blaumen ship was plowing away as fast as her oar banks could beat and the Danes were coming to join us, rowing because the wind was against them.

Bothvar and Yrsa had sunk their grappling hooks into the enemy ship's sheer strake and were heaving to keep the hulls together.

"Here! Take this!" A man with a filth-matted beard looked down at us, then dropped one end of a knotted rope, which Sigurd himself caught. Then the man was gone.

Sigurd sheathed his sword and turned to us with a savage grin.

"Are you whoresons coming?" he said, then began to climb. A spear streaked down, and I turned just in time, so that it glanced off the fur on my shoulder and thudded into a Norseman's shield. All around me arrows jutted from the furs Sigurd had told us to wear, and I knew men were still alive because of that low cunning. I slung my shield over my back and climbed the rope, throwing myself over the enemy's sheer strake without stopping to make sense of the chaos. And it was chaos. The blaumen were fighting one another, but I saw that some of them had to be slaves, for they wore rags and looked as though they had just crawled out of a burial howe but for their shoulders and arms, which were thickly muscled from rowing. Many of them were still chained to one another, but they fought their masters with a desperate fury that reminded me of the Danes, who were now pulling alongside the stern. I unslung my shield and pushed into the fray.

"Kill them!" Olaf bellowed, thrusting his shield's boss into a blauman's face, then plunging his sword's point into the man's foot.

A warrior screamed something at me and slashed his sword, but I caught the curved blade on my sword and lunged forward, smashing the hilt into his face. His eyes filled with shock and his mouth hung crooked, his jaw smashed, and he tried to step back but could not because of the press of men around us. I swung my sword at his forward leg and he dropped his shield, but my move was a feint and I reversed the blade, sweeping it up into his throat, ripping out his windpipe in a spray of bloody gore. These blaumen had lured us into a trap to kill us and take what was ours, and now they were dying because they had underestimated us. Many were shedding their buff leather jerkins and arms and leaping overboard; those men would drown because we were far from the shore, but they preferred that death to the one we offered them.

I saw the man who had thrown us the rope. He was on his knees, throttling a blauman whose eyes bulged like those of a fish dragged up from the depths, and I realized he was not one of the Danes but must be a slave of the blaumen. The veins in his bare arms looked like hemp cords, and his skin looked to have suffered burns and healed over them. Other oarsmen cowered pathetically, two to a bench, half gripping their staves and half shielding their heads.

"The ship is ours!" a Wessexman yelled. To my right the first of the Danes were boarding, eager to earn their own kills. Kveldulf, one of *Fjord-Elk*'s crew, spun around, hot blood spraying me from a gash across his face; then a blauman's spear burst through his chest, and he fell to his knees. Blood flew and men screamed, and the battle joy filled us. Swords rang and shields clashed, and the clamor of it all drenched the world.

"Shieldwall!" Sigurd yelled.

"Shieldwall!" Olaf roared, pushing through the press to stand with his jarl. It was a good idea because in that sort of chaos you are as likely to be killed by one of your own side as by the enemy, especially on a rocking ship. Building a shieldwall would make sense of the tumult, and once it was formed, we could sweep the deck in a line of wicked sharp steel and finish it.

"They won't be trying to snare us again, hey!" Svein the Red said, shoving between two Norsemen to take his place in the growing bulwark of shields that already spanned the width of the deck. At the ship's stern the Danes were making their own shield-wall, and they looked impressive now, if strange, in their new mail and wielding the blaumen's curious weapons. Between those two walls of death our enemies tried to regroup, pulling themselves into some sort of order but not knowing which way to turn. Many of the slaves cowered at their row benches still, chained and helpless or else too frightened to fight. Others lay wounded or dead in pools of blood. The few who had fought free and survived, including the man who had thrown us the rope, had gathered by the mast, where they stooped uncertainly, not knowing where their best chances lay. Men hurled insults at one another, clutched bloody wounds, gasped for breath, bellowed with pain, or died quietly.

"Hold!" Sigurd yelled, and so we made sure our shields overlapped and planted our feet as the ship gently rocked, unlocking our knees with each pitch and roll. Then we waited, our chests heaving and our mouths drier than a dead dog's ashes.

"Norsemen!" It was Filthy Beard, the man who had helped us board the blaumen ship. "Do not kill us. I am from Aggersborg."

"Not another Dane," Bram Bear muttered through a beard whose bristles held beads of blood.

"We are slaves of these dogs," Filthy Beard said, spitting toward the surviving blaumen, who were fear-soaked and staring like wretched, beaten curs. There were perhaps thirty of them still armed and in a fit state to fight, but they could see their sister ship in the distance and see too that her bows were pointing the wrong way. "I have rowed for these dark dogs for two burning summers, but I knew a good crew of Týr-brave men would come from the north and slaughter the whoresons. I am Yngvar."

Sigurd stepped forward, and from the look on Yngvar's face, he knew instantly that Sigurd was our jarl.

"It was you who threw us the rope?" Sigurd asked.

"It was, lord," Yngvar said, dipping his head, though you could see the pride in him.

"That was well done, Yngvar," Sigurd said. The other slaves were all blaumen, and they watched in desperation, not knowing what lay in store for them. "I am Jarl Sigurd, and these are my oathmen. Do you speak the blaumen's tongue?" Sigurd asked Yngvar, pointing his gory sword at the enemy warriors, some of whom were muttering strange words under their breath.

Yngvar shook his head. "Would a Norseman eat goat droppings?" he asked. There were chuckles at that. "But my friend speaks their filthy words." He gestured at a blauman standing proudly among the slaves. He wore no clothes but for a cloth to cover his manhood. He was heavily muscled, his corpse-black skin glistened with sweat, and like Yngvar's, his body was covered in welts from his master's whip. "We have shared these rusting fetters," Yngvar said, moving his leg so that a short length of severed chain rattled along the deck, "and pulled the same oar for a long time. I have taught him our words, but . . ." He shrugged his scarred shoulders. ". . . my dog back home can speak it better."

Sigurd nodded. "Tell the blaumen that I will spare them if they put down their weapons." Yngvar looked horrified, but I knew it was the right thing, for we did not want to risk our lives if we did not need to.

"But my lord, these dogs deserve only your blades," Yngvar said. "They lured you in with that trader and would have killed you all or made thralls of you. Even you, Jarl Sigurd, would have been beaten and treated worse than a beast of burden." His eyes hardened. "Kill them."

"Just give the word, Sigurd, and we'll send these draugar back to their graves!" Rolf called from the stern, his men bristling with violence.

"Kill them all, Sigurd!" Yngvar said.

"Watch your tongue if you want to keep it, cur!" Olaf warned, pointing a finger at Yngvar. "Do as you have been told before I have you standing in your own rancid guts."

Yngvar grimaced and gestured to his friend to step forward, then told him what Sigurd had said. The blauman nodded and turned to those who had kept him in chains for who knows how long. He all but spit the words at their feet. The blaumen did not move.

"Well?" Sigurd said. "Are they in such a rush to get to the afterlife?" One of the blaumen spoke to Yngvar's oarmate, who locked his eyes with Sigurd's.

"They do not trust you to keep your word, because you are heathen devils." It was the strangest thing hearing Norse words from a man who looked like that.

Sigurd laughed. "They sound like Christians even if they don't look like them," he said, then turned to Olaf. "Well, Uncle, these walking corpses do not trust us. Perhaps we should lay down our weapons to prove ourselves."

Olaf grinned. "Aye, and we could bend over and let them fuck us, too. Just to show that we mean what we say." The blauman spoke again.

"They say Allah the almighty will protect them. They will fight," Yngvar's oarmate said.

Sigurd frowned.

"This Allah must be one of their gods," I said.

"There is only one god," Yngvar's blauman friend said.

"They *do* sound like Christians," Sigurd said. Then he shrugged at Olaf and lifted his shield. "Are you ready, Rolf?" he called.

There was a thumping of shields from the Danes behind the blaumen.

"Aye, Sigurd! Gleipnir couldn't hold the lads back!" Rolf replied.

Sigurd nodded. "Leave no man alive," he said to us, and I gritted my teeth and lifted my shield, eyeing the blaumen for the one I was going to kill. Penda loosened his neck, and Svein slapped the haft of his long ax.

Then a sword clattered onto the deck. A gray-bearded blauman stepped from the press of warriors, his chin held high. He studied us down a beak of a nose as though we were a shit bucket that needed emptying. Some of his men stepped in front of him protectively, raising their curved swords at us threateningly, but a few sharp words from their lord stung them into stepping back, heads bowed.

"That's the vicious son of a troll who likes to whip men who are chained to the deck," Yngvar said, the words dripping with putrid bile.

The blaumen's lord barked at Yngvar's friend, and you would have thought the man was still chained to an oar.

"He's got balls, this one," Bram said admiringly.

Yngvar's friend nodded at the blaumen's lord and looked back to Sigurd.

"He says you may kill him but only if you let his men go," Yngvar's friend said. "Otherwise they will fight you and many of your men will die." I did not know how many men we had lost, but surely some were already crossing Bifröst.

Sigurd dragged the knuckles of the hand holding his sword across his chin, then eyeballed the blauman who had offered his life for his men's.

"Aye, Bram; he is brave for a dead man," Sigurd said.

Seeing a chance to appease the gods, Asgot stepped forward, the bones rattling in his braids. "Sigurd, the All-Father will look kindly on a blood offering."

Sigurd seemed to consider this, then shook his head.

"No offering, godi. Ódin might think we had dug up a corpse and killed it again," he said, and even Asgot admitted that perhaps it was not such a good idea. "You say that this man whipped you, Yngvar?"

"Even when we were rowing well, my lord," Yngvar said.

Sigurd nodded again. "Tell him I accept his offer."

Yngvar glared at us, clearly horrified at the thought of letting his captors live. But then he nodded, for it does not do to gainsay a jarl. Besides which, he did not know what we were going to do with him.

When Yngvar's oarmate confirmed Sigurd's acceptance, the blauman dipped his head and muttered something—to his god, I think—but even then he had some nerve, demanding that Sigurd put his men ashore before the heathen brought his filthy blade anywhere near him.

"Gut the draugar, Sigurd," Bram Bear said.

"I will throw his guts to the fish." Svein the Red pointed with his ax, gripping the long haft's throat in one massive hand.

Sigurd shook his head. "Uncle, can a small crew sail this blauman ship?"

Olaf pursed his lips. "In this weather ten men could handle her, I think. If they've any sea-craft." He looked up at the sky, eyeing the clouds, which had thickened into heaped layers of shorn wool drifting northeast. "But if it turns . . ."

Sigurd nodded, turning to Yngvar. "Choose nine good men and tell them I will pay them three large silver coins each if they sail this ship until I can sell it."

Yngvar glanced at his oarmate, whose eyes were yellow as butter against his dark skin. "Her sail alone needs ten men, Jarl Sigurd," Yngvar said. "Especially when the wind is up."

"Then fifteen men will each get two coins or the same weight in silver," Sigurd said, to which it was impossible to guess Yngvar's thoughts. "Uncle, take the rest of the blaumen aboard *Fjord-Elk* and put them ashore."

"You want me to give them food and water too?" Olaf asked, wide-eyed.

"They have their lives," Sigurd said, implying that that was enough.

And so we watched as the blaumen, slaves and erstwhile masters together and none of them armed, were loaded aboard *Fjord-Elk* and rowed to the shallows. Bragi would not risk *Fjord-Elk*'s belly for the sake of those men and so made them jump overboard at the points of his men's spears, about three boat lengths from the surf that rolled up the dark gold sand. Of the two groups there were many more slaves, and the rest of us watched, wondering if they would turn on the others in vengeance now that they were free. But to the disappointed groans of many, the crowd split like an oak and the sorry-looking freed men shuffled off like a herd of sheep, leaving the others staring out to sea from above the waterline. For those were loyal men and hated abandoning their lord to us.

"If a man beats his slave, he must be certain that the slave will never taste freedom," Sigurd said to the blaumen's lord, "for that first breath of free air will bring to his mind every bite of the whip and every blow of the fist." But the blauman did not understand, or at least he showed no signs of understanding, and simply glared at Sigurd with eyes as cold as Hel. "Yngvar," the jarl went on, "it is not right that a man from the fjords should be in thrall to a walking corpse like this. Worse still that this burned goat's prick should beat the men who are pulling his oars." Sigurd glanced at Bag-Eyed Orm, who lay against the hull, bleeding to death from a spear thrust that had split his mail and pierced his belly. Uncle had poured a gruel made with onions down Orm's throat, and now he was on his knees sniffing the wound as Orm bit into a comb against the pain. He looked up at Sigurd and shook his head, meaning he could smell onion in the wound and so Orm's stomach was holed. There was no hope for Orm now.

Sigurd half grimaced and looked back at the blauman. "Do what you want with him, Yngvar," he said.

Now Yngvar grinned; his oarmate stepped forward, but Yngvar batted him away with a brawny arm. "I felt the whoreson's lash more than you. You can have what's left when I'm finished."

But in the end there was nothing left. The blauman had not raised a finger, which some of the Norsemen thought was a pale-livered and shameful way to behave. But I agreed with Floki, who cursed those men for their thickheadedness. For the blauman not to have at least tried to defend himself was not cowardice. It was one of the Týr-bravest things I have ever seen. He stood there on the deck of his own ship, taking blow after blow, until Yngvar's fists were torn to bloody pulp. And even when his face bones were broken and he could no longer stand, he clasped his hands together over his stomach, shaking and pain-racked as the Dane stamped him to death. The man knew he would soon be feeding the crabs. Knew that any resistance would be useless and, worse, would look wretchedly pitiful. And so with iron will he made his death one that others would remember. Perhaps his men on the shore saw the way he died, but most likely they did not. Either way they would not have recognized what was left of their lord when it was over. And yet, even as Yngvar's dark-skinned oarmate tipped the bloody meat of the blauman overboard, I admired the man's bravery. And I thought that this Allah, who was the blaumen's god, must be a powerful god indeed to fill his people with that kind of courage.

chapter
SEVEN

WE NAMED Yngvar's blauman friend Völund. I suppose he must have had a name already, but the chances were that it was one our tongues couldn't wriggle around. And so because he was muscle-bound, and for his skin, which was as black as a smith's covered with the soot of the forge, we named him after the smith god. After the fight Rolf had taken our dead aboard *Sea-Arrow* and beached a little farther along the coast. The Danes buried Bag-Eyed Orm and Kveldulf along with one of their own who had, incredibly, taken an arrow in each eye. Those men went to their graves with decent weapons, for having stripped the blaumen of theirs, we now had so many blades that each of us would need four hands to wield them all. Sigurd said it was a strange thing to bury his men this far from their home, but he also said their kinfolk would be proud to know they had journeyed so far and won so many hard fights, and we could not disagree with that.

We had also found plenty of food aboard the blaumen's ship: bread mostly but also some salted meat, grain, and cheese. There was also a basket of strange yellow fruits that were so sour that when Svein bit into one, being the first brave enough to try it, his face almost turned inside out. We laughed as the juice ran through his beard and his mouth puckered and the cords in his neck looked about to break through the skin.

"This is more sour than Borghild!" he announced at last when he had straightened out his mouth.

"You don't know my wife very well, then, Red," Bram said, waving Svein away. "For nothing is as sour as Borghild." And we roared because Bram did not seem to be joking.

We sailed in an arrow formation like a skein of geese. *Serpent* was the tip, with *Wave-Steed* and *Sea-Arrow* off our steerboard side and *Fjord-Elk* and *Goliath*, which was our name for the blaumen's ship, on our port side. Despite her enormous white sail, *Goliath* was slow and lumbering, and we could only think that the other ship, the one that had fled from the fight, was faster.

"I'll wager the other one would catch their prey and this one would come along to finish the kill," Bragi had suggested when we had taken a closer look at the vessel. We had named it *Goliath* after a story of a giant from ancient times that Father Egfrith had told us one night in Frankia. We had all liked the beginning of the story, how the giant Philistine warrior had stridden from his ranks, his beautiful armor glinting in the hot sun, his sword-brothers chanting his name. But few of the Norsemen had liked the ending. They were troubled that a mere boy had killed the Philistines' greatest hero with nothing more than a smooth pebble, and they sulked when Egfrith told it.

"I think young David finished Goliath off with the giant's own sword," Egfrith had explained in an attempt to rescue his story, but by now men were grumbling and farting and rolling over into their furs to sleep, leaving the monk upset that his tale, which had begun so well, was trickling away like piss in a ditch.

Even so, we had all remembered Egfrith's story, and *Goliath* seemed a good name for the ship because of its size, and so it was. But that ship was like a rock around our necks, for we could sail only as fast as it could. And yet all agreed that it was too rich a prize to cut loose. We must have looked like a force to be reckoned with, though, and from then on we saw many ships' sterns as they changed course to avoid us the way dogs skulk away from their drunken masters to escape the boot.

The jagged mountains and scrub-crowned peaks on our port side gave way to land that sloped gently into the sea, which was warm and so clear in places that you thought you could just reach down and pull in the fish with your bare hands. Even when we were far from the beach, our fat-smeared fathom weights came back up crusty with sand, warning us to stay farther from the shore than we would have thought necessary. It was because of this long slope that the waves gathered such force for their assault on the shore, and we watched them surge and roll from far out until they flung themselves up the strand in frothy white billows and vanished.

Nevertheless, we did risk landfall on a few occasions and so had a chance to learn more about *Goliath*'s crew. It turned out that Völund spoke better Norse than Yngvar gave him credit for, and he was happy to give answers where Yngvar could not. It seemed he had been a raider before Beak Nose's blaumen captured his ship and made a slave of him. He was a fierce-looking man, Völund, and he had muscles on his muscles. But smiles came easily to him, and I admit I liked him better than I liked Yngvar.

It was from Völund we learned that the strange building we had named Gerd's Tit was rightly called a mosque, which is indeed a church for the blaumen's god; it seems they are all built with those bulging roofs the likes of which none of us had ever seen before.

On this latest landfall conversation turned to an island we had sighted to the northeast, which Völund said he recognized from his raider days. It seemed to burst up from the blue sea, craggy white rock studded with dark green bushes. By the water's edge, on the narrow, pebble-strewn margin, giant boulders sat sentinel. Having long ago broken and crashed down from the heights, they would rest there, wave-licked, until the doom of the gods, as immovable as Yggdrasil. According to Völund, there was a mosque on the island's north side where many rich men stopped to pray. As far as I could make out from him, this island's remoteness kept it clean of man's sin, and if you made the effort to go there to pray, Allah would surely reward you, though with what I had no idea. Egfrith said there were storm-bashed Christian churches and monasteries like that where the most devout and God-fearing men could dedicate their lives to Him without the distractions of others.

"We know of such places, monk," Olaf said, winking at Sigurd, who nodded, grinning.

"Gerd's Tit had nothing in it worth stealing," Rolf said, which was true enough, and I said so as the

Dane sat combing his tangled beard and squashing the lice that were left on the comb's teeth.

"That was not our target; we were going to wait near that mosque until a rich amir came," Völund explained, shaking his head at the memory, "but sometimes there is a bigger fox hunting the—" He frowned.

"Chicken?" Sigurd suggested helpfully, to which Völund nodded.

It emerged that it was on this island that Völund's lot had fallen prey to Beak Nose's crew. Most had been killed, though the blaumen's lord had spared the strongest to pull his oars. Sometime after that Beak Nose had tangled with a crew of Danes. Yngvar had been one of the men using oars to heave the enemy ship off their hull, but it had been his ill luck to fall overboard. He was still dripping wet when the fetters went on and he was put on a bench next to Völund. Olaf glanced at me during that part of the story, for I had been put to one of *Serpent*'s oars even as the smoke from my burning village dirtied the sky. Yet that seemed so very long ago now, and I returned Olaf's gaze, trying to remember the fear I had once felt at the sight of him.

"Maybe we should visit this mosque, Uncle," Sigurd suggested, fingering the ridge of scarred flesh on his right cheek where Mauger had desperately clawed at a wound. But Mauger was long dead now.

"Do you need to wash your ears out, lad?" Uncle asked. "You just heard what happened to Völund."

"How many ships did you have?" Sigurd asked the blauman. "One," Völund replied, at which Sigurd turned to Olaf, a haughty smirk lifting his beard.

"And the blaumen lords travel with their silver?" Olaf asked Völund.

"And gold, Norseman," Völund replied, his white teeth flashing. "Much gold."

So now our prows were pointed toward Yebisah, which Völund told us was the island's name, though Sigurd had said we would avoid a fight if we could. Men were still grimacing from cuts and bruises taken against the blaumen, and none of us really wanted another fight so soon, however much we liked the idea of some amir's gold.

We moored in a deserted cove on the island's north-west side. There were hundreds of such bays, but this one could not be seen from the sea, and we probably would have sailed by it if Völund had not recognized a cairn high up on a bluff. It was from the very same anchorage that Beak Nose had swooped out to capture the small ship Völund had sailed in.

"That brave turd would have made a good Norseman, I think," Olaf said admiringly, "for it seems he used to catch ships the way a spider catches flies."

"His web could not hold us, Uncle," I said with a grin.

"That was like a spider trying to catch an eagle," Svein the Red put in, which was well said, especially from Red, who was not known for his clever words.

Those of us who would make up the raiding party prepared to disembark. There were ten of us, and that would be more than enough, Sigurd said, to steal anything worth stealing and get back to the ships before anything went amiss. If there were too many blaumen for us ten to deal with, we would not fight anyway, so ten it was. And we were armed like war gods: Sigurd, Svein, Bram, Floki, Aslak, Bjarni, Penda, Wiglaf, Völund, and me, all in shining brynjas and polished helmets. Völund looked awe-inspiring in Kveldulf's old war gear, though some of the Norsemen had griped about a blauman wearing their dead sword-brother's brynja and helmet. Worse still, they grumbled, was that the blauman spent half the day on his hands and knees for his god, which was no way to treat good war gear. Even Yngvar had moaned that it should be him accompanying Sigurd onto the island and not his old oarmate. But Sigurd had explained that of the two of them Völund was the more useful, blauman or not, because he knew the island and spoke the Allah worshippers' tongue. No one could argue with that, though some clamored that Völund had better put the arms back in Kveldulf's sea chest the moment we returned. Kveldulf had a son back home, they said, and the war gear should be his.

Using *Sea-Arrow* as a tender, we were able to get close enough to some rocks to clamber ashore without so much as getting our feet wet, which is always a good way to begin a raid. We looked around, blinking against the glare of the midday sun off the white rocks, then followed the blauman, scrambling up the rocks, the sweat already soaking our beards and running down our backs. Gods, it was hot! We carried swords and shields, spears and axes, and some had brought bows, for even though we would not be able to carry so much if we did get lucky, it was decided that it was a better thing to be able to kill anyone who wanted to kill us. We also had food, bad-weather skins, and furs so that we could spend a night or two on the island without having to return to the ships.

Apart from some scraggly goats that eyed us indifferently, Yebisah looked deserted. We climbed over rocks that showed no sign that men had ever set foot on the place, yet Völund assured us that the blaumen had built a temple to their god here and that we would see it for ourselves soon enough. I was glad there were only ten of us, as our boots raised a cloud of white dust; if we had been more, that cloud would have been big enough to announce us as surely as a war horn.

The sun was in the west when we climbed, drymouthed, up the last escarpment, picking our way through thorny bushes to get to the edge. Völund gestured for us to make ourselves low, and so we did as he bent his legs and peered over the crumbling ridge. He had taken us around so that we came to the mosque from the southeast and would be able to use this high ground to our advantage, like ernes watching for hares from a craggy peak.

"Gerd's Tit was bigger," Svein grumbled, his face flushed beneath his sweat-soaked red beard.

"We haven't come for the mosque," Sigurd reminded him, slapping the big Norseman's back so that dust puffed up from his cloak.

I used my spear to push aside a bunch of gorse and got my first look at the Allah temple below. An arrow's flight away, it was surrounded by a low wall and had the same rounded roof as the other one we had seen, but this one had no balustrade crowning it from which men could look out. Instead it had a stone tower on its east side, which Völund told us was called a *ma'dhanah*, and the whole thing was as white as *Goliath*'s sail so that I had to half close my eyes against the brightness. The only part of the whole structure that was not white was the doors, which were of dark wood. In the courtyard a succession of stone troughs, each set lower than the one before, channeled running water so that at several places you would be able to fill a bucket from the flow.

"There's no one down there," I said.

"Someone will come," Völund said. But the only person we saw the remainder of that day was a man in white robes who twice climbed the steps of the *ma'dhanah* and sang that eerie song we had heard from the blaumen before. And at that sound Völund would kneel and touch his forehead to the ground and perform other strange acts whose meaning was lost on us. In the morning we were up before the sun and crawled to the ledge to watch as the white stone blushed pink with the new day's light. It had been a hard thing not to go down and fill our skins with that fresh running water that glistened in the sun, for ours was stale and warm, but Sigurd would not risk being caught down there.

"What would you do if you were that blauman down there and you saw us coming?" he asked Bram when the Bear complained that his water might as well have been horse piss for how bad it tasted.

Bram shrugged. "Fight?" he suggested halfheartedly.

Sigurd frowned. "Anyone?"

Black Floki glanced at me, urging me to put Bram out of his misery.

"I would get inside that tower and lock the door if

there is one," I said. "Then I'd light a fire at the top so that my people would know that raiders were here."

Sigurd looked back to Bram.

"Fucking coward," Bram muttered at me, scowling at the grins around him.

So we stayed up there on the ridge and listened to the blauman's strange song and watched Völund perform his strange ritual whenever the undulating sound floated up to us, for it was the job of the blauman in the tower to tell the other Allah worshippers that it was time to pray.

"His god must be a hard bastard to make his followers kiss the damned ground for him five times a day," Penda said in bewilderment. I repeated this in Norse to Völund.

"The key to paradise is prayer," he said simply.

"Then your key will be worn to a worthless stub by the time you need to use it," Bjarni warned him, chewing a mouthful of wind-dried mackerel.

That night it rained, and we took it in turn to keep watch, sheltering beneath grease-smeared reindeer skins and wondering how long Sigurd was prepared to lie in wait for something tempting to come along. As men will when the weather is bad and their bellies are grumbling for food, the others talked of their kinfolk back home. They imagined their loved ones sitting around crackling fires, laughing and gossiping and talking about the jobs that needed doing on the farmstead and complaining that their menfolk were off across the whale's road instead of being home. Winter was coming, and decisions would have to be made, such as which animals would live through the coming winter and which would be killed. Norsemen and Wessexmen talked of these things, and I listened, for I had no kinfolk that I knew of. The closest I had to kin were an English girl who no longer could bear to look at me and the men with whom I shared that miserable night among the rocks of Yebisah.

It was Black Floki who spotted our hare in the grass. Bored with the others' talk of home, he had loped out into the sodden night to watch for sails from the cliff tops, the only man whom Sigurd allowed to leave our camp. He had returned at sunrise, pale, soaking, and grinning, his crow-black hair swept back from his rawboned face and his beard dripping. Sigurd was just wiping dry his helmet against the inside of his tunic, and the others were pissing or rubbing the sleep from their eyes.

"Some blaumen are coming," Black Floki said, nodding to the east and the rising sun. "They spent the night moored a stone's throw along the coast."

"So close?" Bram asked.

"One of Svein's throws," Floki clarified, a rare smile in his beard. "But it was some Thór luck that they did not stumble onto us."

"Lucky for them," Bram rumbled.

Bjarni rapped his knuckles against his head. "Any man with both oars in the water would have been keeping dry last night, not wandering around like a corpse without a grave."

"How many?" Sigurd asked.

"I counted twenty, but there could have been more," Floki said. "They lit no fires. It was dark. But they must be coming here. Ódin knows there's nothing else on this island worth dropping anchor for."

"Good odds," Svein said cheerily.

"The blaumen are brave fighters," Bjarni reminded us.

"I have an idea," I said, speaking even as I untangled the scheme in my mind.

"Does it involve throwing all our silver into the sea?" Bram asked, and Bjarni cuffed him on the head.

"I'm listening, Hugin," Sigurd said. Hugin is one of Ódin's birds, and its name means "thought."

"Aye, spit it out, Raven Deep-Thinker," Black Floki added with a smirk.

"We don't want a fight if we can avoid it," I said. Most, not all, nodded at that. "Völund is a blauman. That wailing whoreson down there is a blauman."

"Frigg's tits, lad! That *is* some deep thinking," Bram mocked, but Sigurd scowled, showing that the time for joking was over.

"Völund goes down there, unarmed of course," I said, "and he tells that man with the long beard that he has come to pray. Then he threatens Long Beard that he will cut off his ears if he doesn't give him his robes."

"Why not just kill him?" Svein suggested with a shrug.

"Because the blood would stand out against those white robes, you thickheaded lump of snot," Black Floki said, shaking his head. Svein sulked at that.

"Will all the blaumen enter the mosque?" I asked Völund.

"Maybe," he said, "but usually the amir will go in and pray alone first. Afterward, he will let his men give their praises to Allah."

I nodded. "So when the amir enters the mosque,

Völund will take hold of him and make his warriors drop their blades."

"And if they don't?" Bjarni asked.

"If they don't, this Allah will be using their lord as a footstool much sooner than he thought." I looked at Völund. "As soon as they put down their swords, which they will if they want to save the man who feeds them, we will come." Völund's thick lips curved in a smile because he knew it was a good plan.

"At least this scheme doesn't end with us being silver-light," Bram admitted as I explained it to Penda and Wiglaf, though they had already caught a whiff of it.

"It will work," Sigurd said, holding my eye a moment.

"We have to be quick," Black Floki warned. "They will be here soon."

We looked at Völund, who was already out of Kveldulf's brynja.

chapter
EIGHT

THE AMIR was the fattest man I have ever seen. We watched from the ridge, sipping the fresh rainwater we had collected during the night, as the blaumen came toward the mosque from the east. Völund was looking up at us from the courtyard below, and Sigurd held up his sword to let the man know that the amir was approaching. Völund had had no difficulty persuading Long Beard to give up his white robes, and it seemed to me that the former slave was enjoying himself as he tucked a long knife into his tunic and waited.

"Maybe he cannot walk," Bjarni suggested, for the fat amir came to the mosque lying among swaths of bright blue and yellow cloth on what could have been a door carried by six thickset slaves. Ten white-robed warriors walked in front, spears in their hands, swords at their waists, and golden shields slung across their backs. But our eyes did not linger on the fat man or his warriors, for behind them walked thirty women in fine loose tunics that reached down to the knee in every color of Bifröst. Beneath them they wore loose-fitting breeks, and their feet were bare. Their faces and heads were covered by more fine cloth that shimmered in the breeze, and from where we were, it seemed that the dark skin of their bare hands and feet was covered with tattoos. Behind the blauvifs walked another ten warriors with the strangely shaped bows slung across their shoulders.

"Never mind his legs not working," Bram said. "I'll wager the fat whoreson's ears have fallen off, traveling with so many women!"

Aslak made a low purr in the back of his throat. "I don't know about you sheep swivers, but I'm now wondering what we're doing all the way up here when all those beauties are down there."

"How do you know they are beauties?" Bjarni asked. "You can't see their faces."

"When your balls are as heavy as mine, they're all beauties."

"We move now," Sigurd said, carefully backing away from the edge, so we did the same, collecting our war gear and putting on our helmets, wincing whenever iron chinked on iron. Sigurd's still had the gold band around it, which, added to the rest of his rich gear, made me think of Týr, Lord of Battle.

"Lord," I said quietly as the others checked straps and buckles and tightened their belts to take some of the weight of their brynjas, "if it comes to a fight, they will know that you lead us." I nodded at the golden ring, which glinted dully against the gray iron. "Their bowmen will go for you."

Sigurd pursed his lips and scratched his chin as though deep in thought. He knew this, of course. Then he nodded, a smile playing at the corners of his mouth. "Then while I'm swatting their arrows, you can kill them, Raven," he suggested as though it was the most simple thing in the world. Svein slapped my back, his beard all teeth, then we were on the move, iron and steel jingling as we followed Black Floki down a dark defile that in places narrowed to the width of Svein's shoulders but was a quicker way down than the track we had taken up. Water trickled among the clacking pebbles at our feet and our breathing sounded like the sea in that cold crevice, but we soon came to the end of the shadow, where we blinked at the white daylight. Black Floki raised a hand for us to stay put while he edged along a wall of white rock and, keeping his cheek to the stone, peered around its corner. He gestured for Sigurd to move up, which the jarl did, taking a look himself only when Floki gave him the nod.

Sigurd turned to the rest of us. "Svinfylkja," he said, and we nodded, knowing that at the mosque Völund was about to make his move on the amir. Then men were shouting, and Sigurd said, "Heya!" and stepped out into the open, his shield raised before him and his spear in his right hand, ready to be thrown. Behind him on either shoulder were Bram Bear and Svein the Red, and behind them were Black Floki, Aslak, and Bjarni, their shields protecting our flanks. I came next with Penda on my right and Wiglaf on my left so that our formation was a solid wedge of wood, iron, and steel that is called *svinfylkja* because it is the shape of a boar's snout. When there are more of you, a svinfylkja is a good thing for breaking through a shield-wall, but for us that day it was the best protection against the blaumen's arrows.

Through the fleeting gaps between the others' heads I saw some of the blaumen turn toward us, their faces full of shock and their weapons and shields raised. Beyond them, Völund had a thewy arm around the fat amir's neck and a wicked-looking curved knife pressed against the dark flesh. The amir's eyes bulged like boiled eggs, and his mouth was wide enough to catch the gull that laid them. But I could not blame him for being terrified, for his god's priest had a knife to his throat and was grinning like a fiend.

"Keep it tight, lads," Bram growled, "and keep those shields good and high. Better to get an arrow in your foot than in your eye."

Völund was yelling something to the amir's men, ordering them to throw down their weapons, I guessed. But they seemed unsure what to do, because we were stamping straight toward them, and this must have made them think twice. When you outnumber your enemies two to one and your enemies still come at you with not so much as a whiff of fear about them, it gnaws at your guts. But Sigurd knew that we risked them making a fight of it if we came any closer, and he yelled at us to stop, which we did, coughing in the dust cloud we had kicked up. The slaves who carried the amir stood by the water troughs, gaping, their sweat-soaked, corpse-black skin streaked with gray dust. Nearby, the women were sitting on blankets, their heads turned toward us but their expressions hidden beneath their colorful shrouds.

Now the amir called to his men in a voice that was piss-thin with fear, and they nodded dutifully, then carefully laid their swords, spears, bows, and shields on the ground, stepping back from them, hands raised passively.

"Shieldwall," Sigurd said, for we did not need the boar's snout anymore. Yet it was no bad thing to look like a wall of gut-ripping death, and so we put our shields edge to edge rather than overlapping them and moved forward as one. The blaumen stepped backward, never taking their eyes off us, and when we had passed their discarded blades, we stopped. Bram was snarling at them, and Svein was eyeballing them with enough violence in that look to half kill a man.

"Raven, Penda, gather their weapons," Sigurd said, gesturing behind us. "We'll take the best of them. Svein, break the rest."

"Shame to leave good iron behind," Bram grumbled. "We can come back for them."

"A wise guest knows when to leave the table," Sigurd replied, eyeing the blaumen.

"Bram wouldn't know about that," Bjarni said, "as no one ever invites him to their house."

Bram spit. "Wouldn't go if they did. The mead your wife served last winter tasted like horse piss."

"It *was* horse piss," Bjarni said, his face straight as a spear.

"Bring the amir to me!" Sigurd called to Völund. "Make sure they do not move, Floki."

Floki nodded and, slinging his shield across his back, stepped forward with his yew bow, calling for Aslak, Bjarni, and Wiglaf to join him. Those four each drew one good arrow from the quivers at their belts and nocked it, standing close enough to the blaumen not to miss but far enough away to throw a spear or draw a sword should the enemy make a desperate charge.

Völund pushed the amir toward Sigurd, and the blauman stumbled and fell, tipping onto his face, so that some of the Norsemen laughed. But Sigurd handed me his spear and walked over and helped the amir to his feet, even brushing the dust off the robes over his enormous belly. "That is no way to treat a chieftain in front of his warriors," he said. Svein threw Kveldulf's rolled-up brynja to Völund, who was already half out of Long Beard's white robes.

"The women do not look like slaves, Völund," Sigurd said.

"Some of them are the amir's wives, Sigurd," the blauman replied, his smiling face appearing through the neck of the brynja. "Some are just for . . . how you say . . . swiving?"

"Aye, lad, swiving," Bram put in. "Good to see you know the important words."

"The blaumen have more than one wife?" Svein asked, looking afraid for the first time since I had met him.

"Some of them, yes," Völund said. "The rich ones, anyway. You can believe they will all be beautiful," he went on, nodding toward the women. A change in the breeze brought their smell to my nose. It was sweet and woody and reminded me of Gerd's Tit.

"Good," Sigurd said, "because we are taking them." The others looked at him, their faces beneath their helmets half astonished and half ravenous like that of a man before a feast. Penda and I had chosen the best of the blaumen's swords—or at least we had chosen the straighter ones among them—and Svein was standing on the ends of the others and one by one gripping the hilts with two hands and bending them. Some bent right over, but some snapped, at which Bram shook his head, still rankled by the waste of it. The amir's men and carrying slaves we herded into the mosque like sheep, and they went peacefully enough, though I could

feel the hatred coming off them like heat. Then we shut
the door, filled our skins with fresh water from the
troughs, and showed our spears to the amir's women
so that they knew that the best thing for them was to
do as Völund told them. The blauman told us that there
was nothing worth taking in the mosque itself, and we
believed him, so none of us even looked inside it. Now
that we knew it was a god-house, we thought it best to
keep our distance. I did wonder what Völund had done
with Long Beard, because there had been neither sight
nor sound of him, but I never asked. We pushed the
amir and his blauvifs southwest toward our ships, our
spears flat across our waists, fencing them in, while
Black Floki, Aslak, and Bjarni hung back to make sure
we were not followed. When we came to the goat track
that wound down to the cove, we found Kalf waiting.

"Ódin spit in my eye!" His mouth hung open, and
his head jutted forward on the neck he was scratching.
The wince that he'd worn in his face ever since he had
taken an arrow in Frankia was gone, replaced by disbelief that became wonder that became joy as his eyes
ranged over our plunder. "What do they look like?" he
asked Svein, who merely shrugged his huge shoulders.
"You don't know?" The wince was back. "So which
one is mine?"

"You can have this one, Kalf," Bram said, yanking
the fat amir forward so that he shrieked pathetically.
He'd been made to carry an assortment of swords bun-
dled together with rope, and his arms shook, and so it
was a wonder he had not dropped them. The poor
man's trembling face was fear-sheened, his disheveled
beard was dripping, and the linen wrapped around his
head was coming undone to reveal wispy strands of

glistening black hair. His once sky-blue and yellow robes were dark now, soaked through with sweat, and a sorrier-looking man I have never seen. Even his shoes, which seemed to be made of the same fine cloth that swathed his enormous body, were tattered shreds, so that his fleshy feet were nudging out.

"Völund, ask the amir which one is his favorite," Sigurd said, gesturing at the women, who were clinging to one another and crying now that we were so close to the sea. Before we left, Sigurd had assured the blaumen that their lord would be returned to them in one piece, and because they had not caused us any trouble, he meant to keep his word. Völund spoke to the amir, whose face suddenly took a grip on itself as though he had at last found some courage. He said nothing but stared balefully at Völund, his beard lifted as though inviting the former slave to do his worst. Völund shrugged, and so, drawing his knife, Sigurd strode over and gripped the amir's fat neck in one big hand. He put the blade to the amir's eye and told Völund to repeat the question, and this time the amir pointed toward one of the blauvifs in a nearby group. The other women stepped back as that one stepped forward, and I noticed that she was a little fatter than the rest. Then this woman lifted the fine cloth covering her face and gave the amir a sad smile.

Her skin was dark as a chestnut, and you could see she had been a beauty in her day. Now, in place of beauty she wore pride, and the amir could not take his eyes off her.

"She stays," Sigurd said, shoving the amir toward her. The woman threw her arms around the amir as the rest of the blauvifs began to wail. "Get the others down to the ships."

I looked at Penda, who nodded in approval of the jarl's small mercy as we turned to make our way down the goat path, leaving the amir and his woman where they stood.

"I knew Sigurd wouldn't let that fat son of a sow get away with it that easily," Bram said. And we laughed all the way down to the ships.

We put the blauvifs aboard *Goliath* and gave them food, skins, and furs. Sigurd threatened Yngvar's crew that they would be carved up and flung overboard if they so much as laid a finger on the women let alone took their bollocks from their breeches. The blauvifs were to keep their faces covered, too, for Sigurd thought that his men would be less sorely tempted to force themselves on them if they could not see their faces. Olaf disagreed with him on this. "Not knowing what is in the pot only makes a man hungrier," he said. But Sigurd had his way, and so we were left imagining the dark-skinned treasures beyond the wind-stirred shimmering cloth.

Völund had suggested we could wait above the mosque for more rich men to come, for surely some would bring their treasures with them rather than leaving them aboard their ships. But Sigurd was more than happy with the catch.

"This is the best kind of treasure," he said, eyeing one of the amir's women, tilting his head to work with the sunlight. In the right light you could sometimes catch a glimpse of a face through the thin weave. "Because it has its own legs, meaning you don't have to lug it around."

"And you can fuck it," the Dane Beiner suggested, which had several men nodding in agreement.

We were sailing north now, though we knew we would be turning our prows southeast again soon enough, for that way lay Miklagard and the rich fame that awaited us there.

After leaving that rugged island we had crossed an angry sea, and many of us had sailed with one eye on *Goliath* and promised Njörd rich offerings if he spared her precious cargo. I even heard one of the Norsemen ask Rán, Mother of the Waves, to take one of the Danish crews to a watery grave if she must rather than the blauvifs. But *Goliath*'s crew, which was really too small for her size, fought with her lines and kept her beaked prow into the swells, and it became clear that Yngvar knew something of sea-craft. Nearer the coast we escaped the great surges that had lifted *Serpent* high and then sent her surfing down steep, rolling walls of water. But there were other dangers. The wind would change without warning, and the sea was a patchwork of dark shades as currents fought one another, in places forming whirlpools that threatened to suck us down into oblivion. *Serpent*'s mast creaked indignantly. Her ropes twisted, and water seeped through gaps where the seething waves forced her hull strakes out of true. Jörmungand snarled, defiant as ever, but Knut was ashen-faced at the tiller and Olaf was struggling to match the sea's ever-changing moods. It was cold, too, much colder than it had been farther south. Winter was upon us, and only a fool sails in winter, so we began to watch the coast and the offshore islands for some deserted place where we could rest and make repairs to the ships while the worst of the weather passed.

That place was an island we would later name Lyngvi after the island on which the wolf Fenrir was chained. It was a barren, wind-whipped marshy place where sandbanks separated freshwater lagoons from shoals of brackish brine, which was surely why no one lived there. But this made it a safe place to make camp, and after two days of wading through freezing water some of us located a large mere in which we could moor the ships out of sight from the open sea. Cold, half drowned, and miserable, we trudged back to the ships, leaving torches burning along the edges of a dozen narrow ditches. Then we guided them through rolling fog, beckoned on by the small flames, back to the place as silence fell like a blanket the deeper we went.

But *Goliath* did not have a dragon ship's shallow draft and got stuck in the mud a short way into the third channel, so we had to leave her behind like a dying animal and hope she would still be there when we moved on.

West of the mooring, past boggy fields of sea lavender and saltwort, the ground rose a little and was covered in tall swaying grass. That was to be our camp. The fog, thick as dragon breath, seemed to swirl forever about the place, though we soon came to see this as a useful thing because it meant we had no fear of lighting cook fires. There were no trees as such, but everywhere were dense thickets of salt cedar, which we found burned well and provided good shelter against the wind. Fires burned night and day, for none of us had ever seen so much waterfowl, and the birds were easy to snare or shoot, so that our bellies were always full of roasted meat.

And we would need both fires and meat soon enough, for the bitter winds came. They tore down from the northwest, cutting across the dunes and marsh and biting into us like blades. To the east, Bram and Bjarni had found a small island thick with trees that were the height of ten men but more resembled giant bushes because of their twisted trunks and enormous rounded crowns, the leaves of which smelled spicy and resinous. Father Egfrith said they were almost certainly juniper trees, though I did not see how he could know such a thing, having never seen their like before. Nevertheless, we took our axes and cut many of them down, using the wood to make a rough palisade against the wind. From this windbreak we ran thick reeds down to the ground to make frames onto which we laid thickets of salt cedar for warmth. Upon the whole thing we piled skins, making passable lean-tos, and inside we laid thick furs. Still we froze. Yet all agreed it would have been worse at sea, where we could not light fires to cook with and dry our clothes.

The blauvifs suffered worst. It seemed that they were not used to that cold, and Völund said they would have all lived together inside the amir's palace and would rarely have been allowed outside. They would have bathed every day in hot water and attended the amir's every lustful desire. There was no bathing now. But there was desire. By now Sigurd had let the men have their way with them. He had waited until the first grumbles had begun around the fires from men who were wondering where the glory and riches were that their jarl had promised them. I had thought Sigurd's intention was to sell the blauvifs as soon as possible, for they were surely worth a great deal, but I might have known my lord had a deeper use for them. The grumbles stopped as the swiving began. And they *were* beautiful. At first many of them clung to one another and wailed and fought, but after a time they seemed to accept their fate. Some wisely sought certain men's protection and got it, too. Early on one clung to Red Svein, and from then on no other man came near her. Sigurd chose a full-lipped beauty for himself, and no one complained about that. And then there was Amina. I had noticed her watching me and had thought she was perhaps curious about my blood eye. But then, as I was building my shelter against the bulwark, my fingers blue with cold, she had smiled at me, shivering beneath a bearskin. I had smiled back. It probably had more to do with the fact that Byrnjolf the Dane was sniffing around her like a randy dog and his breath stank like rancid meat. But by then I was under the spell of those eyes, which were a mix of gray and golden brown and the shape of mint leaves. When I had finished my shelter, she had simply walked over and crawled inside it, and from then on she was mine.

At first I had wondered what Cynethryth thought. Soon, and to my disappointment, I knew that she did not feel one way or the other about it. Neither did she bond with the women as Penda had suggested she might. Instead she was always off among the marshes, hunting and learning the old ways from Asgot, and not even Father Egfrith could get through to her much anymore.

The weeks passed, and eventually we grew sick of waterfowl, especially when some of the Danes who had been out hunting spoke of seeing boar tracks in the mud. So we set about digging pits in the soft ground to try our luck. We would make a large hole and throw salt cedar bushes into the bottom so as not to lose any creature we caught in the water that soon seeped in. Then we laid thin branches across the top over which we scattered long grass to disguise the whole thing. It was in such a pit that Cynethryth caught a wolf. One bitter night, among the constant grunting and croaking of frogs and toads, we had heard a wolf's howl. I did not know until long after the beast was caught that Cynethryth and the godi had been baiting their trap with fresh meat. Eventually, the wolf's curiosity had gotten the better of it, and the beast had ended up in Asgot's pit. There it stayed, and Cynethryth and the godi fed it every two or three days until its fury was spent and its knowing golden eyes had begun to look for other ways to survive. It was a big male, at the shoulder level with a man's waist, with teeth that could tear your arm off. The rest of us would go to the pit to look down at the animal, and men would mutter that it was an ill thing to trap such a beast and keep it alive. For all men had heard of how even the gods had watched in horror as Fenrir Wolf had grown, its hatred of them seething even as they bound it and placed a sword in its jaws. And all knew that one day, at Ragnarök, when the doom of the gods is upon us all, the beast Fenrir will kill Ódin himself.

Eventually, though, on our own Lyngvi, that wolf became almost as tame as a hound, at least while Cynethryth was around. It would still growl and bare its wicked teeth to the rest of us just to remind us that it was a killer and that we should beware, but for the most part it padded behind Cynethryth, its tail hanging low and its tongue lolling out. She named it Sköll after the wolf that pursues the sun through the sky, and I suspected that Sigurd thought its capture a good omen because his war banner was a wolf.

"It's hard to remember the girl she was," Penda muttered one morning as he fed the camp's main fire, which we rarely if ever let go out. "She's a lost soul, that one," he added, shaking his head. We had made the fire in a pit to protect it from the worst of the wind, and behind it we had piled up a wall of branches between two sloping uprights staked into the ground. This wall bounced the heat back at us, so that men would stand for hours before that trench, holding out their hands to the heat and talking. Völund never strayed from those flames. It seemed that for all his muscle the blauman was no match for the cold, and he shivered pathetically so that I feared his white teeth would rattle themselves out of his jaw and be lost in the mud.

The women had their own fire, which they tended themselves, though they often could be found around ours.

"That old goat has poisoned her mind," I told Penda, and he knew I was talking about Asgot. Above, against a gray sky, a marsh harrier circled, beating its powerful wings every now and then, and I remembered that I had used to call Cynethryth my peregrine. I stared into the flames, trying to lose myself in their ravenous dance. After a while I said, "I loved her, Penda." My eyes were dry from the heat, though I could feel still the wind's ice-cold teeth biting into my back.

"I know you did, lad," Penda said, never taking his eyes from the fire.

chapter
NINE

ONE MORNING we woke to a day that the north-west wind had forgotten to flay. We knew it would be back, for it was still winter, but the wind's absence made it feel almost warm. Some of the men had suggested going hunting. Not digging pits and set-ting snares but proper hunting with bows and spears. We had caught two boars in our pits, but there was nothing like facing one down and coming away the winner, and so Sigurd decided to make a contest of it. Some of the men chose to spend the day swiving and sleeping, but those of us who took up the challenge split into four parties of five men each. The first party to bring back a fully grown boar would win the weight of the beast's head in silver; that meant that none of us would settle for a small animal. Five men is a small hunting party if you are after a full-grown boar. One can break your legs without thinking about it. It will slash its tusks up into your belly and rip out your guts. It will even bite chunks out of you. And so we would need every man and spear in our group, which was unfortunate because we were lumbered with Father Egfrith.

"I have always wanted to hunt for boar," he said, huffing into his hands and rubbing them excitedly. "I went with Mauger and the ealdorman once many years ago." He frowned from under bushy brows. "But I can't claim to have helped, because as soon as we got near the beast's nest, Ealdred made me climb a tree." I laughed at that, and Egfrith looked embarrassed. "Then off they went, tearing through the forest after the creature while I was still stuck up that tree like poor Zacchaeus."

"If you're coming, you're going to need this," I said, thrusting a spear into his hand. Penda, Bjarni, and Wiglaf were the other three, and they seemed more amused than concerned that the monk was with us. All around us fur-clad men were grabbing spears and long knives, eager to be on their way. Even Sigurd was grinning with excitement like a boy as he braided his golden hair at the nape of his neck, revealing his scarred face. Black Floki was beside him, sharpening the blade he no doubt believed would soon be finishing a speared boar.

"If more than one is killed," Sigurd called, "then the silver goes to the men whose animal is larger."

"You might as well give the silver to me now and be done with it, Sigurd," Bram said while emptying his bladder. "These young pups couldn't catch a three-legged stool if they were sitting on it."

"Keep the fire high, Uncle," Beiner said to Olaf, who had said he was too old to be chasing through a bog after his food. "My boar is going to need a long time cooking."

And then, clutching spears and hope, we set off into the marsh, each group going its own way.

We tramped northward through the sucking fen, sending startled coots screeching up from the reeds.

Penda and I had decided that the farther we went, the better our chances would be, and we were prepared to put in the legwork. We had wanted to go west, but Bram's group had headed off that way before us, and so we were left with north. Now and then a great egret took to the sky, flapping its white wings indignantly. Any other time we would have hurled a spear at it, but not this day, for we would need every spear we had if we came across a big boar, and to throw one after a bird risked losing it in the marsh.

"This *is* enjoyable," Egfrith chirped, thrusting his spear at the shrubs he was passing. He had hitched up his habit, and his bare feet and legs were covered in watery mud. It was still bitterly cold, but I had come to learn that the monk was a hardy little weasel, and to my annoyance he seemed to cope well with all kinds of hardship. "I shall be ready, Raven; you can rely on me."

"If you keep flapping your tongue, monk, we will never set eyes on anything other than birds." I could see why Ealdred had ordered the monk up a tree and out of the way.

"You're quite right," he said, pursing his lips in determination. "I shall be as quiet as a mouse. I shall be as patient as Job. I shall—"

"Egfrith!" I snapped. He nodded, putting a finger to his mouth, and I caught Penda sharing a grin with Wiglaf.

"Now what?" Wiglaf said a while later, palming his thinning hair back across his white scalp. He rested his spear across his thickset shoulders so that his forearms hung over the shaft. "I don't mind a swim," he said. "It's the bollock shriveling I'm not fond of."

"Aye, it'll be cold all right," Penda said.

None of us had ventured this far north before, and now we eyed the fen in front of us. But it was not a fen. It was a lake, shallow by the look of it but still a lake.

"We'll go around," I said with a shrug. "It can't be far." It looked far. Bjarni pointed, having seen something in the flinty sky. Two golden eagles were attacking a white-tailed sea eagle, taking turns swooping in and raking the other bird with their talons. Asgot would see some meaning in that, I thought.

"Or we could go through it," Penda suggested, nodding at the breeze-rippled gray water. A flock of black marsh hens slid across the small furrows, up-ending now and then.

"I am a strong swimmer," Egfrith said proudly. My face told him what I thought about that idea.

"There's a causeway," Penda said, pointing to our right, where a good spear's throw away an old timber stuck up from the water. Then my eyes saw more of them, and I realized I had not spotted them earlier because they had blended in with the reed beds far behind them on the horizon. Some of the piles were no more than knee-high, but it had definitely been a causeway once.

Folk had used it, but long ago: the walkway looked to have been submerged for years. It was rotten, as soft as mud, so that you felt your feet breaking through. But whoever had built it had run it along a natural ridge of higher ground or piled the earth into a spine to raise it above the flood, and we were able to reach the other side of the lake, staying dry for the most part.

We then crossed a number of pools and sandbars where thousands of terns filled the world with their short, sharp calls. After that the ground became firmer, marshland giving way to meadows of marram grass and heather, and after midday we came to scrub woodland, which in turn yielded to fruit trees and pine.

"This would have made a better camp," Wiglaf said, sniffing the air, which was thick with the pungent tang of foxes.

"Too far from the ships," I said, remembering the backbreaking portage we had done in Frankia, sliding *Serpent* and *Fjord-Elk* over rollers that had not rolled. "But I'll wager there's boar here."

"There's more than boar here," Egfrith said, pointing with his spear through a copse of bare apple trees. A field of winter barley stirred in the breeze like a green sea.

"See there," Bjarni said excitedly, for beyond the barley was a palisade above which we could see a clutter of thatched roofs.

"They are Christians!" Egfrith added, making the sign of the cross, for though the dwellings seemed scattered, the largest roof was aligned east–west, which told Egfrith that it was likely to be a church.

"So we're not in the blaumen's land anymore?" I said.

"I think we're back in Emperor Karolus's land," Egfrith said.

"Frankia?" Penda puffed out his cheeks.

"South Frankia, yes," Egfrith said. "But I should not worry, Penda. The emperor's lands stretch far and wide. I'm sure we are quite safe." Egfrith was already walking toward the place. Bjarni was following him.

"Wait, Bjarni," I said. "If they are Christians, maybe we should turn around and go back."

Without breaking stride Bjarni flung a hand through the air, swatting my warning away. "Penda and Wiglaf are Christians," he said, "and we have our own White Christ slave. What could go wrong? Come on, Raven. Or are you a little girl?"

I set off behind him.

"We're going in there?" Wiglaf called after us. I glanced around and saw Penda shrug and set off behind me.

"Of course we're going in there, Wiglaf," Penda said. "With any luck they'll sell us a bloody great boar."

When we came to the place, we realized it was much smaller than we had thought. You could have walked around it in the time it takes to boil a pot of water. Other than the palisade, which was low and poorly made, there were no defenses. The main gate stood open, and Father Egfrith called out to announce us. No one replied, and so we walked in, spears ready in case it should be a trap. But other than three tired old hounds, two white ponies that stood eating the old thatch from some low eaves, and several hens pecking at the mud, the place looked deserted. Thyme and other herbs grew in neat rows, and I peered into a barrel in which eels rolled over one another, tying endless knots. Sweet smoke leaked from a small hut in which Bjarni found meat hanging. In another small dark place we found butter and cheese and a bucket full of salt. But there was not a man or woman to be seen.

"You have scared them all off, Penda," I teased, for Penda had a face that could frighten a war dog, not least because of the terrible scar that ran from his temple to his chin.

"What kind of men would just let us walk in like that?" he asked, biting into a fist-size lump of cheese.

"There are no men here," Egfrith told him. "This place is a convent."

Penda glanced around, nodding because suddenly, like the rest of us, he understood. The place had felt strange: sparse yet orderly, industrious yet lacking in the buildings you would expect to find, such as a forge and a butcher's stall. We did not know where the Christ women were, but we thought they must have been watching us from somewhere. I remembered Abbess Berta and shuddered.

"I would like to pray while we are here, Father," Wiglaf half asked Egfrith.

The monk seemed unsure for a moment, rubbing his newly shaved pate. "I suppose the good sisters won't mind that, Wiglaf," he said. "But we should not linger. We are interrupting their spiritual dedication, and it does not do to keep the faithful from the Lord." He turned. "What about you, Penda? Will you join us in prayer?"

The Wessexman glanced at me and then turned back to Egfrith and shrugged. "Seems a good place to seek the Lord's blessings," he said. "A man can't be too careful what with living among the heathens."

"Quite right, Penda," Egfrith said, pointing a finger at the sky; then he led the way to the church. I grimaced and followed.

It was a simple timber-framed place with chambers

running on either side of the nave and an apsidal chancel at the east end. On a rough-hewn table in that chancel sat an embroidered cloth, and on that cloth stood a large wooden Christ cross. Next to it several tallow candles flickered sootily, burning into the heavy darkness. The faint scent of unfamiliar sweat still hung in the fug, and in that place I felt far removed from the world outside. It made you not want to speak. So I spoke.

"Perhaps this is how it feels between dying and waking in the afterlife," I suggested to Bjarni in Norse. He shrugged gloomily because it was obvious that the people who lived there were poor and owned nothing worth taking. That was just as well, I thought, for I did not know how Penda and Wiglaf would react if Bjarni were to loot the place.

"That Christ cross would not have dragged Tufi down to the crabs," Bjarni said, gesturing toward the table in the chancel and touching his sword's hilt to ward off the ill luck that had drowned the Dane.

"He should have left that thing where it was," I said, watching two mice scurrying through the dry floor rushes. One of the creatures vanished, but the other scampered over the bare planks where there were no rushes.

"It is time we left," Father Egfrith said, his eyes flicking from me to the floor and then back to the Wessexmen.

Wiglaf scratched his round chin. "I still have some more prayers to get out, Father," he said.

"We have intruded long enough, Wiglaf," Egfrith snapped. "We will leave now so that the sisters may return to their prayer. The poor souls must be terrified out there in the woods waiting for us to be gone."

Wiglaf turned to Penda, who simply shrugged, if anything looking relieved, and so we left the church, blinking against the daylight.

"We could take the goats," Bjarni suggested. "And some cheese." We had found three of the animals tethered on the far side of the church, and beside one there was a pail half full of milk that we shared, though Egfrith would not drink because he said the milk would be tainted by the sin of theft. At which Penda admitted that theft was a taste a man could get used to. But the monk was agitated now and wanted to be away.

"Anyway, a goat is not a boar, Bjarni," I said, dragging the back of my hand across my mouth. The milk was thick and still warm. "Bram will be the first to point that out when we return."

"That won't stop him from drinking two men's share of milk," Bjarni said, eyebrows arched knowingly.

"Are you suggesting stealing the sisters' animals?" Egfrith said. The cunning little weasel had learned more Norse than I had realized. "I will not hear of it! We must go now, Raven, before the Lord sees fit to punish us. Oh, He will," he warned us all. "Do not doubt it."

Penda put a hand on the monk's shoulder. "Father, are you still trying to coax this red-eyed son of a troll into the light?" His eyes flicked to me. "You may as well try to talk the sea into not being wet."

Egfrith narrowed his eyes at me. "*Gutta cavat lapidem non vi sed saepe cadendo.* A water drop hollows a stone not by force but by falling often," he said. "I am a patient man, as you well know. I have not given up hope for young Raven."

"Then you still have wood shavings for brains, monk," I said, turning to leave the convent.

"What about the goats?" Bjarni called after me.

"Do you want to carry them through the marsh?" I asked. And so we left with nothing.

We had come far, and so we spent only a short time searching for signs of boar—of which there were none—because we did not want to be caught out in the fen when night fell. As it was, it would be hard enough to find our way back, but in darkness it would be nearly impossible. There was also the part of us that feared whatever strange spirits might wander abroad in the murky, pitch-thick darkness of the bog, though no one talked about that. And so we resigned ourselves to losing Sigurd's contest. At least we returned with news.

At first Sigurd and the others listened keenly, their eyes glinting like fish scales at the mention of a god-house on the north side of the island. But those eyes dulled soon enough when Bjarni told them the place was poorer than even the meanest farmstead in their homeland. "My uncle had a turned foot," he said, "so he never went on a raid his whole life."

"Old Tjorvi walked like a one-legged duck," Olaf put in, smiling fondly. Those who had known Tjorvi and some who hadn't laughed at that.

"Aye," Bjarni went on, "he was piss-poor, but even he had more loot worth taking. Which was why that whoreson Hogni Ketillson paid him a visit one summer. Hogni and his boys carried off two chests full. And what could my uncle do about it?"

"They say poor Tjorvi limped after them," Svein the Red said, hitching across the soft ground before the fire pit and grinning like a fiend. The men roared. "Until his good foot struck a stone and turned the same way as the lame one!"

Olaf leaned on Sigurd to steady himself. "Old Tjorvi has been walking in circles ever since!"

"At least he never gets lost," another man added, fueling the laughter.

"So you did no killing?" Sigurd asked, serious as the laughter faded.

"We saw no one, lord," I said. "The Christ brides were hiding in the trees. We took nothing either." I added that because I knew why Sigurd was asking. He did not want word of raiders spreading as far as some lord of warriors who might feel strongly enough about it to come looking for us.

"It was a good thing not taking the goats," Bjarni hissed in my ear, rubbing his palms together for warmth. I nodded. And then all our talk was forgotten because Bram was back with Knut, Bothvar, Hastein, and Baldred, and hanging by its legs from a sturdy branch, dripping blood, was the largest boar I have ever seen.

We ate like kings that night. Black Floki's party returned with a boar too, which had charged Ingolf, so that he had leaped into a thicket that had half flayed him. Still, beneath all the bloody scratches he was grinning now because while the beast was going for him, Floki and the others had speared it. It was a large male, but all agreed that Bram's was bigger, and so it was Bram's party that won the silver. It turned out that the Danes were good shots with their bows, for Rolf's men came back with four hares, and all said it was a feast to make us forget for a while the stinging cold of that damp, desolate place.

With our stomachs full we built up the fires, and men began to settle down for the night, leading blauvifs to their shelters or turning in alone. The wind was building from the north again, and Amina was waiting for me, and I knew she was naked under the furs. I was on my knees, half inside the shelter and half out, when something tugged at my cloak.

"Fuck off, Egfrith," I growled, not wanting thoughts of him to sour my thoughts of what was waiting for me among those furs.

"It is important," he hissed.

"Amina, stay awake until I get back," I said, knowing that she did not understand a word and cursing Egfrith for pulling me back into the cold when I should have been warming up between a beautiful woman's legs. "What do you want, monk?"

Behind Egfrith the flames stretched themselves into the cold night, their peaks breaking off and vanishing with a flurry of bright sparks. Some of those sparks died in a heartbeat, but others surged high into the darkness. The monk's face was shadow-shrouded, but his bald head glistened and the whites of his eyes glinted, wide with alarm.

"I overheard some of the men talking," he said. I must have looked surprised. "It is not a difficult tongue to grasp. I *am* a man of learning," he said. "Halfdan and Gunnar and some of the Danes plan to go north tomorrow."

"And?" I said.

"They want to see the convent for themselves, Raven. You know what that means," he hissed.

I shrugged. "What does that have to do with me?" I asked. "Or you for that matter?"

"It will not do for men to go there again," he said, and from any other man I would have felt the edge of a threat in his voice. "Let the good Lord's servants be about their work unhindered. Tell Halfdan and the others to stay here."

"And why would I do that, monk? I am not their jarl." My mind summoned Amina lying there just a few feet away. So warm. "Besides, the Christ brides were not even there. They saw us coming well enough." *Next time we will have to try harder at stealth,* I thought to myself. "They'll be hiding far off in the woods again before Halfdan and the Danes get within a bow shot."

The whites of his eyes vanished for a long moment.

"That's just it, Raven," he hissed. "They weren't hiding in the trees." My mind sifted through what we had seen earlier that day, searching for the tracks that the monk, it seemed, had already followed. "I cannot say more," he rasped.

"You'll spit out what's in your mouth or the next thing you'll hear will be me snoring in there," I said, thumbing back to my lean-to. Though snoring was not what I had in mind.

"God help me, I cannot say."

I turned my back on him, but before I could walk away, a hand grasped my shoulder. I turned back to Egfrith. The fire crackled and spit noisily.

"In the church," he said, his voice barely more than the whisper of leather shoes on stone.

"The floor!" I blurted.

"Shhh!" He flapped a hand at me. I remembered the mouse that had scampered across a small bare patch of the floor. There had been no rushes there because they had slid off when the trapdoor had been opened.

"The Christ brides were hiding beneath the floor," I said, "which was why Wiglaf never got to finish his prayers."

"When I realized that the poor sisters were below our very feet, I knew I had to get you all out of that place or risk one of you discovering them. I thought you had seen, Raven. I feared you were going to reveal their hiding place, but it seems you are as dimwitted as the rest of them, for which, this time, I thank the Lord."

I ignored that. "Wiglaf and Penda wouldn't hurt nuns," I said.

"And Bjarni? And you, Raven; would you?" I scowled because I had put Abbess Berta on her enormous arse with a savage blow. "Men are ruled by anger and lust," Egfrith said. "You must have seen the men's eyes when you told Sigurd there were nuns living to the north of here." He shook his head. "The lust of a man is his shame."

"You tell yourself that when you are shivering alone tonight," I said, thinking of Amina.

"Listen to me, Raven. Tell Halfdan and Gunnar that your gods have warned you not to go to the north of the island."

"You want my gods to help you?" I said, almost smiling.

"Tell them that you suspect there are Frankish warriors patrolling the place. Tell them anything but stop them from going to the convent. Do this for me, Raven, if not for your own soul. I will not forget it. I will pray even harder for your salvation—" He broke off because Hedin Long-Face had emerged from his shelter to empty his bladder, and now the Norseman stood behind him, gathering warmth from the fire. Egfrith leaned in closer so that I felt his breath on my cheek. "I believe Christ will look kindly on you for saving his daughters," he said.

"I will do what I can," I said. Not because Egfrith was asking me but because no matter how hard I had tried, I had never forgotten the black-haired girl from Caer Dyffryn and what I had done to her. "But not now. I will talk to them in the morning when there's less chance of them telling me to go and screw a bearded goat." Egfrith nodded, appeased for now at least. "Now leave me alone, monk," I said, "Amina will be getting cold."

I crouched, pulled aside the bad-weather skin, and crawled into my shelter. Then I cursed. Because Amina was asleep.

chapter
TEN

IN THE morning I woke early. I had slept badly, besieged by dismal dreams that I did not remember when I woke, though their claws were still in me and I could not step out of the cold, dark mire of them as I watched the sun hoist itself in the east, shivering against the damp mist that wreathed the camp. In the stillest depths of the night I had woken and for a few confused moments had thought it was Cynethryth, not Amina, breathing gently beside me. Perhaps that is why I had determined to seek her out at dawn and try to reach the girl I had once known behind the Cynethryth I hardly recognized.

The fire's warmth had barely seeped beyond skin and flesh to chase the ice from my bones when Egfrith breezed over to me, his pale cheeks bristling with the beginnings of a beard.

"I hadn't forgotten," I said, which was a lie.

"I did not think you would," he answered, which was also a lie. Otherwise he would not have been waiting for me like a hound at a rabbit hole.

All around, men and women were stirring as the camp came awake. The low murmur of conversation was strewn with yawns, farts, and the hawking and spitting of phlegm as men cleared their throats.

"It would be better to catch them early. Before they slink off."

"I need to speak with Cynethryth first," I said, and Egfrith must have known I would not budge on that, or else he was intrigued about what I wanted with her, for he cocked an eyebrow and extended an arm, inviting me to get on with it.

Cynethryth had built her shelter on the camp's eastern edge next to Asgot's, which was recognizable for the many animal skulls hanging from a length of twine around the lean-to's entrance. The largest were fox and badger skulls, but there were many others: hare, stoat, yellow-toothed rat. The smallest were birds' skulls, many of which had belonged to crows and ravens, and they hung threaded through their eye sockets. They looked like sharp white arrowheads.

Cynethryth's wolf, Sköll, was nowhere to be seen, which was the first clue that Cynethryth was not in her shelter.

"Where is she?" I asked Bothvar, who was sitting on his sea chest making a fishhook from a piece of bone.

"I thought you had a new woman these days, Raven," he said with a grin, not taking his eyes from the small hook. "One of those pretty dark whores you're keeping all to yourself when you should be sharing."

"Have you seen Cynethryth?" I asked. Bothvar shook his head, his skin as gray as cold ashes, and so I called out to Asgot, but there was no answer from his lean-to. A wind cut through the camp, rippling the skins of the shelters and causing some of the godi's animal skulls to clatter against one another.

"They could be off hunting," Egfrith behind me suggested.

I turned to him, my mind glimpsing again the old godi's eyes when we had talked of the convent to the north.

"That's what I'm afraid of," I said.

I fetched my spear and helmet and slung my shield across my back, and when Olaf saw me arming, he asked what was going on. I told him I was heading out to look for Cynethryth, but Olaf had been around too long to believe that that was all there was to it, and in the end I had to tell him that I feared Cynethryth and Asgot had gone in search of the convent. He swore and strode off to find Sigurd, leaving Egfrith and me standing there like tree stumps.

"What makes you think they've gone north, Raven?" Sigurd asked, clutching a fleshy boar rib left over from the night before.

"You know Asgot," I said. The jarl nodded slightly at that. "As Father Egfrith will tell you, a place full of Christ brides is unlikely to be far from a fort or even a town. If the nuns get word out about us, we'll be sleeping with one eye open for the rest of the winter." I glanced at Egfrith.

"It is true, Sigurd," the monk said, scratching his bristly cheek. "The good sisters are sure to sell cheese, milk, and bread to local folk. That is usually the way. They will have a protector. They must. And he will have spears."

That was Egfrith's second lie that morning. From what I knew, convents were like monasteries and very often to be found far away from normal folk. Something to do with shunning the corrupted is how I'd heard Egfrith speak of it. "Sin is like a stinking fart, Raven; it spreads quickly," he had once told me. But Sigurd seemed to consider the monk's words and eventually nodded purposefully, chewing as he said, "Fly, then, Raven. And make sure Asgot does not bring more Franks down on our heads." He grimaced. "I have met enough Franks to last me till Ragnarök." Those in earshot agreed with that. "Go with them," he said to Black Floki, who nodded and went to fetch his war gear as Egfrith went to gather whatever it was he would need.

Sigurd and Olaf shared a look, and Olaf patted his belly and nodded at the rib in Sigurd's hand. "I could eat some of that myself," he said, "if that greedy son of a troll bitch Svein hasn't eaten it all, nose, arse, bones, and balls."

I was ready to leave, and so I stood there, spear butt in the mud, as I watched a crowd of rooks and crows hugging the edge of the darkness that still clung to the west. A few gruff notes carried across the fen as the black shapes rose into the gray with the guilty aspect of killers leaving a murder. I could feel Sigurd's eyes on me.

"So you fear that Asgot and Cynethryth might poke a bees' nest? That we may have to fight the Franks again?"

I looked into the fjord depths of those blue eyes. "Better to avoid a fight if it can be done," I said. I had heard him say the same thing many times.

He nodded. Then silence rushed in.

"You must let her go, Raven," he said after a while.

"Lord?"

"Cynethryth. She is not the same as she was. We all change, Raven, like boulders worn away by the sea. Chaos has shaped her, and she is lost to you."

My blood simmered then because it was not for any man, even Sigurd, to know my thoughts, let alone give them voice. But now that it had been said, it was like an oar blade in the water and needed pulling.

"Asgot has been gnawing away at her ever since we left Wessex," I said, almost spitting the words. "She barely even speaks to the monk these days. I preferred it when she prayed to the White Christ. Now Asgot fills her head with his black seidr."

"He *does* have some power," Sigurd admitted. "The old wolf should have died many times in many fights. And yet he lives. Cynethryth was lost, Raven, but it was Asgot who found her. Not you." That pierced my heart like steel.

"He has led her from the dark into the mire," I said, "and one day I will kill him."

Sigurd took three steps, reached out, and gripped my shoulder. "Go and find her," he said, his eyes boring into mine. "And then let her go."

Someone called my name, and I turned to see Black Floki standing among the knee-high bristling grass, his shield on his back and his spear gripped loosely. Behind him Father Egfrith waited, a small sack across his shoulders and a stout juniper staff in his hand.

"I'm coming," I said, turning my back on my jarl and setting off into the marsh.

It was cold. The sun was rising pale and watery, and we kept it on our right so we knew we were walking north. By midday it was low and lost somewhere behind a frigid wan sky that stretched in a silent echo of the desolate, wind-scourged fen. But several skeins of geese passed noisily overhead, and so long as we tramped in the opposite direction we could not go far wrong. Besides which, every now and then we saw footprints still visible in the waterlogged earth, and some of those prints belonged to a large wolf, which was how we knew for certain that Asgot and Cynethryth had come this way. What was more alarming, at least for Egfrith, was that there were too many tracks. Floki had been the first to see it.

"There are four, maybe five men walking behind the girl, the godi, and the wolf," he had said, squatting in a foul-smelling reed bed, unraveling the tracks with the practiced ease of a fisherman unsnarling his net.

"We must hurry!" Egfrith said, understanding at once, and because he was not lugging war gear, he took up a half-walk, half-run gait that had our shields bouncing on our backs and made me glad I had not put on my brynja. I was sure he would have gone on without us if we had fallen behind, yet I had a fair idea what Asgot would do if the monk tried to stop him from walking into that convent. So I kept up even though the soft ground sapped my strength.

"This is one way to stay warm," I huffed to Floki as we splashed through shallow water, our shields breaking the stiff reeds as we passed. Egrets waded carefully, stabbing down with their black bills now and then. A weasel emerged at Egfrith's passing and regarded me for a moment before making for cover in its hooping run. Then on to boggy ground where short grass sprouted tenaciously and curlews *quee*'d and tittered, teasing worms from the mud with slender bills that were curved like the blaumen's swords. Suddenly the sky above filled with screeching as a huge flock of gulls passed over us from the west, heading for the seashore.

"We're going to lose them in this!" Egfrith called. The mist that hung over the flat land was thickening. It almost looked like water, as though the tide had swept in to claim the land once and for all.

"We're almost there," I called back, for I recognized a great spread of red saltwort scrub. The day before Egfrith had said that the Franks call the plant Saint Peter's herb, and I had thought that just about said it all: that Ódin should have the mighty ash and the oak and a Christ saint should have a pathetic sprawling bush.

The brightest part of the dull sky was in the west when we came to the lake with the ancient causeway. Gray plovers and sandpipers waded at the margins, and grebes floated along, using their feathers as sails to catch the wind.

"Perhaps they went around?" Egfrith said hopefully, scanning the horizon east and west. "We could yet head them off."

"Maybe," I said, brushing a fat spider from my breeks. My cloak had been wicking water and was soaking and heavy now, so that I was wishing I had left it behind even with the cold. "A wolf wouldn't swim this."

"But that beast is no ordinary creature," Egfrith admitted through a grimace. "I'd wager Asgot has worked some foul spell on it." *Like he has on Cynethryth,* I thought but did not say, as I steadied myself on the first rotting post and waded into the clear, numbing water. Once across, we shivered through the meadows of wind-stirred grass and up the low rising ground to the apple trees, whose buds sheltered from the cold in tiny furlike coverings.

It was among those sleeping trees that we found them. The first I knew of it was when Egfrith stumbled and fell to his knees. For a heartbeat I thought he had tripped, but then he let out a low, whimpering moan.

"Oh, dear God! Oh, God. What have they done?" He was wringing his hands, and we caught up with him and peered through the gnarly trees. There were dark shapes hanging among the branches. "You have murdered God's daughters," Egfrith sobbed, hanging his head and clutching his face, barely able to look upon the carnage. Sourness churned in my gut, and I put a hand on Egfrith's shoulder, perhaps to steady myself. The Christ brides were hanging by their necks, their blue faces and bulging eyes accusing all in turn as their corpses twisted in the wind. Seven hung there, their bare feet skimming grass that glistened and steamed with piss.

I remembered when I had found Ealhstan hung in a tree to die, his guts undone and strung up around the trunk, a victim of the godi's bloodlust. This time those watching were Danes, and now they looked at us, the awe at what they had done still greasing their eyes. Asgot had finished his rites and now stood talking with one of the others as I left Egfrith where he was and walked into that death grove.

"Raven, these Frankish bitches tried to use Christ seidr on us," a Dane called Arngrim said, shaking his head in bewilderment. But I ignored him because I was looking at Cynethryth. She was standing close enough to one of the hanging corpses to reach out and touch it, and she paid me no notice as I came to stand beside her.

"Be careful, men," Asgot said. "The last time we did this, Raven went berserk and killed a man named Einar. Sigurd let him get away with it, too."

I felt some of the Danes' eyes on me, but I was looking at Cynethryth.

"Why, Cynethryth?" I asked. A crunching sound made me look past her, where Sköll had chewed a fleshy lump through to the bone. I grimaced at what or who that flesh might have belonged to. "These Christ brides did you no harm," I said. "Cynethryth?" I touched her arm, and she flinched as though I had burned her.

"Raven," she said, her eyes meeting mine, and for a brief hopeful moment I thought I saw the old Cynethryth in those green eyes. But as soon as that ember had appeared, it hardened and died. "They cannot harm anyone now," she said, her lips twisting into a grin.

"They harmed you?" I said.

She shook her head. *Not these*, I thought, *but others like them.* Cynethryth was staring at the bloodless face of the young woman, whose neck was horribly stretched. She had been Cynethryth's age more or less.

"Listen, Raven," Asgot hissed, his breath clouding in the frigid air. "He is here. He has come to this place." The old godi's eyes flashed in the way they did only when death was in the air. He was talking about the All-Father, and although I could hear nothing other than the creak of the hang ropes and the twisted branches and the men's breathing and Cynethryth's wolf eating, I *could* feel the seidr that had been worked there. The grove was heavy with it.

"We should hang the monk up with them," a Dane called Boe suggested, pointing at Egfrith, who was on his feet now but bent double and retching.

"If you touch him, I will kill you, Boe," I said, and for a heartbeat Boe bristled at the threat. Then he showed me his palms and grinned.

"Heya, Raven, I did not know he was your friend," he said.

"He is," I said, glancing back at the monk, who was walking toward us now, dragging his sleeve across his mouth as his eyes flicked from one dead nun to another.

"This is powerful seidr, Raven," Black Floki muttered with a nod, his left hand instinctively resting on his sword's pommel. "Killing seven Christ brides like this."

He was right. The gods were sure to notice a thing like this. It was like lighting a great fire for the midwinter Yule feast to summon the spirits of the dead.

"We have bought much favor for the voyage ahead," Arngrim said. "The others will be pleased."

"I'll wager Tufi wishes we had done it sooner," a Dane called Ottar said, stirring subdued ayes from the others.

"Sigurd wants us all back at the camp," I said as loudly as I dared in that grove where Ódin lingered, brought there by Asgot though not Asgot alone. Cynethryth had played her part in it too. I had not seen her do it, but I knew it was so. The Danes trod as lightly around her as they did around Asgot. She was as immersed in that potent seidr as the rest of us.

She was letting it seep into her being like pine resin into new strakes, and you would never know that she had once been a Christian. "Did any of the Christ brides escape?" I asked.

"No, they are all here," Ottar said, marveling at the gently swinging bodies. Two crows were sidling closer to a corpse, stopping now and then to cock their heads and eye us.

"Good," I said. "Then let us leave now before it gets dark. I would not like to lose my way in the marsh and run into the vengeful spirits of these murdered women. Do not forget we are in Frankia."

"Raven is right," Asgot said. "The White Christ has some power here. It is done, and we should go."

"Let me bury them!" Egfrith pleaded, his shrill voice threatening to disturb the seidr balance. "Have some pity for the dead and let me cut them down." Asgot hissed at him like a cat, and Arngrim swore under his breath.

I clutched the monk's arm. "Hold your tongue," I growled, "or you'll find a rope around your neck and your feet off the ground." His weasel face was a knot of anguish and misery, and I saw an emptiness in his eyes like the emptiness I had seen in Halldor's eyes before Sigurd killed him. The monk looked broken.

"You will not go far from the camp again without your jarl's leave," Black Floki gnarred. "That goes for you too, Asgot." The Danes grunted their assent, but Asgot curled his lip at Floki, thumbing some small bones over in his hand, which might have been a threat. Floki eyeballed him, and the Danes twitched nervously until Sköll cut the silence with a howl that stiffened the hairs on my neck. The two crows flapped into the sky, *kaah*ing angrily, their stealth undone. Cynethryth knelt in front of the beast, her forehead against its snout, and whispered tenderly. Then, somewhere to the east, another wolf howled, and Sköll narrowed its golden-yellow eyes and pulled back its ears.

"Let's move," I said. Because the darkness was coming and there were gods among us.

chapter
eLeven

"SHE HELPED that bloodthirsty old cunny string them up?" Penda asked me, throwing another branch into the fire pit. I watched the flames lick the new wood, which began to bubble and spit because it was still green. All around us folk were turning in, having heard Asgot and the Danes' tales of their offering and the All-Father's visit to that grove of the dead. They had listened like children, eyes wide, mouths framing unspoken questions. Many had seemed grateful to Asgot. And to Cynethryth.

"I think it's worse than that," I said. "I think the whole thing was Cynethryth's idea."

Penda shook his head. "No, Raven. I know she's changed." I felt his eyes on me as I watched the flames. "She is not the girl she was, I'll admit that, but—" He scrubbed his head with a fist. "She would not do that. By Christ, they were nuns, lad!"

"They think she has power," I said, thumbing at a knot of Danes, seeing no reason now to flinch from the truth. I had hated seeing those Christ brides hanging there, stiffening in the cold. Even if their deaths had bought us the favor some had thought lost, I despised their murder. I have always thought it a cowardly thing to kill a woman, and that night I had known.

I was not alone in that. Some of the men had frowned at the tale, Sigurd among them. Though he knew the power in such an offering, he could not spit out the bad taste it left in the mouth. But what curdled my guts, made me feel like taking my sword and ramming it down Asgot's throat, was the thought of Cynethryth putting the ropes around the nuns' necks. That thought twisted my mind like corpses twisting in the wind. Because I knew then what I had feared for a long time: Cynethryth was lost to me forever.

"And what about you, Raven?" Penda said. "Do you think that she has . . . power?" I heard the grimace through which his words seeped.

"It doesn't matter what I think. The others believe so. That damned wolf, too."

Penda tossed another branch into the flames, sending a dense swarm of sparks into the night sky. I followed their flight, turning over in my mind the black threads that had been woven into Cynethryth's wyrd and wondering if I could have unpicked any of them.

We saw another three full moons on Lyngvi, during which time we made repairs to the ships, grew fat on meat, and humped the blauvifs to keep warm. We spent Yuletide gorging on the flesh from small bulls we had found wandering the fen. They were wily creatures, which is probably why we had not come across them sooner, but once we had found their drinking pool, we just had to wait with ropes downwind among the rushes. At first we had tried bows, but we found that these sturdy beasts could sprout ten or more arrows and still charge off into the scrub, so that when we found them bled out, the meat was tough as leather.

With ropes and enough men we could catch them, hold them, and cut their throats, and that was the best way. But even the beef could not make up for the lack of ale and mead. Bram was not the only one who moaned that this was the first Yuletide he could remember spending sober, to which Bjarni added that it was the first Yuletide he could remember at all, and if it had not been for the dark beauties warming his bed, it would have been the worst Yuletide ever.

As for myself, I had grown fond of Amina and might have loved her if we could have understood each other better. As it was, she taught me scraps of her language and I tried to teach her some English and Norse. Mostly, though, we clung to each other among our furs as the scourging wind moaned across the marsh or the freezing fog hung thick as broth over our camp. Amina and the others had been quick to discard their colorful tunics and shrouds because they were too fine to keep out the cold. Instead they had made clothes from our stock of skins, and so you would hardly have recognized them now as the amir's women. They looked more like some strange wild tribe from old men's tales, yet even when they were drowning in massive furs and pelt hats, you could see they were beauties. Often we would joke about how the fat amir must be missing them though his ears probably were enjoying the peace.

Father Egfrith was cheerless and wretched. He had not shaved his head for many weeks now and had even let his beard grow. If not for the threadbare habit he still wore under an old bear's pelt, you would not have guessed he was a Christ slave. Penda said that the monk had given up all hope of bringing any of us into his god's fold and now carried a burden of guilt and failure.

It is always the way in my experience that when men are in far-flung lands, they observe even more fiercely the habits and customs of their home. So it was with us. Men favored certain trees or deep pools, leaving offerings of food or making animal sacrifices to Ódin or Frey or Njörd. Even those who had listened to Egfrith's talk of the White Christ before, if only because any story was better than none, now had no time for the monk. Asgot had proved the more powerful of the two of them, his blood offering of the nuns keeping us in favor with the gods, so that we had spent a winter if not in comfort nevertheless full with food and safe from attack. The only men who listened to Egfrith now were the Wessexmen Penda, Gytha, Baldred, and Wiglaf. And even they spent less time around the monk these days, perhaps because they, too, enjoyed the company of the blauvifs for which they had had to endure Egfrith's tongue-lashing. So Egfrith kept to himself now, brooding and sour as a crab apple, and I think he would have left us to our sinful ways and gone if he had not been stuck on that sodden island in the heart of winter.

When the northerly wind lost some of its teeth, we began making preparations to leave Lyngvi. Every few days one of us would follow the brackish channels back to the wave-lashed shoreline to judge the sea's mood and the sailing conditions. We marked the sun's journey through the sky, watching it climb a little higher each day and take longer to fall behind the western horizon. Our shadows across the mud-flats shortened, and lone flying insects became swarms best avoided. We watched buds swelling on bushes and trees and looked to the sky for birds flying north, all of which told us that winter was ending.

But the winter had not been kind to *Goliath*. The ship had been buffeted by wind and flayed by icy rain and seething seas. Without men to bail it, the bilge was knee-deep in water and much of the deck was rotting. She was rolling slightly to the steerboard side, too, and Knut and Olaf agreed that if we took her out into the open sea, she would more than likely fall apart at the first sniff of heavy weather. We took what was useful, including much of the rigging and the sail, which we had stored in *Fjord-Elk*'s hold over the winter, and also some of the wood that was still strong, and we left the rest of her to the sea. We struck camp and carried our sea chests back to the ships, and the blauvifs were put aboard the snekkjes with the Danes because Sigurd would not have them on *Serpent* or *Fjord-Elk*. It took Cynethryth a long while to persuade Sköll to walk *Serpent*'s boarding plank. The beast seemed to shrink, tucking its tail between its legs and flattening its ears, but in the end Cynethryth tempted it up with a raw bull's heart, and once aboard, the creature cowered in the bows, whimpering and shivering, so that I almost pitied it.

We could just as easily have waited for the wind to change so that we could sail those waterlogged ditches and channels back to the sea, for a day here or there would have made no difference. But Sigurd said that we had lived softly for too long. That journey from the mere would remind our shoulders and arms how to row again before the sterner test of the open sea, and in truth we were glad to grip the staves once more and turn some of that meat into muscle. The men were in good spirits as men always are when water is turning on either side of the bow after a long time on land. We were happy to be leaving that island too, though we all agreed that it had the promise of being a fine place to live in the summer so long as the biting flies were not too many.

We passed *Goliath* sitting forsaken in the estuary. To me she looked like the rotting carcass of a whale, her plundered hull the creature's ribs where the flesh has been picked away. But our ships had been protected and repaired and cleaned, and we rowed into the open sea, then east toward the rising sun, so that I could feel the warmth on my back, and *Serpent*'s hull shivered with the thrill of being free again. I filled my lungs, letting my hair loose for the sea air to wash the cloying damp smell of Lyngvi from it. When our muscles began to cramp and burn because they were not used to the work, Sigurd made us row some more, and none of us could complain, for our jarl rowed too, sweating as much as any of us. When at last we stowed our oars and sank the anchors with the sun, we were as tired as thralls at harvest time, almost too tired to eat though our bodies craved food. But it felt good being rocked to sleep by the sea's endless rolling furrows, listening to the creaking of the ropes and the mast and the strange yet comforting sound of bubbles playing across the strakes on the underside of the hull.

Next day, we came tired and stiff to the oars, and the day after that was even worse. But by the fourth day our oar rhythm was as good as it ever had been, and the aching in my muscles had dulled to a faint reminder not to leave it so long next time. The men we had freed along with Yngvar and Völund we put on *Fjord-Elk*'s row benches and found them to be good oarsmen, though *Fjord-Elk*'s original crew members were not too keen on sharing deck space with men whose language they could make no sense of. Now and then the lightening sea would swell or the wind would suddenly build, warning us that we had perhaps left the safety of Lyngvi a little early in the season, but we had all itched to move on. So long as we stayed near the shore and kept one eye on the sky and the other on the sea, we believed all would be well. Besides which, trading galleys were thick as gulls around a herring skiff in that sea. Not a day went by when we didn't see a sail or two straining full of the warming air, and if merchants were not afraid to be out, then men as sea-bold as us should not give it a thought, though of course we did. We kept our dragon heads mounted on our prows, but it was likely that these other ships would have avoided us anyway, which was what we wanted for now.

Ten days after leaving Lyngvi, we came to the land of the Romans. Most of us had heard tales about them, how in the olden times their kings had ruled lands and peoples stretching beyond the farthest horizons in all directions. These emperors would send great armies against their enemies, their warriors numbering more than the stars in the sky. They had built enormous halls of stone, much bigger even than the ones we had seen in Frankia, and even the poorest of the Romans had thought himself a lord among the men of other lands. Those days were long gone, but a man of no less power than the emperors of old held dominion there now: Emperor Karolus.

"The Vicar of Saint Peter, His Holiness Pope Leo himself, placed the ancient crown of the Roman emperors on Karolus's head," Egfrith said as we looked for warships among the vessels moored in the harbor off our port bow. It looked like a busy little place, with traders and fishing boats lashed to the wharf and stalls set out along the strand, though most of the buying and selling had stopped as folk stood looking out to sea, shielding their eyes against the glare off the water.

"I am beginning to think that we could sail off the world's edge and still land in this emperor's lap," Sigurd said, shaking his head in wonder. "Perhaps we were lucky to escape with our lives the last time we met Karolus, hey, monk?"

Egfrith's eyebrows bounced. "Lucky? It was miraculous," he said. The monk had been sulking for a week, but having recognized the flat coastline and some of the islands from descriptions he had read in church books, he now seemed gripped by a little of his old vigor. For days we had been following a coastline of soft, inviting, keel-friendly sand beyond which the land was flat enough to spot a war band coming, and seeing this harbor had further whetted our appetite to make landfall. We did not need food: we had smoked enough waterfowl, beef, and freshwater and saltwater fish to last us halfway to Ragnarök. What we wanted was mead.

"Looks safe enough," Olaf said, his lips pursed within his dense beard.

Knut agreed. "I'm happy to take her in," he said, looking for his jarl's approval.

Sigurd nodded. "We'll moor with the prows turned

to the sea," he said, stirring a few grumbles from us, for it would mean we would take longer to berth. But it was the wise thing to do because we could be away much more quickly if something did go bad. Olaf gave orders to drop the sail, and Bram called across to the captains of the other three ships to tell them what we were doing. Then we all fetched our oars and returned to our own sea chests and got ready to begin the difficult task of maneuvering the stern into the berth, which, as it happened, was easier than expected because crewmen from five traders were frantically hoisting sails, weighing anchors, and casting off.

"I don't know what they're afraid of," Bjarni said, turning back with a smirk and pushing his oar.

"What harm could four ships of heathens do to a quiet little port like this?" I said, watching Olaf, who was telling us all when to pull and when to push. When we had moored, Sigurd ordered the other crews to stay aboard their ships until he and a landing party had taken a sniff around the port.

"What is it my father always used to say?" Olaf said, picking up his spear with one hand and scratching his neck with the other. "Never wander too far ahead of your spear. You can't feel a fight in your bones or know when danger's near."

"Wasn't your father killed by a broken neck, Uncle?" Osk said, frowning. Olaf nodded.

"He tripped over his spear," Yrsa Pig-Nose mumbled, and Olaf swung his fist against Yrsa's chin, dropping him to the deck.

"Let's go, then," Olaf said, and I followed him over the sheer strake onto the wharf, leaving Pig-Nose sitting there watery-eyed and confused. Most folk scat-

tered from us like birds from a fox, but not all. Some
of the merchants saw the chance for profit and flocked
toward us, chattering in their tongue about whatever
they had to sell, and not for the first time it struck me
that merchants are often not given enough respect for
their bravery. For we were five warriors, sea-bedraggled
and fierce-looking and armed with swords and spears.
And our eyes had the glint of the mead-thirst in them,
so that if you did not have mead or ale, you would be
better served getting out of our way. Sigurd and Olaf
led, and I followed with Black Floki and Svein the Red.
Behind us scurried Egfrith, trying his Latin on the locals, though from what I could tell, it made as little
sense to them as it did to me.

We stepped from the wharf, and our boots sank
into the sand as we turned this way and that, half
looking for warriors, half looking for anything worth
having. Old fishermen sat mending their nets, having
no need to fear the likes of us, for their only silver was
in their hair. Two boys were pulling the stiff dried
weed and crisp small fish from another net spread
across the sand. Three older boys tracked us, keeping
a safe distance while their leader, the tallest, with a
nest of curly black hair and the spiteful look of the
hungry, seemed to be weighing when would be the
right time to approach us. Another group of old men
were sitting in a beached skiff playing some game that
looked like tafl, though their eyes were on us, too, now.

Instinctively, we had followed the sweet smell of fish
sizzling with onions and herbs, and now Olaf handed
a nervous boy a silver coin the size of a fingernail. The
boy's eyes grew, and he turned to his father, who gave
us a wide grin and threw out his arms, inviting us to

claim the delicious-looking food spitting above the coals. Olaf tossed me a fish, and I threw it from hand to hand, blowing on it, then peeled back the skin and took a bite of the hot, fragrant flesh, grinning at Svein. The giant bit into his own fish and could have looked happier only if he'd had something strong to wash it down with.

"Better than wind-flayed herring," I said, wiping grease from my lips and beard.

"Better than anything Arnvid fishes out of the pot," Sigurd said, flashing a grin at the boy, who gave a gummy smile and puffed his little chest like a robin.

"Arnvid could burn water," Black Floki put in casually, eyes scouring the length of the strand and the line of green scrub inland. Beyond that scrub to the east was a clutter of poorly built dwellings that we guessed belonged to the fishermen who would sell their catch farther inland or along the coast.

The three older boys made their move, cutting across our path, the two shorter ones taking their place either side of the tall thin boy in a fluid maneuver that spoke of practiced ease. Their feet were planted in stride rather than square in case they should have to run for it, and they gave us well-greased smiles that did not touch their calculating eyes.

"I'll wager these are just the little sea urchins we want to talk to," Olaf said.

"Talk, then, Uncle," Sigurd said, at which Olaf shrugged, coughed, and spoke, addressing the boys in Norse. Immediately the leader shook his head and wagged a finger at Olaf, spewing something in reply. Olaf turned to me, palms to the sky.

"Monk!" Sigurd called, and Egfrith tried speaking to them in Latin, at which one of the other boys, a callow-looking lad with a face full of pustules, tugged the leader's sleeve and gabbled something to which the older boy simply nodded, irritation flashing across his face. The older boy then made a ring of his thumb and forefinger through which he poked the forefinger of his other hand. That was clear enough in any language, and Sigurd shook his head.

I raised an invisible horn to my mouth and pretended to drink, following it with an "aaah," then dragging my arm across my mouth. All three boys grinned at that, and Curly Hair snapped an order at a blond-haired boy, who nodded and ran off up the strand as lightly over the sand as a water snake across a pond. Then Sigurd produced an iron ring from his tunic of the kind that went around a slave's ankle and stepped up to Egfrith and took his hand as though about to thrust it into the fetter. The two boys who were left frowned at each other, chattering all the while, then Curly Hair dared to step up to Sigurd and put a hand on his shoulder. He turned the jarl around until they were facing west, back out to sea, and then he pointed a thin arm up at the sun. He held up two fingers, which we took to mean in two days' time, and then the boy thumped his chest with his palm and pointed to our ships at the wharf.

"Clear as a pail of mud," Olaf said, shaking his head.

Sigurd gave Curly Hair a small coin, which the boy examined before nodding indifferently, though he must have worked far harder for much less many times before.

"Uncle, tell the men we'll be staying for a couple of days," Sigurd said, turning his face toward the sun and closing his eyes. The two boys ran off southeastward, which made me think there must be a larger settlement in that direction. "We'll stay here and stretch our legs," the jarl added, breathing deeply of the warming air. Olaf nodded, pulling another fish from a pouch on his belt and biting into it as he turned on his heel. "And tell them to make the most of the blauvifs," Sigurd added, to which Olaf casually raised a hand as though he had already intended as much. "You too, Raven," Sigurd said. "The wolf that eats the farmer's sheep loses its teeth before the wolf that must hunt in the forest."

I glanced at Svein, who now wore the face of a boy who is told he cannot play with the other boys. Then I followed Olaf back to the ships. And Amina.

That night the three boys returned, only this time they came leading an old tired ass. Across the creature's back was slung almost its height again in bulging skins, but it plodded stolidly on, hooves flicking up flurries of sand as the boys beside it beamed with pride. They had barely got among the shelters we had built on the strand before Norsemen, Danes, and Wessexmen fell on their hoard like men who were thirsting to death. It turned out to be not mead or ale but wine, as red as blood and at once sweet and sour and delicious. In some of the skins was fresh water, and after watching Bram swill enough wine to drown a horse, the boys took great pleasure in showing us the proper way, which was to cut the wine with water. Though many of us ignored that advice. When Sigurd had paid them, they seemed more than happy to stay and spent the rest of the night flitting among us, filling our horns and cups over and over again. Fires crackled and popped, and the moon-dappled waves splashed up onto the sand in languid sighs, each breath fresh with the scent of the sea. Having decided we meant them no harm, local folk came to sell us hot pottage made with barley, fish, olive oil, and wine. They brought fresh bread and cheese and spiced vegetables and mice stuffed with pork and herbs. But my favorite dish was crusts of bread that had been soaked in milk, fried in fat, and then covered with honey, and I ate until I could eat no more.

Men and women screwed in the sand, some even swived in the sea, and all sluiced their insides with wine. Yngvar and Völund were part of our crew now, had even agreed to take Sigurd's oath, but no one saw why the other men we had freed should still be sharing our food and drink, and so Sigurd paid them what he had promised and sent them off to whatever lay in store for them in the land of the Romans. We cared about nothing so long as the wine flowed and the food kept coming, and I half watched them stalk nervously off toward the town. Bram challenged men to wrestling bouts, and he won five in a row until he was eventually beaten by the wine, which put him facedown in the sand, something no man had been able to do. One of the local men came with four dark-haired girls who he implied were his daughters. Three of them were beautiful, and the fourth I wouldn't have touched with a long oar, but the man happily sold their services to men who wanted a change from the blauvifs, and some of those men might afterward have wished they'd left the new girls alone judging by

the scowls on the faces of those they usually shared
their beds with.

Penda lay back on his elbows, bare-chested and
sweating, the sand stuck to his skin making him look
white as a new corpse. In one hand he gripped a
drinking horn, and in the other a fleshy joint of meat.
He was almost as drunk as I was.

"You would have thought they had been told that
tomorrow the sky is going to fall on their heads," he
said, squinting drunkenly at the seething camp. He
was right. King Hrothgar's Geats could not have cel-
ebrated more boisterously when Beowulf returned
from Heorot brandishing the corpse-maker Grendal's
severed arm. I tried to reply, but the words slewed out
in a wine-soaked mess. Amina lay in the crook of my
arm whispering her strange words into my ear. I
shuddered as her hand snaked into my breeks.

"Tomorrow, Baldred!" Penda called over to the
Wessexman, who was grunting like a boar, busy with
one of the local girls. "Tomorrow the sky is going to
fall on our heads! Make the most of that sweet honey-
pot. Tomorrow the sky's going to fall."

Which it did. Because the next day we lost our
women.

chapter
TWELVE

I WOKE FEELING as though my brain had shriveled and died inside my skull. My mouth was so dry that I could not speak, my guts rolled over themselves like eels in a trap, and the bile had risen so that I thought I would vomit but didn't know when. Amina was still sleeping after a vigorous night, her glossy black hair spread across the furs and her breathing a soft imitation of the nearby surf. I crawled out but halted, waiting on my hands and knees while my eyes yielded to the harsh morning light. Then I climbed to my feet and stood swaying as I looked around the camp. Piles of white ash still smoldered, and drinking horns lay abandoned, half buried in the sand. Bones and scraps of food were everywhere, and farther up the beach I could see Cynethryth's wolf content as a hound as it chewed plundered scraps. Here and there lay a Norseman or a Dane who had slept where he had fallen, and there were even two or three local men who had been too drunk to make it back to their homes.

"Raven! Here, lad!" I turned, and there was Sigurd in the sea, waving at me to join him.

"I swim like a rock, lord!" I called back, holding the back of my head because I feared it was about to split open.

"That's good! Rocks cannot drown. You will feel better afterward. Svein!" Svein had just emerged from his shelter like a troll from its cave, and beneath that flaming hair he looked as ashen as the spent fires. He was muttering to himself. "Svein!" Sigurd called again. "Pick Raven up and throw him this way!" I looked at Svein, who shrugged and started toward me, but I raised my palms, and he shrugged again and walked off to piss. So I took off my breeks and waded into the surf.

"Makes you feel alive again, hey?" Sigurd said. I could not reply because I was retching.

"Swallowed . . . some . . ." I muttered, watching the vomit float off and trying to find my feet. Sigurd was grinning.

"That was some night," he said, sweeping his sodden golden hair back from his scarred head. There were scars on his shoulders too, like the runes of battle.

"I would rather not think about it," I said, spitting bitter-tasting strings of saliva. Along the strand men were pushing their skiffs into the sea. Some were already far out, nutshells bobbing on the horizon, blurs of movement as crews cast their nets. The smell of onions cooking in fat wafted down from the beach.

"Don't fight it, Raven," Sigurd said. Beneath me my legs were kicking even more frantically than my arms were flapping. "Watch me." He lay back so that even his ears were underwater, and then he let each new wave gently lift him and lower him back down, and somehow his nose and eyes remained above the water. "You just have to take a deep breath and hold it so that you float," he said, staring up at the sky. Then he came back upright and blew snot from his nose.

"Try." A gull dived and snatched a morsel from the waves, but another gull wanted the prize too, and because the loot was too big, the first bird dropped it and the second swooped in to snatch it up again. "Don't be afraid, Raven. Your wyrd is not to drown; I'd wager my sea chest on that." And so, gritting my teeth, I lay back in the water, and just as I did, a wave broke over my upturned face and I choked as the water hit my throat. I came up retching again. Sigurd's laughter was flat as an oar blade across the water. "That's the thing about wyrd," he said, beginning to wade back to shore. "You just never know."

Curly Hair and his urchins came back that afternoon and brought with them a rich-looking man whose clothes were similar to those the amir had worn, though he was no blauman. He came with four bodyguards, big men with big spears who looked as if what they lacked in wits they made up for in muscle. They were nervous now, though, surrounded by shambling, wine-addled warriors, and I suspected they were hoping their master did nothing that would get them killed.

The merchant's name was Azriel, and he was a slave trader. He had come because Sigurd had shown the fetter to Curly Hair and the boy had done enough business on that strand to know when men stepped ashore looking for slaves. Only Sigurd did not want to buy slaves. He wanted to sell them. We had been told to say our good-byes to our blauvifs, and that had been a hard thing to do. Many of the men had grown fond enough of their women to shed a tear at the prospect of losing them, and I admit to having a lump in my throat as I kissed Amina for the last time.

The women had been lined up along the shore, and Azriel had examined each one, often shaking his head disappointedly and clicking his tongue in annoyance. But his dismay was as thin as watered wine judging by how quick he was to make Sigurd an offer, and not just for some of the blauvifs but all of them. That was only to be expected, because as the amir's women they had lived lives of comfort, and that showed in their skin and in their teeth and in every delicious part of them. They may have looked rougher at the edges after living with us these last months, but the merchant knew his trade well enough to recognize good flesh when he saw it.

"I will miss her," Svein said glumly as Azriel opened his blauvif's mouth and peered inside. "She was the best bed partner I have ever had." I nodded, too upset to speak. I knew what he meant, though. Amina had done things to me that I would never forget. "Hey, hey, never mind! There will be another one," Svein added with a smile, slapping my back and then turning to walk back to the camp. From that sorrowful line of blauvifs Amina stared at me with her brown-gold eyes, tears rolling down her dark cheeks. Nearby, Sigurd and Olaf were arguing with Azriel over the price.

"No more tit pillows for a while, then," Bram Bear said, brows arched. "I'll wager you'll miss that dark little treasure, hey, Raven?"

I gazed at Amina, wondering what might have been had the two of us been somewhere else. She was a spear's throw away, yet I thirsted for her as though another kiss might wash away the bitter taste of parting. Leaving her there was harder than I cared to admit. It felt wrong, and those eyes staring at me did not help one bit.

"There will be another one," I said, turning my back on the girl and walking away.

Two days later we set sail. A northwesterly pushed us southeast along the Roman coast past countless small harbors and villages of white stone houses. We passed white beaches, jagged rocks and cliffs, and swaths of dark green pine woods whose sweet scent wafted out across the sea to us every now and then. The wind tended to be stronger in the morning, and we reveled in it, harnessing it to drive past tree-shrouded promontories and blazing white dunes, and none of us had ever seen such shimmering blue waters.

"The roof of the world is higher above these lands than our own, I think," Olaf said one day, scratching his coarse beard and watching a hawk drift high above the pine forest on our port side. Far above the bird, in the vast expanse of blue, a few vaporous white clouds hung, seeming not to move at all.

"It keeps the rain off better, too, Uncle," Sigurd said with a smile. They both stood by the mast step, overseeing the men whose job it was to tighten the stays and work the sail. The rest of us were on our sea chests, making the most of the oars being up in their trees. The air still had a bite to it, but we had stowed our bad-weather gear and used only our furs at night now.

No one talked about our blauvifs. It had been a hard thing watching them sold, though Sigurd had shared out the silver equally and there had been enough for every man to get four silver coins to put in his sea chest. But even that was a bitter draft to swallow because every one of those coins had been stamped with the likeness of King Karolus, the emperor of the Franks, who was our enemy.

"It could be any whoreson," Bram had said, unimpressed, holding one of his coins up and inspecting it closely. "This man has no beard."

"The monk says it has the king's name on it," Bjarni had said, "just there; look." He was pointing to his coin and the writing that ran around the edge of it. We were all looking at our own coins, not for the first time overawed by the Frank king's power. But Bram wasn't having it.

"It does not look like Karolus," he said.

"Well, if you don't want yours, you can give it to me," Olaf said, at which Bram mumbled something and tucked the coin into the leather scrip on his belt.

"I'm just saying it could be anyone, that's all," he said.

"Not you, Bram," I said. "They'd never be able to get your face on something this small. A cauldron, maybe, but not this."

He winked at Svein. "I'm just surprised you haven't thrown yours overboard yet, Raven," he said, rousing moans and mutterings and several insults that were flung my way, so that I wished I had kept my mouth shut. I called Bram a troll-humping goat turd, then stood and made my way to the stern, thinking I would talk with Knut at the tiller, where I hoped there would be no mention of the hoard I had set adrift in Frankia. But my eye caught on Father Egfrith huddled in the port stern. He was staring landward, the wind ruffling the beard he wore now and the messy wisps of graying hair above his ears. Something made me go to the monk instead of to the steersman, and I cursed under my breath because I would rather have talked to Knut.

"It looks like good land, hey, monk?" I said, watching *Serpent*'s shadow crawl along a stretch of rugged sun-dappled rock. The black shape expanded and shrank and looked like a living thing, some seeking spirit.

"You cannot imagine the things that have happened here in these waters, on this coast," he said without looking at me. "Great civilizations were born here. Men whose ambitions shook the world have looked upon the same rocks we see now. Men who valued enlightenment and learning and wisdom, not just the sword and the ax."

"I thought you said that the Romans' greatest king was a warrior who killed thousands of men from a hundred lands," I countered, "just because they would not obey his laws."

He nodded. "Caesar. His name was Julius Caesar, and yes, he certainly shared your heathen bloodlust. But he was a great man, too. Unfortunately for him, he lived and died before Christ's light illuminated the world."

"The Romans believed in many gods, didn't they? Like us." He nodded. "And some of them were warrior gods like Ódin and Thór and Týr?" I asked.

"Like all men they had faults. We are all sinners." Now he turned and stared into my eyes. "Though some sins cannot be forgiven." I thought that was aimed at me, but then I saw that those tired eyes, though they were fixed on mine, in truth looked inward. I knew the shadow that lay across his face for what it was. Shame. He stared again at the shore.

"You could not have saved the nuns," I said, and the twist of his thin lips told me I had struck true.

"No, I could not," he said. "But had I saved the men first, then the nuns would still be alive." I knew by "saved" he meant turned them into Christians, and now I tried to keep my own grimace hidden in my beard.

"You have not had so long with the Danes," I said, "and as for Asgot, surely you don't think you can make a Christian of him." If he did, Egfrith was more of a fool than I thought.

He hoisted his brows. "I have failed, Raven." The sail thumped, and I felt a gust from the east on my right cheek.

"You helped get your precious Jesus book to King Karolus," I said.

He almost smiled at that. "That is true. A small triumph but not enough."

"Sigurd must value you," I said. "Loki knows why, but he does. Otherwise you'd have been thrown overboard with the fish guts by now. You don't row, and I have not seen you in the shieldwall."

"Sigurd could teach a fox slyness," he said, this time letting a smile creep into his beard. "He feeds me crumbs of hope that I might one day win his soul for God, and in return . . . ? In return I go along with whatever iniquitous schemes you vile creatures fall into. I am a wicked whore, Raven. I have sold my soul, and for what?" I had no answer to that, for truly I believed that there was more chance of the ocean freezing over than there was of the Wolfpack bending their knees to the White Christ. "And the worst of it," Egfrith went on, "is that I am a thrall to my own pride." He cocked

Giles Kristian

one eyebrow at me. "Do not think you warriors are the only ones ruled by pride. Knowing that I have failed, that the Lord is disappointed in me, ought to compel me to abandon this damned ship and return to the fold, to my brothers, and there pray for forgiveness. I ought to quietly seek some lesser task to which I might, God willing, be equal."

"Sigurd would let you leave, I think," I said. "You are no good to him sulking like this anyway. You've been as sullen as a sober Norseman for weeks now."

"That's just it, Raven," he said, clutching at *Serpent*'s sheer strake, "I cannot leave. My damned pride will not let me. I have met Alcuin of York, the greatest scholar of our times. I have spoken with Karolus Magnus, the emperor of Christendom. I may yet live to see the glorious domed churches of Constantinople." I frowned. "Miklagard, Raven, the heartbeat of the Eastern Roman Empire." He shook his head. "A curious mind can be a burden. Did you know that we must soon pass the mouth of the Tiberis River?" I shook my head. I had never even heard of it. "That river leads to Rome itself. Sigurd knows it because I told him." I glanced at Sigurd, who was now in the foreship working the bowline while Olaf wound the tacking rope around the boom, lashing it to the clamp. The two men were enjoying themselves, each seeming to anticipate the other's next movement. "Even now your jarl is weighing in his mind the risks against what might be won. Rome's glory has faded, her eminence overshadowed by her sister empire in the east, yet she must surely make Aix-la-Chapelle look like the humblest village."

"You think we should sail up this Tiberis?" I asked,

scanning the shoreline for the turbid, angry water that would betray a river's mouth. I saw no river. A ravenous flock of screaming gulls wheeled above something dark that the sea had coughed onto the sand.

After a while Egfrith said, "I think my reasons for wanting to go to Rome would be very different from Sigurd's." His eyes flashed hungrily for a heartbeat. "But yes, I would see the city with my own eyes after reading of it in vellum leaves." He closed his eyes, then nodded slowly as though in answer to a voice I could not hear. When those eyes opened again, they were dulled by a layer of ice. "Greed is greed, lad. Whether it is a heathen's silver greed or a failed monk's hunger to visit the places he has only ever imagined in his feeble mind. At least I now see why I have failed. I failed because I was too ensnared in my own ambitions to give myself fully to the Lord's work."

"Well, you did not kill those nuns," I said, not knowing what else to say. "That much I *do* know. And if your god is as mild and forgiving as you say, he'll overlook a little wanderlust." I stood and made my way over to Knut, hoping to draw from the steersman some inkling as to whether Sigurd was going to take us up the river Egfrith had spoken of. "As for making Christ slaves of us all," I added over my shoulder, "there is still time." Even the gloomy monk chuckled at that.

Eight days later, after a night of heavy rain and dark dreams, we left behind the clear blue coastal waters and the boundless vault of the sky and entered the mouth of the Tiberis. We stowed Jörmungand, and the other ships did the same with their prow beasts, because we did not want to risk offending the local spirits, who we suspected must be ancient and perhaps still powerful. In the end Sigurd had held a ting, a meeting at which all were allowed their say, and the word from each ship was that almost every man had voted to sail up the river come what might.

"How could we go back to Wessex and tell our kin-folk that we had sailed past Rome because we were too pale-livered to clap eyes on it for ourselves?" Wiglaf had said, which was the way the rest of us felt about it too. So now we were rowing. Hard. Because somewhere far to the east, spring meltwater was en-gorging the river and our arms were having to over-come the force of the current. As I rowed, I tried to summon again the pictures that had filled my mind as I slept, for though the form of the dreams had dis-sipated like smoke, a grim, dread feeling had clung to me from the moment of waking. Even now, as I pulled at the oar, my heart hammering, the dream's claws were still in me, but I could not see the rest of the beast.

Where river and sea entwined, we had passed whole villages of crumbling stone that had been abandoned long before. Perhaps, too often attacked by sea raid-ers, the folk had moved inland, leaving their homes to the slower but no less certain onslaught of creeping vegetation. Now, beyond the silt-stirred mouth, the river's banks were thick with evergreens and gorse that billowed down to the water's edge as though the whole verdant valley sought to drink the freshwater. The sun, rising somewhere beyond the river's source, infused thick blankets of morning mist with red dye, and above that, swaths of cloud that were thin as the blauvifs' shrouds curled out of the east, hung to dry below a gray and golden sky.

The low roar of the sea became a murmur and then faded away completely, taking with it the shrieks of gulls and the languid whisper of waves on the shore. All sound was subdued so that even as we bent our backs to the oars, we were aware of some ancient and weighty seidr clotting the air. Our oar blades plunged in their ceaseless way, stitching *Serpent*'s course through the dark water, the staves clumping in their ports, and men's labored breath further fogged the air about us.

"At least this damn spate means we shouldn't run into any shoals," Bjarni said through a grimace.

"Still, it's not much of a river," Gap-Toothed Ingolf put in. "I've pissed more ale the morning after a good feast."

I knew what Ingolf meant. Every tale I had ever heard of the Romans told of the enormous buildings against which, it was said, men looked like insects. I had not believed most of it, thinking that like all tales, it had grown legs in the telling. That was until Frankia. In Frankia I had seen things I would not have thought possible: churches and halls of stone that you would have believed could have been built only by giants. And according to Egfrith, those places were as nothing compared with the ancient constructions of Rome. That was why I expected more of a river than the one we now navigated, for it did not feel like the "artery to the heart of the world" as Egfrith had put it.

The river snaked northward. We passed a fighting galley crammed with blaumen coming downriver, its oar banks beating quickly on the back of the current, and although Völund might have been able to learn something from them, he did not get the chance, because we were yelling curses at them and they were yelling back. It was harmless enough, though some of the Danes neglected their rowing long enough to loose a few arrows at the blaumen for the sake of appearances. We passed three heavily laden barges being pulled against the current by oxen, and their drivers were struck with terror when they saw us, but we did them no harm and did not even stop to discover what cargo the barges held. Because the wind had changed. In the morning the wind had been against us, and that, coupled with the current, had meant we had to row. But now the wind was coming from the west, and Sigurd decided there was enough of it to make it worth hoisting the sails. You could have walked along the bank and beaten us to Rome, but we did not mind, for it gave us time to put on brynjas and swords and string bows. We did not know what we would meet up this river, and it is always better to prepare for a fight that does not come than to fight unprepared.

And so it was under sail that we came to Rome, our shields lying at our feet in case we should need to slot them in the rail or make a shieldwall. It was late afternoon, and the wind that had blown us up the Tiberis had drawn a shroud of black cloud across the roof of the world, and so we had put on our greased skins over our mail. We did not have to wait long. Caught in that black shroud above us was a broiling hailstorm that now came in a great rush, driving into the river and pelting us angrily, the pebbles of ice thudding onto the deck and bouncing off the sheer strakes. Within moments, ridges of hail had gathered against *Serpent*'s ribs and among the oars piled in their trees. Svein was happily catching the ice in his mouth until a hailstone struck a tooth, making him curse in pain. Father Egfrith sheltered under a spare shield, the hail tonking off the iron boss, and I watched the yellow river thicken and swell and absorb the countless ice stones piercing it. Then, as quickly as the hail had come, it vanished. Brown light seeped through the trees lining the banks, and the smell of those trees filled the air. Men grabbed gourds and drinking horns because they knew what was coming.

Serpent pushed on, the other ships behind, their crews quiet because the trees had thinned, and on the next coil, where the river slowed, we could see wharves jutting out on both sides. A white flash as quick as a blink was followed by a *crack* that decayed with a rumble that seemed to go on forever. Then the rain came. At first it hissed against the river's surface, but before long, rods of water were plunging deep into the river and the noise was immense.

"So this is Rome!" Sigurd shouted from the prow. His sopping hair daubed his head, sticking to his cheeks and beard as he looked up at the great crumbling wall that filled the world along the bank on our steerboard side. It was pitted, and much of its brownish brick skin had come away, revealing bloodless flesh beneath, but it was huge, at least nine times a man's height. "How can men build such things, Uncle?" Sigurd called through the rain's roar. Olaf did not answer at once because like the rest of us he was standing now, beard soaked, jaw unhinged, eyes wide and staring at the wall.

"Such a wall as this must protect Asgard," he called back after a time. Every hundred feet or so along its length stood a square tower, and it was at those points that we could see that the wall was some two spear lengths thick.

"Against this, Offa's wall would look like a pig fence," Penda said, scratching the short hair at the back of his neck.

The Tiberis snaked northeast, and we passed between the walls, for that bulwark carried on along the far bank, running north to enclose Rome. That meant that we were now inside the ancient city.

"Well, that was easy enough," Bram Bear said, sweeping his soaking hair back over his head. We had not even been challenged.

"What good is a wall Gymir would struggle to peer over if you're going to let savages like us just sail through it?" Olaf asked, peering through the rain fog for signs of a trap.

"It's a bloody rat's nest," Gytha said, wide-eyed.

We had all emerged from hats and bad-weather gear now, caring nothing about the driving rain or the fact that we were wet through to our bones. For we did not want to miss any of the wondrous sights around us not already hidden behind the veil of rain and gray mist. Wharves lined both banks, stretching off toward the next bend of the river, and they thronged with vessels of all shapes and sizes and groaned beneath the weight of barrels and great long pots up to a man's waist and crates and two hundred types of cargo, from chickens and pelts and spices to grain and stone and timber. Horses whinnied, stamping against the quay because they knew they were going to sea and feared it. Men bartered, made last-minute deals, or argued about a ship's capacity or the likely journey time or the weather. Soldiers pushed among the crowd after eel-slippery thieves they would never catch. Whores with red lips and blackened eyes paraded arrogantly, silver lust battling whatever pride they still clung to, and men stood holding barrel lids over smoking braziers, trying to keep their hot food dry. We had sailed into a thick soup of every kind of smell; one moment your mouth watered, and the next your eyes streamed and you thought you would retch.

"Oars!" Sigurd called, for Olaf had been reefing the sail to slow us with so many other ships about, and now the rake was juddering down the mast as he and three others lowered the yard and the sodden sail. We took to our sea chests and sliced the blades into the river to slow *Serpent* further, watching that our oars did not hit other vessels. Behind us, *Fjord-Elk* and the snekkjes did likewise, and we were lucky that although the wharves were lined with ships, few of those craft were in the channel, because the wind was still blowing toward the city and their captains were waiting for it to change.

Buildings lined both banks beyond the wharves, some with their red-tiled roofs fallen in and white walls crumbled, others still in use by their looks. Yet others were rising anew from the debris of the old, their ancient shaped stones climbing skyward one atop another once again, but overall the impression was one of decay. On our steerboard side the ground rose, though our view of the city was partly obscured by long stone buildings that appeared to have been repaired countless times and that followed the river for as far as I could see. Open on their river sides, they were stacked to their roofs with goods and guarded by ruddy-skinned warriors with spears, clubs, and hand axes. Out of the rain, men sat at tables writing. Others counted barrels in or out that were lugged by bare-chested muscle-bound slaves whose skin glistened with rain and sweat. Some pushed carts or led back-bowed asses, horses, or oxen to and from the wharf.

Another ancient wall bent eastward off our steer-board side, and this one had soldiers on its heights who would glance down at the chaos below every now and then but mostly seemed oblivious to it. At the wall's base a great gate yawned like an open mouth, through which spewed a continuous stream of men, women, children, and animals.

"We'll find a mooring farther on," Sigurd called, pointing off _Serpent_'s port bow beyond the long line of swarming vessels. So we rowed on until the wooden wharf ended and the old cracked stone wharf began. There were few vessels this far up, for much of the quayside was underwater, another effect of melt-water flowing off faraway hills, perhaps. Besides which, the wooden wharves were nearer to the gate and so were bound to be more popular.

"Bram, Svein, Bjarni, take your oars and make sure there's not another level to that quay that could rip our belly open," Olaf said. "Bring her in nice and easy, lads; there you go. Folk will be watching, and we don't want to give these Romans a good story to spout over their ale tonight." At the stone wharf's high end there was a berth easily long enough for _Serpent_, though not for the other ships as well. They would have to moor alongside, hull against hull, so that their crews would all end up walking over _Serpent_ to get to shore. I have seen this lead to fights when a man's be-longings go missing after other crews have tramped past his gear. But we were a Fellowship, every man oath-tied to every other, and I could have laid every bit of silver I had on my sea chest and gone ashore knowing I would find it untouched when I returned.

Beast heads had been carved into the stone wall, and we argued as to what kinds of animals they were, for they had a wolf's teeth, a mouth more like a bear's, and broad, fur-wreathed heads. In those snarling, teeth-filled maws were set iron rings through which we passed our mooring ropes, and we had barely finished the knots, when the reeve turned up demanding the port tax. He came with another man, who carried a sack over one shoulder, and twelve bored-looking soldiers, and none of them seemed the least bit surprised at the sight of us or our ships that crawled with motifs clearly not carved by Christian hands. The reeve was a small, brisk bald man with busy hands who reminded me of a squirrel as his keen eyes probed our four ships for clues to what manner of men we were. He seemed unimpressed with what he saw, which Penda suggested was because it was clear from our ships with their relatively small holds that we had not come to do any serious trading. But luckily for us, it was not long before he and Father Egfrith found either end of a great twine of the Latin tongue so that they were able to follow the thread and meet in the middle.

"I have told Gratiosus here that we have traveled very far and braved dangers of every kind in order that our eyes may feast upon the sights of his wondrous and ancient city," Egfrith said to Sigurd, a thin smile hiding in the beard I was still not used to seeing on his face.

The jarl nodded. "How much does he want, monk?"

Egfrith's smile grew now. "Gratiosus says he is used to dealing with our kind. The price for *Serpent* and *Fjord-Elk* is six solidi and three solidi for the two smaller ships. But he knows barbarians do not trade in coins, so he has brought scales." Then he said something to Gratiosus, who clicked his fingers, at which the man with the sack came forward and pulled from it a large pair of scales, setting them down carefully on the quayside. "If we wish to pay in silver, we must simply balance the scales," Egfrith said with a shrug. Now Sigurd smiled, because Gratiosus had been rummaging in the sack himself and now produced a large brick of iron, which he held up for all to see before bending and placing it into one of the scales' silver bowls.

"That lump must weigh more than Svein's head," Bram muttered.

"Let me put my cock in the other dish, Uncle; that will do it," Hedin called, rousing chuckles all around.

But Sigurd, being Sigurd, had already prepared for this moment. "If that's all this Roman wants, let's be done with it," he said, throwing his sodden cloak off his right shoulder to reveal his arm, which bore seven silver warrior rings, each one thicker than a man's thumb. At his signal Bothvar dropped the plank onto the wharf, and so it was that with four long strides Sigurd was the first of us to set foot in Rome. He gave Gratiosus and his men that wolf's grin, then twisted five of the silver warrior rings off his arm and dropped them all onto the scales. The iron brick almost took to the air as the other bowl clattered against the stone quay, and Gratiosus's eyebrows, too, leaped in astonishment. Then, just because he could, Sigurd pulled off another silver band and tossed it into the dish with the others, which were already half submerged in rainwater.

Gratiosus stared at Sigurd as though he did not know whether to run for his life or embrace the Norsemen, then spoke in a voice that was more breath than sound.

"What did he say, monk?" Sigurd asked, half turning back to *Serpent*.

Egfrith swept the rain from his face, then made the sign of the cross over his chest. "He said welcome to Rome."

CHAPTER
THIRTEEN

I WAS WALKING along the stone-paved streets of Rome! Gratiosus had sent us a guide: a man of about my age with sun-browned skin, warm eyes, and a quick smile. His name was Gregororovius, but none of us could remember that let alone say it, so we called him Gregor. Every man had itched to go ashore, but we could not leave the ships unguarded, and so lots had been drawn to choose the fourteen men who would stay behind. Those men had cursed their ill luck and moaned and flung insults at the rest of us as we got ready to go ashore. Then we had followed Gregor through a gateway he called the Porta Trigemina that was framed with smooth stone pillars as tall as oaks, and in passing I had pressed a palm against the cool stone, wondering how many other jaw-slack visitors to the ancient city had done the same.

"Good of that Roman to send us a guide," Bram said as we passed between two long red-tiled buildings and into an open space so that for the first time we could see something of the city. "But he could have sent us one who speaks Norse." Gregor spoke good enough English, though, and I found myself appointed translator for those who did not understand that tongue. Whenever he pointed something out, those Norsemen and Danes would roll their hands at me in a hurry-up gesture or huff or scratch their beards in irritation because I was not quick enough explaining what we were looking at.

"He's here to keep an eye on us, Bram, you great ox-brained brute," I said, "because that harbormaster took one look at you and decided that a man who has more beard than face needs to be watched."

"And he'd be right," Bram said, "because— What in Ódin's eye is that?" He was looking at a round stone building that was ringed with glistening columns and had a roof like that of a roundhouse, only this one was made of hundreds of red bricks instead of straw.

"It was a temple to the old Roman god Hercules," I translated, "but now it is a White Christ church." Some spit at that or touched amulets or sword hilts, for they had liked the sound of the hero Hercules who was half man and half god and thought it a poor thing indeed that his temple had been taken over by a god who had never even held a sword. As for ourselves, we had left our mail shirts, helmets, and shields on the ships but had brought swords and long knives, though we did not expect trouble. Rome, it seemed, was well used to the likes of us. You only had to look around to see that whatever it once had been, Rome was now like a snarled net. There were more types of folk in Rome than there were types of fish in the sea. As we walked among its crumbling glory, I saw men and women of every skin color you could imagine, from shaven-headed blaumen to the ruddy-cheeked and red-haired. I saw a woman with the slitted eyes of a cat and yellow skin. I saw fine-boned men who were as pretty as the blauvifs we had lost. Some even had painted faces like women, which we all agreed was a bad thing for a man to do. I saw others who were black as soot with great bushes of curled hair on their heads and eyes like Völund's, as yellow as butter, and I passed yet other men who had brown hawklike eyes and long noses and deep sun-scourged lines in their skin, and they I imagined were the descendants of the old Romans, because they had a haughty, knowing look about them. There were also crews fresh off the water like us, men who walked the streets wonder-struck, their necks craning, taking in every enormous pillar and building and statue. Many were armed like us, and we were glad we were not bladeless among the twist and tangle of it all. Rome was as chaotic as a battle, and I said as much. Even the air seemed to crackle like dry kindling just lit, and there was a sense of violence just happened or about to erupt.

"Damned place is making my eyes itch," I heard Olaf complain through the seething downpour.

"I have never seen anything like it," Sigurd admitted. "Which is half the reason we are here. More than for the curiosity of it and the silver to be made, I suspect Rome might arm us . . . up here," he said, tapping his head, "for what lies ahead in Miklagard. We can learn much here, I think." I smiled at his deep thinking. "Do you think Asgard looks something like this?" he asked me.

"I reckon it might, lord," I replied, "though without all the lean-tos." For against almost every solid stone wall there was a timber dwelling, many of them owned, according to Gregor, by farmers and families that worked the vineyards and fields both inside and outside the Aurelian walls. Even those temples that had not been taken over by the Christians had found new uses as granaries or houses. Almost every stone building that could be used had been built on and against. Though some of those timber lean-tos had been burned, recently too by the look of it, and were nothing more than twisted, blackened skeletons now.

"Actually, I had always thought of the gods living in great timber halls," I said, "like our own but much bigger of course and carved with such skill as a mortal man could never match. But now?" I shook my head, flicking water off my hair. "If the Romans built all this in stone, I don't see why our gods could not do the same."

Sigurd pursed his lips. "It is astonishing," he said, peering through the rain, which showed no signs of giving up. "I would not have believed it if I had not seen it with my own eyes. But don't you think there is something cold about the place? All this lifeless stone?" A memory flashed in my mind like the first glimpse of a fish on your hook before you pull it in. "Whatever spirits were here have left this place," Sigurd said. I looked around me. Though many of the enormous structures still stood proud, many more had fallen into disrepair, their stones plundered to patch other buildings, and the whole city had the feel of being at once dying and yet reborn in a different, humbler form.

"I dreamed of it," I said, suddenly filled with gloom. The previous night had lain heavy on my spirit, like a burial mound through which I had clawed my way out and emerged into the new day, still cold and damp to the bone.

Sigurd stopped walking and turned to me. Many of

the others had gone their own way by now. Too impatient to wait for my translations, men had wandered off in twos and threes, having given their word to Olaf or Sigurd that they would stay out of trouble, for there was trouble to be had in Rome; we all felt it.

"You dreamed of this place? Of Rome?" Sigurd asked. He swept his soaking hair back and tied it at the nape of his neck.

I shook my head. "No, not like this," I said. "I dreamed of a corpse. It had been dead a while. The flesh was rotting, and some of the bones were sticking out. Maggots were all over it. It was just a dream, but I could hear them sucking on the flesh." I felt the grimace eat into my face. "I think that somehow that corpse was Rome." I let my eyes follow a pretty girl as she threaded her way through the crowds, but I soon lost her. "All these people, they're the maggots," I said, "and the bones poking through the rotting flesh are these stone buildings."

Sigurd frowned, his eyes fixed on my face, though mainly on my left eye, or so it seemed to me. Men always tended to favor my blood eye even if they did not want to, the way a moth will fly into a flame because it has no choice.

"It was just a dream, Raven," he said. "We all dream of death." He smiled then, water dripping from his golden mustaches. "It reminds us not to get ourselves killed."

"Are you not impressed with our city?" Gregor asked, coming and putting a soft hand on my forearm.

I smiled at him. "We could not have dreamed of such wonders," I said, at which my smile jumped onto his face and he nodded and happily turned to continue leading us. "We have never seen so many people in one place, Gregor," I called.

"That is because everyone wants to come to Rome. Rome is the light of the world!" he yelled, spreading his arms and drawing glances from several passersby, though he did not mind at all. "You know who said that?"

"Yes," Father Egfrith said under his breath, too quietly for Gregor to hear. I had thought we'd lost the monk to one of the many churches, but there he was again, his old habit so full of holes that it was more water than wool.

"It was an Englishman," Gregor announced proudly, "the great Alcuin of York, the man to whom our emperor turns for advice."

"We have met Alcuin," I said, unable to resist. But Gregor simply swatted my words away without even breaking stride, for he must have thought our meeting Alcuin was as likely as him becoming the next emperor.

"The light of the world!" he hooted again, this time to an old man pushing a cart piled high with golden loaves of bread that were covered with rainproof cloth. I noticed the old man was armed, a long-bladed knife even older than he tucked unsheathed into his belt. He stopped so that we could pass, cursing Gregor and shooting the rest of us a look that would wither a nettle before going on his way.

"There remains to you now only a great mass of cruel ruins," Egfrith chirped.

"What's that, monk?" I asked.

"That's the rest of what Alcuin said about Rome," Egfrith replied, "because he could see what it once was but is no longer. Gregororovius must have forgotten that part."

It *was* strange, I thought, that even amid all that chaos, the farmers and traders and whores and travelers, I yet felt engulfed by the immense and towering silence of the massive ruins around me.

"Where are you taking us, Gregor?" I asked, my head nearly twisting itself off my neck at all there was to see. I saw Penda looking up at a stone likeness of one of Rome's emperors from hundreds of years ago. Patches of color still clung to the figure, who gripped a sword as firmly as he ever had.

"To the Palatinus," Gregor said. "Rome sits on seven hills, but the Palatinus is the centermost of them. It is where it all began."

"These short swords are what beat our ancestors time and again, Wiglaf," Penda called to the Wessexman, who was making an offering of a coin to a bunch of Christ slaves who were singing one of their miserable songs beside another temple.

"That's it, Wiglaf!" I yelled. "Pay them to shut their mouths."

"It's a stabbing sword," Penda went on, thrusting an invisible blade under an invisible enemy's rib cage, "and when the Romans fought in their shieldwalls, these short swords made good gut rippers." How someone had carved a man with all of a man's features out of stone was almost unimaginable. That this stone warrior, even after all the years, yet looked as though he was about to slaughter enemies hundreds of years in their graves was enough to make your mind feel it was drowning.

The view from this hill was staggering. Even through the lashing rain, which was thick as a hide curtain, I got an idea of the hugeness of the place. Rome was a great sprawling confusion of a city. Some of the enormous buildings seemed to fight for the same ground, with none winning outright. Others had claimed small rises upon which they were safe from other stone buildings, though not from poor men who had built timber shelters against them so that they might own at least one wall of solid stone.

"Now I know how a mouse must feel looking up at Svein," I told Penda, who nodded dumbly, running a scarred hand through his short hair.

"To the south is the Aventine Hill, to the east the Caelian." Gregor pointed northwest. "There, between the Forum and the Campus Martius, you see the Capitoline Hill with its temples unequaled in beauty, and to the east is the Esquiline Hill. Beyond them to the north, which you cannot see for the rain, is the Viminal, and north of that the Quirinal." Gregor shivered and plucked at his sopping tunic. "It has not rained like this for weeks." He seemed embarrassed.

"Where we come from, we never take off our helmets for fear of the rain flattening our heads," Sigurd said, at which Gregor gaped until he realized that the jarl was teasing him. Our guide went on telling us the story of this place or that, but I was only half listening, and so, I think, were most of the others who stood there on that hill, almost oblivious to the rain now because they were too caught up in the seidr web of that incredible place. For we were staring to the northeast at such a building as I believed even the gods would be hard-pressed to equal in magnificence.

"It is the Amphitheatrum Flavium," Gregor announced, his voice breathy with awe. "And it has stood there for nearly eight hundred years. It is not what it once was, of course, but even now it has the power to capture our imaginations, no?"

"What is it?" I asked. The building was so enormous that it towered above many others that were themselves the largest places I had ever seen until that day. More egg-shaped than a perfect ring, it had been built in four layers of columns, one upon the other, and between each pair of columns was a rounded opening identical to the one next to it so that the whole building was full of perfect holes as neatly done as the finest stitching.

It was mostly open to the sky, for surely not even the Romans could have put a roof over it.

"Don't tell me it's a Christ house," someone said in Norse.

"In the old times the people would go there to watch men hunt fierce beasts that were brought here from the far corners of the empire. Fifty thousand Romans at one time could enjoy the spectacles."

"Do we look like fools to you, lad?" Wiglaf challenged Gregor. "Fifty thousand people in one building? This beardless whelp must think we're idiots."

I could not even imagine so many people. Were there so many people in the whole world?

"It is true on my life," Gregor said, shocked that one of us should suggest that he was lying.

"And now?" I asked. "What is it used for now?"

"Many things," Gregor answered, shaking his head. "But recently some things I am too ashamed to speak of." The smile had gone from his face as he gazed down toward the impossible structure. "It is a place of death," he said, wiping rainwater from his forehead. "It has always been a place of death."

"Take me there," Sigurd said. For a moment Gregor seemed unsure. Gone was the cheerful, energetic young man, and in his place was someone burdened by troubles he would not speak of.

"Gratiosus said I was to put myself in your service for as long as you are here in Rome." He glanced at me and then at Penda, Wiglaf, and Father Egfrith. "If you really want to go there, I will take you the day after tomorrow."

"Why not now?" Sigurd asked. "This pissing rain means nothing to us."

Gregor stepped closer. I could smell wine on his breath, which was fogging in the rain. "Forgive me, lord, but it is better not to speak of it. You will understand the day after tomorrow. For now let me show you some of our other wonders. Come! There is so much more to see." The carefree young man was back again, as though he had never left us. "You will be amazed by the Circus Maximus," he said, turning north and setting off down a cobbled path along whose gutters rivulets of water were gushing. "It was used for chariot races. Two hundred and fifty thousand people used to take their seats and watch the charioteers and their horses go around and around as fast as lightning!"

"Two hundred and fifty thousand?" Wiglaf spluttered. "Now listen carefully, you smooth-faced whoreson," he shouted after Gregor, striding down the hill in the guide's wake. "If you lie to us again, I'm going to kick your Roman arse around your Circus Maximus until your farts scream for help!"

It was late by the time we followed the smell of duck shit and slick green weed back to the river and the ships. The men we had left behind were furious at us for not relieving them sooner, especially seeing as it was nighttime now and they would have to wait until morning to look around for themselves. As it was, the best they could do was listen to the rest of us wearing our jawbones thin with stories of a hundred different marvels, our eyes wide and shiny as coins and theirs resentful slits of skepticism. Still, they listened, and I do not believe we exaggerated much, because the truth was hard enough to swallow as it was. Afterward they got over their disappointment by getting under some of the local whores who sold their goods down by the river where there were always bored men guarding their boats. It stopped raining, too, and so we took the opportunity to change into dry clothes, wringing out sopping tunics and breeks and hanging them over the sheer strakes.

The next day, I was one of those who had to guard the ships while the others went ashore clamorously, eager to lose themselves within the ancient, astonishing city, and the sun had barely begun to warm the morning air before I was picking out my own whore from a bunch that Svein brought aboard.

"They were the best I could find." He shrugged apologetically.

"You can take the pretty one if I can have those two," he suggested, nodding at two girls with thin yellow hair and the ashen skin of those who mostly work at night and sleep during the day. They looked identical, too, but for one of them having three black teeth and the other having no teeth at all that I could see.

"Sisters, I think," Svein said, guessing the question before I said anything. I was about to tell him that his suggestion about the split was a good one, when Cynethryth came aboard hefting an ass's leg over her shoulder.

"I'd rather chew a handful of nails, Svein," I said loudly enough for Cynethryth to hear, "but I wish you luck with them. Though I'd be gentle with that one," I said, nodding at one of the yellow-haired girls. "If you rattle her bones too hard, I'll wager those last few teeth will fall out."

The giant frowned and scratched his head, then Cynethryth called for Sköll, and Svein turned, clapping eyes on the girl, who was showing her wolf the ass's leg he would soon be chewing. Svein swung back to me and shook his head, and there was more pity than annoyance in that gesture, so that I had to look away for shame.

Why should Cynethryth care if I took a whore? After all, I had shared my shelter with a blauvif on Lyngvi for the winter, and Cynethryth had said nothing about it. But when it came to Cynethryth, my feelings were a knotted ball of twine I doubted I would ever unravel. Perhaps I wished that she did care, that she was even jealous and longed for things to go back to the way they had been between us. And that made it all the worse, for it was clear as rainwater that she did not.

Svein, it seemed, did not need any luck in dealing with the three whores. From the squeals and yelps and giggles and grunts coming from his berth between *Serpent*'s ribs just forward of the mast, it sounded as if the Norseman was doing fine.

I played tafl with Bjarni, and along with some of the Danes we collected a bucketful of muddy pebbles and laid wagers on who had the best throw. The target was a stone statue of some long-dead Roman that stood across from us on the far bank, and the best thing about it was that its head had been replaced with a wooden one that made a loud *crack* when you hit it with a pebble. Not that I did, though I claimed to have grazed the Roman's left ear. Black Floki was the best. He could strike the head over and over, and in the end he grew bored with the game and left us to it. When we ran out of stones, we sat around making up verses either about the adventures we had already had or about the ones yet to come. The Dane Arngrim was the best skald among us. He wove a rich verse brimming with kennings that took such vivid shape in the eye of your mind that you felt you could reach out and touch them. Arngrim's only trouble as far as the original Wolfpack was concerned was that he had not been with them from the beginning, and so his stories were the Danes' stories, not theirs. However, his verse about the rotting Frankish hall in which I too had been chained brought hot bile into my chest and sweat onto my palms, and in this way Arngrim was perhaps too good.

Next morning, we waited for Gregor. The ancient city around us stirred to a new day as it had innumerable times before, its people going about their lives in the shade of Rome's golden past. The river exhaled a putrid damp mist across the wharves, which rolled among the poorhouses and pissy alleys near the water and up between the grander buildings of the lower Palatinus. When the sun had burned the river mist away and it began to look as though the day would be bright and warm, and the traders and merchants of Rome began to crow about their goods and the guide had still not shown his face, many of the men lost patience and went ashore. But we waited.

"I knew we couldn't trust that lying bloody Roman whelp," Wiglaf growled just as Gregor called down to us from the quay. Wiglaf flushed red beneath his beard.

"Are you ready to see the arena, Wiglaf?" Gregor asked, shaming the man further by knowing his name.

"Arena?" Wiglaf said, bushy brows arched.

"The Amphitheatrum Flavium!" Gregor said, spreading his arms. "And you, Raven; are your eyes prepared to see our great city as it used to be, before the Roman people found the light of Christ?"

"My eyes itch to see what Rome was like before the nailed god," I said, glancing at Penda, who looked just as eager as me despite his being a Christian.

"Very well," Gregor said soberly. "We will go now. But if there is trouble, I will not be able to help you."

"What kind of trouble?" Sigurd asked, climbing over *Fjord-Elk*'s sheer strake to come aboard. He had been talking with Rolf and Bragi since sunrise.

"You will know if it happens," Gregor said, "for the city has become a dangerous place these last weeks."

He seemed to wrestle with the next words on his tongue. "You may want to bring some silver. Coins this time," he added with the shadow of a grimace. "They don't deal in warrior rings in the Amphitheatrum Flavium."

chapter
FOURTEEN

I NEVER HEARD Arngrim the Dane weave a verse about the arena, but I would have liked to. For I am no skald and do not have the tongue-craft for telling it so that you can feel and smell and taste it the way I did that day. Before we entered the place, we stood outside, and our necks snaked as we looked up at the immense, unimaginable mass of perfectly cut stone, tree-size smooth glistening pillars, and fine red bricks. From the Palatinus we had seen Rome and the Amphitheatrum Flavium as just one of many giant remains from a long-dead past. From the ground, though, among the stalls and statues and lean-tos and traders, I could not fit the place into my eyes. We stood at the threshold of one of the entrances but had to move aside soon enough. It seemed we were not the only ones who had come to the arena that day. Groups of two and three and even whole crews by the look of it were coming from every direction. Warriors and merchants, women and gangs of filth-smeared boys, were streaming through the many pillar-framed openings, all of them chattering like birds at dawn. There was a low hum like that of the ocean coming from beyond the walls before us, reminding me of a packed mead hall before the food is served. And talking of food, the air was thick with the smell of frying onions and mush-rooms, fish, spices, and garlic from a dozen crowded stalls, the owners of which had that frenzied look that merchants get when they're doing a better trade than normal.

"This one building covers more ground than any village back home," Sigurd said, admiring the statue of a naked woman that stood on a ledge above the entrance. The woman's breasts were so plump and soft-looking that I was half tempted to climb up just to check that they had been carved from stone like everything else. There was another stone figure next to the woman, but only the legs and lower torso remained now. A dark thought slunk through my head of some Roman being killed by a stone man's torso falling from the sky.

"How many men standing on each other's heads would get to the top?" Sigurd asked.

Olaf pushed out his bottom lip and scratched his beard, looking up at the heights and shielding his eyes against the midday sun. "Thirty?" he suggested. Sigurd nodded, satisfied with the guess. "But by all the gods, Sigurd, I cannot think how they did it. Raven, you're a deep thinker. How could men build such a thing?"

I shrugged as two warriors with tattooed faces jostled past, reeking sourly of wine and garlic. "Perhaps their gods helped them, Uncle," I said.

"Pah!" Olaf backhanded that suggestion flying. "When I built my mead hall, I didn't see Frey or Heim-dall or Thór there hefting planks or bashing their damn thumbs with a hammer. We even bled my best bull in their honor, too. Remember, Sigurd?"

"I remember, Uncle," Sigurd said, smiling. "I remember Halldor falling off the roof, too."

"He was ill-lucked, that one," Olaf said, remembering poor Halldor whom Sigurd had killed so long ago now it seemed. "He would have liked to see Rome."

"We will have much to tell him when we meet in Ódin's hall," Sigurd said. "Bjorn, too, and all the rest."

"Well?" Bram said, slapping Olaf on the shoulder. "Are we going to stand outside in this garlic fug all day or are we going in there?" He nodded at the entrance, where a father and son, hand in hand, were passing beneath the stone woman with the big tits.

And so we followed, leaving behind the bustle of the city and entering a place whose seidr hung in the air as thick as barley porridge.

"Frigg's tits," Olaf growled, his hand instinctively clutching the sword grip at his hip.

Sigurd whistled, his eyes shining, and my breath escaped from me as though my lungs had been pierced. I spun around, almost losing my footing. "All of Rome must be here," I said, even more awestruck by the inside of the Amphitheatrum Flavium than I had been by the outside. Thousands of people were standing or sitting among the countless levels that ran around the inside of the place, encircling an open space in which you could have built my old village of Abbotsend five times over. And yet, bristling as it was with so many people, it was not even half full. We had walked through dark, damp-smelling tunnels, our voices changed by the cool stone walls, blindly following the man to our front. Then we had made our way up through the shadows, climbing endlessly, so that I soon lost count of the stone steps, the hairs stiffening on the back of my neck and the blood chilling in my veins. The boots of men whose faces I could not see scuffed against the ancient stone, and it seemed to me that we were like a procession of the dead abandoned by Óðin's Choosers of the Slain and left to tramp our gloomy way to the afterlife. Shafts of light sliced that cold warren, and eventually one of them drew us blinking and unbalanced out into the white glare of midday. We had emerged a third of the way up the inside of the giant bowl, and for luck I touched the scrag that was all that remained of the raven's wing Cynethryth had once tied in my hair, which was part of the thick braid hanging against my right cheek.

Each tier of long stone benches was separated by low walls and curved passages and cut further into wedges by steps emerging from other tunnels evenly spaced all the way around. Many of these dark mouths were disgorging their own eager crowds that spread along the age-pitted rows, looking to claim their piece of the Amphitheatrum Flavium. Folk took their seats excitedly, called and waved greetings to friends on different levels, rubbed their hands eagerly, or gaped around in astonished wonder.

"This place is buzzing like a kicked hive," Bram Bear said, shoving a big Roman out of his way. The man turned angrily, took one look at Bram, and backed away, palms raised.

Around the edge of the arena floor were lean-tos and wooden dwellings and even some stone-built Christ houses outside which crosses had been driven into the ground. Across the rest, shadows, foundation trenches, and scraps of timber and brick betrayed where other buildings had stood until recently, and more remains sat piled here and there against the base of the walls.

"People have been living here," I said, looking to Gregor. "What happened to them?"

"Men have lived here since they stopped using the arena more than three hundred years ago," he said. "Perhaps these men were paid to leave," he suggested, nodding down at the scars in the earth. "But I don't think so." Just then a war horn bellowed somewhere below.

"Here we go," Olaf muttered. The ocean's roar of the crowd shrank to a murmur as thousands of eyes looked down into the empty space. The horn blew again, the sound small and flat and far away.

"I must go now, Sigurd," Gregor said. He made the sign of the cross, which made me think of Egfrith, who was not with us. Instead, he was off visiting Rome's churches and in particular one to the south of the city beneath which Saint Peter lay buried. As far as I could make out, Peter had been the White Christ's second, as Olaf was Sigurd's, and the Christ followers still worshipped the man's ghost though it was nothing more than a fart in the wind by then.

"Where's he going?" Bram asked, nodding at Gregor's back before it was lost among the crowd.

"He made the White Christ sign and scurried off like a mouse from a burning barn," I said.

"Well, the damn fool is going to miss whatever is just about to happen," Bram said, turning back to the arena. Three men walked out into the open and turned their faces up to the crowds. Even they looked impressed, yet surely they knew what was about to happen. Two of the men were warriors, each armed as though he was about to go into a battle, which he was. One was a big, fair-haired man, Norse or Dane, perhaps. The other was dark and, though slight, was well muscled and moved like a hunter. The third man looked wealthy, a long red cloak stopping above tall boots of soft-looking leather. He was dark like the smaller warrior, and though his fine clothes hid any obvious signs of his being a warrior too, he had a sword scabbarded at his hip.

"Hólmgang?" Sigurd gave the word the weight you'd expect from a man who was half killed in one.

"Aye, they're going to fight all right," Olaf said with a nod. "I can smell it." That was when I noticed several clusters of men gathered along the bottom row just two spear lengths above the arena floor and the three men waiting there.

"They're making wagers," Svein the Red said, pushing through the crowds to get to us. He, Black Floki, and some of the others had become separated from us in the tunnels, but now they'd found us. "We have money on it, too!" He thumbed behind him and shook his head, a wide grin splitting his beard. "Black Floki has wagered three silver coins on the small man. Anyone can see that the other man is much stronger. That puny sheep's dropping does not have a hope." Black Floki's face was as cold as the stone bench against the backs of my knees as he eyeballed the warriors below. "Where has that beardless pup gone? He could have told us what that Roman is saying," Svein said. To me it looked as though the rich-looking man was introducing the warriors, for the big Norse-looking man bowed to the crowd, raising a cheer. Then with a flourish he threw off his brown cloak and bent his right arm so that the muscle below the short sleeve of his brynja bulged. The crowd roared again. The Roman-looking man paid his opponent no attention at all. Instead, he was rolling his shoulders and stretching his back and chest, loosening his muscles for the coming fight. He wore a polished helmet from which hung strips of fine red cloth that fluttered in the breeze. Curved iron plates protected his shins, and beneath his bright white tunic he wore a lamellar brynja whose scales glinted. That all showed he was proud enough in his own way and must have known how to fight, too, to own such fine arms.

Then the two fighters were told to pick up their shields and pace in opposite directions to put some distance between them. The man who had called up to the crowds strode to the edge of the arena and gave an order, at which sixteen warriors armed with shields, spears, and swords spilled from one of the nearby passages and ran to take their places, forming a circle around the fighters. When the brown dust had cleared and the guards were all in place—to ensure that neither man tried to run, we guessed—the richly dressed man nodded to another man, who blew the horn again.

"Don't cry, Floki," Svein said, "I will buy you a wineskin with the money I win."

"It feels good being one of those watching this time," Sigurd said, a half smile in his beard. For the heavy sweat stench of the crowd was cut now with the tang of violence, and the fight had begun.

Neither fighter risked throwing his spear. Instead, they closed on each other, making quick thrusts with the weapons, searching for weaknesses and testing each other's speed. As was expected, the smaller man was the faster, his spear blade whipping out and back out of harm's way in fast neat moves. But his opponent was fast for his size and his thrusts came with the power to break a shield, and so the smaller man was using much of his speed to avoid his enemy's blade. He was moving his feet well, trying to keep the other man off balance because a man cannot put his weight behind a thrust if his feet are dancing. A spear blade thudded against a shield, glanced off a helmet, deflected off mail. Boots scuffed dust into the air, teeth flashed, and the crowd roared. The darker man's blade sliced into his opponent's right arm, gouging out a piece of flesh that flapped against the man's biceps, hanging by a scrap of skin. I saw the roar of pain but could not hear it for the baying crowd. A moment later the man's whole arm was sheeted in bright blood that dripped onto the earth.

"That big bastard is getting angry now," Penda said as the injured warrior lunged at the cause of his pain, missing again because the other man was already moving to his right, his quick feet taking his torso out of harm's way. In and out of range he moved, his spear jabbing here, cutting there.

Then, because he needed to wipe the blood off his hand or risk the spear slipping from it, the big man shook the shield from his left arm and flung it behind him. It was a brave thing to do against a fast opponent, but he knew he could now get more control over the spear and both arms behind his thrusts.

"I think this fight doesn't end with the first blood, either," Sigurd said, brows raised as the other man discarded his shield. The crowd clamored because a fight without shields cannot last too long. I remembered the hólmgang between Sigurd and Mauger, which had ended with the Wessexman's mutilation and death and Sigurd leaking blood from a dozen wounds. I had never seen a fight like it. If Sigurd or Mauger were in that arena now fighting either of those two warriors, it would have been long over. I said as much to Sigurd.

The jarl shook his head. "The dark-haired fighter is good. He is dragging this thing out to please the crowd. He could have killed that ox five times over, and the ox knows it, too."

"Why would he take such a risk by keeping the fight going?" I asked. "If the ox lands that spear, it will likely be a killing blow."

"Because he is Red Cloak's man," Sigurd said, nodding down toward the rich man who waited at the arena's edge. "So are they," he said, gesturing at the warriors with the spears and long shields that formed the enclosure of iron and flesh around the two fighters. "More than once the fighter has glanced at Red Cloak for approval. Men have silver riding on the back of this fight," he said with half a smile, his eyes flicking across to Svein, who was cheering for his man. "And those men will feel better about losing that silver if it has at least bought them some excitement and a tale to tell." I shook my head at my own callowness. Now that Sigurd had said it, it seemed obvious. All the smaller man's movement, all his feints and parries and dust-whipping footwork, even the pride-stinging arm wound—all of it had been to keep the fight going for the sake of those who had come to see a real contest.

The two warriors circled, each knowing that a single mistake now could mean his death. They probed, and their spear staves *clack*ed time and again. Then the big man swung his spear from far right, around his head, as if to sweep aside his enemy's spear before thrusting, but the other man was ready and stepped back, dropping his spear so that the big man's stave hit nothing. Then the small man stepped inside, bringing his right arm up and smashing the butt end of his spear into his enemy's chin. The blond man staggered backward from the blow, which would have felled a horse, then thrust again for the other's lead arm, and this time the small man used the oar block, rotating his spear down and deflecting his opponent's blade wide. Then he whipped his blade up, gashing open the big man's throat in a spray of gore. The blond warrior took three steps forward and then fell to his knees, still jabbing his spear toward his enemy. Around me folk were yelling in languages I could not understand, though it was clear some were happier than others. The small warrior glanced at Red Cloak, who looked up at the raucous crowd before nodding sharply at his man. The fighter nodded back and, thrusting his spear into the ground, strode forward, drawing his sword. Then he stopped because the big man, whose neck wound was spilling blood like a waterfall, had dropped his spear and was fumbling for the sword at his waist. Not because he still thought he could fight but because he was a Norseman and wanted to drink with his ancestors in Ódin's hall. The small man waited until his blood-drenched enemy had drawn his sword and then moved closer, and the big man gave an almost imperceptible nod. The blade plunged into the gaping wound, down into the chest, where it ripped into the big man's heart. He shuddered and died, and the last sound he heard in this life was the cheering of the thousands who had won money by his death.

The corpse was dragged away, and Red Cloak's man drew his spear from the ground and walked between two of the long shields, sharing a look with his lord before disappearing back into the tunnel from which he had come, his work done.

"That was a good fight, hey!" Bram said, folding his brawny arms and nodding contentedly.

"My man must have gotten dust in his eyes," Svein grumbled at Black Floki, who gave him a wicked grin.

"I wonder what they were fighting about," Bram said.

"A woman," Svein suggested. "It is usually over a woman."

But the bloodshed was not done, for no sooner had men claimed their winnings than two more warriors stepped into the arena. One was a blauman with a curved sword and a small leather shield, and the other was a Frank with no shield but two wicked-looking hand axes.

"This has nothing to do with women," Olaf said, shaking his head. "It's about hard, cold silver." The others nodded and ayed, and I suddenly remembered what Gregor had said about the Amphitheatrum Flavium having always been a place of death. "Raven, take this," Olaf said, handing me five small silver coins, "and put it on the Frank." He rubbed his hands together like a man who has just traded a thread-bare, flea-ridden pelt for a good knife or a pair of soft shoes. "Move your arse, lad," Uncle called after me as I fought through the press. "That Frank has the look of a proper killer, and he's going to make me some money."

As it turned out, the blauman won. He cut off half of the Frank's foot, which caused much beard shaking among us, for we thought that was a low thing to do. The Frank had no balance without his toes, and for all his skill with the axes, all the blauman had to do was walk circles around him until he fell over. Then the curved sword sliced off his limbs one by one, and even those in the crowd who had wagered on the blauman groaned to see that.

The next fight made up for it. Two skilled blaumen fought long and hard, and both took bad wounds before eventually Red Cloak stopped the fight because neither had the strength left for a killing blow. The one who looked most likely to live was proclaimed the winner, and I made two gold solidi, and we all thought it was the best fight of the day.

The crowds poured out of the Amphitheatrum Flavium buzzing with the strange thrill of having watched men fight to the death, and we made our way back to the ships as dusk's dark blue blanket draped itself across the ancient city and the air turned cold enough to make me shiver. We found Gregor waiting for us on the quayside.

"I thought you were supposed to keep your eye on us," Wiglaf said, gnawing the flesh from a spiced pork rib and slapping Gregor's shoulder as he passed.

"Aye, why did you leave, Gregor?" I asked, slapping the small scrip at my belt. It clinked satisfyingly. "You could have won some money."

He shook his head, glancing around nervously. "What is happening at the arena is an abomination," he said. "I could not stay and be a part of it. The worst of man is tainting this city as it did when Rome was young. I am a Christian, Raven." He shot an accusing look at Wiglaf, because he must have known that the Wessexman was also in thrall to the White Christ, though sometimes even I forgot that. "How can a Christian in good conscience enjoy watching men maim and kill each other? Worse still to profit from it." He shook his head again. "I told you it was a place of death. Men have killed and been killed in the Amphitheatrum Flavium since it was built. And all for the crowd's delight." There was accusation in that.

"Those Romans were blood-loving bastards," Penda said. "Still are, I would say."

"Not all of us," Gregor said, wrapping his cloak tighter around his shoulders against the chill coming off the river.

"Enough of you are," Penda added. "There are going to be more fights in two days." He must have seen my surprise, and he shrugged. "I met a Mercian coming out of the arena. Been here for two years, he has, and we got to talking."

"Don't you usually kill Mercians?" I asked, grinning.

"This one shared a wineskin with me. If not, I would have gutted the whoreson." He grinned back. "The fights began two weeks ago, he said. At first not many people came to watch. They were afraid that the Pope or the emperor would cut off their balls for putting wagers on the fights. It's not Christian. But neither Pope Leo nor Karolus has made a move to stop it."

Gregor nodded. "I have seen the Holy Father's soldiers outside the arena. But they never stop the fights."

"Of course they don't stop the fights." The voice cut through the river's ceaseless surge. It was Father Egfrith, and I had not even noticed him sitting on the edge of the wharf, his cowled face toward the Tiberis's west bank. He turned now so that the glow of the city's myriad torches touched his weasel face. "They don't stop the fights because they can't." Sigurd and Olaf came over, eager to hear what the monk had learned while we had been watching men die. "Ask Gregororovius about the mood of the people these last months. Blood was being spilled upon the well-worn streets before they reopened the doors of the Amphitheatrum Flavium."

We looked at Gregor, who made me think of a worm that is trying to burrow into the ground because the birds are around.

"Men were hungry," he said. "Their families were hungry. A man expects to be able to buy food to feed his children. But we could not even get bread. Some blamed His Holiness, others the emperor. Armed bands roamed the city, stealing what they could and killing any that did not give them their food. So the traders who had supplies hid them away, and that made it worse. Powerful men fought for control of the city, and as Father Egfrith says, much blood was spilled."

"Did Karolus do nothing?" Sigurd asked. "The Romans are his people, yes?"

"The emperor is far away," Gregor said.

"Lucky for us, hey," Olaf put in, half smiling.

"Maybe His Holiness Pope Leo has enough soldiers to beat the gangs, but . . ." Gregor turned his palms to the night sky. "Maybe the lords of Rome would join their forces. Maybe they would attack Saint John Lateran."

"Attack a saint?" I said.

"Saint John Lateran is the basilica—the church in which His Holiness the Pope lives," Egfrith explained. I nodded, feeling stupid. "Leo has his enemies. The lords of Rome resent his humble beginnings and would rather their Pope was of noble stock. He is also accused of adultery and perjury and many other crimes of which I am sure he is wholly guiltless."

Gregor nodded. "Only four years ago His Holiness was attacked by men whose purpose was to root out his tongue and gouge out his eyes." He grimaced. "We thank God that those evil men failed. We are fortunate that now he enjoys the emperor's protection, for it was Pope Leo who put the crown on Karolus's head. And yet His Holiness still has enemies in Rome who would bring him down."

I told this again in Norse for Bram and Svein and some of the others who were standing nearby sharing wineskins and bread soaked in butter and garlic and admiring a new flock of whores who had blown in on the breeze.

"This Pope is the lord of all the White Christ followers," Bram said, "and he lives here in Rome?"

"Their god whispers in his ear day and night," I said, snapping my fingers and thumb together.

"I'll wager that sheep-swiving son of a rancid cunny has some treasures worth plundering," he said, sharing a vicious grin with Svein, and I wished then that I hadn't mentioned it, for it would be just like those two to kick down Pope Leo's door and yank the rings off his fingers regardless of the consequences. I left them with those silver-heavy thoughts and turned back to Gregor.

"Since the fights began in the arena, peace has returned to Rome," he said. "Bread is being baked. People are eating."

"Men are happy when they are making money," Olaf pointed out, tapping his scrip, which was much heavier than mine by the look of it.

"Word has been sent to the emperor," Egfrith warned. "Those barbarous fights in the Amphitheatrum Flavium will be stopped. Karolus will not allow Rome to return to its godless days."

Gregor made the sign of the cross and looked sheepishly at Egfrith. "I pray that you are right, Father Egfrith. And I for one will be nowhere near the arena when the emperor comes."

chapter
FIFTEEN

TWO DAYS later we made sure we were even closer to the fighters than we had been the first time. The dark-haired fighter Floki had put his money on was known as Theo the Greek. We watched him kill the blauman who had butchered the Frank who'd fought with two short axes, and I lost the two solidi I had made earlier. There were two more warriors who had, it seemed, made names for themselves in the arena: Berstuk the Wend and the man they called the African. Berstuk had won five fights, the African four. Both were fearsome-looking warriors who bore the scars of countless fights, and both were natural killers. Big, powerful, fast, and skilled, they had everything a great warrior needs, and over the next two weeks, in between trading and provisioning the ships, we watched them kill again and again.

"There's a stink to it all, Sigurd," Olaf said one night, passing a wineskin to the jarl and dragging the back of his hand across his lips. We lay among pelts on the wharf, where half of us had put up rough shelters to give everyone more room. No one had stopped us because the Pope did not want any trouble, and so we did what we liked. "Why is it that the Greek, the Vindr, and the African never fight each other?" Olaf went on.

Farther down the wharf a group of men were arguing. Someone nearer belched loudly. We were drinking ourselves stupid and arguing about which of the fighters we had seen was the best.

"They are worth too much to Red Cloak alive, Uncle," Sigurd said. "They bring in the crowds, and so long as his best warriors keep fighting, there will always be men who think they can beat them."

A fight had broken out on the wooden wharves, and we half watched a maelstrom of punches and kicks. Then blades were drawn, and that must have persuaded some of them that the disagreement was not worth dying for, because the knot of men split, both sides backing off amid insults and curses. Ships of all shapes and sizes were arriving daily, their crews spilling off the river into Rome and most of them armed to the teeth. There was no sign of the harbormaster Gratiosus nowadays, and not even Gregor knew where he was, which was good for us because it meant he was not around to squeeze us for more berthing money. "He's likely pulled those scales of his out in front of the wrong crew and they've fed his Roman guts to the river rats," Bram had suggested, and we thought that was probably the truth of it.

"But Red Cloak must be losing money in wagers," Bjarni said, coming up for air from a pretty whore's tits. "Who would wager their silver *against* those three? It seems to me that we have not seen anyone half good enough to beat them."

I sluiced my insides with a great splash of wine and shuddered because it was sour. "Red Cloak is weaving their fame," I said. "That's what it is about." Eyes turned to me then because I talked of fame and fame is what a Norseman craves even more than silver. "Gregor told us that in the olden times, even when Rome was the most powerful kingdom in the world, its emperors still feared their people."

"That's because there were so many of them, like fleas on a damn dog," Bram said. *Or maggots in a carcass,* I thought.

"To win favor and keep the peace, the emperors would hold fights between slaves." Someone barked a laugh at that. "Not just any slaves," I said. "These men were trained by the best fighters in the world until they were ready for the arena." I looked at Sigurd. "Can you imagine that place choked to the sky with blood-hungry Romans?"

Sigurd shook his head. "The noise must have been like thunder."

"So this Red Cloak thinks he's an emperor," Bjarni said, picking his teeth with a sliver of wood.

"He's a crafty son of a goat, that's what he is," Olaf said, "because he is getting rich while other men are getting dead." There were chuckles at that because it was well said. Yet even through the false light of flames and the moon glow off the foam-flecked river, I could see the men's eyes as they talked of meaningless things and of home and women and friends gone to the grave. They drank sour wine and weak ale and ate pork ribs cooked in garlic oil. But their eyes shone like golden solidi. And I wished I had not talked of fame hoards, for that was like putting a fleshy bone beneath a hound's nose at night and expecting the meat to still be on it in the morning.

———

Some days later Sigurd told us to fill our ships' bellies with food because we were leaving Rome. If what Egfrith had learned from his brother Christ slaves was true and Emperor Karolus really was on his way to support Pope Leo and put the lords of Rome back in their places, it would be better for us if we were not there. We had crammed our eyes with the countless impossible wonders of the ancient city. We had eaten foods that tasted so good that you didn't want to finish eating them and other things that tasted so bad that they turned your face inside out. We had made some money, too, selling furs, amber, bone, and some of the weapons we had taken from the blaumen, though we had lost most of it again in the arena. It was time for our prows to taste the salty ocean once more, for we had set our hearts not on Rome but on Miklagard, the Great City. And so we were leaving. Little did we know that that was not what the Spinners had woven for us.

"Tell them, Raven. They'll lap this up!" Penda, Gytha, Baldred, and Wiglaf had returned from the market at the foot of the Esquiline Hill, where Gregor had told us we could buy the best smoked cheese in all of Rome. Each of the Wessexmen had come lugging a greased linen sackful, the sweet, woody fug of that delicious treasure billowing in their wake. But it was not the cheese that had them slobbering.

I felt my brows bend like drawn bows. "I think we should say nothing about it, Penda," I said, thinking back over the story I had just heard. Gap-Toothed Ingolf passed, and I slapped the fragrant slab of smoked beef ribs on his shoulder. The men were thrumming as they always did when we prepared to leave a place and take to the sea road again.

"I'd tell them myself if it were not for my honest Christian tongue," Penda gabbed, grinning at Gytha and the others. He rolled it over his bottom lip. "Just can't find its way around those filthy heathen words of yours," he said.

"I'm not telling them," I said, pointing at him. "Besides, we're leaving in the morning. It's too late."

"Tell them."

"No."

"Tell them."

My eyes rolled in their sockets.

"At least tell Sigurd," Baldred put in, several black teeth showing within his even blacker beard. The Wessexmen were glistening with sweat because the afternoon was warm and they had walked far.

"Hey, Raven, what are the little Englishmen bleating about?" Svein said, stopping nearby to get a better purchase on a barrel of ale he was hefting across the rain-slick quayside toward *Serpent*. Rain had blown in from the northeast, and it was the same wind, which seemed to come every morning and last till midday, that we would catch in our sails the next day to push us back down the Tiberis to the sea.

I knew I should keep my lips riveted together. I knew I should swallow the words that were rising in my throat like bubbles in good ale. But there is a part of me that loves chaos, that revels in the clatter of the runes across the deck in that moment when nothing is certain and anything is possible. All warriors, I think, hear the echo of sword against shield in the beat of their own hearts and are savagely drawn toward it. That is why I told

Svein and Bram and anyone else within earshot what Penda had told me: the word jumping like a flea across Rome was that Red Cloak had issued a challenge. Three warriors had beaten every man brave enough to fight them. Theo the Greek, Berstuk the Wend, and the man they called the African were, so Red Cloak said, the greatest fighters to wield a blade since the days of the gladiators. Now these three would fight together as sword-brothers in the greatest spectacle the Amphitheatrum Flavium had seen in four hundred years. Were there any three men in all of Rome to match those three in courage and skill? African, Moor, Northman, Frank, Wend, it mattered not, so long as they dared.

"And supposing there are three half-witted men foolish enough to accept this challenge," Egfrith piped up, "and suppose by some miracle they defeat those three killers. What would they get for it?"

"One thousand two hundred and fifty libra," I said, "which is—"

"Which is five men's weight in silver," Sigurd said, glancing at Olaf, who tugged his beard at the thought. Men whistled and murmured and tried to imagine that much silver.

"What's the bone in the broth?" Olaf asked, suspicion slitting his eyes.

"That whoever fights those three will probably die, Uncle," I said. "And that they have to pay Red Cloak five hundred libra for the pleasure."

"Then they just make sure they win, hey!" Svein said with a shrug of his massive shoulders.

"And whatever happens, Red Cloak will make enough silver in wagers to become an emperor after all," Sigurd said. "Uncle, get everyone together at sun-

down. Here, by *Serpent*. Tell Asgot to bring the runes."
Olaf nodded and marched up the wharf. "Raven, go
and find Red Cloak. Tell him that Ódin's Wolves who
are moored in the embrace of the river's coil accept the
challenge and will pay six hundred libra tomorrow if
he turns down any others."

"Lord?" My head was swimming, my ears trying
to grip the words coming out of my jarl's mouth.

Sigurd eyeballed me fiercely. "Raven, do you think
men like us can ignore such a challenge? Did we come
to Rome just to see the ruins of men long dead? You
knew, Raven." His brows lifted. "Even before the
words tumbled out of your mouth, you knew that it
would be this way." He was right. I had known. Yet I
also knew that part of me loved chaos. And so I nodded to my jarl as Norsemen, Danes, and Englishmen
simmered like water above coals and forgot all about
setting sail. And I went to find Red Cloak.

Father Egfrith went with me because he could speak
Latin, which might be useful for all we knew, having
no idea where Red Cloak was from. At first the monk
had refused, saying that he wanted nothing to do with
our bloodthirsty schemes and would rather spend his
last days in Rome visiting shrines and churches and
the grave of a saint called Paul. Sigurd threatened to
leave him behind if he did not help us, and I believe
Egfrith half liked the sound of that threat, for in his
gloom he believed he had failed as far as converting us
into kneeling White Christ followers went. But Egfrith
was also as inquisitive as a crow. As much as any man
he thirsted to see Miklagard, or Constantinople as he
called it, maybe even more so now that he had seen
Rome. And so he wandered the city with me, and we

asked a hundred people if they knew where we might find the rich dark-skinned man who held the purse strings in the arena. The ones who understood us eyed us suspiciously and refused to speak of the arena, perhaps thinking we were in the pay of Pope Leo or the emperor and were trying to trick them into confessing they had attended the fights.

"They're not so tight-lipped when the blood starts flying," I moaned as we turned our backs on another man who claimed he did not even know where the Amphitheatrum Flavium was. "You should hear it, Egfrith, the noise of so many people. It's a wonder your ears don't burst."

"It is barbarous," he said. "It hurts God's ears; I am sure of that."

I thought that might be true and said so. "But I think our gods would pull up a bench, fill their mead horns, and watch until the last blood sprayed the dirt," I said.

"You *would* think that. Because you are a vile heathen, Raven, and your soul is damned." The crowds were thinning out as merchants packed away their goods and folk began to make their way home. There was still an edge of menace to the night because the soldiers who normally would patrol the streets were instead guarding the Lateran and Pope Leo. "What are we doing here, anyway?" Egfrith asked, stopping suddenly and sweeping an arm through the air. We were in the Forum, between the Palatine Hill and the Capitoline Hill, and our ears rang with the clamor of countless hammers and chisels striking stone. Men were building towers from ruins, great strongholds from which they could watch over the city and, perhaps, their enemies. Workers, as white as bloodless corpses from all the stone dust, yelled to one another and argued. Others clambered up and down the wooden frames that surrounded the half-built towers like rib cages around beating hearts. Boys played among the ancient rubble. Dogs fought over scraps of dropped food. Whores waited patiently for newly paid men to finish for the day, and the whole place stank of sweat and shit from the oxen that were everywhere, dragging sleds stacked with shaped stones.

"I thought you would like it here," I replied, wincing. "Look at all the White Christ houses." Around the edge of the Forum were many Roman temples that had been turned into churches. "Besides, it seems to me that if you are a rich man in Rome, this is where you build your stronghold. Near the river but not so near that you drown when it floods and far enough from the Pope that you can do what you like. And you build it high, by the look of it, so you can piss on other men's heads."

Egfrith had to admit the sense in coming to the Forum, though in the end it was Red Cloak who found us. Or rather his men did. We had come across a fat man selling honey-coated figs, which I had learned should be eaten sparingly if you did not want to spend the whole day squatting over a bucket, and that man spoke enough English to understand that I was going to cut off his balls and throw them to the dogs if he did not tell us what we wanted to know. Egfrith had scolded me in front of the man, pissing on my threat somewhat, but I was tired and my feet were aching, and I had not realized it would be so hard to find a man whose face was known to thousands who had seen him in the arena. Only when a small rat-faced boy returned with five armed men did my memory pluck from somewhere the sight of that boy running off the moment I had grabbed the fig-seller by his fleshy neck.

The fat man ranted to the soldiers, who had surrounded Egfrith and me though they had not yet leveled their spears at us, pointing at me as though I were a two-headed mountain troll. "You would have thought I *had* cut his balls off," I said, sickened by the fat man's whining and his terror-filled eyes, for I sometimes forgot about my own blood-filled eye and the effect it had on others.

"They want to know why you seek Lord Guido," the fig-seller said. *So he has a name, then*, I thought. As it turned out, that wasn't Red Cloak's name at all, but we were not to know that yet.

"Ask these sour-faced, maggot-arsed fart-eaters how we are supposed to accept Lord Guido's challenge of fighting those three pale-livered lumps in the arena if we cannot find him," I said. The fat man's eyes bulged so much that I thought that they might pop, but so far as I could tell, he asked my question of the soldiers. To Egfrith's obvious surprise, and mine too, I admit, one of Guido's soldiers smiled, and so I shrugged and delivered the rest of Sigurd's message. By dusk we were back at the wharf.

The men had gathered beside the ships, and there was not a single face missing. Even Cynethryth and her wolf, Sköll, were there, the beast nowadays as much a part of Sigurd's Fellowship as those who had taken the new oath in Frankia. I caught Sigurd's eye and nodded to say that our challenge had been accepted. His eyes flashed, and he nodded back. There were no whores, no men selling pork fried in olive oil, garlic-laced mushrooms, and bread. There were no men offering to sharpen blades or leather workers fixing holes in shoes or boys bringing plump wineskins from across the river. There were just the men of *Serpent* and *Fjord-Elk* and *Wave-Steed* and *Sea-Arrow*. Their eyes were on their jarl, who stood at their center like the boss of a shield, his golden hair in two thick braids, a green cloak fastened with a wolf's head brooch over his granite shoulders, and his father's sword at his hip. Warriors' pride hung thick as green leaf smoke in the air.

"You are all the equal of any warrior Red Cloak can find," Sigurd said, his voice easily matching the river's gush. "You are all killers, skilled with the tools of death. But I have spoken with our godi, and he agrees that in such matters as this, it is about more than a man's cleverness with a spear or sword. The Norns have a hand in this, as well you all know. That is why it is not for me to choose which of you shall fight." I saw Svein's face drop then, because I knew him well enough to be certain that he wanted nothing more than to fight in the arena and must have thought that he would be chosen. The blauman Völund and Yngvar the Dane stood at the front of the press, and I guessed they wanted to fight, too, to earn their place among Sigurd's wolves.

"Asgot will tell us how the choice will be made," Sigurd went on, lingering on a face here, a face there, "for the runes have spoken to him, and we would do well to heed them." He stepped back, and Asgot came forward. He had threaded the tiny skulls of five mice into his greasy ashen beard.

"This is the battle god's domain," the godi said, his yellow eyes scouring us. "His hand will be in this up to the elbow, mark me." He pointed a knotty finger across the moon-silvered Tiberis. "On the other bank, a short walk northwest of the stone warrior, there is a ruin that has been swallowed by briars. Hanging from a branch of the tallest tree there is a sack. Between now and sunrise, any man who wants to fight in the Romans' arena must place some token in the sack, though he must not look inside."

"What kind of token, Asgot?" the Dane Beiner asked, clawing at his beard.

"It must be something that has traveled the sea road with you for a long time," Asgot said, one eye half closing, "long enough that it carries your stink. It will be a keepsake that you could pick out as yours though your eyes were blind and your fingers cut off." There were murmurs at that. "In the morning the battle god will help us choose whom to send." Men nodded and talked in low voices, careful of being boastful, as is wise when your godi tells you that one of the Aesir's hands is moving the pieces on your tafl board. For the gods can be cruel, and it is a brave man or a fool who crows too loudly when they are near.

Then Olaf stepped from the crowd and lifted two wineskins out wide, like plunder won after a hard fight. "Seeing as we're staying a little longer, it seems to me we might as well get on the outside of a few drops now, hey!"

We cheered that idea, for the gods never had a problem with men getting drunk, and we spent the night celebrating because thousands of people would soon watch three warriors of our Fellowship beat the champions of Rome. There was a shining fame hoard waiting for us in the arena, and by its brightness the Norns were spinning our wyrds.

The wineskins were passed from man to man and, judging it safe to mix with us again, the food-sellers and whores and ale boys moved in like hawks, all smiles and nods and clinging like fleas, until Byrnjolf threw one of them into the river, which carried him off never to be seen again, after which the rest gave us a little room to breathe, at least for a while.

I explained to the Wessexmen what they would have to do if any of them wanted the chance to fight.

"I don't need to fight some big black bastard in the arena to prove I know one end of a sword from the other," Baldred said, putting a wineskin to his lips.

Red-faced Wiglaf nodded, his little finger digging something foul from a nostril. "Let these blood-loving savages get themselves cut up for the crowd's pleasure," he said, wiping his finger on his breeks.

"What about you, Penda?" Gytha asked.

Penda reached inside his tunic and pulled out a braided length of red hair that was tied at both ends. I had seen the warrior put that lock to his nose many times before but had never asked him about it. The head it had come from was far away now.

Baldred rapped his knuckles against his head. "Your brains are addled, Penda," he said, because Penda was going to put that lock of hair in Asgot's sack.

"If I get into that arena, God help the man who faces me. I don't care which of those bastards it is, I'm going to gut them," he said simply, holding out a hand for the wineskin, which Baldred passed him. I shared a look with Wiglaf because we both knew that coming from Penda that was no boast. It was the cold truth, because Penda was the kind of man who was born with a sword in his hand. In that way he reminded me most of Black Floki, though they were different in every other way.

"And you, Raven," Baldred asked, tilting his head toward Penda. "Tell me you've got more sense than this son of a rabid bitch."

I smiled. "I'm in no hurry to see what my guts look like, Baldred," I said.

"Good lad," he replied with a satisfied nod. Penda nodded too, pleased with my answer, and we ate until we thought we would burst and drank ourselves to sleep. Several times during the night I stirred and caught glimpses of shadow-shrouded figures coming and going. And I knew that somewhere across the river, Asgot's oiled sack was beginning to swell.

chapter
SIXTEEN

I WAS WOKEN by a clamorous, ear-pounding bellowing. Nearby, on the large square base stone of some long-vanished statue, a massive bull was fighting ten men who were red-faced and straining to hold it still so that Asgot could get into the right position to cut its throat. The dawn was mostly gray and dank, and the river mist seemed heavier than normal, clinging to the banks of the Tiberis and soaking into our clothes. But neither that nor our aching heads could dampen the mood that was spreading through the camp like fire through dry grass. Today was the day. Soon we would know which of our warriors would have the honor of fighting in the Amphitheatrum Flavium. Onions sizzled on hot iron. Men shredded fried fish onto warm bread, and others were cutting wedges from a wheel of smoked cheese; excited voices interwove, creating a hum to equal the river's murmur.

"I've got a good feeling in my bones about this," Bram said, tossing Bjarni a fish straight from the iron, which Bjarni caught and passed from hand to hand, blowing on it. "I'm itching to show these scrawny Danish whelps how we do things where we come from," Bram went on. The bull gave one last bellow of rage, and then Asgot's blade sliced deep; an impossible amount of blood gushed out, splattering onto the stone and steaming in the fog. The beast's forelegs buckled and its knees crashed down, then it slewed sideways, and men were suddenly leaping clear, narrowly avoiding being crushed as other men laughed and Asgot invoked Týr, Lord of Battle.

"I'm sure the Danes and the people of Rome will enjoy watching a warrior who was taught how to fight by Grendal," Bjarni said, trying not to smile, "but I imagine that they would rather watch someone with some skill. That is why Týr will choose me."

"Hah! I'll wager the only reason you left your furs last night was to piss in the river," Bram said, and men chuckled at that.

"It's time," Sigurd said, placing a hand on Bram's shoulder. A flock of screeching gulls passed overhead, following the river toward the sea and the fishing boats that would be casting off. Suddenly everyone was talking at once and converging on the bull, around whose corpse was spreading a pool of blood and piss. The beast was a worthy sacrifice, and I hoped it had been enough to lure the one-handed god Týr, who was the bravest of the Aesir. "Asgot will draw from the bag three times," Sigurd said, holding up three fingers. His cloak, I noticed, was fastened with a leaping stag brooch that shone dully in the gray morning light, and I guessed that his wolf's head brooch was in the bag in Asgot's grasp. "Each possession drawn will reveal which of us the gods want to see fight in the Romans' arena, for it is the Aesir that grip the tiller on this journey." But it was Asgot who gripped the leather bag in his bloodstained hands, and when everyone was gathered, Sigurd gestured at him to get on with it. The godi's old fingers worried at the draw rope until the bag yawned open. There was just the sullen gush of the river and the flat voices of men farther along the bank on the wooden wharves as Asgot, his yellow eyes turned to the gray sky, plunged a hand inside the bag. The words he muttered to the gods were ancient, perhaps older even than Rome, and then out came the hand, and in it was a comb. It was an old comb, many of its teeth missing, and I had thought to have seen the last of it long ago, but Svein must have kept it after all, and now we who recognized it turned to the giant, whose red bush of a beard was split by a great savage smile. Then we cheered, because there was no better man to fight for our honor than Svein, and the giant stepped up and took the comb from Asgot, then turned and held it aloft as though it were a silver jarl torc, and we cheered even louder. Roused by the noise, Sköll howled, adding his own approval of the choice, and I wondered what the folk of Rome must have thought to hear that blood-chilling sound from the bank of the Tiberis.

As Svein stepped back into the press of men, the portentous silence closed in again, thicker than the river mist. Nervous hands tugged beards and clutched amulets. Teeth chewed fingernails, throats hacked clear, farts squeaked and ripped, and men wondered what their wyrds might be, for there were only two more choices to be made.

In went Asgot's hand, slower this time, as though he half feared that one of his sharp-toothed creatures might be hiding inside, cowering from the knife.

"Watch him pull out another of Svein's combs!" a man barked, but few men laughed. The godi drew his hand out, and someone yelled, "Frigg's tits!" and there was no mistaking that voice, for between Asgot's thumb and forefinger, held up for all to see, was a bear's claw: a black, shiny finger-length curl of wicked sharpness. I grinned, turning to look for Bram Bear. But his eyes were already on me, his brow hoisted, and others were staring at me, too.

"You damned fool, lad," Penda hissed. Confused, I turned back to Asgot, whose eyes were also riveted on me, and then my bowels turned to ice water and my knees threatened to give way. The godi still held up Bram's bear claw pendant, the leather thong hanging down, but somehow tangled up with that cord was a battered old scrap, black and frayed but still recognizable for what it was—a raven's wing. The same one that Cynethryth had tied into my hair long ago in a forest in Wessex.

"Does that count?" someone asked.

"Put the bird back in," Bjarni called. "It only came out because it was caught up with Bram's claw."

"Put it back," Bram agreed, and men nodded and ayed, but Asgot shook his head.

"Fools! Can't you see Týr's hand in this?" He glared at them. "The three have been chosen. We cannot change it."

"If Asgot says this is the god's doing, who are we to interfere?" Arngrim said, his brows sewn together.

"Sigurd, the lad will get himself killed," Olaf objected. Sigurd frowned but said nothing, so Olaf turned back to the godi. "Asgot, draw another," he said, pointing at the sack.

"He cannot, Uncle," Sigurd said loudly enough for all to hear, and the twist of a smile touched the godi's thin lips. "That the wing came out even without Asgot laying a finger on it tells me that some scheme is being played out here."

I wanted to yell out that I had not put the raven's wing in the godi's sack. I did not want to fight in the arena. Even the thought of it was madness, for I had watched Guido's fighters slaughter much better warriors than me. I would die, my guts unraveled in the dirt beside me, my ears stuffed with the crowd's baying. Besides which, even if I *had* wanted to fight, I had been so drunk the night before that I had slept where I lay on the wharf, an empty wineskin beneath my head. I would have more likely fallen in the river than found my way over the bridge to the tree on which Asgot's sack hung, and that, I realized, must have been how Asgot was able to take the raven's wing from my hair without my knowing. I scowled at the godi, my eyes promising him a hundred painful deaths, but held my tongue.

"I will look after you, little brother," Svein the Red boomed, throwing his arm over my shoulder. It felt like an oak beam.

I tried to smile, but my face was frozen. If I told them the truth of it, who would believe me? Who would believe that Asgot had, in the dead of the night, cut the wing from my hair while I slept? I would look like a nithing coward trying to wriggle out of my wyrd. I would be marked as a man without honor. Then there was the fog around how it had happened. Asgot had taken the raven's wing and put it in that sack of his— I was sure of that—but had he tied it to the thong on Bram's claw pendant? Or was it just ill luck that it had snagged like that? Or perhaps that part really *was*

Týr's doing? I tore my eyes from the godi, the hot hate still in them when they settled on Cynethryth at his right shoulder. Had she known? No, I could not believe she wanted to see me killed in the arena. Her green eyes were silent as the grave, and I looked away.

"Let's hear it for Týr's chosen men!" Bothvar hollered. Cheers rose with the mist, and men slapped our backs, and some went to fetch wine to celebrate even though it was early in the morning. My head still thumped like a sword hilt against the inside of a shield.

Over the next few days we trained hard. At the foot of the Aventine Hill, in the shadow of the crumbling Servian Wall, was an area of scrub among which a man named Paschal pastured his sheep, goats, and some horses. Sigurd gave the man a drinking horn full of amber for which Paschal happily gave over half his land for us to tramp around on. Sigurd and Black Floki worked me half to death until my whole body trembled and I vomited. We mostly used spears whose blades we had sheathed in leather, for if you can use a spear well, you will be better with the sword and the ax, too. Sigurd and Floki would attack me together so that I had to fight desperately, twisting this way and that, blocking again and again until my saliva was thick as porridge and my chest was fit to burst. If I showed any weakness or began to tire, one of them would crack his shaft against my leg or shoulder, and I had no choice but to fight harder or else suffer later. After each bout, when I counted the tender purple and green bruises on my body, I convinced myself that they had been careful not to do me any serious injury before the big fight, though my battered flesh took no comfort from that.

We worked on our strength, too. Svein, Bram, and I would stand together, our shields overlapping, facing a skjaldborg of six or seven or even ten men. Then it was a simple shoving match, and our hearts hammered and our lungs seared as we put our shoulders into it and drove on. But even with Svein on our side, we would always be pushed back, our feet plowing up great sods of earth and our faces red as Roman wine and sweat-soaked. And yet no amount of sweat and bruises would change the truth, which was that I was not even half good enough to beat Theo the Greek, Berstuk the Wend, or the blauman known as the African. Everyone else knew it too. Leading up to the day of the fight, some of the men were cold toward me, and I suspected they were angry because they did not think I was worthy to fight for the Fellowship's honor. Or perhaps they were simply envious because as they saw it, Týr had favored me with the chance to claim a fame hoard that they believed should be theirs. That was not how I saw it. It was not how Penda saw it, either.

"By all the saints, lad, I still don't know what you were thinking. They're proper fighters, not some ham-fisted farmers called up to the levy. The Greek is fish-quick and has all the skill you could want. He's clever with it too. The African could probably out-wrestle Svein, and the Wend has a born instinct for killing men that would keep me awake the night before I fought the bastard."

"I've killed better fighters before," I said, drinking weak ale. It was the night before the big fight, and

Penda had held his tongue while he helped me prepare, running through the moves and techniques that made him one of the best fighters I have ever seen. Perhaps the wine had unstuck his tongue, which was, as far as I was concerned, ill timed, seeing as I'd be fighting for my life soon.

He shook his head, the whites of his eyes shining in the flame light. "You've been lucky, lad. And you've got instinct too, but you're not ready. I've seen better footwork from an eel," he said with a smile that faded before it reached his eyes. "Are you still trying to make up for ditching their damned silver in that Frankish river?" He gestured at the nearest Norsemen, who, like everyone else, were talking in low voices, counting out the silver they intended to put on us winning and arguing over who they thought we should be matched with to give us the best chance of leaving the arena alive.

I shook my head. "They might not like it, Penda, but they know that our bones would be rotting in that river if we had not put that hoard over the side."

"Is it about the girl, then?" he asked. "Does Cynethryth have a part in your wanting to get yourself killed?"

My stomach twisted at her name. "I care nothing for her now," I lied, and the Wessexman shook his head in frustration because my wish to fight far better warriors than myself made no sense at all to him. And so because Penda was my friend and because I knew he could sense the fear in me the way a hunting dog catches a fox's scent even if the fox is hiding underground, I chose to tell him. I told him the truth of how it was that Asgot had pulled my raven's wing from his sack, and as I spoke, his eyes bulged. His jaw dropped, and his fists balled into hard knots.

"The wily, venomous bastard!" he exclaimed. I shushed him.

"You will not say a word to any of them," I hissed. "On your oath you'll say nothing."

"But you don't have to fight," he said, barely able to keep his voice down. "They can draw another man's fucking comb, and you might get to live a while longer."

"What's done is done," I said with a shrug. "There is no way out of it, Penda, not without looking like a pale-livered coward." Penda thought about this for a long while, scratching the scar that carved its way down his face as he tried to fathom a way by which I might avoid the arena.

"A man's wyrd is inescapable," I said, holding out my hand for the wineskin leaning against his leg. The ale had not clouded my mind nearly enough, and if this was going to be my last night, I would not have it filled with thoughts of death. Penda handed me the bulging skin, and I got to work on it.

"You'll just have to bloody well win," he said.

Just then there was a great cheer from the men camped nearest the stone bridge that spanned the Tiberis. Many of us climbed to our feet and peered through the flame-licked night, eager, I think, to shake off the sense of apprehension that sat heavy upon the Fellowship. I saw Sigurd and Olaf and Rolf striding up the quayside, each with a pig's carcass across his shoulders.

"Has someone died?" Sigurd yelled. "Have we lost a ship to this stinking Roman river? No? Then why are you all sour-faced? Hey, Uncle, have you ever seen such a gloomy crew? Such miserable-looking men?" He was grinning.

"Only Christians," Olaf said, shaking his head.

"Tomorrow, Svein, Bram, and Raven will hoist our fame high enough for all of Rome to see," Sigurd shouted, unburdening himself of the pig so that Arnvid and Bothvar could spit it above the cook fire. "If that is not worthy of a feast, then I cannot say what is."

The men needed no more encouragement than that. Bjarni found some Romans who could make music with pipes and a lyre with strings of twisted horsehair, and Bork and Beiner brought the women. We all came together around one great fire and drank and laughed and watched the fat drip from the pigs in glistening strings to hiss and seethe in the flames. When we had gnawed one of the carcasses to the bone, Olaf climbed unsteadily to his feet, ale sloshing over the sides of his silver-inlaid drinking horn.

"To Ódin, All-Father!" he yelled, thrusting the horn out before him.

"Ódin, All-Father!" we yelled back.

"Now I would like to hear from our champions," he said, pointing into the crowd with a wandering finger. "Svein, you red-haired son of an ox! I pity the poor whoreson who has to face you tomorrow. Will you give him a quick death?" There were shouts of "no."

"Stand up, Svein Thór's son. Let's see you."

The giant stood, a smile nestled in his great beard, and we cheered him. "Being so tall has both benefits and drawbacks, hey, Svein?" Bjarni shouted, turning to the rest of us. "Svein is the first to get soaked when it rains but the last to smell it when someone farts!"

"What will we see from you tomorrow, Svein?" Sigurd's voice cut through the laughter.

"I will cut my enemy's belly open so that you will all know what he has eaten for breakfast," Svein said. "Then I will pull out his gut rope and strangle him with it." The men liked the sound of that. "If he is still alive after that, I will introduce him to my ax, which some of you know is called Skull-Biter. I don't think he will like Skull-Biter." He shook his head sadly. "And that is a shame, for I think that Skull-Biter will like him very much."

Everyone agreed it was well said, for this was the time for a warrior's boasts, and the more outlandish they are, the better as far as a Norseman is concerned. Svein raised his horn to the Fellowship, then sat down again.

"Bram, Bram, Bram!" The Bear let the chant ring a while before standing up, the glow from the greasy flames bronzing his face and beard. One hand gripped a saggy wineskin.

"Well, Bear? Are you going to let your opponent walk from the arena tomorrow to screw the night away and boast of beating a Norseman?" Sigurd asked, lighting the tinder beneath Bram's famous pride.

"Hah! If he can walk on his face!" Bram bellowed. My head was beginning to swim now, which might have been the wine but might also have been fear. "I am Bram. Some call me Bear. I fought for King Gorm at Fyrkat, where the blood ran in streams and the wolves and the ravens glutted themselves so that the wolves could not stand and the ravens could not fly. I killed King Hygelac Storm-Temper's champion, who was called Olof, and many other men besides." He could not resist looking at the Danes as he said this, for Hygelac was a Danish king and they must all have heard of the champion Olof. "At Ribe I killed the brothers Randver and Hreidmar, who were known as great fighters." Some ayes at this. "When I was young, I swam the Kattegat Sea from Grenen to Læsø island. The man who challenged me drowned. I have never heard of another man swimming so far." No one challenged this, though I do not see how any man could in reality swim that far. Even a fish could not.

"Didn't you once kill a troll?" Osk said. The stubs of his broken teeth flashed in the firelight.

Bram grasped his bird's nest beard and gave an embarrassed smile. "It was an ugly beast as I recall," he said, pulling his beard through his fist. "But I have been wondering if rather than a troll it might have been some relation of Svein's. A cousin maybe." Even Svein laughed at that, and Bram shrugged. "It was dark, and I had been drinking."

"Drinking? You?" Sigurd's eyes were wide with shock. "I do not believe my ears."

"Aye, and that's another thing," Bram said, swinging the wineskin up as a challenge. "I've outdrunk the best men who ever tipped an elbow."

"Heya!" Sigurd cried, lifting his drinking horn in Bram's honor. We all did the same.

"The ill-wyrded snot-eating son of a sow who fights me tomorrow is going to wish he'd never slipped out of his pig mother's cunny." Men roared their approval, and I began to feel eyes on me, which slickened my palms and dried my tongue like wind-lashed cod.

"On your feet, Raven," Olaf called. "Don't let those two puffed-up whoresons outcrow you."

"Give them what they want, lad," Penda muttered as I stood.

"I wouldn't want to fight the lad!" the big Dane Beiner said. "I've seen him spear a blauman who just wanted to talk. The lad's unhinged."

"He doesn't fight fair; I know that much," Yrsa Pig-Nose added. "Remember that big Frank who jumped aboard *Serpent*?" They did. "I'll wager he never thought to be killed by a damn brooch pin." Laughter rang out, but Sigurd shushed them so that I could speak.

"I am grateful to Týr that I will fight beside these two," I said, gesturing to Svein and Bram, "for I know of no braver men. Or better drinkers," I added, at which men raised their horns, cups, and wineskins again. "But the man who fights me will not have an easy time of it. Since I joined this Fellowship, many men have tried to kill me. Most of them have long since been eaten by worms, but I am still here." A murmur began, and men leaned together to share it. "Some have said I am Ódin-favored because I have walked away from fights that should have been my death. They whisper behind my back. *Blood Eye cannot be killed*, they say. *The Spear-Shaker's seidr protects him.* I have heard many of you hiss as much when you have thought me asleep," I accused them. "I have even heard it said that death clings to me like a black cloak and that men should keep their distance from me if they want to live." They were not cheering as they had for the others, but the murmur was swelling like a river in spate. I held my tongue for a moment, scouring men's faces with my gaze, letting my blood-filled eye work its seidr. "It is all true," I said. "The man who fights me tomorrow will learn it to his cost. I am Raven Corpse Maker. He will not see another sunset." Some of the eyes looking up at me were pebble-wide so that I could see the fire reflected in them. Others were slits beneath heavy brows. Not knowing what else to do or say, I bent and grabbed the wineskin Penda and I were working on and lifted it high. "For Ódin!" I yelled. The men raised their own drinks and some of them repeated my dedication, but the whole thing was lack-luster.

"I'm a piss-poor boaster next to Svein and Bram," I muttered, sitting back down. I put the wineskin to my lips to take a swig, but my head was spinning and so I thought better of it.

Penda did not answer, and when I looked up, I saw that he was staring at me just like the others. I said again that I ought to practice my swagger.

"I couldn't make sense of most of it, lad," he admitted, "but nobody cracked a rib laughing, that's for sure."

"I would have liked to wipe the smirk off that putrid old goat's face," I said, nodding toward Asgot. The old godi was casting the runes across a tafl board, his eyes rolled back in his head, looking where other men could not see. Cynethryth was beside him, stroking the wolf Sköll's silver back as it slept, its head on its paws. "If I live past tomorrow, I'm going to kill him," I said, only half meaning it, for I knew that by killing the godi I would be breaking my oath to the Fellowship and to Sigurd.

"What *did* you say to them, Raven?" Penda asked then, glancing around. "Because whatever it was, they're still talking about it." By the look of it, Penda was right. A shroud had fallen over the camp again, and it did nothing to ease my pounding head. So I cursed and sluiced the inside of my neck with wine anyway.

Someone said my name at the same time as he touched my shoulder. It was Sigurd, and he nodded at Penda and then looked back to me. "Walk with me, Raven," he said.

We followed the Tiberis north and cut east as far as the first swell of the Palatine Hill, letting our ears latch on to the muted rush of the river and the distant din of the city: drunken laughter, dogs barking, men shouting.

"The men didn't think much of what I had to say, lord," I said glumly, breaking the silence that had stretched too long between us.

"It lacked a little gilt, Raven," he said, taking in the torch-lit churches and convents that nestled brightly on the hill among the enormous white-stoned decaying temples and palaces that men no longer had the skill or the wealth to repair.

"It lacked more than that," I said.

He smiled, but it was strained. "Beowulf's boasting when he came to Hrothgar's hall was better," he admitted. After a few more paces he stopped and turned to face me, the scars glistening on his high cheekbone and temple though his eyes were in shadow. "Raven, I cannot let you fight tomorrow."

For a heartbeat—only a heartbeat—my spirit leaped.

"But I must fight," I said.

He shook his head. "Why did you do it? You have already proved yourself to this Fellowship. Many times.

There is bravery, Raven, and there is fools' pride. No one would have known if you had not put that withered bird's wing in the sack. That was why we did it that way, so that I would not have to declare before all which men are our best fighters but still knowing that only the best would come forward and the others would be spared any shame."

"I thought it was so Týr Lord of Battle could choose," I said, my face tight beneath a frown. His darkened eyes burrowed into mine. I was tempted to tell him the truth of it. How Asgot had had a hand on the tiller of my wyrd because he hated me and wanted me dead or else was curious to know once and for all if I was Óðin-favored. Perhaps, if I survived the arena, the godi would accept that I was and then that would be an end to it.

"I was proud, though," Sigurd said, "I will say that. When that wing came out with Bram's claw. I was surprised and angry but proud, too." That last made me swallow the truth. "But you must not fight."

"Lord, I must fight. That is my wyrd. Everyone saw it."

"They saw something else, too," he said through a grimace as though the words had broken free of his mouth cage.

"Lord?" I felt my blood chill then.

"Your face, Raven, when you were speaking. Your face turned bone-white. It happened like that," he said, clicking his fingers. "We all saw it. Your eye looked like a bloodstain in fresh snow."

"The wine?" I suggested. "I have tasted better. Or perhaps I stood too quickly." Sigurd shook his head. My scalp prickled and my saliva soured because I knew what dark thing it was that Sigurd was edging around.

"You think I'm feigr," I said. It was not a question. I had heard it said that if a man's face suddenly changes color, it betokens his doom. The men thought that I was feigr, that my doom was on me. Sigurd did not reply, which was louder than any answer.

"If I am feigr, then so be it," I said, trying to swallow the fear that was stuck in my throat like an arrowhead. "My wing came out of Asgot's sack, and I must fight tomorrow."

"I am your jarl," he said. "I could command you not to fight." His voice was firm, but he had turned into the silver wash of the moon, and by its pale light his eyes betrayed what his voice had not. Which was that he knew as well as I did that I had to fight alongside Svein and Bram the next day. That I had no choice but to follow the Norns' weave wherever it might lead.

"You would not ruin my reputation, lord," I said, realizing all of a sudden that that *would* be worse than dying. At that very moment I was actually more terrified of Sigurd preventing me from fighting than I was of anything else in the world.

"No, I would not do that," he said unhappily, resigning himself to what would be. I had never seen his eyes look so heavy, as though his brows were house eaves dangerously laden with snow. He looked sad.

"Raven," he said after a silence swollen with unspoken words. "If it comes to it, fight it. Do not give in. Do you understand me?" His eyes were riveted to mine once more, and now they held their old spark. "The gods have their patterns for us, but I say fuck the gods." And this was Sigurd's burden. His whole life had been a battle against the gods. Asgot had said that Sigurd did not respect the gods as he should, but Sigurd had long ago broken free of the fetters that bound most men. I believed that the gods admired him for it. Though one day they would tire of him. And now the jarl was telling me to defy my wyrd. "You must live tomorrow," he said, his lips curled in ire. "Fuck the gods and their feigr. When death comes for you tomorrow, I want you to fight with every part of your heart and marrow and spirit. You live, Raven. And together we will weave a tale that will keep skalds' tongues flapping for a thousand years."

I tried to smile, but the skin over my face bones felt as though it had shrunk. My friends thought I was feigr. They knew as surely as wounds bleed that I would be dead before the next day's end. And now I was on my way back to them to drink more wine and boast of killing.

chapter
SEVENTEEN

THE AMPHITHEATRUM Flavium was all seething madness. It was different standing at ground level, looking up at the stone terraces that were filling with the crowds that had come for blood. The place was filled with their sound, like the whir of a thousand arrows through the air, and the sweat stink of them was thick enough to taste. It was like being at sea in the eye of a storm. All is strangely calm, yet you know what is coming. I could not see clearly the individual faces, but I knew well enough where the Fellowship was. They had come in war gear in case of trouble with the Pope's or emperor's men and were massed on the bottom level on the west side, as far away from any of the White Christ churches and altars that had been built into the stands as they could get. They had hung Sigurd's banner— a wolf's head on a red cloth—from the wall below them, and I kept looking at it because it gave me courage. Had he been sitting among them, Svein could have hurled a spear in any direction and not hit anyone, because the Romans and other crews had not dared get too close to so many iron-sheathed, battle-ready men.

I wondered whether Cynethryth was among them; I could not see her, but that was not to say she wasn't there. Besides, I knew Asgot would be present, for he would be drooling at the prospect of seeing how his scheme would unfold, and so there was every chance that Cynethryth had come too.

"If you get the Vindr Berstuk, go for his left side, lad," Bram said, rolling his shoulders and stretching his neck. "He's got an old injury in his lower leg that makes him favor his right. Hides it well, but it's there all right. Go for his left and you'll either get lucky and cut him or he'll overcompensate and leave his right side open." He grinned. "And then cut him." The crowd was chanting now. They were happy because the sky was blue and the sun was shining and there was money to be made. Lord Guido stood behind a table on which three iron-bound chests sat with their lids open. His soldiers were trying to keep order, corralling the hordes into lines so that they could place their wagers. Men were eyeballing us, weighing what kind of men we were before they parted with their silver. "Now, if you get the African, run him around for a while," Bram went on. "Keep moving. Make the whoreson chase his own tail like a damn dog." He pressed a thick finger into my chest. "But when you can, go for his legs." He tilted his head toward Svein. "These big trolls always leave their legs vulnerable. I've never seen a tree that couldn't be cut down with a good blade on the end of a strong arm."

I nodded. My mouth was as dry as a long-dead corpse's fart. "What if I get the Greek?" I asked. Bram thought about this for a while and then gave a slight shake of his beard.

"Then run, Raven," he said. "And I'll kill the cur just as soon as I've finished with my own snot-swilling son of a crone."

"We could just take those chests," Svein suggested,

nodding toward Lord Guido and his long shields. Svein was right. There were enough of us to kill the long shields and carry the silver back to the ships. I doubted the Romans or the visiting crews or anyone else would try to stop us.

"You know as well as I do, Red, that this isn't about the money anymore," Bram said, and I too knew he was right.

Svein nodded, finishing off a thick red braid, for it does not do for a man's hair to fly in his eyes when he is trying to avoid sharp steel. "We'll leave this place with a fame hoard that'll outshine Baldr's golden ball sack," Bram said, tightening straps and tugging a fold of his brynja up and over his belt to spread the weight of it.

Lord Guido had made us walk into the middle of the arena so that everyone could watch how we moved and get a look at our weapons. And we must have looked like war gods. The rings of my brynja glinted in the sun, and my helmet was polished so that it looked more like silver than iron. I was wearing my tall boots and had sheathed my lower legs and forearms in boiled leather because I had seen too many men take cuts in those parts. It was not for nothing that many men's swords were named Leg-Biter. I had sword, long knife, short knife, shield, and spear. Bram was armed the same way, but Svein hefted the long two-handed ax, and its edge was honed to the keenest, thinnest, most wicked smile. We wore no cloaks, because a cloak can snag a blade or trap your arm, but were iron men ready to plow flesh and sow death. Whatever the reputation of the three champions we were to fight, if I were in the crowd that day, I would not have been quick to put money against us.

"Here, lad, give me your hand." I turned to Olaf, who had come to wish us luck. Cynethryth was with him. Wide-eyed, she was looking up at the crowds, perhaps imagining what the place must have been like in the time of the old emperors. I held out my right hand, letting Olaf tie a braided leather thong around my wrist. The thong had a slip loop on the other end. "If it comes to sword work, pull that tight over the grip," he said, nodding at the looped end. The thong was so that when I died, I should still be able to grip my sword, and that thought soured my guts even more. "It's just in case, lad," he added, slapping my shoulder and smiling through his beard. "I expect you to spear gut your man before it ever gets to swords."

"Thank you, Uncle," I managed, rolling my tongue around my mouth, trying to stir some saliva. Olaf reached into the scrip on his belt and pulled out a silver coin.

"Put this under your tongue. It will help." I did, and it did. "I'm proud of you, Raven," Olaf said then, looking up at the time-ravaged walls of the Amphitheatrum Flavium. "Sigurd is too. More than he'd ever like you to know."

I took the coin out of my mouth and smiled weakly. "He told me to fuck the gods," I said. Olaf turned back to me, his eyes blue as glacier ice.

"Then fuck them," he said.

Olaf went over to speak to Bram, and my eyes met Cynethryth's. I had not been this close to her for a very long time, and at that moment we were the only two people in the Amphitheatrum Flavium, so that I was only faintly aware of the din of the crowd like the murmur of some distant seashore and of my blood gushing through my veins.

"Did you know, Cynethryth?" I said, the frost in those words making my face bones tremble.

"Know what?" she asked. Her hollow cheeks were pools of shadow that defied the midday sun. Her once golden hair was a greasy tufted crop, and her skin was as pale as the dismembered statues that still looked down on us from the heights.

"That Asgot put the raven's wing in his sack," I said. Her green eyes flickered at that. "You think I would be standing here if I had a choice?"

She frowned. "All I know is that Asgot fears you," she said. "He believes you are Ódin-shielded, though he will not admit it. He thinks that shield is our curse, Raven." Try as I might, I could not penetrate her gaze. It was as though she were the other side of a smoky hearth. "For the Father of the Slain's name means frenzy, and his love of chaos clings to you."

"So you believe in our gods now, Cynethryth?" I said. One brow lifted, and her lips twitched like a fishing line between finger and thumb.

"Death follows you, Raven. Or perhaps you follow death."

"Then I am well named," I said through my teeth. She came closer, and I could smell her. A sweet, pungent burned sage smell. It sickened me because she smelled like Asgot. She took something from around her neck—a small purse on a string of twisted horsehair—and reached up to place it over my head.

"Do not take it off until the fight is over," she said,

tucking the purse into the neck of my brynja. "Do not even open it. Just give it back to me afterward."

"What is it?" I asked, my chest so tight that I could hardly breathe.

"Something to keep you safe," she said.

"You have barely looked at me since Frankia."

She stepped back, and for a heartbeat I saw through the bitter smoke the girl I had known. "You once swore to protect me, Raven," she said. "How can you do that if you are dead?" And with that she walked away, and the sound of thousands came crashing down on me like a great wave.

"It's time, lad," Bram said, gripping my shoulder.

"Kill them," Svein snarled, slapping the haft of his ax.

In front of us Lord Guido's champions stood waiting, their deadly-looking weapons glinting in the sunlight. "Gods help us," I whispered, because those grim-faced men looked terrifying. At the arena's edge men were near enough to throw their coins at Guido and his men, desperate to make their wagers while there was still time. The rest of Guido's long shields marched into the killing ground and formed a large ring of steel, their sun-browned faces fish-eyed so that it was impossible to tell what they were thinking. In this way they were as different from Norsemen as cats from dogs.

Guido strode over and stood before us, his dark eyes probing, the faintest keel twist of his lips betraying a man who loathes the mired path he must take to get to the feast. He was a warrior, this one. His were an eagle's eyes, keen as rivets and predatory. His mouth was the tight line of a man who takes no joy in food or drink, and the only hair on his face was a short black beard trimmed to a perfect wedge.

"What are we waiting for, Guido, your damned beard to grow? It looks like a girl's cunny pelt," Bram growled as Guido eyeballed him. Guido said nothing and, seemingly satisfied with Svein and Bram, turned those eagle's eyes on me. He could not have known how it was that we three came to be standing before him and would have expected us to be the best fighters Jarl Sigurd had. That was why that keen gaze lingered on my stripling's beard and the clench of my jaw that kept my teeth from chattering with fear. For my feigr was upon me, clinging to me like the stink to a shit bucket, and Guido's beak nose must have been full of it.

He spun on his heel, pointing at Svein with his left hand and the bald-headed African with his right. The two giants glared at each other with enough flint and steel to start a blaze, which I took to mean that they were both happy with the match. Then Guido matched Bram with Theo the Greek, which meant I would fight the Wend Berstuk. Guido gestured that we should step back to put some ground between us and the men we were soon to fight, which we did, edging back to the long shields.

"Remember what I told you, lad," Bram growled. "He's weakest on his left."

I had watched the Wend fight and kill over and over again and had seen nothing weak about him, but I nodded to Bram anyway as we spread out, each against his opponent as the noise inside the arena surged. It was not even a third full, yet the clamor was horren-

dous. *It has always been a place of death.* Gregor's
words rolled around inside my skull.

"Thór be with you, little brother," Svein boomed
above the crowd's din. I could not look at him because
I did not want him to see the bowel-melting fear in my
face. It was bad enough that Guido had seen it, but
rather him than my oath-brothers. I rolled my shoulders because the shield on my left arm felt as heavy as
Serpent's anchor. My feet were rooted to the ground
like Yggdrasil, the World-Tree, so that I feared I might
topple over onto my face the moment I tried to move
my legs. My heart was thumping against my ribs. The
hairs on my neck bristled. Cold sweat sluiced between
my shoulder blades, the muscles in my thighs began to
tremble, and I eyed the spear in the Wend's hand. *The
Aesir must use such a weapon,* I thought, *to gut
Sæhrímnir, the giant boar that those in Valhöll feast
on.* The iron-sheathed shaft was two heads taller than
Berstuk, and the blade was Frankish, huge and winged
to stop it from sticking too deeply into a man's flesh.
My flesh.

He wore no brynja, instead protecting himself with
furs and boiled leather, but he is a fool who thinks a
man with such poor war gear will be easier to kill,
for such armor will often stop a blade better than any
brynja. Besides, Berstuk must have killed men enough
to own spoils that included a brynja or two, yet he
spurned iron in favor of animal skins, which told me
he was confident enough in his own way of fighting.
No one had killed him yet, and many had tried.

His helmet was iron, though, taken from a dead
blauman, I guessed, for it was pointed like those we
had found beneath the blaumen's turbans. This one

looked too tight for Berstuk. As it was, the Wend was an ugly troll, all grizzled beard, bulbous nose, and pus-spilling boils, but that helmet squeezed his brows so that his eyes were little piss slashes in dirty snow. It made a scowl not even a mother could love and was enough to wither my balls and make me wish I had died in my sleep the night before.

He must have untangled his name from the tumult of voices, for he turned to the crowd and raised his shield and spear as I had seen him do before.

"Norseman, do you know the name Berstuk?" It was one of the long shields who had called out, his English thick with another tongue's twisting. He was a short, thickset man with a neat beard and deep dark holes for eyes. "You have not heard the name?" he asked. I shook my head. "Berstuk is the name of an evil god that his people believe in. A god of the forest." He dangled those words before me like a hooked and baited line, his eyes waiting expectantly.

"Then the god must be uglier than an old sack of arseholes," I said, "if this lump of stinking pig shit is anything to go by. Little wonder shame makes him hide in a forest." I felt better for that, perhaps because the dark-browed soldier's eyes widened a hair's width in surprise. Then Guido was gone, and the others began to close the distance, eager to stop standing and start fighting. So I put one foot forward, relieved because I did not fall, and went to face my doom.

Svein and the African struck first, their shields clashing like the antlers of two great bull elks. The crowd roared, and that sounded like the thunder a burning hall makes when the thick roof beams catch and the fire makes its own wind.

Then the Wend came. He swung the spear like an ax, and that heavy blade would have scythed my head off my shoulders, but I got my shield up in time and the blade clattered against it. He edged around to my right and made a straight thrust that I parried with my shaft, and then I rammed the point at his face, but he ducked and the blade glanced off his helmet, at which the crowd cheered.

I could hear the clashing of the other men's weapons: of Svein's ax against the African's shield boss, the Greek's spear clacking against Bram's. I could hear their visceral grunts, but I dared not tear my eyes from the ugly Wend whose big iron-sheathed spear was light in his hands and seemed to come at me from all places at once. That winged blade bit splintered chunks from my shield, and I kept my feet moving, desperate not to give the Wend an easy target. He stabbed under my shield, the blade sliding off the leather shin guards, then he thrust high and I was not quick enough, and the point burst into my brynja, sending broken rings flying like water in the sun. The blood-hungry mobs yelled, and I staggered backward with the searing pain, but when I looked down, there was no blood and I knew that my leather gambeson had held. *Go for his left side . . . he's got an old injury . . .* Bram's voice growled in my head, and so I lunged for Berstuk's left thigh. He shield blocked. I lunged again. And again. He crabbed left so that I had to turn with him, and even then I could not get through. I knew that without all that hard training with Sigurd and Black Floki, I would already have been bleeding out in the dirt. And yet feigr is feigr.

"Some fight, hey!" Svein yelled, but I had not the

spit to waste on words, and I don't think Bram had, either. He was a raging storm of steel in my peripheral vision, but the Greek was quick and strong and was dealing with everything the Norseman could throw at him like a man bailing out the bilge.

I shield blocked a high thrust, sending the blade higher, but Berstuk used that momentum, turning the shaft end over end and then stepping wide and ramming the butt toward my face, which I dropped, taking the blow on my helmet. It must have knocked my eyes spinning in my head, for I was blind and stumbling. Berstuk came on, plunging that blade again and again, and somehow, by luck more than skill, I got my shield in the way.

"Stand, Raven!" Bram yelled. "Stand!" But my knee bones were slipping in their joints, and I was slewing sideward, foot over foot. Then I hit a wall. Not a wall. Svein.

He took a massive blow on his shouldered shield, grimacing as he levered me upright. "Kill that ugly fucking Wend," he sneered, launching at the African with a brutal ax dance that put the blauman on his back foot as I squinted through blinding pain and circled left. The Wend's spear was too long, and I could not get near him with my own. I strode backward, needing time, and luckily for me the Wend took the opportunity to crow to the crowd, raising his arms again as though I were dead already. He had more swagger than a jarl with a golden cock, that one. Changing to an overarm grip, I rolled my shoulder, threw back an arm made brawny by rowing and spear work, and let fly. But Berstuk's instinct was as sharp as his Frankish spear, and he spun back, lifting his shield so that my spear clattered off it, falling harmlessly somewhere over his left shoulder. And then he grinned because he thought I had wagered and lost.

"You look like a troll whore's armpit," I growled at him, spitting a thick string of spittle over my beard as I drew my sword. The crowd was baying for blood. "Your mother must have fucked a rancid corpse." I could not tell if he knew what I was saying, but it made no difference, for the Wend wanted to kill me badly enough anyway. And now he thought it would be easy because I had lost my spear. He came within spitting distance, and I realized he was even uglier than I had thought. A twist of a smile split an angry boil above his lip, spilling yellow slime into his beard, and he was growling like a stiff-hackled dog. A man bellowed in pain, and the crowd roared, but I did not know who was hurt.

"Come, then, Wend," I said, showing my teeth. I beckoned him on with my sword, for I realized then that the fear had gone out of me, knocked out by Berstuk perhaps, and if I was feigr, so be it. I thought I heard Olaf's voice cut through the surge, and my blood began to simmer like broth over the hearth fire. "Come and cut my life's thread if you think you can," I snarled.

His winged blade probed low, and I blocked it with my blade, then the Wend reversed his spear and stepped into my low thrust, binding it to the right. Our shields clashed, and for a heartbeat I smelled him; then we broke, Berstuk shoving me off because he knew that inside his spear blade I was dangerous. Now that blade flashed like lightning, and my shield was everywhere at once, the arm behind it burning with the effort. I was strong, but so was the Wend. I cursed because I was not good enough to find his weakness, and I wanted to wipe the stinging sweat from my eyes but knew that to take my eyes from that spear even for the beat of a bird's wing was to die. His eyes flicked to my chest, and my sword was already coming inside to block, but then he pulled the thrust and my blade wheeled down and out, hitting nothing. His blade streaked in, gouging into my brynja and sliding along my ribs. Vicious, molten iron pain scorched my flesh, and I did not have to look down to know I was cut. From the crowd's thunder, they knew it too.

Berstuk swung the spear from far right, around his head, no easy thing one-handed, and the iron-sheathed shaft hammered against my sword, knocking it from my grasp. But I did not lose it, for it hung from Olaf's leather braid as I blundered out of reach of his killing blow, grasping for the sweat-slick grip. Then the spear scythed down onto my shield's rim, and Berstuk yanked it back so that the iron wings hooked on the shield's edge, ripping it from my grasp.

My feigr reared like a dragon prow mounting a spumy rolling wave, and I knew death was coming. So I roared defiance to the All-Father, blindly swinging my sword with all the strength I possessed, and it cut through iron and wood, lopping off the last three feet of Berstuk's spear. I threw my left foot forward and slammed my sword's hilt into his beard, but his neck was thick as a young oak and the blow did no more than anger him, so that he hurled the broken shaft aside and pulled his sword, which rasped from its scabbard. Then the swirling rage of sound leaped like a flame, and I turned to see Bram on his knees, blood cascading over his gaping eyes and streaming from his beard. One arm hung limp, but the other stretched out like a crooked branch, fingers grasping. Even Berstuk watched as Theo the Greek bent and picked up Bram's sword by the blade, offering the Norseman the grip. The Bear's trembling hand grasped it, and he slumped back, his great shoulders caving in and his blade biting dirt.

The Greek turned to Lord Guido, palming sweat from his eyes, his chest billowing. Guido glanced up to where Sigurd and the rest were sitting, then nodded to his man, who stepped up neatly, putting the point of his sword on the inside edge of Bram's collarbone. Svein and the African were still fighting, and I was too far away, and then, with two hands on the hilt, the Greek plunged the blade deep into Bram's chest, ripping into his great heart. Blood spewed from the cave of his mouth, and he toppled sideward; Svein must have known what had happened, for he bellowed loud enough to shake the beams in Valhöll.

Berstuk grinned savagely and came again, hungry to finish me himself before the Greek could join the kill. Our swords clashed, and the right side of my chest screamed in pain. My brynja's rings were blood-slick, and life must have been sluicing from the wound, because shadows were crowding my vision and my head felt light as feathers, as though my spirit was halfway out of my body. I was still swinging, sometimes hitting his shield, mostly hitting nothing, and I spit another curse at the gods and the Norns whose warp and weft had led me to that place and no farther.

Then the Greek was there behind Berstuk, still puffing, but the Wend snarled at him to stay back. This would be his kill, another hacksilver death for his fame hoard. I staggered backward, my hands losing feeling, so that I thought I must drop my sword. I was in a shadow world now and was no longer even aware of pain, just of pieces of myself floating away like jetsam on the tide.

Our swords clashed, and the crowd's roar was as muffled as distant thunder. I was aware that my sword was hanging again from Olaf's rope at the end of my numbed arm, and then Berstuk rammed his blade into that loop and sawed through it. I did not hear my blade hit the ground. Over the Wend's shoulder I saw Svein's great ax slice the massive African's head from his shoulders, the Norseman's mouth cavernous with a triumphant howl that I could not hear. Berstuk kicked my sword away, and somewhere in my mind I heard a god laugh because I would never cross Bifröst, the Rainbow-Bridge, and sit at the high seat of Ódin's hall.

I felt no pain as I bit into my bottom lip, bursting it, but I did smell the Wend's fetid breath as he snarled a curse at me, which was all slaver and snot hitting my face. He took hold of my neck and brought his sword up to shoulder height, pulling it back for the killing thrust. And that was when I blew a mouthful of hot blood into his eyes, at the same time pulling my long knife. Blinded, he thrust the sword, which slid across my shoulder as I hammered my blade into his mouth, breaking through the back of his skull. I smelled his piss as he died, then yanked my knife free, sending wet gray gobbets flying, and stepped back to let the corpse fall face-first onto the ground.

The noise of the crowd flooded back in, and I bent and snatched up my sword, striding and stumbling toward where Svein, his helmet off and his long red hair lank with sweat, now fought the Greek. His ax wove a deadly pattern through the air, and the Greek, having no shield now, could not get close enough with his sword. Neither had he seen me coming, and most likely he thought me dead. Then Svein turned his opponent so that Theo's back was square on to me and I could not fail to hack him in two from neck to arse. But before I could, the long shields came at us, closing the ring of iron and steel, their spears leveled, and Theo spun, backing into that ring as neatly as a knife into a sheath.

Svein looped his ax, inviting the long shields to come and die, and then I heard the howling of wolves and looked up to see Sigurd and Floki and Penda and all the rest pounding across the arena, blades and teeth glinting in the sun. The short soldier who had told me about the Wendish god of the forest was yelling at the other men, including Guido, who had drawn his sword, ready to fight, his eagle eyes wide as coins. As one, soldiers threw down their spears and shook off their long shields, raising their hands to show they were unarmed, which was either very brave or very stupid with a Fellowship of warriors coming to kill them. But Sigurd hollered, and his men heard. He yelled at them to sheathe their blades, which they did just in time, and I was glad to see it, for sometimes killing cannot be stopped even by a jarl.

Penda and Bjarni came to me, throwing my arms around their shoulders before I could fall. The others were slapping Svein's sweat-drenched back, and still others were gathering over Bram's corpse.

"You are Jarl Sigurd?" the short soldier asked of Sigurd. Guido stood at this man's shoulder, eyeing Sigurd fiercely.

The jarl nodded. "And these are my men," he announced, chin high. Then he glared at Guido and pointed accusingly. "Bring your money," he said. "We have won." Now he pointed at Theo the Greek, who stood ashen-faced among his men. "That worm would be dead now if your men had not stopped the fight."

"You will have your money, Norseman," Guido said. "But you will have to wait." He looked up at the baying crowds who perhaps felt cheated of the blood they had come for. "I could not risk keeping so much near these savages," he said.

Sigurd shook his golden head. "My friend is crossing the shimmering bridge," he said, his voice heavy as storm clouds, "and I must see to him. We are camped at the stone wharf west of the Palatine Hill. You will bring the money tomorrow at dawn." Guido nodded. The short soldier eyed Sigurd like a man who stares at the sky wondering if rain is coming.

"You will have your silver, Sigurd," the short man said.

"If not, I will flay the skin from your flesh and nail it to my ship's mast," Sigurd threatened him. Then he turned his back on them and went to see to his friend, whose blood was mixed with the dirt of that ancient place of death.

chapter
eighteen

W<small>E HAD</small> won, but it did not feel like it to me.
They carried Bram's corpse back to the wharf,
where they laid him on a fine bear's pelt and cleaned
the crusting blood from his head, beard, and face. He
was death-stiff now, and his hand still gripped his
sword so that it would have taken a stronger man
than Svein to prize his thick fingers from the grip,
and Black Floki muttered that that was how it should
be, given the warrior that Bram had been.

I had been barely conscious by the time we came to
the river, but I was alive enough to be surprised when
Asgot came to help Olaf see to my wounds. I lay on a
pile of furs on the quayside next to *Serpent*, looking up
at the dark blue sky in which gulls wheeled and cried.
Bjarni said I was corpse-white like Bram because so
much blood had leaked from the gash between the
third and fourth ribs on my right side. But when I suggested through torn bloody lips that I was perhaps still
feigr, Bjarni barked a laugh.

"That scratch won't do for you," he said, nodding
at the wound as Olaf washed it with clean water
hot off the boil. It stung like Hel, but I knew worse
was coming. "It seems even the gods can't kill you,
Raven."

"Perhaps it was they who spared him," Asgot suggested. Bjarni considered this deeply, then smiled.

"That blood-spitting trick was Loki-cunning," he said. But I could not answer. My teeth were clamped down on a leather knife sheath because Asgot was bringing a red-hot iron toward my torn flesh. I cannot explain the pain of it. I do not have the skald-craft to whet those words sharp enough. But when Asgot pressed that searing iron to the wound because I had lost too much blood already and could lose no more, I would have chosen death if I could. I did not even pass out from the pain as men usually do at such things, and perhaps that had something to do with the herbs Asgot had tipped down my throat in the arena. Or perhaps it was the All-Father's way of punishing me for defying my own wyrd, for surely I was supposed to be dead, another corpse bled out for the people of Rome. I spit the sheath out and screamed as the blood hissed and the smoke bloomed and the iron stink of my own burned flesh brought tears to my eyes. I was half aware of Olaf telling me to scream louder, to wake Rome's rotten dead and bring them whining from their graves, in between trying to pour neat wine into me.

"At least you won't feel the other cuts and bruises for a day or two," Penda said, coming to see how it was going. "Christ, Raven, I lost count of the hits you took." But luckily most of those hits had been from the butt end of Berstuk's long spear.

"The bastard was playing with me," I squeezed through my teeth. "Killing me slowly."

Olaf's brows hoisted. "Aye, well, he won't do that again," he said, cutting newly bought linen into strips.

Asgot spread a foul-smelling poultice across the ravaged, blackened furrow, and Olaf bound it tight. The wine stung my burst lip but not enough to stop me from trying to drown myself in it, and Penda was good enough to keep filling the horn I clutched white-knuckled. The Wessexman pointed out happily that I was not leaking from the wound, which I took to mean he was relieved I was not belly pierced. Then he said: "It wouldn't do to waste half-decent wine," and filled his horn to the brim.

The others were building a hero's pyre. You need a lot of wood to burn a man properly, but the only wood near the river was from gorse and thickets and good for nothing more than the cook fires. Neither were there many proper trees in the city itself, and so Sigurd had offered a crew of rough-looking Frisians more silver than they could refuse for their boat, which was moored downriver against the wooden quay. It was bigger than a faering but smaller than our snekkjes, and as a boat it had seen better days, the kind of craft good only for rivers or island-hopping. But Sigurd did not want to sail it, and now Svein, Knut, Bragi, and Gunnar were breaking up the timbers with axes while others laid the pyre.

"We will burn our brother tonight so that the flames of that great warrior will sing in the darkness," Sigurd said, crouching and lifting the fur covering me to appraise Olaf's handiwork. "We won, Raven," he said, the words as hollow as the horn I still clutched.

"Only just," I said, trying to keep the pain out of my face in front of the jarl. Truth was, it didn't feel as though we had won, not with Bram stiff and cold.

"You fought well. You're still clumsy as a beardless boy with his first whore," he said through a sad smile, "but your spear work was almost good. The Wend was a great fighter."

"The Wend was ugly as a week-old turd," I said. Then I remembered the small leather bag Cynethryth had hung around my neck before the fight. Gingerly, I felt under the fur and was surprised how relieved I was that it was still there. "Will you tell Cynethryth I would speak with her?" I asked. The wine was at last taking the edge off the pain and filling my head with wool. Sigurd looked at me skeptically.

"There are some fights a man should walk away from," he said. "You know that, don't you? Blades or Loki-cunning cannot help you when it comes to women."

"I just want to talk with her," I said, those words sliding off Sigurd like water off greased leather.

"Get some rest, Raven," he said, standing. "Speak to the girl and then sleep. I'll wake you when we light the fire." I nodded, easing myself up onto a rolled fur bolster as Sigurd steered Rolf and some of the others away who had come over to see how I was.

Just moving my right arm brought fresh waves of agony flooding over me, and so I tried to keep it stone still, with my left hand yanking the purse from my neck to break the horsehair thong. I worried the drawstring loose with my teeth and tipped the contents of the purse onto my chest. And I felt Yggdrasil, the World-Tree, crash down so that my insides shook with the force of it. On the white linen bindings on my chest, glossy as a mussel shell from a thousand clutchings, was Bram's bear claw charm. Now I clutched it, hoping that no one had seen it, shivering with the fjord-cold omen of it.

"I told you not to open it, Raven." Cynethryth's voice pulled me to the surface, where I gasped for breath. I had not heard her coming, but something in her face told me that she had been there a while. She stood on the wharf's edge, the sinking sun over her right shoulder blinding me and making spun gold of the strands of her hair that were lifting in the breeze. Behind her, their timbers sun-gilded, like treasures from Fáfnir's hoard, *Serpent* and the other ships rested hull against hull. "It would have been better if you had never known."

"What have you done, Cynethryth?" I could nearly smell the seidr magic in it.

"You were feigr." She said it like an accusation. "I took that feigr and put it on Bram instead." She shrugged. "You would be dead otherwise." She was watching the men breaking up the last strakes of the Frisians' old boat, seemingly lost in the dull hammer rhythm of the ax heads on seasoned wood. Where her tunic sleeves ended I saw she had cut runes into her skin, the lines dark with old blood and charcoal.

I closed my eyes, hoping it was all some wine- and pain-woven dream or perhaps a stupor wraith summoned by Asgot's healing herbs. But when I opened them again, Cynethryth was still there. "Are you a völva now, then?" I asked, and now I was accusing, because a völva is a witch and it was not so long ago that Cynethryth was a Christian.

"Asgot says I have talent." She was glaring at me, her dark green eyes made black by the sun's glare behind her.

"Asgot is a putrid lump of goat shit," I said. "He tried to kill me and came within a flea's cock of doing it, too." I took a fur from the pile and threw it at her, wincing with the pain of it. She laid it down next to me and sat, hugging her knees the way she always did.

"I told you. He was testing the gods," she said. "He needed to know if you really are Ódin-favored like they say."

"And what does he think now?" I asked, hatred for the godi snarling my words.

Cynethryth considered this for a moment, then cocked her head to one side.

"He doesn't know what I did. He is surer than ever that you are favored." I grunted and shook my head. I did not feel favored, lying there with a gash of seared, stinking flesh as long as a drinking horn between my ribs. "But he is also certain that other men die because of you," she said. "The All-Father loves chaos. He demands blood." She gave a poisonous grin. "And so men bleed." Men like Bram, I thought.

"You should never have done it," I said. And then, because I was angry with her and heartsick that my friend had, through Cynethryth's foul seidr, been saddled with my feigr, I tried to hurt her. "Weohstan would hate you now," I said, watching where that arrow landed. Weohstan, who had been her brother and whom Cynethryth had loved so dearly. But Weohstan was in the grave now.

Her eyes fogged, and she turned her face away so that I would not see her tears, and even after everything, I wished I could take those spite-curdled words back, wished I could hold Cynethryth and make things between us golden again as they used to be.

"I have to tell them what you did," I said, gripping

the bear's claw as though by holding it I could somehow hold on to Bram. "They have to know."

"If you do, they will blame you for his death," she said, turning back to me. I knew she was right. And perhaps Asgot was right, too. Maybe I *was* the poisoned blade in the Fellowship's side. Maybe I was the raven, the herald of death, the scavenger of the slain. I had brought death to the men and women of Abbotsend. Bjorn was worm food because of me, and now Bram was gone, dead because my feigr had become his. How many others sat in Ódin's hall waiting for me that they might avenge their deaths? "Take this for the pain," Cynethryth said, offering me another purse. I kept my hands by my sides. "It is just herbs," she said, putting the purse on my chest and standing. "In water it will taste foul, but in wine or mead it is not so bad."

She walked away, leaving me with the boulder weight of Bram's death, and I yelled at Penda to bring more wine.

There was no pissing rain to spoil Bram's death pyre. The moon had waned, and much of the ancient city was cloaked in night's thick pelt, but the stone wharf and towering walls built long ago to keep Rome's enemies out glowed red with a hero's flames. The Tiberis was a sluggish flow of molten iron upon which our blaze-kissed ships waited patient yet eager to ride that flow back to the sea. As were we all eager now. But first we would honor our fallen sword-brother with a feast worthy of the Aesir. Beasts were slaughtered, and their cook fires added a greasy glow to the night sky so that folk came from all around, drawn by the unnatural dawn that flooded our camp. Men traded and argued and wenched and ate, but mostly they drank in honor of Bram, who had enjoyed mead more than any man ever did. The Bear's name rang around the camp like the kiss of swords. Stories spilled from greasy lips, weaving a saga-tale too great for any one skald, and the golden weft in all those tellings was Bram: Bram who killed King Hygelac Storm-Temper's champion and swam the Kattegat Sea. Bram who had once knocked out a bull with one punch and whom no man had ever outdrunk. Bram who had killed a troll.

Penda came over to where I lay, his hair sticking out like hedgehog spines and his scarred cheeks red from the fires' heat.

"You've got the right idea, lad," he slurred, waving his drinking horn through the air and sloshing wine across my skins. "If you drink lying down, you can't fall over." Sigurd and Olaf had all but carried me between them over to Bram's pyre so that I could pay my last respects before flint and steel summoned the flames, and I had laid the pouch containing Bram's bear claw in the crook of his folded arm. Neither Sigurd nor Olaf had asked what was in that pouch, for which I was glad, and they had taken me back to my bed because just being upright made my head swim and my side scream with pain.

"Seeing as you're here, you can empty that for me," I said, nodding at the half-full piss bucket by my feet. "This wine runs through me like brine through a fish's gills."

"I can see that," Penda squeezed through a grimace. "But it's the least I can do for the man who has made us all rich as bloody kings. That sly-looking bastard Guido is here with the silver you won us."

"He's here now?" I twisted, ignoring the searing

pain to look for Lord Guido among the sea of firelit faces. "He was supposed to come tomorrow."

"Sigurd was hardly going to turn the man away, was he?" Penda said. "Not with that much silver burning a hole through Guido's sea chest." All in all I'd had enough of burning one way or another and said as much.

"Hurts, does it, lad?" Penda asked, nodding at my right side, where the flesh still smelled burned. I didn't dignify that with an answer, instead telling Penda to help me over to where Sigurd was hosting Guido and his men.

"This is Raven," Sigurd announced to Lord Guido, who nodded respectfully from his furs, showing that he remembered me from the arena.

"I hope your wounds heal quickly and cleanly, Raven," Guido said. "You fought with great heart today, as did your friend," he added, glancing at Bram's charred shape at the heart of the raging pyre. The heat made you have to dip your head or else risk blistering your cheeks. As it was, there were plenty of us with singed beards.

I nodded at Guido, but my gaze was drawn to the man with the stockier build and deep-set eyes sitting beside him. He was the soldier who had spoken to me before the fight, though now he wore a long silken tunic with three-quarter arms and over it a blue cloak embroidered with white crosses. His boots were studded with pearls.

"Must be a White Christ man," Svein muttered through his beard. Though he was nothing like Father Egfrith, this one. He was a man of some standing.

"We have brought you that which you won fairly

by skill and bravery," Guido said, sweeping a palm toward the ironbound chest around which seventeen of his long shields stood sweating like a Norseman after a roll in a whore's bed. Theo the Greek was among them, I noticed, and I was not surprised to see the sweat glisten on his face, seeing as he had killed the man we now honored with fire and drink.

"One thousand two hundred and fifty Roman libra," Guido said, which meant nothing to me, but I remembered Sigurd saying it was five men's weight in silver, and that I understood well enough.

Sigurd nodded, eyeballing the two men sitting across from him on thick furs.

"I said to come tomorrow," he said, pointing his mead horn accusingly. "Why have you come now? You can see we are burning a sword-brother. It is no good thing to be busy with scales and talk of money at such a time." The jarl's eyes flickered in recognition of Theo, who stood with his head bowed like the other long shields.

Guido was about to reply, but the smaller man stopped him with a hand. His beard, which glistened like a wet otter, half hid a smile just as well greased.

"Sigurd, please forgive my English. I learned the tongue from a priest many years ago, but . . ." He shrugged. ". . . a blade soon rusts if it is never used." I suspected that the man's English was better than Sigurd's, and the jarl suspected that too from the squinch of his eye, though he was not going to admit it. Instead he circled two fingers in a gesture telling his guest to spit out whatever was on his rusty tongue.

"My name is Nikephoros, and this is General Bardanes Tourkos."

"Not Guido, then?" Sigurd asked, to which the man we had known first as Red Cloak, then Guido, and now Bardanes shook his head and inclined it toward Nikephoros as though to warn Sigurd that his companion was not a man to be interrupted. Father Egfrith drifted over to us like a silent fart.

Nikephoros said: "I am Basileus Romaiôn. Emperor of the Romans and God's anointed protector of the true faith." Wine sprayed from Sigurd's lips, and some of it struck Nikephoros's face. Bardanes looked horrified, but Nikephoros dabbed at his cheek and beard with the long sleeve of his tunic, never taking his eyes off Sigurd. "You do not believe I am who I say I am?" he asked.

"Oh, I believe you," Sigurd said, grinning at Olaf. "And did you know that Olaf here is the Christhumping son of a dog they call the Pope?"

Nikephoros shook his head. "That *I* do not believe, for I met with Pope Leo three days ago, and he certainly looked nothing like this rough fellow."

"He's got me, Sigurd!" Olaf barked, slapping a tree-trunk thigh. "There's no fooling this fox." We were all grinning like fools, except for Nikephoros and Bardanes and his long shields, who did not seem to understand English at all.

"Besides," Sigurd said, "I have met the emperor. I have . . . traded with Karolus. We are old friends." His wolf grin gleamed in the fire's glow.

"The barbarian Karolus is not without power," Nikephoros admitted, "which is why Pope Leo needs him, indeed, why Leo placed the crown on his head. But my kingdom in the east outshines anything the west can boast. For five hundred years men have called it New Rome." He threw out his arms. "This city is a ruin, Sigurd, a shadow of what it once was. Ruins lie on ruins, and all is tainted by unbelievers. Pope Leo is not strong enough to keep the wolves out of his fold." Sigurd hitched an eyebrow at that. "But Constantinople? My city is blinding in its glory."

"Constantinople?" Sigurd said, scratching his cheek.

Nikephoros nodded, glancing at Bardanes. "I believe you men of the north know it by another name, Miklagard." He smiled at the simplicity of that name, for Miklagard means "the Great City."

"You are from Miklagard?" Olaf growled, his eyelids heavy with wine.

Nikephoros and Bardanes shared a look of bewilderment, then Nikephoros gave an order to one of the long shields, who unslung a leather bag from his back and, approaching Nikephoros, unthreaded the straps from their silver clasps. Nikephoros climbed to his feet, and the soldier knelt, offering the open bag like a hard-won prize.

What's he got in there, Ódin's frothing mead horn? Bram gnarred in my mind. I looked at his death fire and saw the Bear's rib bones pulsing black and copper at the heart of the flames. Then an intake of breath brought me back, and I saw what Nikephoros was clutching. My eyes fed on it. It was a crown of wrought gold with a gold Christ cross on top and two more golden crosses dangling from strings of pearls on either side of the brow band. But those White Christ things could be pulled off and tossed in the river or melted down, and then it would be the kind of treasure a jarl would weigh anchor and go raiding for. It was the kind of treasure my mind had summoned before with the tale of Beowulf ringing in my ears. And in my mind it belonged to the hoard Beowulf found in the cave dwelling of Grendal's mother. To look at the thing was to want it. The flame-licked gleam of it wrenched men from whores' clutches and drew them over, their fire-bright faces hard as cliffs and their eyes wide and hungry.

Nikephoros placed the crown on his head, and those crosses hung down below his short oiled beard, and every man whose eyes drank the gold blaze of that crown imagined its weight on his own head. But none, not even Sigurd, would sit so comfortably beneath it as Nikephoros did, and I would have put money on the man's belonging to the crown.

"If you are the emperor of Miklagard," Sigurd said, tearing his eyes from the whispering gold, "then what are you doing here?"

"Aye." A thrum came from somewhere deep in Olaf's throat. "If your city is as Freyja-fair as you say, why are you here with us and the stinking river rats?" He slapped the back of his hand. "And the arse-biting flies," he added, wiping the mess on his breeks.

Beneath the golden band Nikephoros's eyes narrowed. "Maybe it would be better if we came back tomorrow, Jarl Sigurd, when you have honored your dead."

Sigurd eyeballed Nikephoros, his head slightly cocked toward his right shoulder. "Bram liked a story as much as any man," he said. "But a story told with a dry tongue tends to be a dry story." He looked up at Wiglaf, who was half listening and half fondling a plump gray-haired woman who looked old enough to be his mother. "More wine for our guests!" Sigurd said, then glanced at the ironbound chest that sat between Nikephoros and Bardanes. "And bring my scales."

Nikephoros's story was a good one, the kind that Norsemen like regardless of whether there's a spit of truth in it, because it was full of betrayal and murder and feuds and fights. For the sake of the tale Sigurd said he was happy to believe that Nikephoros was indeed the emperor of Miklagard, for, he said, men who have the most to lose often have the best stories to tell. And so it proved, because the basileus had lost his throne to a noble he had himself raised up, a man called Arsaber. Olaf pointed out helpfully that no one with any sense would trust a man whose name sounded so much like the way drunken Wessexmen pronounce "arse," but that was by the by. This Arsaber and his nest of vipers had turned on their master, and it was only by the grace of God that the basileus escaped with his life. "The grace of God and General Bardanes's unfailing sword arm," Nikephoros added, heaping high praise on the eagle-faced Bardanes, who accepted the flattery with both hands. It turned out that the emperor and some of his loyal men—those long shields who stood now among us—had fought their way to the royal berth, losing many to Arsaber's spears, and by the hairs of their balls caught enough wind in their sail to outrun the traitors.

"At least they didn't have to row," Svein rumbled, that sore memory of our escape from the Franks never far below the surface for any of us. It seemed that Arsaber's heart was not in the chase now that his hands were on the key to the emperor's treasury, and this, Sigurd said, showed that for all his low cunning and treachery Arsaber was not a deep thinker after all.

"If you steal a man's hoard, you had better steal his life, too, or you will sleep with one eye open for the rest of yours," the jarl put in, which stirred grunts and nods of agreement for the cold truth of it.

Nikephoros had pointed his prow toward the one city where a Christian emperor might hope to find friends or money or men or all three: Rome. But the high lords who serve the White Christ—Karolus, Pope Leo, and Nikephoros—though they share their god, would not be seen sharing a drinking horn, so we learned from these Greeks.

"I will take back my throne and see the traitors dead before anyone discovers this shameful betrayal," Nikephoros said. "I cannot have men look at my empire and see cracks in the stone," and by men I was guessing he meant Emperor Karolus and Pope Leo. "We have greater enemies than Arsaber and his rebels. The Moors have coveted my city for many years. They shall not have it while I live."

Although this might have been the truth, we had heard that Nikephoros had withheld the tribute that the last empress, Irene, had promised Caliph Harun ar-Rashid. The Moors would have blood if they could not have gold.

"Forgive me, lord, but I would ask a question if I may," Egfrith said, shuffling from the shadowed press of men so that his weasel face was dyed red with flame. I saw Bardanes's lip curl as though he did not think Egfrith worthy of speaking to his master, and this did not surprise me, for with his scruffy beard and straggled, untonsured head, Egfrith looked more like a farm thrall these days than a monk. But Nikephoros nodded, extending a hand as an invitation to speak. "These ungodly spectacles in the Amphitheatrum Flavium," Egfrith began, "these barbarous fights that have dragged Rome back to the dark, bloody years before her emperors found Christ . . ." He let that word rope hang, unsure, it seemed, how to tie it off.

"The basileus does not answer to any man, only God," Bardanes lashed, but again Nikephoros stilled him with a gesture.

"Seven weeks ago we came to Rome, our plan having grown over many days at sea," Nikephoros said, turning his gaze back to the man who counted—Sigurd. "General Bardanes became Lord Guido, a cloth merchant from Venice, and I became a common soldier in his guard." A smile touched Nikephoros's lips at this part, which told me that he was a man who enjoyed a good Loki-scheme for all his love of the White Christ. There were Christians and Christians, it seemed to me. "We had money. Not enough to buy the soldiers we would need but enough to upset the grain cart."

"Grain cart?" Sigurd repeated, twirling the end of his beard around a ringed finger.

Nikephoros smiled, pleased with himself. "My men buzzed through the city like bees from flower to flower, buying up every loaf of bread, every sack of grain." He glanced at Olaf. "If you want grain, you have only to ask," he said, brows arched, his short black beard glistening wetly. "At night we sabotaged the aqueducts, sank rotting animal carcasses in the public fountains, lit fires here and there. We killed men's pigs and oxen. Took animals from one man's pen and put them in another, anything to encourage suspicion and feud."

"That'll get men feuding all right," Olaf said appreciatively.

"We did whatever we could think of, sowing seeds of disorder that began to sprout all across the city. After four weeks of this Rome was like dry tinder waiting for a spark," Nikephoros went on. "You could smell trouble in the air."

"But not bread," Olaf muttered into his mead horn. I had smelled that trouble myself and seen the burned lean-tos and fountains guarded by armed men.

Bardanes glared at Uncle, but the Norseman simply dragged his forearm across his bushy beard and flapped a hand at the emperor of Miklagard to continue.

This Nikephoros has patience, I thought, and patience can make a man a dangerous enemy, which was another reason Arsaber should have tried harder to catch Nikephoros and kill him before making himself a nest in the man's throne.

"Lord Guido," the basileus went on, smiling like a fox, "secured an audience with Pope Leo. Armed mobs were roaming the streets. Murder and theft were rife. The poor blamed the rich, and the rich blamed Pope Leo."

"The Pope has soldiers," Sigurd said, as though that should have been enough.

"He has some," Nikephoros said, "but not enough to keep the peace. He needed them to guard his palace and his churches."

"Like all rich men Pope Leo wants to stay rich," Bardanes took up at a nod from his lord. "He sent for

Karolus, of course, but the Frankish king is up to his elbows in heathen blood, and meanwhile the people of Rome are battering down Leo's door." Bardanes sipped at his wine, more for show, I felt, than because he enjoyed it. "I gave Leo what he needed."

What Pope Leo needed was peace in Rome. And Lord Guido the cloth trader from Venice sold him the idea of peace steeped in blood. He suggested that if the people of Rome could be distracted, they would forget about their hungry bellies. Give them a reason to stay off the streets and, better still, give them the chance to make money. The idea of staging fights in the Amphitheatrum Flavium had appalled and disgusted Pope Leo. He had raged at the iniquity of the idea, the foulness of letting the arena be used for spectacles of death as it had been in Rome's past. But Lord Guido had been persuasive. Let a few willing fighters die in the arena and keep the good people of Rome safe on the streets, he had said. Four weeks was all he would need, Guido assured Pope Leo, by which time Karolus would be here with enough soldiers to restore order.

This was the gist of it so far as I could tell through my wine- and herb-soaked pain. There was no doubt Bardanes was as slippery as a snot-covered eel. He seemed to me the kind of man who could talk a bear into stepping out of its skin and rolling it up for you. As for Pope Leo, the way I saw things, he could not have been a fool or else he would not have risen so high among the White Christ followers. And yet he went along with Guido's plan or at least turned a blind eye to it, and I was thinking that strange until I heard the bit where Guido had promised Leo a cut of the money he made from folk's wagers. The Pope's coffers were light these days in large part thanks to the warships and crews he maintained to protect the coast from Moors.

"There was never any shortage of fighters," Nikephoros said. "Dozens came to fight and thousands came to watch, and my chests began to fill. Openly, Pope Leo condemned the fights. He had to, of course. Some of his soldiers broke a few heads to make a show of it, and the crowds watched the fights with one eye on the doors. But they still watched the fights. After two weeks we let the grain flow again. The people had their bread. After three, the fountains were clean and there were no more riots."

"And now?" Sigurd said, his eyes reflecting Bram's dying pyre.

"Now we have silver to raise an army, and the Pope has his city back," Nikephoros said simply. "Leo will never know we were here. He will bury all evidence of what has happened in the Amphitheatrum Flavium. Perhaps he'll build another church over the blood. And he will minister to his flock."

"Why did you stop the fight?" Sigurd asked, his eyes meeting mine for a half breath, then riveting back on Nikephoros. It was a good question, I thought, for there was no denying that the way it had ended had taken a little of the shine off our winning.

"Theophilos is one of my best men," Nikephoros said, scratching his oiled beard. "As you can see, I don't have the army I once did. I will need men like Theo in the days to come."

Sigurd greeted this with a low grunt. "That was a good tale," he said, raising his horn to Nikephoros and Bardanes and sweeping sweat-lank hair out of his face.

"There could have been more fighting in it," Olaf moaned, one eye closed and the other pointing Thór knew where, because Uncle was as drunk as the Thunder God at a Yule feast.

Then Sigurd frowned while Bjarni leaned over to refill his horn from a wineskin. "The ending was poor, though," he said, shaking his head. "Uncle is right. A good ending must have a generous spattering of blood or else no one is happy." He scratched the back of his head as though there were a mouse nesting in his hair. "Now I am thinking about it, it wasn't a good story at all."

"I could not tell you the ending because it hasn't happened yet, Jarl Sigurd," Nikephoros said, one dark eyebrow hitched. "But I can assure you that there will be blood. Arsaber will die, and his snakes with him."

"Good," Sigurd said. "I am happy about that. My friend Bram would be happy about that too. He liked a bloody tale." Olaf banged his horn against his jarl's, and wine spilled.

"Perhaps you want to see how this story ends for yourself, Sigurd," Nikephoros suggested, and though it shames me to admit it, that was the first time I saw through the smoke the pattern that these Greeks had been weaving since they came to our wharf and sat among our furs. Here was an emperor sharing piss-foul wine with rough men and heathens. He could have sent any of his men to deliver what he owed us, but here he was, biting his tongue and biding his time, and I had been a fool not to see it sooner. This emperor wanted us.

"At last, Uncle, I think we are through to the bone!" Sigurd bellowed. Men looked at one another with shrugs and beard scratching. I levered myself up onto a higher bolster, swearing at Halfdan and Gunnar, who were blocking my view.

"Your men fought well in the arena today, Sigurd. They did you great honor. Truly, I did not think my fighters could be beaten."

"Every one of these wolves wanted to fight your men," Sigurd said, which was not quite true but near enough. "We drew lots for the honor." Nikephoros shared a look with Bardanes then that told us they were even more impressed, for surely they had thought we had simply sent our best fighters.

"Then your reputation as great warriors is well deserved," the basileus said to the growing press of men around him, though the flattery was mostly wasted on the blind drunk and those who knew no English. "What impressed us most was your men's loyalty to one another." He grinned, revealing good teeth. "You flew down like hawks to protect the giant and that young warrior when we moved to guard Theophilos. I admit that I sweated a few drops at that moment." Bardanes stifled a grimace at that, and I guessed he was still pride-hurt from yielding to a few crews of heathens. If he truly was the emperor's war leader, he must have been used to commanding thousands. Now he led eighteen men.

"We were a flea's ball bag away from carving you into joints of meat for Rome's mangy curs," Olaf said in drunken Norse, forgetting to use English. The men cheered. "That would have gotten the crowds stiff!" he barked, making a fist and shaking his forearm.

Nikephoros ignored him and pointed to the iron-bound chest that now sat between Sigurd and Olaf, its contents having been weighed and found to be as promised. "Compared with the riches that lie in my treasury, that which you have won today is like a candle against the sun," the basileus said.

"I think it is not your treasury anymore," Sigurd pointed out, drinking. Wine spilled into his beard as he smiled. Those words stung Nikephoros like a wasp.

"My people are loyal, Jarl Sigurd. They will rejoice to see me back on my rightful throne. As for the army, they are simple men. They fight for whoever carries the pay chest." He nodded resolutely. "With your help that will be me again."

Sigurd laughed. "All the men I have are here as you see them. Aye, they are killers. Every sharp-clawed growling one of them. But I have seen Roman armies before. They are like swarms of flies or fleas on a dog."

Bardanes glanced at Nikephoros, who nodded his permission for the general to take the reins of the conversation.

"All we need to do is cut off the serpent's head," he said, "and then the rebellion dies. It has always been this way in Constantinople."

"It is true, Sigurd," Egfrith said warily. "Just three years ago the Empress Irene ruled in Constantinople." Nikephoros's eyes bulged, and Sigurd waved a hand at Egfrith.

"He is a Christ monk," the jarl said, as though that explained everything.

"As the emperor has told you," Bardanes went on, "we will kill Arsaber and secure the treasury. Then it will be over. Help us do this simple thing and we will make you richer than kings."

"I have heard this before," Sigurd rumbled.

"Not from the emperor of the richest city in the world, you haven't," Bardanes said.

Sigurd pursed his lips at this. "As it happens, we were going to Miklagard anyway," he said, at which Olaf nodded, biting into a hunk of meat that was cooling on the end of his knife. Sigurd gave Bardanes his wolf grin. "We were coming to raid. We were going to fill our ships' bellies with as much treasure as they can take. But it seems to me that the All-Father's hand is in this. How else can it be that the emperor of Miklagard happens to be sitting on my furs drinking my wine?"

"So you will fight for me?" Nikephoros asked, tiny flames dancing in the whites of his eyes.

"We'll put your Greek arse back on your golden chair," Sigurd said, nodding. "If Ódin wills it," he added. "And you will fill our ships to their sheer strakes with silver." He nodded at the crown on Nikephoros's head. "And gold," he said. "What say you, Uncle?"

Olaf frowned, meat juices glistening on his lips.

"Anyone with a name that sounds so much like 'arse' needs to be kicked," he said. The four men leaned together and grasped one another's forearms in the warrior way.

And we were going to Miklagard.

chapter
NINETEEN

WE SPENT ten more days in Rome. We found young Gregororovius again, or rather he found us. We had not seen hide nor hair of him for days, and it turned out that he had been made the new harbormaster because Gratiosus, to whom we owed several weeks' berthing tax, had never been found. Penda suggested to Gregor that he might be better off finding another trade unless he wanted to end up food for the river rats, which probably had been the last harbormaster's fate. But Gregor gave his handsome smile and assured the Wessexman that he would be safe enough now that the trouble in Rome seemed to have passed and His Holiness the Pope's soldiers were patrolling the streets again. Whether that was true or not, he let us off the money we owed, and this made me think that Gregor would be just fine, for he had enough cleverness in him to tell which way the wind was blowing and rig his sail for the smoothest ride. He also took Sigurd to the best blacksmith in Rome, who worked a forge in the shadow of the great wall east of the Amphitheatrum Flavium, because there were still seven Danes who needed good mail. The smith had four brynjas already, which he altered to fit the Danes, but he and his workers made the final three brynjas from the first ring to the last, and to do this in ten days was unheard of by any of us. Still, it cost Sigurd no small part of the coin we had won with our blood, and for a hoard like that I was willing to wager the smith would have gone happily without sleep for a month.

The day we slipped our moorings, our four prows sniffing the sea air on the wind, was the day we heard that King Karolus had entered Rome from the north. We had no desire to meet the warrior king again, and neither had Basileus Nikephoros, and all in all we felt like mischievous children creeping out of the orchard at the bark of the farmer's hound.

It turned out that the emperor of the Romans needed more than our swords. He needed our ships too if he was ever going to get back to Miklagard. They had scuppered the imperial dromon on the coast south of Rome and walked three days across country, arriving at the city's walls as footsore as common peddlers. It had been quite some ship, Nikephoros told us sorrowfully, but they could not afford for it to be recognized, and so now it sat broken on the seabed, scoured by sea wrack and lived in by fish. This was the part of the Greeks' story that Sigurd found the saddest. "It is a dark and gloom-stirring thing to sink your own ship," he had said, shaking his head at the misery of it. "But you will like *Serpent*," he announced, pride shining in his eyes. "She is the best ship in the world." Bardanes had raised an eyebrow at that, but it seemed to me that Nikephoros took pleasure in the jarl's obvious pride, and he nodded appreciatively at every part of *Serpent* that Sigurd pointed out to him.

So the basileus, his general, and the warrior Theophilos sailed with us aboard *Serpent* while the remaining sixteen long shields pulled *Fjord-Elk*'s oars, so that she was no longer crew-light. But they were not sailors, these Greek Romans. Bragi called across from *Fjord-Elk*'s stern fighting platform that he had seen cows with more sea sense than the new men in his thwarts. Of course *Fjord-Elk,* being short of rowers, had not been the only reason Sigurd had put the soldiers aboard a different ship from their masters. We did not know these men well enough to trust them and could not risk their trying to take one of the ships, but we now realized there was more chance of Bragi sprouting braids, a bird's nest beard, and a bristly arse. They shipped oars like a forest in a storm, hitting one another with the staves and sending Norsemen ducking for cover. They rowed too deep or too shallow and raggedly, their blades hitting the water like a handful of lobbed pebbles.

"They are palace guards," Nikephoros explained, embarrassed, watching *Fjord-Elk*'s skipper trying to establish some order aboard his ship. "They are good fighters," the basileus added, clenching a fist, "with iron discipline. You will see, Sigurd."

Sigurd frowned, still watching *Fjord-Elk* off our steerboard stern. "Maybe," he said, "if they don't drown themselves and sink my ship before we reach Miklagard."

I wasn't rowing. The wound in my side showed no signs of rot no matter how often Penda or Olaf or Egfrith came to sniff at it like dogs around a bitch's arse. But to row risked tearing it open, and so I was free to perch on my sea chest, letting the sun warm my eyelids and bailing every now and then when a pool slewed my way. Bram's death and my part in it still scuttled around my thought cage like a spider, nibbling away at my mind and spinning a gloom web that wrapped me around and around. It was an anchor weight in my gut, too, and I wanted desperately to tell someone how Cynethryth had put my *feigr* onto Bram. But I knew I could not. Not because they would hate me, though that thought was no mood lightener, but because they would hate Cynethryth for doing it, for Bram had been to the Fellowship what her oak keel was to *Serpent*.

On the journey back down the Tiberis to the sea, Bjarni had looked up from a carving of Týr he was working on and said to me that at least no one had mentioned for a while the silver we'd lost in that Frankish river, for which everyone knew I shouldered the blame, they having slung it squarely on me.

"You've just mentioned it, Bjarni," I'd said.

"Ah, so I have," he'd admitted, brows hitched.

"I haven't brought it up for a while," Svein had said, tugging his red beard.

"Nor me," Aslak had chipped in. "All that silver you pitched overboard never to be seen again. I have not spoken of it for weeks."

"You're all piss-dribbling goat fuckers," I had gnarred at their grinning faces. At least they could smile about it now, with their jarl's sea chest half full of coin and the promise of much more to come. I had helped buy those smiles with my blood and the fame hoard we had won in the arena.

Now we were on the open ocean again, back on the

sea road, the ancient city of wonders far behind, and to a Norseman there is nothing better. Gulls tumbled and wheeled above, shrieking noisily. The warm sea turned an even paler blue so that it was unlike any sea most of us had ever seen, for the cold, endlessly deep waters of the fjords can be black as night. Osk said that if it was his wyrd to drown, he would rather drown in this clear blue sea than in the Norsemen's black one.

"At least I'd be able to see your crying faces as I sank to the bottom," he said thoughtfully, pulling his oar.

"More likely you'd see us sharing out your gear and banging our mead horns together," Bothvar corrected him, getting a few laughs, for it was a sleeping sea and the rowing was easy. Not that General Bardanes thought so. We had been barely out of the river's mouth when Sigurd had ordered Theo and Bardanes to heft an oar from the trees and row. Theo had simply done as he was told, taking his place amidships next to Svein, but Bardanes had glowered at the jarl with those eagle eyes, and I'd wager I was not alone in wondering what kind of talons the man had if it came to it. He was broad-shouldered and well muscled by the look of it, but that does not always make a good fighter. Sometimes those things are no more use than the decoration on a sword hilt collar, as Bram had told me once.

Sigurd could have shown the man a little more respect, but then, why should he? His ship, his rules. And instead of asking again or leaving Bardanes on his roost to preen his feathers, Sigurd gave the man a choice. Either he could row with the others or he could be given a knife and lowered over the sheer strake to scrape the barnacles off *Serpent*'s belly. The Greek had looked to his emperor for support, but Nikephoros had flashed his palms, wanting no part in the dispute, and still Bardanes had refused, seething like hot iron in the quench trough. Until Sigurd fetched a coiled rope, an old knife, and Svein the Red. Now the general was rowing and sweating with the rest of us. To the man's credit and our surprise, he handled an oar well, keeping his rhythm neat as a sheathed blade, which is a sound way to earn a Norseman's respect.

I was healing well because I was young and because Asgot and Olaf were good with wounds. By burning the gash in my side they not only had stopped the blood but also sealed it so that the wound rot could not seep in, which was the least the old godi could do since it was his fault I had ended up in the arena at all.

Now there was a glossy welt of new skin that looked much worse than it felt, and soon I was able to row again, though I was careful not to stretch my arms above my head for fear of ripping the scar open.

The days and weeks passed uneventfully, and we enjoyed fair weather and fairer seas. All must at some point have reflected on what a strange company we were nowadays. Norsemen, Englishmen, Danes, Greeks, a woman, a monk, a blauman, an emperor, and a wolf, all sharing labor, food and drink, and the rolling sea road and all destined for the Great City, Miklagard. We passed the country of the Langobards and rounded the southern tip of the land that marks the western edge of Basileus Nikephoros's empire of the Romans, as the Roman Greeks call it. Then on we plowed into the Western Sea's cauldron of cultures, as Father Egfrith put it. He also called it the womb of civilization and many other names that flew into my right ear and out of the left, claiming that the sun-scorched islands had been home to heroes, deep thinkers, and master craftsmen since long before we men of the north had learned to rob the earth of iron or hew oaks into oceangoing craft. We knew nothing of the truth of all that, but we did know it was hot as the smith god Völund's anvil on that glittering blue sea. Tunics, cloaks, and bad-weather gear were stuffed into sea chests. Our backs and shoulders blistered, peeled like dry hoggorm skin, then turned brown as leather. When we were not rowing, we sought the shade of *Serpent*'s sail, and often, when the sun was low in the sky but still hot enough to melt the pine tar between the strakes, we mounted shields in the rail and slunk into their cool shadows.

I had never seen so many craft, and neither had anyone else apart from the Greeks. Vessels of every size and shape harnessed the sea breezes. Huge beaked dromons rose and dipped, their bows raising billows of white spray, oar banks dipping even with the sails up. Broad knörr-type boats swayed like wide-hipped wives on their way to market, and fishing skiffs bobbed free as the gusts. White sails were everywhere, and it was a hard thing not to wriggle into brynjas, put men and axes at the prows, and see what we could pilfer. Bothvar said it was like laying a slab of meat before a hound and telling it not to lick its lips, and he was right, for patience in a raiding man is as rare as a happy marriage. Even if he tries to cling to it, it almost always proves as fleeting as a belch.

On we sailed, each dusk mooring in a different sheltered bay, for there were so many pine-fragrant islands strewn across that glimmering sea that it was an easy thing to let the wind lift us and carry us from one to another like bees from flower to flower. The waters being so clear, we would peer over the sides to look out for hull-splitting rocks or else use a fathom weight smeared with tallow to discover what the sea-bed was made of. If we could not get close enough to use the planks, we sometimes dropped our anchors offshore and used the snekkjes to ferry us in because their drafts were more shallow even than *Serpent*'s and *Fjord-Elk*'s. We would go ashore to stretch our legs, light fires, and cook our night meals, hunting hare, boar, and fox among olive, cedar, and a green tree that Egfrith called Saint John's bread because some long-dead preacher who baptized the White Christ had survived on the tree's seed pods in the wilderness. We found them good eating when roasted, though we all agreed life would not be worth living if that were all there was to eat. We saw many creatures we had never set eyes on before and tried eating all but the most ugly ones. The best tasting was a sea creature that would scuffle ashore to lay its eggs. Some of these were almost the size of a shield, with broad backs as hard as toughened leather that could stop an arrow. Not that we needed to shoot them, for once ashore they were the slowest creatures I had ever seen, and even a man with one leg could have caught one without breaking a sweat.

Rome was a distant, sun-faded memory now. Miklagard, the Great City, the golden thread of our future wyrd, was still far away. The scorching days had begun to weigh heavily on the Fellowship, souring men's moods like old milk, and the truth was that we were restless. It was only a matter of time before Bothvar's hound licked its lips. Bardanes was the flint and steel of it, our own silver-thirst was the kindling, and a Moor galley was the slab of meat. This is how it began: three days before, we had caught a gusting westerly wind, letting it push us across a wide stretch of glittering sea called the Aegean, before pointing our prows north and hugging the dry, jagged coast of Nikephoros's eastern empire.

Dawn was rich molten copper seeping up the sky's deep blue hem. We had cast off from a deserted island off the coast of a place called Ephesus, and as usual Olaf and Bardanes were goading each other for want of something to do, using Egfrith and his Latin as the sling for their taunts. Those two got along like ring-mail and rain. From what I could gather of it that morning, Bardanes was saying that though we Norsemen were brave fighters, we could not match the Greeks for ingenuity and war-craft. Olaf had taken the bait, claiming that there was more truth in a fart than in anything that comes from a Greek's mouth. He went on to ask why, if he was so cunning and crafty a warrior, Bardanes had let a man whose name sounded like "arse" steal the throne from under his emperor's backside. Sigurd and Nikephoros usually kept their distance when Olaf and Bardanes locked horns, but this time they were drawn into the rut, which had turned to the matter of sea-craft now. Perhaps the jarl and the basileus were bored, too, but when Rolf yelled across from *Sea-Arrow*, pointing north at a billowed sail through the hot wind's shimmering haze, I knew what was coming.

"If we were aboard the basileus's ship, we could run down that Moor galley," Bardanes said, shaking his head.

"Ha! You think your ships are faster than ours?" Olaf said, hoisting his brows at Sigurd, who raised his in return.

"My people have been sailing these waters since long before the Lord Christ's disciples were casting their nets in the Sea of Galilee," Nikephoros said, a proud tilt to his chin. Then he stepped up onto the raised fighting platform at *Serpent*'s stern and gripped the sheer strake with both hands. "Galleys like her prey on my people, Sigurd. The Moors are a plague on us."

"She is laboring like a pig in mud," Sigurd replied, a sour curl to his lips. "I'll wager she cannot sail as close to the wind as we can." The jarl was right, for even as we watched, the distant galley showed us her length as she turned into another long tack.

"And I'll wager that you can't catch her, Sigurd," Bardanes said, smoothing his oiled beard through finger and thumb.

"You hear that, Sigurd?" Olaf said in Norse, thumbs tucked into his belt. "This slippery badger's cunny of a Greek wants to lose more money to us. You would have thought he'd given us enough."

"Who are we to piss on such generosity, Uncle?"

Sigurd replied, then turned to Bardanes and accepted the wager, suggesting that whoever lost would have to fill the other's helmet with coin. Bardanes blanched a little at that, for it was quite a hoard to lose, more silver than a man could hope to get his hands on in four or five decent raids. He avoided his lord's eye, though if he had looked at Nikephoros, he would have seen the basileus shake his head and steel his eye enough to show his disapproval. But Nikephoros kept his tongue locked up behind the wall of his teeth, because he knew warriors and their pride well enough not to get between them, especially now, having fallen so far from power and a throne that was being fart warmed by someone else.

When Osten blew our war horn, signaling to the other ships that we were hunting, Rolf replied with three long bellows of his own horn, which meant he wanted to talk to his jarl. *Sea-Arrow* came alongside, and it turned out that Rolf and his Danes wanted the honor of being the first crew to strike the galley, like the lead wolf that sinks its teeth into a deer's haunches to sever the tendons so that the prey cannot escape. Then the rest of us would hit, ripping out its throat and eating our fill. Sigurd warned Rolf of the wager he had with Bardanes, but this only made the Danes grin, for they were eager to prove themselves now that they were armed like war gods, with ring-mail and good helmets and swords that were hungry for blood.

"We will be close as a jealous wife, Rolf," Sigurd yelled.

"Don't concern yourself, Sigurd," Rolf called back.

"We will leave you some scraps and a seat at the table."

And then all four ships were squalling, with crews working ropes and fighting sails, trying to yoke the shoulders of that hot wind so that we could run down our prey, so that we could show these Greeks what dragon ships could do. *Sea-Arrow* was true to her name, streaking across the shimmering sea like a shaft shot from a good bow, her crew thronging the thwarts like penned beasts. I remembered how those Danes had fought the blaumen, and I shuddered because they were savage as Ulfhédnar, the wolf skins whose battle frenzy can chill the blood of even the most skilled and bravest of men.

I was wriggling into my brynja now, wishing I had kept it in the cool of my sea chest longer, for the rings were scalding to the touch.

"Who is the other prow man with me?" Svein the Red asked Sigurd, his eyes wide with the realization that Bram would not be up there with him this time. You always put your strongest warriors on either side of the prow beast to strike fear into the enemy and land the first blows. But Bram was gone, and no one felt his loss more keenly than Svein, for those two had been as close as brothers. The giant gripped his long ax, its head and his enormous brynja glinting in the sun. His red beard was already dripping sweat in that fierce heat.

Sigurd's hesitation revealed that he, like the rest of us, had simply expected Bram to muscle his way to the bow, his prideful swagger parting the crew like a hot blade through butter.

"Penda, hang your English balls around Jörmungand's neck!" he said, at which the Wessex warrior grinned like a troll in a nunnery. I slapped his back because he deserved the honor of being the new prow man, had earned it long ago. Svein nodded, pleased with the choice even if some were not, for there were some rumbles that Penda was not big enough to be a prow man. But those rumbles had no real grouse in them because, honor or no, being at the prow in a fight was like smearing your naked self in honey and wandering into a bear's cave, and no one else was volunteering. Besides which, every man aboard knew that the Wessexman had a gift for killing and would work well with Svein.

"That crew would be better off jumping over the side while they still can," Bjarni called, tying the helmet strap under his chin and grimacing as the nasal bar singed the skin between his eyes.

"They'll wish they had when the Danes climb aboard," I said, tucking a hand ax into my belt. A short ax is a useful weapon in a ship fight because it is easier to use in a press of men than a spear or even a sword. We were gaining on the Moor galley fast and were now close enough to see her crew. They wore white robes and turbans, but that was not to say they were not wearing armor beneath, and that put the idea in our heads to keep our cloaks on so that they mostly covered our brynjas and kept the sun off the iron rings. I took a deep breath that was hot and stale as old water and did not seem to fill my lungs. The puckered scar along my rib cage thrummed like old men's bones before a storm, and I was suddenly filled with the fear of being cut again, of steel slicing into skin and flesh and the searing agony of it. I told myself that Rolf and the Danes would have savaged the enemy before we sank our grappling hooks into their hull. Or else the Moors would yield without giving us a proper fight of it.

"She is fast, Sigurd," Bardanes admitted, putting a foot up on the mast step and strapping an iron greave over his lower leg. Beneath the scarlet cloak his cuirass glittered with hundreds of golden scales, each of them like a miniature sun, so that the armor looked like something Baldr, Ódin's handsome son, fairest of all the gods, would wear into battle. Mine were not the only eyes scouring it.

"You think it could stop a good sword blow?" Wiglaf muttered, his face still burned red though other men's had long since turned brown.

"I think the thing is more likely to blind you before you could get close enough to wallop him," I said, tearing my eyes away from Bardanes and back to *Sea-Arrow*, which was now less than twice an arrow's flight behind the galley.

"They look like bloody golden fish," Baldred spit through his dense black beard, because Nikephoros was there now, and he too wore scale armor, gold greaves, and an iron helmet with a gold cross on it, the cross's upright stretching from nasal to crown.

There was a knot of blaumen at the galley's stern now, nocking arrows and preparing to defend her thwarts. Shield bosses reflected the sun, which was climbing into the sky on our steerboard side and would burn more fiercely still before the real killing started.

"Go on, Rolf; rip the whoresons apart," Bjarni hissed, fist clenched around a spear's shaft. Men were slotting spare shields into the rail to give height to the ship's side, creating a bulwark for when we came alongside the enemy vessel, for it had higher sides than *Serpent*, which was something we were getting used to though we liked it not one bit. We could see arrows flying from the galley's stern now: black shafts streaking up into the blue and then swooping down like starlings to barley stubble.

"Fools are shooting too early," Olaf growled. "Something must have them spooked," he added with a smirk.

The Moors had turned and were running with the wind toward the shore, perhaps hoping to outrun us on land because they knew they could not outrun us out here. So said Sigurd, adding that either way we'd win, for we'd take their ship if nothing else. But Rolf saw what the blaumen were trying to do, and suddenly *Sea-Arrow* was slashing east, having caught the wind in her sail and flung her rudder hard over so that she was heeling wildly, no more than a hand's length of freeboard between her and the hungry, drowning sea. She righted again, and the Danes began loosing their arrows—no easy thing on a moving ship—banging swords against shields and yelling threats and insults at the blaumen. I saw big Beiner and Gorm hurl grappling hooks into the galley's foreship, and I heard the Danes cheer as those iron claws gouged into the wood and held fast. The Danes hauled on the ropes, but the blaumen cut one of them, flinging a knot of Danes back into the thwarts.

We had turned too and were racing toward the

shore and would hit the galley's stern in the time it takes a drunken man to piss. I stood between Black Floki and Bjarni and pressed my helmet firmly down, gripping a long spear and a shield. The air was thick with the smell of sweat and leather and iron. Behind me men were nocking arrows and readying throwing spears. Others clutched ropes and grappling hooks, and still others had long spears with winged blades that were good for stabbing at faces over men's shoulders but also for hooking on to another ship's sheer strake so that you could haul it closer. At the stern, Egfrith was on his knees praying to his god and Cynethryth was comforting Sköll, for the beast was shaking like a hound before a beating, its ears flat against its huge head, eyes wide as coins.

Wave-Steed and *Fjord-Elk* were swooping like eagles on the Moor ship's port side, their crews brandishing their killing tools and whooping with the thrill of it. The sun was like a god's golden shield, blazing down on a sea that was bright blue and burnished white, and we were sea wolves.

"Sigurd!" Svein roared from the fighting platform at the prow. He was pointing to a low scrub-covered island off our enemy's steerboard bow.

"Thór's hairy arse," Olaf rumbled.

"Not another fucking trap," Gytha said, spitting over the side, because two more dromons had burst from behind the island, their oar banks beating like enormous wings as they came against the wind. Sigurd was already barking orders, and men were hauling on ropes, trying to get the wind across the sail so that we could turn back out to sea. Osten was blow-

ing the horn so that the other skippers would know
that they were to fly from this like carrion crows fleeing from a carcass when a fox comes, for we did not
need a full battle with its carnage and corpse piles.

Nikephoros fought his way through to Sigurd,
teeth flashing white against his neat black beard.
"You need to get your men away from the Moor ship
now!" he said.

"Rolf is no fool; he knows what to do," Sigurd
snarled between hurling orders here and there. But it
was no good, and the jarl knew it. The wind was behind us, and it would take too long to try to turn
under sail, and so he yelled at his men to lower the
yard, which they did, others desperately reefing as the
sail came down.

"Holy Christ on his cross!" Penda clamored. "Fire!"
The two dromons had come around the Moor ship's
stern so that the wind was behind them, and now,
though I hardly believed what my eyes were seeing,
fire was spewing from the dromons onto the Moors'
deck, and suddenly men were flailing and burning
and screaming. *Sea-Arrow*'s crew had cut the ropes so
that the two ships were no longer tethered together,
but they were struggling to disengage from the bigger
vessel because the wind was pushing them onto it.

"Don't just stand there, you slack-mouthed sons of
whores!" Olaf screamed, grabbing Osk by the shoulder and yanking him back from our shieldwall. "Get
your damned oars in the damned sea and row, you
feckless goat farts!" And so we dropped our weapons,
scrambled to the oar trees, grabbed our staves, and
took to our sea chests, our minds reeling from what

we had just seen: ships breathing fire like dragons. The sail was down, meaning we had a clear view over *Serpent*'s stern, though I wished we had not. Because *Sea-Arrow* was burning.

"By all the gods, how is it possible?" Sigurd gnarred. We were rowing hard, putting water between us and the fire-breathing ships now, but *Wave-Steed* had not heeded Sigurd's command to flee. She was swooping down on her sister ship despite the fire and the arrows that were flying in dark flocks from the two dromons, and that was Týr-brave.

"They are my ships, Sigurd," Nikephoros called from the side, where he stood gripping *Serpent*'s sheer strake, knuckles white as bone. "I know their captains. They will attack any warships they come across."

"Your ships?" Sigurd took off his helmet and swept sweat-drenched hair from his forehead. "Greek ships breathe fire?" he said, eyes flaying Nikephoros.

"If not for our liquid fire the Moors would be hammering on the gates of Constantinople by now," Bardanes put in through clenched teeth. He was not rowing, having claimed that his duty was to protect his emperor. Sigurd had not had time to argue.

"What in Hel's hole is liquid fire?" Olaf asked, eyeballing Bardanes and Nikephoros both.

"See for yourself, Norseman," Bardanes replied, and Olaf turned his gaze back to the inferno that was the Moor ship now. Blaumen thrashed in the water, their screams of agony carried off east by the wind, and by some foul seidr magic they were still flame-shrouded. They were burning even as they drowned.

"Water cannot kill liquid fire," Bardanes said, a cold

edge of pride to his voice that I did not like at all. There was no saving *Sea-Arrow* now. Her pitch-lined strakes were burning wildly, belching thick black smoke that added to the chaos, blooming dirty against the bright blue of sea and sky. The Greeks were now raining arrows on the blaumen, their archers bunched thick as gorse in a wooden castle by the main mast.

"Good for Burlufótr!" Bothvar called. Egill Ketilsson, bynamed Burlufótr, "Clumsy Foot," for his limp, was *Wave-Steed*'s skipper, and it was because of his crew's bravery that the men of *Sea-Arrow* were not joining the blaumen in flaming, drowning death. Burlufótr had *Wave-Steed*'s stern against *Sea-Arrow*'s prow, the only part of Rolf's ship that was as yet untouched by fire, and from there her men were helping pull their fellow Danes aboard. The Greeks were streaking arrows over the burning ships, but for the moment the smoke was the Danes' friend because it meant that the Greeks were shooting blind. Not for long, though, as the farther of Nikephoros's dromons was nosing around the doomed vessels, skirting the wind-whipped flames to attack the other snekkje.

Sigurd raged like the burning ships, violence coming off him thick as black smoke as he stood at the stern, his back to us, watching *Sea-Arrow*'s doom. We knew he wanted nothing more than to turn his own dragons around, give their beast-headed prows sight of the Greeks, and strike them with cold iron and fury. But fire is a ship's worst enemy. It will devour seasoned, pitch-lined timbers with insatiable fury, as it did now, our eyes full of the blazing horror of it.

One of the basileus's ships belched another stream

of fire, but in their impatience the Greeks had loosed that fire too early and the wind was not with them, so that the searing red gush fell a spear length short of *Wave-Steed*'s stern as she pulled away. Her oar banks were beating fast as crow's wings, every available blade chopping into the sea, and some of the Danes were loosing arrows while others hefted shields, protecting the rowers. Behind them the sea burned, and around me men cursed and shook their heads because flaming water is about as natural as a talking corpse.

"There's some god's hand in that, mark me," someone gnarred behind me.

"Ah, we've all seen Finna breathe fire when she's caught you swiving one of your small-titted thralls, Hastein," Bjarni said, though there were few laughs at this as we pulled the oars, watching the black bloom of smoke stain the sky now that we could no longer see the blazing ships over *Serpent*'s stern. I looked over to see *Fjord-Elk* matching us stroke for stroke, Nikephoros's men apparently rowing well enough now that the alternative was burning to death.

"At least the bastards don't have the arms for the chase," Penda said a while later when it became clear that the Greek dromons were not pursuing us. They had raised their enormous white sails now and turned their bows northwest, retreating back up the throat of the Aegean like spiders back to the middle of their webs. That meant we had stowed our oars and raised our sails again, keeping them reefed and catching just enough wind to keep us moving toward the eastern shore while we decided what to do next.

"They know they'll get nothing from coming after us," Sigurd said, peeling off his heavy brynja. "There are too many islands for them."

"Aye, it'd be like chasing someone around a table," Olaf put in, palming sweat from his face.

Svein the Red emptied a bucket of seawater over his head, then spit and blew snot and swept the tangle of hair back over his forehead. The great slab of his face was dark with confusion the way it often was before a question, so we knew just to wait for what was coming. "If they're the emperor's ships," he said, water dripping from his beard, "why doesn't he wave his bloody crown at them and have them kiss his Greek arse? It seems to me that we should be getting better treatment than this."

It was a fair question, and Sigurd said as much, then asked Nikephoros the same thing.

"It would be like putting your hand in that wolf's mouth and hoping it would not bite it off," Nikephoros replied, pointing at Sköll, which was lapping water from the bilge because Cynethryth was not there to stop it and no one else cared enough either way. Those who understood what the emperor had said nodded and ayed, for we all knew the story of how Týr had had his hand chewed off by Fenrir Wolf. Nikephoros bent his knees as *Serpent* rolled over a wave. We were not going fast enough to cut the water cleanly. "It is impossible to know which men remain loyal to me and which are traitors," he said. He had swapped his scale armor for a knee-length tunic of white linen that was belted at the waist with a blood-red sash. I noticed he was hardly sweating at all, unlike the rest of us. "When you ascend the throne of Constantinople, you are wise to buy yourself some powerful friends even before you put on the purple robes." A sour twist gripped his lips. "Arsaber has no doubt had his hand in my treasury by now. He will have replaced many good and loyal men with his own."

"That's what we did," Bardanes said, earning himself a scolding look from Nikephoros. The general shrugged, then slapped at a fly that had landed on his wrist.

"Then how *do* we get past those fire-spewing monsters of yours?" Olaf asked the emperor. "I for one do not like sharing the sea with them." Nikephoros clenched his jaw like a man who dislikes being asked questions; perhaps, if he really *was* as powerful as he would have us believe, he was not used to answering them either.

"We nestle into the shore like you would a cool, plump pair of tits," Sigurd said, nodding toward the brown coast off *Serpent*'s steerboard bow. Waves that we barely noticed swelled and billowed as they sped toward land, then churned in the shallows, hurling white spume up onto the strand. We were close enough to hear each breath of it, and just the sound of it cooled the skin a little.

"It is the best way, my lord," Bardanes agreed, answering the questioning look he was getting from Nikephoros. "Our ships have deeper hulls than these and cannot go so close to the shore." He turned to Sigurd, a half smile twitching his otter-slick beard. "We have not had to defend our great city from men such as you, Jarl Sigurd. The Moors' ships are like ours and need deep water. Our captains will not patrol the shallows. They have no need to."

"I'll remember to tell my sons that when they're old enough to go raiding," I said, at which Sigurd and Olaf chuckled. Bardanes did not see the funny side of it, and maybe that was because I was only half joking. But that man's displeasure was my enjoyment, for I had decided that I did not like General Bardanes. Not one bit.

chapter
TWENTY

FOR THE next few days we plowed the shallows an arrow-shot from the polished pebble shore. At first, Knut had shaken his head and rumbled like a distant rockfall. His long smooth beard swishing, *Serpent*'s steersman had said that sailing so close to an unknown shore was the same as humping another man's wife. There is a certain thrill in the danger, he said, but everyone knows that no good can come of it. Still, even Knut agreed that if it came to it, he would rather drown than burn and then drown. For we were all still reeling from the horror of the Greeks' fire-spewing ships, and none of us wanted to meet them again. It was only by some rare luck and the bravery of *Wave-Steed*'s crew that none of the Danes had been killed. Three or four had burn wounds to hands or faces, and those burns blistered and leaked fluids but were not serious in themselves. Three men had arrow wounds either from the blaumen or from the Greeks, though none of the shafts had fully penetrated their brynjas, for which they owed their jarl, who had given them war gear that few warriors could ever hope to own. Even the loss of *Sea-Arrow* could be borne, as there were enough empty oars on the other three ships to accommodate her crew, and that meant that none of the ships was now crew-light. But the blaumen had not been so fortunate, and in my mind I kept seeing them flailing, writhing in flaming robes, and leaping into the sea, which should have put out the fire but did not.

Rolf was pride-sore, which was only to be expected given that he had been forced to leap from a handsome snekkje and watch it burn, narrowly escaping by a singed arse hair. It was clear that the Dane felt he had failed his jarl by losing the ship, but Sigurd had tried to lighten his burden. "Who could have foreseen liquid fire?" he had said, dark-browed with the loss of *Sea-Arrow*. And that was a fair question, prompting more beard shaking and mumbles that those Greeks must know some powerful seidr and that we would have to be prepared the next time we met them.

Which would be soon. Because it was a sleeping sea, still and flat as a jarl's feast table, and we were clinging to the coast, rowing so that we had *Serpent* on a short leash and could better guide her through the shallows. We had stowed Jörmungand, and *Fjord-Elk* and *Wave-Steed* had removed their own prow beasts because we did not want to anger the spirits of this land. For Asgot said that judging by the land itself, those spirits were likely to be ancient, dry-humored, and capricious, and we had never been farther from our own lands. Sun-bleached white rock rose from the sparkling sea; the hills were studded with dark green brush and, higher up, poplar, chestnut, pine, and fir as well as plenty of other trees and plants we could not put names to. Above the high ground dark shapes soared against the endless blue. These black birds were twice the size of the largest raven and barely flapped their wings as they traced great wheels in the sky. We saw sea eagles too, as well as herons, cormorants, wagtails, and swallows that twisted and turned almost too fast for the eye to follow as they snatched insects from the warm air. A shrieking cloud of gulls billowed in our wake, the birds hoping for scraps and splashing white turds across the stern and those who rowed there, so that some of the men wore skin hats despite the heat. Sometimes Sköll growled and leaped at the birds, but mostly it ignored their mocking cries, too hot in its fur to do anything but follow the ever-moving shade or cool down in the bilge water, though even that was hot. For the sun was so fierce that I feared the air itself would clot so that we would not be able to suck it into our lungs and then would suffocate and die.

It had not rained for many days, and the only water we had left was stale and stinking. We still had a few skins of Roman wine, which we added to the water to improve the taste, sipping gingerly even as sweat dripped from our skin. But in that heat the watered wine made your head swim so that all you wanted to do was lie down and sleep, and what we really craved was cold barley ale. Yet with the loss of *Sea-Arrow* still sore as a fresh burn in our minds, we dared not make landfall to replenish our supply.

"Your men will want for nothing once I am returned to my throne," Nikephoros had told Sigurd as he watched us sharing what there was, wetting our tongues and passing the horn to the next man. But the jarl had laughed at that.

"A Norseman who lusts for nothing more than what he already has is as rare as a happy Christian," he had said, at which the emperor had frowned as though to prove Sigurd's point.

So we rowed and sweated and roasted beneath that relentless southern sun, passing fishing boats and small trading vessels but not coming across the fire dromons, and eventually we came to the strait known as the Hellespont. We moored in the clear calm water on the eastern edge of its great gaping mouth, the land on both sides flat and barren, and there we watched the shield-round sun sink toward the darkening sea. When heated iron turns a red-gold color, the swordsmith knows it is time to start hammering. The sky was that color now, rich and molten and ablaze, though soon, like sword iron, it would cool to dark red and then gray. Just above the sea a thin dark streak of cloud stretched across the horizon so that as the sun passed behind, it created the picture of an enormous dragon's eye watching us balefully, burning at the world's edge.

"So this gullet leads to Miklagard," Olaf said, scrubbing his beard, eyes turned to the northeast.

"Aye, Uncle," Sigurd said, his teeth dragging his beard over his bottom lip, "to the empire of the Greeks who call themselves Romans."

"More bloody White Christ men who'll want to chew us up and spit us out, hey, Raven," Olaf said. Men were settling down in the thwarts, nesting among skins and furs as though they had every comfort a man could wish for.

"I think the fish keep spitting my hook out, Uncle," I moaned, leaning over the sheer strake and peering down into the water. I'd had a line over the side long enough for the twine to have pressed fine furrows in the flesh of my fingers, but so far I had caught nothing. Some of the others had pulled up fish we had never seen before, our favorite being one with stripes the color of iron rot whose flesh was sweet and delicious.

"It's true you are not much of a fisherman, lad," Olaf said thoughtfully. The bedimmed ocean was still clear enough for me to see small fish darting around my line as if to humiliate me.

"But the lad has patience, Uncle," Sigurd said with a smile, "and patience is a good weapon against fish."

Olaf nodded and said this was so. "There are two things I know about fishing," he added, holding up two thick gnarled fingers. "The first is that the least experienced fisherman always catches the biggest fish." There were ayes at this. "And the second is that fish are like women. They both stop shaking their tail soon enough after you've caught them." We laughed at that, and it was a comforting sound in that redgold dusk, for in truth we still felt Bram's loss keen as a seax blade. It was a knot of iced rope in my guts, which was why the warmth of laughter was so welcome.

Bjarni twisted around on his sea chest, knife in hand. He was trimming his beard, pulling and sawing off tuft after tuft and peering into his polished sword blade to see that he made a decent job of it.

"I once caught a fish that measured one foot," he said.

"Ha! That is not so big," Svein barked, unimpressed.

"One foot between the eyes!" Bjarni said, and we laughed again because Svein had walked into that one right enough.

And still I caught nothing, but at least I was not one of those woken by a dig in the ribs from the butt end of Olaf's spear. For it turned out we had not moored there for the night at all. We had simply been waiting for darkness, though no one had told us that, and now men who had settled down for the night were cursing and grumbling as they climbed out of their dens like bears roused early from their winter sleep.

Nikephoros, Bardanes, and Sigurd had spun this plan, deciding that night's shroud would give us the best chance of slipping unseen down this moon-silvered gullet to Miklagard. "Farther in it gets narrow, lads," Olaf had explained, pointing into the murky throat of the Hellespont beyond *Serpent*'s bow. "Bardanes says at one point a man can shout from one shore to the other and be heard if he's got a big mead hole and the wind with him." His grimace gleamed white in the gloom. "The Greeks have got more of those fire-breathing ships in there," he said, and men touched Thór's hammer amulets to ward off that strange and powerful seidr. Our minds were still trying to unravel the knot of fire that burns even in water. "So it would be better if we did not have to get our bollocks burned fighting them." Even those whom Olaf had poked awake agreed with that, and so we had taken to our sea chests and plunged the blades into the sleeping sea and were rowing again.

It is bowel-melting work rowing in the dark. You don't talk. You don't even think about singing. You listen, your staves clumping in their ports. After each wet plunge of the oars your ears draw tight as a rat's arsehole around every sound. You are waiting for the scrape of the keel along submerged rocks or the wash of the waves on a shore that is closer than you thought. You half expect your oar blade to thump against something granite-hard and wood-splintering, and your sweat sluices as cold as glacier runoff. *Serpent* led the other two ships, and all of us had hidden our blades and helmets and anything else that might reflect what little moonlight and starlight there was. At our bow Olaf and Sigurd stood on either side of the stem post peering into the channel ahead and looking down into the water. Cynethryth and Asgot watched from the port side, Cynethryth's young eyes combined with the old godi's experience, and Nikephoros and Bardanes leaned on the steerboard side sheer strake. Sigurd did not make the general row now that we were getting close to Miklagard and needed the man's Greek eyes more than his arms. Theo rowed, though, and rowed well, which was only right given that he was the man who had killed Bram and now churned the sea in our old friend's stead.

It was lucky for us that there was not much wind and the Hellespont was smooth, because it meant Knut and the steersmen of the other ships could hold a true course without too much trouble. Besides which, our Greek companions claimed to know the strait better than the fish knew it, which I doubted of course. I reckoned those Greek fish were cunning enough bastards who knew a baited hook and a nettle-hemp line when they saw one and were probably still laughing at me somewhere down there in Rán's cold wet dark. Still, when we came to the narrowest part of the strait, mine were not the only eyes riveted to the Greeks, for the truth was we needed them now. It was worse than rowing into the unknown, and the fear of it was worse too: a cold dread that stirred in your guts and then crawled up your spine to slicken the back of your neck and make the hairs stiff as bristles. Miklagard, or Constantinople as the Roman Greeks called it, was, we had learned, a kingdom of unequalled power. Tens of thousands of people lived in the city, safe behind enormous walls that Nikephoros claimed were impregnable. Having seen the ancient walls of Rome with my own eyes, I now knew some things were possible that most men would dismiss as the lie-weave of skalds, so that I think I would have believed Nikephoros if he'd said the stars hung as lanterns from Miklagard's walls.

Now we sweated, scuffing our slick faces against our shoulders because we could not break the even pull of the oars that sent us gliding through the pinched part of the strait. On both sides we could see the land looming charcoal dark, pinpricks of flame here and there along the shore. No one uttered a word, for Bardanes had warned us that this was where three of their dromons prowled and even now their captains would be peering into the murk as we were. Except they would be ready with flint and steel to ignite the liquid fire should a Moor ship's silhouette ghost out of the gloom. Or a dragon ship, come to that. And so every creak of timber or rope had men wincing. *Fjord-Elk* and *Wave-Steed* plowed our wake, silent as shadows as their oar blades stirred a white froth with each plunge. With each lift those blades dripped water in broken silver strings, and now and then Máni, whom men call the moon, gave me a gray glimpse of a rower's back and shoulders as he toiled.

I expected that at any moment the dark would be

devoured by ravenous flame and we would be sheathed in fire, tight as a sword in a scabbard. I was waiting for it, the knot of fear in my stomach growing with each dip of my oar because I thought we must be coming closer to the Greek ships and their vicious seidr fire. I could still see the blaumen leaping overboard, trailing flame that could not be quenched, and those are the kinds of memories you can do without.

My body labored, warmed by the endless repetition of the stroke that had piled muscle on my chest, shoulders, back, and arms, but my soul was frozen ice-still in clenching fear. And yet fear, it turns out, has more layers than an onion. Just when you think you cannot be more afraid, something happens that stops your heart and squeezes it as small as a mouse stuffing itself through a tiny hole. That thing was Sigurd hissing like a goose. I caught the glint of his eye as he threw up a hand and turned an ear toward the moon-licked open water on our port side. We lifted our oars clear and heard the other crews do the same; then we listened to the soft gush of our bows through the still sea.

A flame licked somewhere out there, rising and falling with a ship's roll. Fire streaked up into the night. I heard the muffled whisper of it as it soared, lingered for a breath, then fell. It was not the liquid fire that so terrified us; rather, this was the work of any man: a clothbound arrow set alight and shot into the gathering dark. Another flaming arrow went up, inscribing a brassy gray smoke arc in the pewter sky, then vanishing again. Ódin's arse, but I don't think I breathed until the third arrow went up. But then I blew out a stale breath because that arrow flew south, meaning that though the Greeks must have suspected they were not alone out there on the Hellespont, they did not know where we were.

The water was slapping our hull now as *Serpent*, her impetus spent, gave herself over to wind and current, and still we waited, *Fjord-Elk* and *Wave-Steed* drifting silently in the gloom off our stern. Part of me wanted to yell out, to break through the thick ice of that mute terror, for even chaos would be better than waiting, than expecting the fire to reach out of the night and eat your flesh. But I clamped my jaw shut as tight as my fists were on the smooth oar stave, and in my mind I heard Bram growl that he was fed up with skulking like naughty children and would rather face the slick-bearded Greeks and be done with it.

Someone farted. There were some choked laughs at that, and then, turning back to us, Sigurd rolled an arm, which was the signal for us to start rowing again. I think we were all glad to pull the oars again, for the strokes were deep and strong, dragging the sea past *Serpent*'s hull and goading her to slick speed from a standing start. I saw Nikephoros nod to Sigurd, his handsome face still clenched tight, though touched now by the finger ends of relief at having gotten past his own dromons. The emperor must have been sweating like a blacksmith's arse throughout all this. Whenever we weighed anchor and came to new lands, we could expect trouble, for we were raiders, but Nikephoros was an emperor. It would be a cruel wyrd that saw him burned alive by the very men whose pay came from his treasury.

"Part of me wanted to see those ships vomit their liquid fire again," Gap-Toothed Ingolf said a while later when the rowing was steady and we were sure that the Greek ships were far behind.

"That's because you have all the sense of a shrew, Ingolf," Black Floki said without turning to look at the man. Ingolf glowered as he pulled the oar, and I chose not to say that I knew how Ingolf felt and that part of me had wanted to yell out and turn that still night into seething madness. Instead we had crept even closer to Miklagard like three hungry wolves stalking up to a rich, well-stocked farm.

chapter
TWENTY-ONE

IT WAS still night when we came to the island called Elaea in the Marmara Sea. There were several islands we could have moored at, but this one had a ragged coast of creeks and sheltered bays in which we could hide easily once we had dropped the tallow-smeared fathom weight over the side to test the depth and seabed. In daylight we would have been able to use our own eyes, for the water was clear, but even so it is better to use a knotted line than to find yourself cursing another man's eyes as the sea gushes in through a torn hull.

We had come out of the dark narrows, and suddenly what moonlight there was had flooded across the Marmara Sea, so that we felt about as inconspicuous as Svein the Red in a White Christ church. I could even see Kjar's face at *Fjord-Elk*'s tiller, and I should think he could see all of our faces who were turned toward *Serpent*'s stern as we rowed. But it was a wide sea compared with where we had come from, and on the open sea we Norsemen are without equal. We had Sigurd. And Sigurd was the most sea-bold Norseman of all.

Not that we needed boldness now. What we needed was sleep, which is not easily gained when your blood

is still up and the fingers of fear are still grasping. Yet
other than the soul peace that swamps you after a
good swiving, the sound of waves rolling themselves
onto the shore is the best thing to get you into sleep
and keep you there. Someone must have stayed
awake, taking first watch from the stern and gawking
out at the moon-played waves, but it wasn't me. Nor
did anyone wake me for my turn, which was probably because we were already at the arse end of the
night and dawn was swelling somewhere in the east.

The early part of the morning, when there was still
a breath of freshness in the air, was far too short. I
had barely been upright long enough to work the previous day's rowing knots out of my shoulders before
the crushing heat filled the world. You could see it
shimmering like water above the brown rocks on the
shore, and Penda moaned that he thought he was
drunk until he remembered he hadn't had a decent
drop of anything for weeks and his mouth was drier
than a burned bush. I told him he had that right
enough, for we were all thirsty. Even what little wine
we had was sour and foul-tasting now, and we would
look up at the endless blue sky, hoping to see rain
clouds that were not there. Men had gone ashore
looking for freshwater, and others had begun rigging
skins in the thwarts for shade.

Some of us gathered as close as we could to Sigurd
and the Greeks who stood on the fighting platform at
Serpent's bow. It was always the same faces these days,
those men who were close to Sigurd or who felt they
wanted their say in whatever schemes the jarl wove.
Olaf, Black Floki, and Asgot were there, of course, as

were Svein the Red, Bjarni, Aslak, Knut, Penda, Bragi the Egg, and a couple of other *Fjord-Elk* men. Of the Danes, Rolf, Beiner, and Yngvar were always nearby, along with the blauman Völund. More often than not Egfrith joined us, too, though he was a different man these days. Whereas he used to chatter like a bird, now he rarely spoke and looked nothing like the monk he was, for his beard was brown streaked with ash gray and his thinning, unkempt hair was almost down to his shoulders.

Cynethryth joined the gathering, too, though I could not look at her these days without thinking of Bram and the black seidr magic she had spun, taking my doom and putting it onto him. A heavy secret that, like a pair of quern stones grinding in my soul.

"This will be no simple raid," Sigurd told us, ignoring the streams of sweat coursing down his sun-browned face and dripping from his golden beard. He spoke in Norse, which I translated for Penda, though I suspected the Wessexman no longer needed me to. Nikephoros, his general, and the warrior Theo stood dumb as posts but watching us all.

"I would like to tell you it will be as easy as burning Jarl Alrik of Uppland's hall," Sigurd said. There were some happy rumbles at that memory, though not many, and Sigurd seemed to reflect on that awhile—how many faces he had lost along the way, men who now drank in the hall of the slain. "But you all know that the farther a man rides along the whale road, the more dangers he will face."

"There are more ways to die than there are fleas on an old hound, as my father used to say," Olaf put in, sweat glistening on his scarred barrel chest. Most of us were bare-chested, letting every slight breeze off the sea cool our skin, but Sigurd wore a light blue tunic whose neck and sleeves were edged with criss-crossed red braid. He was silvered, too, with a jarl torc at his neck and rings braided into his hair. He looked every inch the Norse chieftain, a ring-giver, and even though he knew his men were oath-tied and loyal, there was no harm in reminding them whom they served, especially when there was an emperor around.

"Emperor Nikephoros has laid bare the bones of it," the jarl went on, glowering at us. "He has a son, and the chances are that the man who is now eating at Nikephoros's table has the boy locked up with a knife at his throat in case his father should come looking for his favorite mead horn."

"It's what I would do," Olaf murmured, though I was not clear whether he was talking about the knife business or the mead horn part. Still, we all agreed that an all-out attack probably would see the emperor's son Staurakios killed if the traitor Arsaber was holding him, and though that did not overly concern most of us, it was something the Greeks were keen to avoid.

It was time to start Loki-scheming, then, and I said as much, at which Sigurd nodded.

Nikephoros leaned on the rail and looked out to sea. "We are not the first men to cast our anchors into Elaea's waters on our way to war," he said, turning his face back to Sigurd. "A king of Athens called Menestheus brought fifty black ships here on his way to fight against the Trojans in the great war. Though from what I have read, I do not think he was a brave man."

"I have heard this story," Egfrith said, frowning with the mind strain of digging up the memory. "The war was over a woman, I believe. Thousands of fools died over a woman."

Nikephoros said this was true but added that any man would have given his life for Helen of Troy. He cocked one dark eyebrow. "She was the most beautiful woman in the world."

"No point in dying for the wench, then," Olaf put in, shaking his head at Svein. "You can't swive a beauty if you're dead. She'll be off rolling around with someone else while you're left with the maggots."

"Being dead is the only way an old fart like you could get stiff enough for swiving," Bothvar said, rousing some good laughs and earning himself a glower from Uncle. But Sigurd silenced them with a hand.

"I want to hear more about this war over a woman," he said, gesturing for the emperor to continue, and it seemed he was not alone in thirsting for a good story. Men were clustering like flies on a carcass, tilting their ears toward the Greek, bracing to catch every word. For such men a fine tale will almost make up for a dry throat and an empty belly.

Nikephoros nodded, and I sighed because I was getting tired of turning English into Norse.

"King Menestheus was one of Helen of Troy's suitors," Nikephoros said, "though she married the Spartan king, Menelaus. Things turned bad when a Trojan prince called Paris, who was visiting King Menelaus, stole Helen. He carried her off back to Troy." He smiled then. "I suspect she had fallen in love with this Paris," he said, "but that would have been harder for the Spartan king to swallow."

"All this talk of marriage and love is sending me to sleep," Bjarni moaned at me as though it were my fault. "You can leave those bits out, Raven."

"You'll get what you're given and be thankful for it, Bjarni," I gnarred as Nikephoros continued with the story.

"Either way the Greeks wanted her back, and King Menelaus gathered the mightiest army the world has ever known."

The tale was a long one and got better as it went, ending with some low cunning by the Greeks involving a wooden horse and plenty of killing and plunder, which is the way all good stories should be.

At the end of it Nikephoros looked exhausted, and Egfrith whispered that he suspected the imperial tongue was not used to flapping quite so much because in Miklagard, Nikephoros had others to do his talking for him.

No one had enjoyed the story of the Trojan War more than Sigurd, who seemed to like the idea that a warrior king had moored on this same shore all those years ago.

"I will go to Miklagard myself and see with my own eyes what we face in helping Nikephoros back onto his throne," he said, looking north. There were some ayes and nods at this but more rumbles and moans, perhaps because they did not want their jarl putting himself at risk or perhaps because they were jealous that he would see the Great City before them. "The emperor will stay here." He grinned at Nikephoros, who gave a slight nod, thumb and forefinger worrying at his crow-black beard. "How can he pay us if he's caught or dead?" Sigurd said, which stirred murmurs of approval. "General Bardanes and the warrior Theo will show me what I need to see."

"You can't go off with them alone!" Svein the Red gnarred. He spit drily. "I don't trust either of those two. Slippery as two snakes in a bucket of snot they are."

"Black Floki and Raven will come too," Sigurd said, which did nothing to wipe the frown off the giant's face, because Svein had not heard his own name mentioned.

"I speak some Greek," Egfrith said with a shrug, easing those words between us all like a twist of resin-soaked hair between two ship strakes.

Sigurd stared at him for a heartbeat, then nodded. "The monk comes too," he said, piling more misery onto Svein.

As for me, my skin was prickling at the thought of being one of the first to see the golden city. The hairs on the back of my neck were still bristling at dusk two days later when *Wave-Steed* sneaked back into our cove with her captured prey—a fishing boat—trailing at the end of a rope lashed to her sternpost.

The fisherman was silver-haired, brown as old shoe leather, and spindly and shrunken with age. His boat had been repaired many times and looked less than seaworthy, which was all to the good, said Sigurd, for no one would pay such a boat approaching Miklagard any notice. As it turned out, its owner was a better fisherman than I, for the bilge of his skiff was choked with a great mound of shifting silver. Maddened by their own silver lust, gulls wheeled and tumbled above, the bravest of them diving now and then but veering off at the last moment.

We would have taken the Greek's fish anyway, but we did not need to, for when Bardanes told him he was in the presence of his emperor, he fell to his knees and began to tremble so that I thought his old bones would crumble with the force of it. As all he had was his boat and his fish, he offered all his fish to Nikephoros, which was at least wiser than giving away his old boat. Bardanes questioned him and was none too friendly about it either, so far as we could tell from the bits Egfrith translated and some scraps that Bardanes himself threw our way. In a stuttering voice as rough as oak bark the man said he was a simple but loyal subject who knew nothing of imperial affairs. He claimed he did not even know that Basileus Nikephoros had been usurped, which, looking at him, I thought was likely to be true.

"This man is a free man?" Bjarni asked, scratching the bristles on his upper cheek.

"He's free," Olaf said, "but I know what you mean. Even the most worthless of my thralls back home doesn't show me the respect this shriveled old hole shows his lord."

Bjarni shook his head. "He's terrified, Uncle," he said. "He's wearing the same face I'd put on if Thór appeared before me bollock naked with Mjöllnir over his shoulder still dripping giant's blood." We all thought that was well said by Bjarni, and it made us look at Nikephoros again. Here was a man as powerful as King Karolus, or at least he would be if some upstart hadn't stolen his throne from under his imperial arse. Now it was our job to get him back on that throne, and one of the first things that had to happen for us to do that was for the fisherman to take us to the Great City.

chapter
TWENTY-TWO

It was farther than I had thought, especially in a leaky old fish-stinking skiff with five other men to upset the balance every time one of them moved to scratch his arse or undo a cramp. Bardanes had not come with us as it turned out. Nikephoros would not risk his general being recognized in the city, and this was probably wise because if the emperor's enemies captured Bardanes, they would know that Nikephoros was not far away. So Theo was to be our guide, and that itched more than a little. It is hard work trying to be well mannered toward a man who has killed your friend, though I suppose that the fight being fair should have made it a touch easier. And so we five, simply dressed and armed only with knives, along with the fisherman, were crammed into that boat like salted cod in a barrel, hoping the wood would not split and spill us out to sink to the bottom like wyrd-cursed nithings. But the fisherman, whose name no one cared to use or remember, was as good a sailor as he was a fish killer and handled the small sail deftly, hopping in and out of our tangle of legs and arms to get the most out of the wind, for with us aboard his boat was heavier than it should have been.

Through the milky fog of breaking dawn we saw

one of those terror-stirring Greek dromons tacking down the eastern coast, making great sawtooth turns against the wind. But we had no reason to fear it in that worthless skiff. There was more chance, Black Floki said through a twist of lips, of some sea creature thinking we were an insect fallen onto the sea and swallowing us than of our being burned.

"Like Jonah and the whale," Egfrith chirped, though no one knew what he was talking about and we didn't ask.

Through the dawn mist we began to see many other craft coming and going, yet none took any interest in us, and it was not until daylight broke, a pale gold wash flooding out of the east, that we saw it.

"By the gods," Sigurd breathed.

"Merciful Father," Egfrith murmured, making the sign of the cross.

Black Floki's eyes looked as if they would burst, as if they were simply too small to hold such a sight. I felt my mouth gaping, warm air on my tongue, and Theo half smiled, clearly pleased with our reaction.

Miklagard! The Golden City revealed itself like a treasure hoard through the smoke of a burning hall, the great domes of Christ churches and palaces pushing head and shoulders above the vast swath of tightly packed white dwellings and all tumbling off seven hills in a glittering array. It was a sight that sucked your breath out of your belly, casting it windward to leave you gasping like a fish.

"Don't tip us out now, Greek!" Black Floki growled to the old silver-hair whose yellow teeth worried his bottom lip as he worked the sail ropes, threading us between two larger trading vessels that were passing in opposite directions. Some men peered over one of those ships' rails and laughed at us—five men and a monk packed into a skiff that boasted barely a hand's breadth of freeboard so that one good wave would swamp us and be the end of it. Sigurd snarled at the indignity of it and hurled a curse back at Rolf on Elaea for not finding a better boat to take his jarl to the Great City. Then, unbelievably, one of the jeering men lobbed a chicken's leg bone at us, which hit Egfrith. The monk grabbed the fleshy bone and held it up like a rune stick.

"*Utinam barbari spatium proprium tuum invadant!*" he called.

"Don't waste your prayers on those goat fuckers," I said, eyeballing the Greeks as we cleared their stern.

"Prayers?" Egfrith said. "I told them may barbarians invade their personal space!" This made us laugh as we drew into the great harbor, which was noisy with shrieking gulls, creaking boats, and men calling from ship to ship. What was even funnier was that we had thought to raid Miklagard with fewer than fifty men, and I said so, at which Sigurd shook his head bewildered, glaring up at the enormous dawn-stained harbor walls.

"You could not do it with five hundred men," he said, and that was true enough.

The closer we came, the larger Miklagard grew. It seemed to swell, rising into the sky before our eyes, so that I suddenly knew how an insect must feel when it looks up at a king's hall. You cannot imagine such a wonder, all glitter and gleam and whitewashed brilliance blazing beneath the pink-blushed morning light. All rolling off its seven hills on that fat thumb peninsula thrust into the sea. Tendrils of smoke from countless hearth fires coiled and wove together, drifting upward to swell the huge filthy brown pall hanging over the heights.

We were among smaller craft now that we were so close to the cliff face that was the harbor wall rising up from the sea. Tenders ferried crews out to larger vessels and skiffs carried food and other goods from place to place along the waterfront, and everywhere was chaos. Men were calling to us from the quayside and from several boats, fighting to get our attention with waving arms and smiles so that I grudgingly accepted that we were lucky to have Theo with us, for a few Greek words from him was enough to deflect their offers of help and trade onto others. On we went, slowly now because there was not much wind in the lee of that huge wall and what there was seemed to swirl in all directions, so that after a while old Silver Hair muttered angrily, wriggled between us, and thrust his oars into the water. But his spindly arms were about as useful as throwing a drowning man both ends of a rope, said Sigurd, and so I took the oars from the old man and rowed us the rest of the way, which was harder than pulling an oar on *Serpent*.

Several times I had to use an oar to push other craft away, for as we drew nearer to one of the many thronging mooring places, the boats became thicker than flies on dung.

"We could walk to the shore from here without getting our boots wet," Black Floki suggested only half in jest. But someone was bound to take offense at us tramping across his boat to get ashore, and even Floki had to admit that a fight would probably not help our chances of entering the city unnoticed. Theo pointed to a narrow gap at the wharf between two larger fishing boats, and I aimed for it, though before I had pulled three strokes, a rope slapped the inside of the hull, thrown by a boy on the dock. Theo pulled us in and we clambered ashore, but not until the Greek had threatened the fisherman with some horrible death or other if he told anyone about having seen the basileus alive.

"He could have just paid the poor man," Egfrith said unhappily. "We took his day's catch after all and made him come all this way."

Sigurd slapped the monk's back, making Egfrith wince, then said: "And he'd have taken the coin to the nearest tavern, drunk like a jarl at Yuletide, and told anyone who would listen that he now supplied fish to the emperor himself." Which was all true of course. Though Theo did flick a small coin at the boy who had thrown us the rope, and that didn't really seem fair to old Silver Hair.

The wall was the height of ten men, a huge curtain of red stone that we followed east, half gazing up at its heights and half watching the chaos out in the harbor. Armed men in red cloaks collected harbor taxes from ship captains. Boys ran up and down, shrieking and making deals and offering themselves as guides to new arrivals. Barrels, chests, huge clay storage jars, and boxes were piled everywhere along the wharf's edge, and the air was thick with the yells of buyers and sellers and captains and crewmen. Every few steps brought a different food smell to my nose—meat, onions, garlic, spices—and we were not even inside the city yet. But there was also the foul stink of shit and slops and refuse of all kinds, which wafted up from the thickly scummed water.

Then we came to a seething throng of folk before one of the massive gates in the red wall, all eager to gain entry to Miklagard. Spear tips glinted in the morning sunlight, and so we knew there were soldiers manning the gate, checking who was entering the city. I looked down at my hands, noting how brown my skin was now after sailing the southern sea road. Yet we would still not pass for Greeks, not least because Sigurd's hair was as gold as Cynethryth's and most of the Greeks I had seen had black hair. Then there were our scars and our bulk, for the Greeks were certainly smaller than us on the whole. I was thinking all this when Black Floki stopped us by clasping Sigurd's shoulder, so that the jarl turned to him, the crowds flowing around us like a stream around a boulder.

"An old one-eyed crone with a skull full of spiders would know that we are warriors," Floki said, "and know too that we do not follow the tortured god, come to that."

"He is right, Sigurd," I said. "They will not like us any more than the Franks did."

"We're in the Greek's hands now," Sigurd said. "We are pieces on his tafl board until we know more about this place." I glanced around and was just about to ask where Theo was anyway, when he suddenly appeared, that chafing half smile on his face and a bulging sack over his shoulder. Behind him, through the crowd, I saw two poorly dressed merchants counting coins and grinning from ear to ear.

"What game is he playing now?" I grumbled, hat-ing the idea that we might have to be grateful to Bram's killer for getting us into the city.

Which is what he did. The guards peered into the sack, and one of them shook his head wearily, took the money Theo offered, and waved us all through as easy as that. It was only once we were inside the gate that I got a look at what had bought our entry. Theo thrust a hand into his sack and pulled something out. It was a trinket made of whitewashed clay: a dome the size of a man's fist with a flat bottom and a Christ cross set on the top.

"What in Heimdall's hairy arse is that?" Sigurd asked, instinctively turning to Father Egfrith because the object had everything of the White Christ about it. But it was Theo who gave us our answer. He pointed west, and we turned to see, up on one of Miklagard's hills and nestled among other domes, tiled roofs, and palaces, a giant version of what the Greek held in his hand.

"It's a White Christ church for ants," Black Floki spit, shaking his head in disbelief. "Even the insects cannot escape this nailed god."

"Pilgrims must surely buy such things," Egfrith said, grinning as he gazed up at the miracle that was the Golden City. "They take them home with them to remind them of their time within the shining city." Theo's sack was full of the things, all exactly the same as one another.

"There must be fifty of the things in there," Floki said.

"Whoever pays good money for something like that must have a hole in his skull leaking all the sense he was born with," I said, and both Sigurd and Floki nod-

ded in agreement with that, though Egfrith seemed
rather taken with the things for some reason I could
not fathom.

The city we now entered reminded me of Rome except that Miklagard had an overwhelming sense of
order about it whereas Rome had been twisted into
many shapes by many hands and ravaged by time.

The wide street was made of small square stones all
the same size and sunk into the ground to create a
solid surface that meant your boots wouldn't become
clumps of mud. Not that there was any mud. I even
saw boys spading horse dung into sacks, which I
pointed out to Floki, who shook his head in wonder at
it all. But the street *was* clotted with people, many of
whom looked as awestruck by the place as we were,
so that I thought we could have been a family of slobbering trolls and no one would have noticed us.

We turned into a narrower side street that was much
quieter where I could gather my swimming thoughts
and sift them into order. Even this street was lined
with countless statues of gleaming white stone and all
of them the size of living men, which to our eyes was
very strange, as though some seidr spell had turned
them all to stone where they stood.

For a time we simply watched the ebb and flow of
the crowds and perhaps would have stood there jaw-
slack all day if Theo had not grown bored with waiting and stalked off. We looked at one another, and
Sigurd shrugged, so we followed Theo wherever he
might take us. Which was deeper into the city. We
joined the murmuring tide of hundreds of folk with
skin more or less sun-blackened, who dressed in every
color of Bifröst. We gave ourselves over to wonder and

confusion in equal measure as we gazed at endless rows of stone dwellings three times the height of a jarl's hall, with wind holes at several levels that were covered with glass! Many of the dwellings had platforms that hung out over the street and from whose edges flowers and plants cascaded, besieged by bees. Other streets shot off in all directions, lined with even taller buildings, though many of them were not richly adorned but shabby and clearly built so that several families could live one atop the other. They stood cheek by jowl with rich churches, palaces, and trade houses, making me think of those tall white mushrooms that can spring up overnight.

I had half expected armed men on the streets ready to stamp on any trouble, for the emperor had been deposed and new hands were on the reins. But Egfrith explained that in such a city as Constantinople life goes on as normal no matter who is calling himself emperor. "Nothing," he said, "can stand in the way of greed, and even a usurper knows that trade must flow on like a river. Nothing must stop his subjects from making money." He wriggled through the press to keep up with us. "There is twice the wealth here that there is in Rome!" he went on. "See what man can achieve, Sigurd, when he lives within the true faith under the protection of a God-fearing prince." I had thought the monk had given up trying to make a Christ man out of Sigurd, but it seemed the Great City had renewed him. Which was worth a muttered curse or two by my reckoning.

"The White Christ followers in your land still live in shit, monk," Sigurd replied, and if Egfrith had an answer for that, I did not hear what it was for I was muscling through the throng to get to a wine seller who stood in the shade of a tree with a vast green canopy. In the time it takes to drain a horn of good mead we were on our third cup of watered wine, thanks to Theo's Greek coin. It was sweet and delicious, and it sluiced the dry sting of sea salt from our throats, making us grin like gormless fools.

"Aah, now I can think straight," Sigurd announced with a smile, dragging a palm across his lips. I blinked at that.

"I do not think straight thinking is what is needed in Miklagard," I said, lifting an eyebrow. Black Floki and Sigurd shared a look, then the jarl turned back to me and his smile stretched into a grin.

"That is well said, young Raven," he said, for though we had only just arrived in Miklagard, it was already clear as new ice that there was nothing straightforward about the city.

We walked east along a wide tree-lined street, the sun fully risen now so that it squashed us with strength-sapping heat. Yet even the wine sweat burning our eyes could not stop us from gawking. Every house looked as if it could belong to the emperor. Each was set within its own abundance of trees and flowers and protected by a wall twice a man's height. The wooden doors in those walls were elaborately carved and so huge that Thór himself could have staggered through drunk and swinging his hammer and still not scuffed the edges. The houses themselves boasted painted lintels, and some even had statues standing guard on ledges on either side of the wind holes or peering down on us mortals from flat, flower-strewn roofs.

On we went, passing fountains flowing with cool, clear water and bridges set on tall columns, which we soon learned carried not people but water to every part of the city. We had seen similar things in Rome, but there you would see a ruin next to a palace or a hovel up against a church. Here almost everything looked as though its purpose was to impress, and Sigurd said as much. "Where we are from a rich jarl may have a hall, a good ship or two, and Baldr-beautiful war gear. Then he is less only than a king. But here it seems that everyone is as rich as a jarl. Richer!"

"It is easy to see why this Arsaber wanted the city for himself," Black Floki said as though he appreciated the traitor's silver lust.

"And why Nikephoros wants it back," I said, cuffing sweat from my eyes as we reached the top of a church-crowned hill on which a whisper of breeze brought a welcome respite from the oppressive heat. With the gust came the sweet scent of flowers and honey. Egfrith hurried over to the church, which was so bright white that I could barely look at it, then rapped on the door. When I next looked over, he had disappeared inside. The rest of us were gazing down to the east. Below, spreading out from the foot of the hill, was the largest market we had ever seen. The hum of thousands floated up to us, sounding like the sea or, as Sigurd said, a distant battle, as merchants and customers traded word blows among a vast tapestry of richly colored canopies. It was like a seething ocean and far more tumultuous than the real sea into which the peninsula stretched a little farther to the east. But before your eyes got to the huge curtain wall with its many soaring towers, they fell upon the place

Nikephoros had tasked Theo with showing us: the Great Palace. It sat behind an enormous blade-shaped arena on the southeastern edge of the peninsula. Farther north, set upon a low hill, was the biggest White Christ church I had ever seen, whose roof was the same shape as the blaumen's church we had named Gerd's Tit, but this roof was all blazing gold and had a cross on the top. As for the palace itself, it seemed to be a sprawl of rounded roofs and buildings, some white, some painted red, but all grander and more richly adorned than anything we had seen in Frankia or even in Rome.

"Basileus . . . emperor. Live here," Theo said, nodding down at the palace. Black Floki muttered that he had gathered that much for himself, but then the Greek warrior seemed to point beyond the palace, and at first I thought he was pointing at the sea or one of the many craft gliding across it.

"Where's the damned monk when we need him?" Sigurd snarled.

"He means that building which is detached from the main complex," I said, squinting into the shimmering midday glare.

Theo spit a stream of words of which I only caught one, which was "Arsaber," though the hate smeared across his brown face said more in its own way.

"My Greek is, I'm sorry to say, very poor," Egfrith said, appearing suddenly, "but I think Theophilos is trying to tell you that the traitor Arsaber prefers to live in the Bucoleon Palace, which is that grand-looking building on the shore. Do you see it? The one incorporated into the harbor walls."

"I see it, monk," Sigurd said, clenching his jaw as he took his golden hair in two hands and tied it back with a leather thong.

"Now, Raven, tell Egfrith why this Arsaber is an arse-witted fool," he said, the twist of a grin threatening his salt-cracked lips.

I glanced at Floki, who nodded encouragingly because he knew the answer was sitting on my tongue.

I felt the warm air across my teeth. "He is a fool because he lives a spear's throw from the breakers," I said, eyeballing Egfrith. "And we are wolves of the sea."

chapter
TWENTY-THREE

THAT NIGHT we slept in a thunderously noisy tavern on the waterfront outside the harbor wall. It was a stinking place choked with whores and drunks, rough men from the port who could afford the wine there because they had pilfered most of it from their own cargoes and sold it cheaply to the tavern owners. As soon as goods passed through one of the city gates, their price tripled, which was for two main reasons as I understood it from Theo through Egfrith's rough translating. First, the merchants had to cover the tax imposed on them for the privilege of selling their goods within the Great City, and second, because Miklagard's inhabitants were so rich that they would pay stupid prices just because they could.

But we weren't there for the cheap wine, though we had plenty of it. We had come for the blather, and by the time I was raging drunk and staggering like a dancing bear, I had to admit a grudging respect for Theo because he'd gathered two earfuls of it and told us more besides. It turned out that Staurakios was not only Basileus Nikephoros's son, he was coemperor of the Eastern Roman Empire, crowned less than two years previously by Nikephoros himself.

"I can't fathom why Nikephoros made no mention

of this," Black Floki slurred, chewing the words and then belching loudly enough to wake the dead.

"I can," Sigurd said, swallowing. "I might have doubted his ability to get his hands on the silver he's going to owe us if I had known there was another emperor with keys to the hoard."

This seemed as good an explanation as any to me, and even Floki admitted as much with another belch.

"Arsaber captured Staurakios as he made his move on the throne," Egfrith explained as Theo quenched his thirst and eyeballed the room, "albeit they seem to be treating Staurakios well so as not to upset the other lords of Miklagard or provoke plots against Arsaber. He is guarded day and night and kept somewhere, no one seems to know where exactly, in the Great Palace. But . . ." A grin stole onto the monk's face at this bit. ". . . he is permitted to pray to God once a day in the Church of the Holy Wisdom, which the Greeks call Hagia Sophia." Sigurd's eyes lit up at this. "By freeing Staurakios," Egfrith went on, "we would rob Arsaber of that leverage."

In my head I heard Bram say that sounded easy enough. *Cut up the guards and take the son,* he growled. But I knew it would not be that easy, for we could never get enough armed men inside the city, never mind getting out again. Also, if we made a proper fight of it, Arsaber would know to expect an attack and would plant a forest of spears around himself.

"We'll go to this Christ church tomorrow," Sigurd said, scrubbing his beard as though hoping a scheme might jump out of it. "If there is a chance to do it then—take the boy quietly—we will. But if not, we will get a better look at the problem." You have never seen

two more different faces than Father Egfrith's and
Black Floki's, both of them sculpted by the same prospect of visiting the biggest god-house in Miklagard.

"If you're going to make me go into that White
Christ house," Floki said to Sigurd, pointing a finger
at the jarl accusingly, "you are going to have to buy
me more wine." And I seconded that.

If I had not already felt green and bilious from the
wine the night before, the Church of the Holy Wisdom
would have done it to me anyway. Try as I might, I just
could not reckon how men could have built the place,
and neither could the others, including Egfrith. With
its round golden roof it had looked enormous from the
hill to the west the day before, but now it filled my
world, pulling my eyes up and up so that the gristle
pulled taut in my throat and my mouth hung open. It
was huge beyond imagining, a great soaring mass of
stones piled one upon the other up into the sky.

"Are you sure this house belongs to the same god
that you worship, monk?" Black Floki asked, looking
askance at the monk as though he was not looking
forward to the reply.

"Of course!" Egfrith said, those words smearing a
full-on grimace within Floki's crow-black beard. I
knew what the Norseman was thinking. He was
thinking that the white god must be much more powerful in these parts than he was back in the north for
men to have built him such a place. For surely there
was magic involved in the massive carved stones of
Hagia Sophia. How else could they have risen to the
sky like that?

It was past midday now and hot enough to hard-boil your bollocks. From dawn we had waited in the shadow of a stand of trees whose leaves had fluttered green and silver and rattled in the morning breeze. We were by the god-house's southeastern entrance, making a show of trying to sell Theo's ant churches to the constant stream of White Christ followers who entered the place. Egfrith was prattling, using what Greek his tongue could navigate to hawk the useless objects to folk who for the most part couldn't give a gnat's fart. Black Floki and I were grinning like fools, brandishing the clay baubles as though they were silver jarl torcs and anyone who did not want one at the price we were selling at must be blind, moon mad, or both.

Meanwhile, Theo and Sigurd stood a little way off by the southeastern door because that, so said Theo, was the entrance used by Miklagard's emperors. They leaned against the wall of a fountain, pretending to play a game on a board inscribed with squares that Theo had bought from a street stall. I think it was like tafl except that the pieces were miniature horses and other figures skillfully carved from bone, though whether the two of them were actually playing I could not tell. I suspected they were, but what they were also doing was watching for the arrival of Staurakios and Arsaber's men.

They came in the late afternoon when the sun had rolled into the west, mercifully taking some of its ferocity with it. There was no mistaking Staurakios. The ten red-cloaked soldiers with their long shields surrounding him gave him away, but once I got a look at him, I knew without a doubt that he was Nikephoros's son. He was taller perhaps and younger of course, but he had the same thin face and intelligent eyes as his father. His beard was short, neat, and oiled in the Greek way, and his dark hair was arrow-straight to the chin, where it then curled out, glistening like a wet otter. He looked as much an emperor as his father, too, which of course he was, and despite being clothed in a simple long tunic and brown cloak, he walked with the pride-stiff back of a man who has no other way to defy his circumstances.

Sigurd had given his birdcall to alert us, and with that we stashed the sack of baubles beneath a thorny bush and joined the spate of chattering folk converging on the massive stone entrance to the church with its carved lintel. It seemed to take an age to pass the threshold, for there were soldiers there checking everyone who entered for weapons, but we got in without any trouble, having stashed our knives too.

If the outside had stretched my mind's fathom rope to the point of snapping, the inside finished the job. There were no beams or columns supporting the enormous, glittering golden billow of the roof, yet somehow all that gold hung there above us when it should have crashed down on our heads. Whereas we were used to leaving true light behind when we entered a place, relying on flame to light the dark, this place was a blaze of light both from the sun's rays lancing in through countless wind holes high up and from the gold mosaics, glittering purple bricks, glistening pillars, and huge bronze doors. Pictures of the Christ and of his saints and angels were everywhere you looked, so that I felt the hairs stiffen all over my body and could only imagine what Black Floki was feeling. I half expected to see his skin blistering, for no one hated the tortured god more than he. Except maybe Asgot. But here were pictures of men and women too, some of whom looked like Nikephoros, and these I thought must be past emperors long in their cold graves.

Men and women were lighting candles, the whisper of hundreds of prayers fluttering in the cool of the place like moths. Somewhere high above, in one of the many passageways that ran around the inner wall, monks were singing their dreadful songs, the languid miserable dirges tainting the air like damp. Somewhere else someone was burning a spice that filled the place with a sweet, musky smell. But I did not have the time to marvel at the painted faces looking down from the walls or at the gold and glittering black of the stonework. I was searching through the meek, prayer-muttering Christ folk for the red-cloaked soldiers. For when we found them, we would find Staurakios.

It was Egfrith who found them. The monk caught my eye and nodded to the eastern end of the place, where, in a separate chamber, Staurakios was on his knees, head bowed before an altar of green stone. He looked asleep to me or dead from boredom, and I whispered as much to Egfrith, who tutted because he thought I was being deliberately impious. Which of course I was. The guards stood around talking, though every once in a while one of them would eyeball the worshippers to make sure all was as it should be.

"I know that face, lad. What are you thinking?" Sigurd breathed, dropping a coin into a silver dish and taking a beeswax candle from a pile. "I can hear ideas squirming in that skull of yours."

I had paid nothing for the candle I now held against another's flame, and I felt strangely guilty about it. *It's the Christ seidr gnawing at you, Raven*, I thought with a shudder, placing the candle in its holder without looking at Sigurd.

"I'm thinking there are a lot of soldiers," I murmured, at which the jarl nodded suspiciously. What I was really thinking about was Freyja, called Gefn— the giver—and Mardöll, sea-brightener, who is more beautiful than any sun-glistened fjord. She is the goddess of love; all Norse know that. But men say she is a warrior goddess, too, a spear-wielding Valkyrie who claims half the battle-slain alongside Ódin; a strange thought, surely, but not as strange as my mind filling with thoughts of Freyja, like a god-house glutting with kneelers. Odd given that I stood in that powerful Christ place with dead saints' eyes boring into me like ship rivets. I was thinking of the goddess's tears, for she is said to weep tears of red gold. Freyja, who is also bynamed Thrungva—"throng."

"We should leave now before someone gets suspicious," Egfrith hissed. I nodded. So did Black Floki, and from the look on Theo's face, he was coming up short in the way of ideas, too.

"It is hard to think of schemes with that monk song curdling the air," Sigurd gnarred through a grimace. "We will come back tomorrow when we have thought of a way." The others nodded, and Egfrith made the sign of the cross over his chest and turned to leave.

And then it came to me: *tears of red gold*.

I was moving. I could hear my boots scuffing against the flagstone floor and was vaguely aware of Floki hissing at me to come back. Candles flickered, and burnished stone glittered. The musky air thrummed with whispered prayers, and the mournful voices of monks swam around my ears and made my blood prickle.

Red gold.

I was close enough to Staurakios now to see that in contrast to the drab tunic and cloak, his shoes were lavish affairs of red cloth, pearls, and glossy jewels. I saw a gold ring gleam on his laced fingers and heard his prayer mumble bouncing off the stone around him. Then, just as two of the red cloaks turned, spears coming up, I skewed left and into an adjoining chamber, where a white statue of a woman stood on a plinth, illuminated by candles. I fell to my knees before it, feeling the cool stone seep through my breeks and hoping that what I was doing was something that a Christ follower might do. Though who this stone person was I did not know. It was not Freyja, not in this god-house. I knew that much. Still, she was beautiful whoever she was. Her face had a kindness to it and a calm that I have rarely seen in a real woman other than when she has been asleep or is cradling a newborn. She looked sad, too, and I wished Bjarni could see the craft that had gone into the carving of stone so that it looked like flesh and almost had life.

She was a forgotten woman, this one, alone in a chamber whose walls were cracked and whose paint was old and faded. Platforms raised on wooden frames hugged the walls so that men could climb up and fill the cracks, as we pack daub into wall crevices or thumb tarred hair between ship strakes. Yet there were no men here. Just me. And thoughts of the goddess. And so I pinched out most of the candles, and I climbed, the acrid smoke following me and filling my nostrils. Up I went, the trestle creaking like a ship at sea until I reached the highest board, which was just over three men's height from the ground and to my mind not a good place to be. My heart was thumping against my ribs like a smith's hammer on an anvil, and I was sweat-soaked despite the coolness of the place. The platform was about the size of a normal door, and I peered over the edge, cursing my foolishness. To my relief the chamber was empty.

Then it was not. Father Egfrith was there, peering around the darkened room, his fingers clawing at the back of his head as though it had woodworm.

"Here!" I hissed, and he looked up, his eyes bulging. Then he dropped to his knees before the stone woman just as I had done, which at least told me I had gotten that part right.

"Come down, you fool!" he rasped through tight lips. "You'll get us killed, you brainless ox!" His neck twisted as he glanced behind him. "Come down!"

"I'll kill you myself if you don't shut your mouth, Egfrith!" I seethed.

Tears of red gold. All I had was my small eating knife, but it was more than enough. I sliced into my hand, pulling the blade along the full flesh between thumb and wrist. Blood brimmed at the slit, and I made a fist, edging out until my hand was directly above the stone woman. Then the first fat drops fell.

Egfrith's mouth fell open. Crimson spattered on white stone, and the monk closed his eyes for two heartbeats. Then, still kneeling, he threw up his arms and yelled in Latin or Greek—I was not sure which, but I heard the word *miraculum* in it. The man shrieked,

his voice cutting through the Christ-thick air, and my
heart stopped beating. Folk were coming, feet slapping
the stone as they ran. I took one last look down and
saw that most of the drips had missed, landing in dark
stars on the stone floor. Three or four, though, had
streaked down the woman's breast. Not tears, perhaps,
but strange enough coming from a statue. Then I
shifted back against the wall, making myself tight as a
sleeping mouse and hoping that I could not be seen
from below.

Voices filled the chamber as folk realized what
Egfrith was yelling about, and then others were bellowing too and women were howling and crying.
That dark forgotten place was suddenly all madness, and still more were coming, their yells adding
to the din. I had made a rat's nest of the god-house.
It was chaos.

Which was just what Sigurd and Floki and Theo
needed.

But then my platform began to shake, the timbers
chattering like loose teeth, and I flattened myself even
more, for there was nothing to grip on to without
showing my hands to those below.

"Raven!" *Why is the damned fool calling me?* I
thought, cursing Egfrith. Then I realized why, just as
the frame shook like thunder and I began to bounce
on the platform and the clamor turned from wonder
to fury. They knew!

"Raven, get down!" Egfrith's reedy English cut
through the squall, and I gripped the uprights, fearing
a broken back more than the rage of Christ kneelers. I
looked over the edge into hundreds of shocked, hate-
filled, and maddened faces just as the whole frame

struck the wall once, twice, then began to tip beyond
the balance point. Folk screamed, and I clenched my
teeth and clung on, not knowing what else to do, and I
thought I saw the flash of red cloaks among the throng.
Freyja Thrungva—throng, I thought as the whole
frame fell and me with it.

I landed on three women, which was bad for them
but good for me, as the frame snapped and splintered
with a great *crash*. Then Egfrith was there, hauling
me up with one arm and brandishing a broken timber
at the crowds, screaming at them. I'd had the wind
knocked out of me and could not get a breath, but that
didn't stop the little monk from dragging me to my
feet. He lashed about him wildly, spit flying from his
mouth, and pulled me bent double through the seething madness. A man grabbed at me, and Egfrith cracked
the stick against his face, dropping him, then snarled at
another man, which was enough. Soldiers were fighting among the crowd, and I saw one of them on the
floor and recognized Floki's eating knife sticking from
his neck; then we broke through the tight press, and I
gasped, filling my sore lungs, and ran.

Into the dying heat of the day.

"Where now?" I heaved, turning to look back up at
the Hagia Sophia to see if we were being followed. We
had taken a shady path off the south-side courtyard,
following others who were running to escape the violence, but had seen nothing of Sigurd and the others.
We would have to recover our stashed gear later.

"Somewhere quiet," Egfrith wheezed, putting a
hand to his face to see if he was bleeding. He was, but
only from a scratch where someone had made a grab
for him in the snarl. I ached all over after that bone

rattling, but nothing inside me was broken so far as I could tell.

I shook my head. "No, monk. Crowds. We want crowds," I said, knowing that losing ourselves among Miklagard's hordes would be the best thing we could do. Egfrith thought about that for a moment and then agreed with a curt nod, and so we loped off to the east, the sun at our backs, heading for the Mese, which Egfrith had said was Greek for "middle" and which was, at twenty-five paces wide, the main thoroughfare of the Great City.

The street was not swarming as it had been earlier in the day, but there were still enough folk on it for us to become inconspicuous, the thinnest gray thread among a great colorful weave of merchants, pilgrims, traders, and Greeks. We did not walk in the middle, instead sticking to the darker, shaded column-lined porticoes that ran along both sides of the street, which housed permanent stalls selling every type of goods imaginable.

"There can be no other city like Constantinople on God's earth," Egfrith said as much to himself as to me as we stood for a few moments catching our breath and glancing around for signs of danger. It seemed we were safe enough for now, and I said as much as we went on, following the road past the Hippodrome—the sword-blade-shaped arena used for horse races—and two palaces either one of which any Asgard dweller would be proud to own. After about six hundred paces we came to the Forum of Constantine, which was to me as impressive in its way as the grandest buildings we had already seen. An ocean of smooth stone with huge monumental gates to the east and west, it was dominated by a gleaming red column that must have been taller than any of Thór's enemies in Jötunheim and upon whose top stood a naked spear-armed warrior of bronze. Islands of men and women stood here and there talking and laughing. Christ priests traded words, beggars rattled dishes at passersby, and all clung to the cool shadows of countless other statues and monuments like clusters of mussels in tide pools.

This is where the jarls would hold great tings, where warriors would talk of raiding and ships and plunder to be had, I thought, *if Norsemen lived in Miklagard.*

Here was yet another of the Great City's wonders: a statue of a hulking beast with massive ears and a long snaking nose. One monstrous foot was raised as though the beast were about to stamp down and crush its enemy, and I asked Egfrith what story ever mentioned such a creature.

"The Greeks used to invent monsters to make their tales more exciting," he said, shaking his head disapprovingly. But I smiled because at last I had found something we shared with the Greeks, though even then there were no people better than the Norse at weaving color into a story to make it brighter.

We decided to go south, agreeing that the harbor was where we would find the others if they had not been caught or worse. And find them we eventually did. Sigurd and Black Floki were sitting on the edge of the bustling quayside, each gripping a wooden cup as they looked out across the glittering, ship-strewn harbor. A saggy wineskin sat between them, and they looked as if they had not a trouble in the world.

"I can see you are worrying yourselves sick about

us," I said, at which they both twisted their necks, grins splitting their beards. "But we are safe, so do not concern yourselves about it." I raised a hand to allay their absent fears.

"We were just saying what a black thing it was for you to meet your life thread's end in a White Christ house like that," Sigurd said, shaking his head. They both wore felt hats with wide brims of the sort that many in the Great City wore, and the jarl seemed rather taken with his, though I thought they looked ridiculous. "It is no lie that Black Floki was just about to sail to Asgard," he said, pointing at a tiny skiff bobbing at its mooring, "to burn the Norns' loom for their being such cruel bitches. But here you are!"

"You've saved me some hard rowing," Black Floki said through the twist of a smile.

"Anything for you, Brother," I said with a smirk and a bow. "The truth of it is I might have been dead if not for Egfrith," I added, as surprised to hear it as I was to say it. "He can be fearsome with two feet of Greek wood." The Norsemen looked at the monk dubiously from under their hat rims. Egfrith wafted the praise away.

"I took no pleasure in Raven's ungodly deceit," he said, making the sign of the cross, "or in my own base actions. Violence is the last course, only taken when there is no other way." He touched the sore-looking cut on his cheek. "I delivered some poor man quite a blow," he said, shaking his head, though I felt sure there was the smallest sliver of pride in him all the same, like a splinter from a short length of cedar.

"Quite a blow? I'll wager he choked on his own

teeth," I said, unable to tame my grin. "I think I saw his ears fly off and slap some woman across the face."

"That's enough, Raven," Egfrith snapped, raising a finger at me and turning back to Sigurd. "What of Staurakios?" he asked. "And where is Theo?"

"Sit down, monk, and you, Raven," Sigurd said, "before you give away our disguises." We sat watching the boats coming and going as Sigurd told us how it had gone for them in the Hagia Sophia. When Egfrith had screamed that the statue—which he told me was of Mary, the White Christ's mother—was weeping blood, the kneelers and groaners had rushed from every corner of the place to see the miracle for themselves. In the tumult the soldiers guarding Staurakios had panicked and, grabbing their charge, tried to force their way out through the crowds.

"I think some of the Christ folk thought they were trying to stop them from seeing the weeping stone woman," Sigurd said, "and they got angry as wasps about that." He shrugged and grinned. "In that chaos the red cloaks did not see us coming at them."

"I near enough had to step over one of them," I said, glancing at Floki, "and I recognized the knife in his throat."

"That was a good knife," he said wistfully.

"So you got him?" I said, meaning Staurakios.

Floki nodded. "We got him."

"But we feared the Greeks would first come here to the harbor looking for him," Sigurd added. "They do not know our faces, but they know Staurakios. For now Theo is hiding him deep inside the city where they will never find him."

It turned out that Staurakios had played his part

too, dropping two red cloaks with a ferocity, if not skill, that had impressed Sigurd.

"But what I am itching to know, Raven," Sigurd said, wincing as he removed the felt hat and scratched his head, "is how you came up with it."

I was watching two skippers yelling at each other furiously, arguing over who had been first to the quayside and so had the right to the berth from which another vessel had just slipped her moorings. One of the traders had had its bows half in the berth when the other had nosed in, so that now the ships were clunking together with the harbor's calm sway while their crews hurled insults across a foot of sea.

"I had been thinking of Freyja," I said honestly, then shrugged. "The goddess put the scheme in my head."

"Not Loki?" Black Floki asked, surprised. I shook my head. "Then you have more luck with goddesses than you do with mortal women." I suspected he was alluding to Cynethryth. With a grimace I admitted that was true and said that if not for that worm Ealdred, Cynethryth and I might have been married and breeding pigs on some small farm in Wessex by now. But the Norsemen laughed at that, Egfrith too as it happened, though why they thought that idea was so funny I could not say.

We stayed long enough to see which crew won the mooring, and it turned out that neither of them did, because some plume-helmed harbormaster, all gold, mouth, and strut, came at the prow of some runt of a Greek dromon and threatened both captains and sent them on their way, leaving the berth free for some trade cog full of wine jars. That was just as well given that we needed a boat to take us back to Elaea. The skipper of this boat had barely tied up before he was casting off again, his purse heavy with Sigurd's silver and us in his bows, sampling the wares.

"Which god put this scheme in *your* head, lord?" I asked, pouring more wine into Sigurd's cup. I was enjoying this journey a thousand times more than I had the one in that cramped fish-gut-stinking skiff. Sigurd banged his cup against mine, sloshing wine into the bilge.

"Ah, this one was all my own," he said, his face toward the westering sun that was turning the sea to burnished bronze.

chapter
TWENTY-FOUR

BACK ON Elaea and in reach of his sea chest, Sigurd bought every last drop of wine the Greek had and almost all his water too, which was the sensible thing to do for two reasons I could think of: first, because the men were able to slake their thirst and had fostered a strong liking for wine, and second, because having sold all of his stock for a good price, the merchant would head off south again the next morning to resupply, meaning he would not return to Miklagard with news of a heathen war band camped out on Elaea. Of course, there was a chance he would pass another crew and tell them about us and they would take that rumor to the Great City, but Sigurd had told the wine merchant through Egfrith to stop at Elaea on his way back, for there was every chance we would be thirsty again by then. And men set on becoming rich rarely tell others where to find good customers. Besides which, we had far bigger problems than that, as Sigurd was now telling everyone by the flickering glow of the dying meal fire.

The men's faces had changed over the course of the telling and were now as grim as cliffs and dark-browed. They had been waiting on the sand and shingle when we had returned, hurling questions at us against the wind even before we had cleared the breakers, more thirsty for news than for the cargo we had brought. They had wanted to know if the buildings in Miklagard were really made of gold and how many rich Christ houses there were ripe for plundering. They were eager to hear what the women looked like and how much silver it would cost them for a roll with a pretty whore. Even Svein had gotten over his sulking at being left behind, the scowl I had seen as we came ashore slowly melting until he was grinning like Grendal chewing a leg bone as Black Floki came to the fighting part.

The story grew taller as the wine jars grew lighter, so that now there had been twenty red cloaks and the raised platform I had fallen from was as tall as an oak. Father Egfrith had even killed two men in our escape, which had a few of them slitting eyes and scratching chins but clearly impressed others, and we let them lap it all up, revisiting the Great City's marvels through the men's changing faces as the sun slid into the Western Sea. They particularly enjoyed the telling of my trick with the statue of the Christ mother and her tears of blood, shaking their heads and growling about how that was as low and cunning a ruse as they had ever heard of.

Sitting among his own men, his patience worn thin as a hen's lip, Bardanes had demanded that we get to the part about Staurakios, but Sigurd had refused to humor him, saying that he who rushes a good story makes himself almost as unpopular as he who demands the ending before the end. So the Greek had glowered at the jarl from then on, his eyes murderous as an eagle's and the muscles beneath his black beard pulsing restlessly. But when, after deliberately dragging it out, it seemed to me, Sigurd finally announced that Staurakios was safely stashed and Theo with him, Bardanes and Nikephoros had nodded soberly and the emperor had taken himself apart and knelt to give thanks to his god.

"Bastard ought to be thanking Sigurd," Penda growled at me, and I could not disagree with that.

Now, though, Sigurd was finished with the skald weave of it and deep into the cold hard truth, which sobered men up like a walk through snow. There was no way, he said, that we could get ourselves and mail, shields, and blades into the city. Even if we got past the dromons guarding the port, into the harbor, and on to the quayside without the Greek soldiers knowing about it, the city walls would stop us. Perhaps we could fight our way through the gates, but by then every soldier in the city would have come, and according to Bardanes, there were many thousands of them. They could close the gates and trap us inside the city, and we would die. If by some miracle we got inside the city and fought our way to the palace, the dromons would return to the harbor, burn our ships, and spew more men for us to fight.

"Miklagard is rich beyond anything you have ever dreamed," Sigurd said, at which wolf grins glinted by flame light. "But it could not have become the city it is if its people did not feel safe enough to make themselves rich instead of pissing their breeks about who might be coming to kill and steal. It is my thinking that not even King Karolus and all his Franks could sack Miklagard." Lips sheathed teeth once more, and I heard some grunts and gripes.

"So you have told us how it cannot be done," Beiner the Dane rumbled. "Now tell us how it can be done." This got a chorus of ayes from men who had been with Sigurd long enough to know that he would be sitting on a plan as a hen sits on its egg.

Only this time there was no plan, and Sigurd said as much, telling Beiner that he needed more time to come up with one. This sank like poor Tufi with that Christ cross snagged in his belt, though it made me think that nothing was as heavy as a jarl torc, which Sigurd knew better than anyone. Men give their oath to a jarl, and in return he must give them fame and silver, neither of which they can enjoy if they are dead.

"What about you, Hrafn Refr?" Beiner said, turning to me. Hrafn Refr—"Raven Fox," the fox part because my reputation for low cunning was growing among the Fellowship. But like the rest of them I had been expecting Sigurd to pull some scheme from that silly hat he was still wearing.

"This Arsaber lives in the Bucoleon Palace," I said, "which is so close to the water, it might as well have oars poking from the wind holes. We can swoop in like eagles and make our kill." Yet even as I said it, I knew it could not be done like that after all, though until that point I had thought it could.

Sigurd shook his head. "I have seen it over and over in here," he said, tapping two fingers against his head, "and every time we fail." Beneath the hat's rim the jarl was dark-browed and sullen. "I thought as you did, Raven, when we stood on that hill looking down onto the palace and the harbor beyond. But that, I think, is the thing about the Great City. Everything seems possible when you are there."

"The gods have always favored us for our bold-ness," Svein the Red said. "This is no time to become old women." This got some rumbles of agreement, but they were muted ones because the whole Fellow-ship knew that if Sigurd said something could not be done, the chances were that it could not.

"You are wise, Jarl Sigurd, not to risk a direct as-sault on the Bucoleon," Nikephoros said, gesturing at one of his men to feed the fire. "Its walls rise from the water more than six times the height of a man. With a hundred men the traitor Arsaber could defend those walls until Judgment Day." The fire flared, staining Nikephoros and his dark-eyed Greeks red. "There is a small harbor," he said, "but there will be three, maybe four imperial dromons moored there. Your dragon ships will not get close."

"If Arsaber sees us coming, it is over," Bardanes said, staring into the flames. "We are like the snake that has only enough venom for one kill. If we strike and miss Arsaber—" A sneer slithered across his face. "—they will crush us."

Penda dug an elbow into my ribs, making me spill wine across my breeks. I called him a rancid goat turd and followed his gaze to where it rested on Sig-urd. It was dark, and men's faces were all shifting shadow and flame, but I saw what Penda had seen, which was the lightest twitch of a smile tugging at the jarl's lip like a minnow on the hook in the dark depths.

"Nikephoros," Sigurd said, which clearly annoyed Bardanes, who thought that the emperor should be addressed with his titles, of which, as far as I could tell, there were dozens. "Tell me again about the war between the Trojans and the Greeks." He removed his hat, and his eyes glinted in the red half-light, though he kept that minnow-twitch smile below the surface. "Don't waste your breath with the women and the fighting and the half-god warrior Achilles." Some grumbles at that because the men had come to like Achilles. He had reminded us of Beowulf. "Tell me again about the trick the Greeks played on the Trojans when it seemed they had lost the war." Sigurd stroked his beard, his eyes becoming slits. "I want to hear more about that wooden horse."

Nikephoros thought about this for a long heartbeat and then nodded, and it seemed to me that he enjoyed playing the role of skald for all that he was a piss-poor storyteller. So he began, and most of us filled our cups again while others built up the fire and the sea lapped at the edges of Elaea. And as the night drew on and men began to snore and fart themselves to sleep, Sigurd's minnow grew into a codfish.

We came at night, a full crew pulling *Serpent*'s oars with more men standing in the thwarts and at bow and stern. Our painted shields were slotted in the rails for effect, and Jörmungand, our snarling prow beast, was mounted. The moon was almost full, a great burnished shield suspended against the immense black warp of the night sky. Moon-silvered clouds were the weft, weaving themselves in and out of the darkness as they moved westward on a warm breeze that brought the exotic scents of Miklagard to our noses.

From a distance it had seemed that the stars in the north were tumbling down to earth, but as we drew nearer to the great harbor, we could see those flickering lights for what they were: pinpricks of night flame leaking from the thousands of dwellings, palaces, and Christ churches spilling off the hills.

If Basileus Nikephoros was afraid, he showed no sign of it, which was impressive given the risk he was taking in going along with Sigurd's plan. If I'd been him, I would have been bladder-clenched and trembling like a drunk the morning after with each oar stroke that brought us nearer to Miklagard. Instead, Nikephoros was grim-faced and straight-backed, his short beard trimmed and glistening and his eyes hard as rivet heads.

"Here she comes, lads," Olaf yawped from the mast step, his face moon washed white as a corpse. "Keep it nice and steady now."

A dark shadow loomed off our port bow, the creak of timbers and the wash of its wake whispering out there in the night.

"I'll wager the whoresons are stoking up that liquid fire ready to light us up like a king's pyre," Gap-Toothed Ingolf called from three benches back.

"Shut your hole and row, Ingolf," Olaf barked, "or you'll spend the rest of the night looking for my boot up your arse cave!"

Ingolf had only said what we were all thinking, which was why we were all twisting our necks every few strokes, watching the moon-dappled Greek dromon for the first flame that would tell us we were about to be roasted like pigs at a Yule feast. Nevertheless, we rowed, and those of us doing the work were the lucky ones because the other men had nothing to take their minds off grim thoughts of burning. Soon, though, we were into the sheltered water of the harbor, among the hundreds of other ships anchored and tethered and bobbing in that sleeping sea and manned by skeleton crews while the rest were ashore. If the Greeks were going to burn us, they would have done it before now, for here they would risk us slewing into any number of other craft and setting fire to the whole damn lot.

So far, so good, I thought, watching Cynethryth, who stood at the bow as still as the stone woman from the Hagia Sophia, one hand snarled in the silver fur of Sköll's neck. The beast was tense and quiet, its tail pointing sword-straight behind it, which a wolf will do when it is hunting. I shuddered at that because it seemed that Cynethryth and the beast could somehow understand each other.

"Not long now, lads," Olaf growled.

My bowels melted. I felt naked as a bairn and almost as helpless. We were wearing tunics and breeks, and that was it, not a blade, spear, or brynja among us, so that you would have thought we were giving a new boat her first sea trial in a peaceful summer fjord. We were unarmed and all but defenseless, but that was what we had to be for Sigurd's scheme to have a chance of working.

I pulled my oar and breathed the strange spice smells of Miklagard, wondering if our gods were watching, wondering if they could even see so far, for surely we were as far from the fjords of the north as a Norseman could go. But then, the Norns had woven our wyrds, and so they must know Miklagard well enough. And if the Spinners knew it, then so must the other Aesir, which meant that the gods must be watching, and if they were, they would admire our daring to go among our enemies as defenseless and thin-skinned as old men. It was that thought which I rolled around my skull to try to keep my mind off the sting in my bladder.

"Now I know how Týr felt," Beiner said, leaning on the sheer strake and watching the Greek ship, which we could see better now because of the flaming braziers lining the quayside. It was well said by Beiner, for Týr had put his arm in Fenrir Wolf's mouth, and that was what we were doing, except we were putting our heads right in there too and having a good look around. Týr's bravery had lost him his hand.

"This place makes Paris look like a dung heap," Penda muttered beside me. We had passed the main ship-strewn harbor now, the sound of men carousing in the harborfront taverns fading off our port side as we approached the western edge of the Bucoleon Palace. Behind the great walls the city rose into the black sky, its domes and palaces night-shrouded and only half glimpsed by the winking lights of countless small flames.

"Paris *is* a dung heap," I said. "If we're still alive come sunrise, I'll show you some sights that will make your eyes sweat."

"Hold your tongues, you blathering women!" Olaf growled.

The oars dipped and pulled in even strokes, and I tried to lose myself in the rhythmic soft *plunge* sound of it. Somewhere off our steerboard side a seabird took off shrieking into the night, its wings slapping noisily, and I wondered how Nikephoros's long shields were faring out there in the dark. For they were rowing *Wave-Steed* to Miklagard's southwestern harbor. They would convince the harbormaster there that they were from one of the imperial dromons patrolling the Marmara Sea and that they were bringing in a captured ship. That had been Bardanes's idea, and I had to admit it seemed like a good one, for we would need those men soon enough.

Sigurd, Bardanes, and Nikephoros stood at the mast step, talking in low voices, and Bardanes was unhappy by the look of it. The general was shaking his head and pleading with Nikephoros, when Sigurd stepped up and backhanded the emperor across the face, sending him staggering. Wide-eyed, his balance recovered, Nikephoros put a hand to his mouth and examined the blood on it. Bardanes was glaring at Sigurd, his hands balled into white fists by his side. Then Sigurd took another step and smashed his fist into the emperor's right eye, and this time Nikephoros fell to his knees, clutching his face, and Bardanes spit rage at Sigurd as he bent to help his lord and master. But Nikephoros pushed his general away and climbed to his feet, and his blood-smeared lips were clenched in a tight smile. He nodded at Sigurd and the jarl nodded back, and we pulled our oars, hoping that the weaves of our lives stretched beyond this warm, gut-twisting night.

"Back oars!" Olaf called, and I twisted my neck to see that we were fast approaching the Bucoleon's small berth and would have to slip between two tall-sided dromons. In that glance I had also seen warriors lining the quayside, their shields, helms, and spear blades glinting in the brazier light.

"Looks like a good turnout," I muttered.

"Fifty or five hundred, we're screwed either way," Halfdan said as we churned the water, killing *Serpent*'s momentum. We pulled our oars in for fear of them hitting the Greek ships, and then Olaf and Sigurd threw our bow mooring ropes to the men on the quayside, who tied us up before any words were spoken.

"Stow oars, then back to your benches," Olaf barked, and men repeated the order throughout the tightly packed ship. We took longer than usual putting our staves up in the oar trees because we were busy getting an eyeful of the soldiers and the Bucoleon and the lie of the land, but when we had done it, those of us who could sat on our sea chests, facing the palace. The Greek spearmen lining the wharf were silent, as were the archers who suddenly appeared along the sides of the dromons, their bows drawn and their arrow points aimed down at us. *That is not good,* I thought to myself with a shudder.

"Jarl Sigurd! Welcome to Constantinople!" The Greek shield line—you couldn't call it a shieldwall, not with two feet of space between the soldiers— parted so that a gaudy cockerel of a man could make the scene he'd so obviously played out in his thoughts before now. He was sheathed in fish-scale armor, and his helmet sported a great plume the same purple as his cloak, which was fastened with a gold, jewel-encrusted brooch. At his right shoulder stood another man dressed in the same armor except that his plume and cloak were red. His face was all sharp angles in the firelight and bore a warrior's scars.

Sigurd stepped onto the bow fighting platform and greeted the cock, who in snot-slick English introduced himself as Patrikios Arsaber. "I hope you have honored our agreement and come unarmed," Arsaber said, directing some of his torchbearing men forward to hold their flames over our bow as their eyes scoured us for weapons.

"Get those flames away from my ship," Sigurd growled, but Arsaber ignored him until his men nodded at him that we were bladeless.

"I thought only the Roman emperors could wear purple," Sigurd baited the man, for the moment ignoring Nikephoros, who stood bound and shoulder slumped behind him.

By the light of the hissing brazier flames Arsaber's smile was as thin as air. "I am emperor, Sigurd, in all but name. We shall make it official soon enough."

Sigurd nodded and gestured at Olaf, who shoved Nikephoros forward onto the platform. "Here is the emperor," Sigurd announced, which brought a twist to Arsaber's lips. Then Nikephoros lifted his head proudly so that Arsaber and his men must have seen the blood-oozing split in his lip that had soaked his disheveled beard. Perhaps they even saw the purple-black bruise blooming around the man's right eye, though they kept their faces stony.

"You have done well, General Bardanes," Arsaber said, at which Bardanes stepped out of the press of Norsemen behind Sigurd.

"My lord," he said simply, bowing his head, then

turning it away from Nikephoros's red-hot withering glower.

"I will have use for a man with your enterprise, though I will have to keep one eye on you, it seems." The big man to Arsaber's right grinned at that. Then Arsaber glared at Sigurd. "Well, heathen? Hand the prisoner over. I am a busy man."

"The silver first," Sigurd demanded.

Arsaber stepped up to the wharf's edge, close enough to reach out and touch *Serpent*'s stem post. "Look around, Sigurd," he said in a voice only just loud enough for the rest of us to hear. "Even a barbarian like you can weigh up this situation." There was that piss-thin smile again. "You are in no position to make demands of me." Sigurd made a show of looking up at the archers in the dromons on either side of us.

"Olaf, hand the goat bladder over," he gnarred, at which Arsaber turned and nodded at his companion. The planks were laid from sheer strake to quayside, and Nikephoros stepped reluctantly ashore, dark-browed as any man would be who knows he walks toward his death.

"Now the silver," Sigurd said, at which Arsaber waved forward two men hefting an ivory-mounted chest. They set the thing down and lifted the lid, and four spearmen closed in as Sigurd stepped ashore.

"Where is the rest of it?" Sigurd demanded, eye-balling Arsaber.

Arsaber held out his hands and shook his head so that the purple plume on his helm swayed stiffly. "It is more than enough," he said, "for giving me one man."

"For giving you the emperor," Sigurd pointed out.

"He is not the emperor now, Sigurd, any more than you are." Arsaber made himself chuckle with that. "Take the money and go," he said, flicking a few ringed fingers toward us.

"Pay me what you owe me, Greek," Sigurd boomed. Arsaber winced at that. We did too.

"Or what?" Arsaber said. "You'll hurl your stinking shoes at us?" The man had a point, for we had not so much as a crooked spear among us. "What will you do, Jarl Sigurd?" Arsaber had a slimy look about him that made you think he had been raised by snakes and killed them all before leaving the nest. The man had a face you just wanted to hit.

Sigurd scratched his chin and seemed to ponder what he had heard.

"Come on, Sigurd; we are all eager to know what you will do to us if we do not give you what you think we owe." Arsaber's eyes slithered over his spearmen, but they had no smiles for him, which made me wonder if some of them would be loyal to Nikephoros given half a chance.

"My men who have the other emperor will take him wherever he wishes to go," Sigurd said, laying the words *other emperor* as thick as a winter pelt. "Maybe the Pope or the Frank King Karolus will help him raise men to lever your arse off his mead bench."

Arsaber blanched at this, though his narrowed eyes showed that most of him thought Sigurd was bluffing.

"You do not have Staurakios," he challenged. "That witless fool is likely wearing the habit by now. Hiding in some monastery and knee-sore from prayer."

Sigurd fished inside his tunic and pulled out something small and shiny, which he threw at Arsaber. Arsaber flailed for it but missed so that one of his spearmen had to bend and picked the thing up, passing it to his lord reverently. It was Staurakios's ring, the one I had seen him wearing in the Hagia Sophia, and from the look of it Arsaber recognized the thing, though he fought to keep the surprise off his face.

"I have no need of greasy-bearded Greek emperors," Sigurd said, showing Arsaber his palms. "Give me the rest of the silver and you can have Staurakios, too. I know nothing of your snake dealings, but it seems to me it will be easier to become Miklagard's emperor if there is not already an emperor somewhere out there raising spears against you."

Arsaber squirmed like a hooked eel. He turned and spoke in Greek to his scarred companion, and we waited, barely breathing and half expecting Arsaber to give the order for his bowmen to loose their arrows. Then, after a while, Arsaber turned back to Sigurd.

"Agreed, Sigurd," he said loudly enough for all to hear. "Tomorrow you will have the rest of the silver, and then you will take us to where you have Staurakios."

"We have to stay here overnight?" Sigurd asked as though that idea stank like pig dung.

"If any man steps ashore, he will get a spear in his belly," Arsaber said. "But you will find me a generous host, Sigurd," he added, smearing a grin across his face. "I will have wine and food brought to you the likes of which you have never tasted. You will find it manna of Heaven compared with the horse blood or sheep's piss or whatever it is you barbarians drink."

Sigurd mumbled a curse and nodded, playing the wine-bag barbarian perfectly.

"Now you will excuse us." Arsaber's smile grew teeth. "We have much to talk about with Nikephoros," he said, spitting the basileus's name. "Stay with your heathen friends tonight, Bardanes," he added, looking at the general. "I have not yet decided what to do with you." Bardanes inclined his head obediently. Then, with a swirl of purple and a scuff of boots, Arsaber turned his back and strode toward the Bucoleon. And Nikephoros followed like a faithful hound.

chapter
TWENTY-FIVE

A RSABER'S SCAR-FACED bodyguard and war adviser was a man called Karbeas. No sooner had Arsaber turned his back on us than this Karbeas came aboard *Serpent* with five soldiers and searched the ship properly for weapons. We had emptied our hold of the richest booty, leaving it at Elaea with *Fjord-Elk* and a mere handful of men under Bragi to guard it, for we wanted to appear silver-poor so that Arsaber believed that for all our bellyaching and bluster, we would do whatever he asked in return for a hoard. Karbeas had looked less than impressed by the few skins and pieces of amber and antler he found, though he did seem satisfied that we were unarmed. We had treated them to a few growls and curses when they began lifting the lids of our sea chests, but to give the man his credit, he did not so much as flinch. Yet for all that, he was soon ashore again, where it seemed he was more at ease, leaving us like dogs waiting for scraps and wondering whether a man like Arsaber, who had betrayed his own lord, would keep his word about the food and wine.

"The last I knew, he was a captain in the palace guard," Bardanes told us, nodding sourly toward Karbeas, who was barking orders at the captain of the dromon on our steerboard side. "Now it seems he holds the reins to the imperial army."

"He's risen faster than a hard-on, then," Olaf mumbled into his beard. There were some strained grins at that. "But can he fight?"

Bardanes nodded.

"Will the red cloaks follow him?" Sigurd asked, which was the more important question.

Bardanes pulled his slick beard through his fist and shrugged. "Perhaps. We will see," he said.

"They're moving, Sigurd," Bothvar called from the bow.

"Ódin's arse, so they are," Olaf said, a grin nestled in the briar tangle of his beard as we watched the dromon on our steerboard side prepare to cast off, her crew slotting oars amid a torrent of yelled commands. And it was not long before the ship on our port side moved off, too, so that by the time the first wine jars arrived at the quayside, both dromons were anchored an arrow shot off our stern, two grim shadow shapes guarding us like hounds. Sigurd said this proved that Karbeas was no fool.

"He knows that without weapons we cannot threaten him," he said when Svein asked why the Greek ships had moved, "but he has no intention of letting us leave, either, until they have what they want from us." And what they wanted was Staurakios.

"It seems Arsaber is a man of his word, after all," Sigurd said now as Greeks carried several tall wine jars aboard. But Sigurd's grin was not caused by the sight of the wine or even by the brass bowls of steaming food that began to appear, which got our mouths watering with their delicious smells. Sigurd was grinning because, standing on the wharf in a knot of flowing gowns and veils every color of Bifröst, were women. There were perhaps twenty of them, all slender as willow shoots, dark-haired and made to turn men's heads, and they smelled even better than the food as they waited to be invited aboard, their scent wafting over us on a warm night breeze.

"Get a tjalda up, lads," the jarl said, pointing at the spare sail that was folded in half across *Serpent*'s hold aft of the mast. "And run a comb through those beards, you ugly trolls." He winked at Olaf, who was well aware what a stroke of luck it was to have whores coming aboard. The men got to work, singing an old drinking song as they pulled and poled *Serpent*'s spare sail into a passable deck awning, and I began to think our gods really were watching. For that humping shelter meant that those spearmen lining the quayside could not see what we were up to.

It took Svein, Bothvar, Beiner, Gytha, and me to haul the sodden, green-haired anchor rope up from the black water off our stern, our grunts adding to those now coming from the humping tent.

"No reason to waste good whores," Byrnjolf had suggested, which had stirred a chorus of ayes and not a few sad-hound faces from men appealing to their jarl for one last screw before the blood started flying. So while we hauled, other men were at it, swiving as though their lives depended on it, which in a strange twist they did. The flame-lit spearmen before the Bucoleon could see men drinking in the thwarts, could hear them singing and humping and enjoying themselves, but they could not see us at the stern.

But there was no anchor on the end of this rope.

Sigurd gave the word, and together we hoisted the great burden out of the water, where it hung dripping for a long heartbeat before we heaved it over the sheer strake and onto the deck.

"Strange fishing, this," Olaf muttered, staring at the catch. There were eight bundles of skins, all tightly lashed so that their fat-smeared treasures could not fall out. Now we dragged each of them under the flap into the humping tent, and those men who were busy either finished quickly or discarded their women like half-eaten apples and watched us instead, grinning like fiends by the dim glow of horn lanterns and grunting and growling now and then as though they were still swiving, which would have been funny at any other time.

We were on our knees, working at the sopping knots and desperate to get the bundles open. Then Floki had one undone, and we shared a wolf look as men threatened the Greek whores and guarded the tent's edges so that they could not leave. There, wet and cold and sharp, were our swords. The other bundles were opened, each revealing more war gear—axes, helmets, long knives—all dragged through the depths on a rope lashed to *Serpent*'s stern. It had been a dark and desperate plan putting good blades into salt water even if they were greased to protect them at least a little. But it had worked. We were no longer defenseless. And the war gods were watching.

Only eleven of us had brynjas because they had taken up so much room in the bundles and made them so heavy. I did not know if that made me one of the lucky ones, for the mailed men would be first into the fray, hacking a way through for the others to follow.

The basileus's sixteen long shields would by now, we hoped, be lying in wait somewhere on the northern side of the palace. They were the spike pit toward which we would drive our prey so that there would be no escape for Arsaber should he try to flee rather than fight. That was the plan, anyway, but we all knew there were still too few of us, which was why we had to keep General Bardanes alive at least until we had killed Arsaber and found Nikephoros, assuming the basileus was still breathing. For only Bardanes could lead us if we managed to fight our way into the sprawling Bucoleon.

My brynja was cold and stiff, and I shrugged my shoulders to loosen the rings, grimacing because I knew the iron rot was already doing its work. But standing there in the gloom of that tent, the air thick with the sweet musky scent of beautiful women, I welled with pride. Only the mailed men stood around me now, and they were the ones Sigurd had chosen to lead the attack. Svein the Red was there, pulling his belt tight, his granite face clenched and his helmet touching the tent's roof. Big Beiner was there and Bothvar, Bjarni, and Aslak, all bone and muscle. Olaf was wiping the grease off his sword's hilt, purring in the back of his throat. Penda was tying his helmet's chin strap, the long scar down his face glistening in the candlelight and violence coming off him like a stink. Black Floki was strapping his scabbarded long knife across his lower belly so that he could draw it as fast as a wolf's bite, and Sigurd was doing what Sigurd did, becoming a battle god. The last of us in mail was Bardanes in his fish-scale armor that glinted and winked like a jarl's hoard and was worth as much.

"You stay near the back, General," Sigurd reminded him, glancing at the dark-haired whores whose eyes, wide with fear, gleamed white as they sat huddled in the dark, bound and gagged now because we could take no chances. Bardanes nodded, discarding his scabbard like the rest of us because the wool inside was sopping and might suck the blade and ruin the draw. We had no need of scabbards anyway, for something told me our swords would be in our hands until this was over, one way or another.

Eyes met in the darkness then, and the sailcloth rippled around us, which was strange because the breeze had dropped some time before so that it was a still night. The hairs on my neck stiffened and a shudder went through me like a trickle of ice melt, because I knew that it was no breeze but rather the Valkyries riding among us—drawn by the scent of coming death—that was making a furrowed sea of the tent cloth. The Choosers of the Slain had come.

"You are my brothers," Sigurd said, wolf-eyed in the sweet dark. "We are oath-tied. Bound by chains no man can break. This night may be your last, but the hero that enters Ódin's dwelling place does not bemoan his death." His voice was low but powerful like distant thunder before a storm. "Our ancestors wait for us in the shield-roofed hall, their mead horns full and their welcome as warm as a good hearth fire." The jarl showed his teeth then, the scars of old fights etched in his face like runes on a stone. "But they will have to wait a little longer for me," he said, eyes glinting like blades. "I have come to feed the wolf and the raven. My sword is thirsty, and I will let it drink. I will fight for you, my brothers, and they will have to drain every drop of my blood to stop me."

My mouth was as dry as sand, which was just as well, for any spit I might have had to swallow would not have squeezed past the lump in my throat anyway. I caught Penda's eye, and he nodded. Bjarni gripped my shoulder, and I tried to smile.

"When we go, we go like Thór-farting thunder," Olaf growled, his bird's nest beard resting on his barrel chest.

"It is easy," Black Floki said with a grimace. "Just kill them."

Shields began appearing where the others had managed to slip them out of the rail and slide them under the tent wall without the palace guards noticing. The rest would have to get theirs at the last moment. The rancid stink of our greased brynjas started to catch in my throat.

"Ready?" Sigurd asked. I slipped my arm through the shield straps, wiped a trickle of sweat from my cheek, and nodded. Then we followed Sigurd. Screaming.

We were off *Serpent*'s bow and onto the quayside in a few heartbeats so that the Greeks barely had time to level their spears. Sigurd hit first, knocking a spear aside and reversing his blade, scything it across the man's face in a spray of blood and teeth. Svein the Red was bellowing like a bull, and I saw him swing his long ax at a man who desperately raised his shield only for the ax head to cut through both the shield and the arm holding it so that the man dropped to his knees, the gory stump spurting blood. I put my shoulder into my shield and slammed into a Greek, expecting to knock the man aside, but he was strong and took the blow, planting his feet and yelling. I glanced down and saw his foot beneath my shield, so I plunged my sword into it, and his yell turned to a shriek. He pulled the foot back, and my weight turned him, allowing Bjarni to slice the length of his sword across the man's exposed neck, drenching me.

"Kill them!" Olaf roared. "Kill every goat-fucking one of them!"

Blades flashed and men grunted, and we were through their ragged-arsed shieldwall like an ax through kindling, the others fast on our heels, yelling battle cries and curses as they rolled over what was left like a killing wave. But two of the Greek soldiers had run, disappearing into the colonnaded passageway that ran from the quayside along the front of the palace. We ran into that brazier-lit tunnel, our boots scuffing against the wide steps that led to an iron-bound door on which we found the two spearmen hammering, their pleas slapping noisily around that stone passage, and we hoped the door would open. But it did not, and the two men turned to us, and one of them pissed himself as they cowered and fell to their knees. They died like dogs beneath Penda and Floki's swords, their blood flinging itself across the door that those inside wisely kept shut.

Then Svein and Beiner were there, hacking into the wood with their axes, sending splinters flying. They would have to be quick, for the dromons would be coming now, drawn back to the wharf by the clash of swords and the screams of the dying.

"Stand back!" Sigurd clamored, but it took Bothvar yelling in Svein's ear before the giant, his red beard full of frothing spit, lowered his ax and stepped back, eyes wild and chest billowing.

Bardanes thrust a key into the lock, and the iron *clunk*ed. With a roar to shake the boughs of Yggdrasil, we pushed the door open and swarmed into the Bucoleon.

Four Greeks half blocked the candlelit passageway, their shields overlapped, the faces above them grim because they knew they were about to die. One of them threw his spear, which clattered against Aslak's shield boss. The Norseman grinned, and we barely broke stride as we made our own shieldwall and smashed into them, our flanks closing around them so that the Greeks were hacked into red clumps with their death shrieks still in their throats.

I stepped around the stinking, steaming mess, and we took a ragged-breathed moment to look around. Coming from the dark outside, my eyes sifted through the flame-lit interior easily, flicking over marble columns and walls brightly painted with dark-skinned, arse-naked hunters and sharp-clawed beasts. Sigurd ordered five Danes to bar the door we had come through and hold it against any harbor guards or soldiers from the Greek dromons who could otherwise attack our rear. The rest of us followed the narrow passage, which widened as it went, coming to a large open space that blazed with light from dozens of polished candelabra. There were two wide marble stairways, one going left and the other right, and in between at the bottom there was a massive golden cage full of shrieking birds of every color you can imagine, such as we had never laid eyes on before.

"Heimdall's hairy arse! What now?" Olaf panted.

His face was blood-spattered. Somewhere men were yelling, their voices swirling so that you could not tell where they were coming from.

"Do you think they know we are here?" Bjarni asked through a grin.

"That way," Bardanes said, pointing with his sword toward the right-hand stairway, and I wished he had said the other way, because men were gathering where his blade pointed. Lots of men, their mail and helms gleaming dully. These Greeks made a wall of their long shields a few steps from the top, which was good battle cunning, for it meant we could not outflank them, and from behind that wall spears began to streak down at us, slamming into shields and clattering across the glittering marble floor. More soldiers lined the marble rail on either side of the stairway, and I saw two with bows.

Sigurd sent Rolf and ten or more men up the left-hand stairway, and they ran howling like beasts after prey. We mailed men bunched and raised our shields, five behind five, and began to stomp up those stone steps, beating out the rhythm with guttural "hey"s as we climbed. I was in the front line with Floki and Penda on my left and Svein and Aslak on my right, and that climb never seemed to end. I slammed each foot to the stone, trying to stamp the shaking out of my legs. My face was into the shield so that I could smell the limewood and the leather and the iron tang of the rivets. Something hit my shield hard, but I could not stop because Beiner was behind me, growling like a beast. We were close now. I caught the onion sweat stink of the Greeks, smelled the fear wafting off them, and heard the shallow breaths of the men behind those long shields. Then I felt Svein expand like a sailcloth caught in the wind and knew it was time to fight, and so I swung my sword over, and it crashed into a shield. But my job was not to swing like a blind man trying to piss in a bucket. My job was to lean the shoulder in and push so that the men behind me had a rampart from which to kill.

Blades flashed and probed, seeking flesh between wood and iron. Stinging sweat filled my eyes, blurring my sight, but it did not matter so long as I pushed. So long as we held. For if you build a shield-wall, you had better make sure you lay the foundations well, and that means having hard men at the front. Men grunted with the strain, their neck cords bulging, lips drawn back across teeth, and beards white with spittle.

"Kill them!" Beiner bawled. "Cut their rancid guts out!" Someone clearly listened to Beiner, for a few hammered heartbeats later a slew of purple gut rope slapped to the steps and slithered down between our feet. Up we went, one agonizing step at a time, my legs burning with the effort of pushing the Greeks back and my boots threatening to give way on the slippery gore of blood and piss. Sigurd was plunging forward, wedging himself between me and Floki and hacking at men over our shields, his eyes wild and spit-drenched curses flying from his lips.

An arrow *tonk*ed off my helmet, and I swore savagely because it hurt, having been shot from less than a good spit away. Our men had wisely kept hold of the spears the Greeks had thrown, and now they thrust those spears back into our enemies' faces and gouged shins with them. The man on the other side of the shield I was shoving was yelling in panic now, calling for help perhaps, and so he might, because a gap had appeared on his left where Svein, in his eagerness to get among the fray, had driven into them like a rock slide and they had been unable to hold him, so that the giant was now two steps higher than the rest of us. That fissure in the Greeks' wall was all Bjarni needed. He lunged from my right, skewering my Greek through the neck so that he dropped his shield and I saw his face properly for the first time. He glared at me as though I had killed him, and then Bjarni's blade ripped free, the gory mouthlike hole spewing warm blood across my face and lips. I lifted my shield up and over the dead man, and the others came with me so that we were now stepping over corpses. Every breath was searingly hot, and my spit was thick enough to clog my throat and mouth, so that when I yelled and cursed at Floki and Penda to move up with me to plug the gap, it came out like an animal's bellow.

Then Svein went down. He must have slipped on the iron-stinking mess, and the Greeks cheered and lurched forward. Svein was now on one knee, his shield raised before his face.

"Push! Push, you Norse whoresons!" Olaf yelled, swinging his sword high and pivoting his wrist to bring the blade over the shield of the man opposite Aslak. Aslak drove his left shoulder into his own shield, pushing his right foot against the wall to get more purchase and give Svein a chance to stand. Svein's roar rolled like thunder as his oak legs braced against the strain and began to unfold, his face blood-red with the effort.

"Ódin! Ódin!" someone hollered. Through the clamor I could hear dull thuds somewhere behind and guessed that the Greeks were smashing the door we had left a handful of men guarding. I heard Aslak curse and glanced across to see an arrow sticking from his exposed leg, yet he kept it wedged against the wall as Svein forced himself up, the giant's fury like the worst storm I have ever known. I heaved with every sinew, my teeth clamped so tightly that my whole skull pounded; then something buffeted my legs, and I looked down to see Asgot. The godi was squirming and writhing through men's legs like a snake through gorse, his wicked, blood-hungry knife in his hand. He was getting a battering so that I thought his old bones must crack or be ground to dust inside the bag of his skin, but on he wriggled, and the next moment one of the Greeks screamed. And another, his leg strings sliced or his balls sawed off. And the Greek shieldwall shuddered at Asgot's nasty work, its lifeblood running down the steps.

With a great Thór effort, we climbed and the men behind us hacked and stabbed, and then someone shouted that there were Greeks behind us. They had broken through the door and were fighting the men at our rear. I was filled with ice dread then because I knew Cynethryth must be back there somewhere.

Up we went. I looked down and saw Asgot, his yellowed eyes glowing dully in a face sheeted in gore, and then I was past him and we had reached the top. The men behind us would not stay there any longer. They pushed down the flanks and tore into the Greeks, who were panic-gripped now. A shieldless man lunged at me with his spear, and I ducked so that the blade scraped my helmet; then I threw my shield arm up, deflecting the blade, and hacked into the Greek's left shoulder. My sword lodged in bone, and the man vomited into his black beard as I tried to shake him off. Another man swung a sword at me, and I let go of my grip and grabbed my shield, taking the blow on the boss. He swung again, and again I took the impact on my shield; then Black Floki ran him through from behind, the Norseman's sword bursting from the man's mailed chest in a spray of iron scales and blood. I turned back and found the other Greek still standing there, puke-covered and with my sword wedged in his shoulder meat like a butcher's cleaver. His eyes were swollen like boiled eggs, his mouth oozed slime, and he just stood there with the chaos swirling in clamorous eddies around him.

"I've got you, lad," Penda called, half crouching, scanning the carnage around us. "You'll want that sword back." I stepped up and gripped the hilt with two hands and put my knee into the Greek's side and yanked, trying to free the blade from bone and sucking meat. This seemed to bring the man back to the moment, for he began to wail, and I suddenly thought I should have finished him off with my knife first. But battle is red madness, and you don't think rationally. You just cut flesh and try not to let another man cut yours.

"Hold it tight!" Penda yelled at me, then swung, hacking the Greek's arm off at the shoulder so that it hung from my sword, and I was able to put my foot on the pulsing wrist and pull the blade free. The Greek crumpled and bled out, and I slammed my shield into another man, the blood thirst on me as never before.

Then the men who had taken the left stairway appeared and made a shieldwall, crashing into the flank of the last of the Greeks and sending a shudder through the press of the enemy.

"We need to end this now!" Olaf yelled, taking a sword blow on his shield and replying with a massive blow that cleaved his opponent's shield in two. Men were fighting below in the main chamber, their screams and yells mixing with the frantic shrieks of the caged birds, and we knew we had to find Arsaber before it was too late.

The Greeks were trying to regroup. They closed ranks and hefted shields and backed away, obeying the orders of the one man they hoped could keep them alive. That man was Karbeas. I saw him for the first time since the blood had started to fly, and he looked as composed as any man could who was fighting for his life. I saw him clash shields with Bothvar, the Norseman eager to kill him and stop the rallying cries that were flying from his mouth. But Karbeas was strong and managed to turn Bothvar, enabling another Greek to ram his spear into Bothvar's face. Bothvar twisted horribly, and the spear came away spilling wet gray chunks, and I knew that was the end for him.

"That way! Now!" It was Bardanes yelling, his sword red and slick and his face a wild grimace because he knew time was slipping away like the tide for us. Sigurd edged forward, and we fell in behind him, making the boar snout and moving as one mass of iron, wood, and steel. We carved into the knot of Greeks, who tried to part to allow a big bare-chested man through who seemed keen to die. He shoved toward us, whomping an enormous sword into Beiner's shield, splitting the thing in half before the Dane had a chance or the room to swing his long ax. Then Beiner's face turned white as snow and he looked down, and so did I. Once through the shield, the sword had sliced through his brynja too, and his gut rope was a straining purple knot bulging from the tear in mail and leather. Penda plunged his sword's point into the big Greek's armpit and then twisted the blade for good measure before tearing it free and moving on, leaving Beiner on his knees, trying to stop his insides from coming out.

A spear blade and some of its shaft burst through the inside of Bjarni's thigh, and he roared, unable to move or do anything other than grip his shield and take blows. I saw Ingolf trying to hack the blade off that spear and heard Bjarni bellow with the red agony of it as I brought my sword inside my shield and sawed the fingers from a hand that was trying to pull the shield away. The fingers fell like runestones and were lost, the ruined hand smearing blood across my shield's rim as I punched it forward, crunching the man's face bones and dropping him. I stamped my left foot down onto his head, keeping the Greek still as I thrust my sword through the iron scales into his stomach, releasing a gush of foul stinking air. Then the Greeks broke and ran, and we ran after them, leaving those behind to fight the new men who were pouring through the south door and forcing their way up the marble steps as we had.

The passageway passed in a blur of color, the walls adorned with painted men fighting—those silent scenes of long-dead men as much like real battle as a gilded pleasure karvi is like a raiding ship, it seemed to me. For there was no mad fear in them, no din to fill your head, and no stink to get up among your nose hairs. Then we came to a vast chamber whose domed roof was held up by sixteen marble pillars. Soft chairs and silk-covered cushions were scattered everywhere so that you could have dropped a freshly laid egg almost anywhere in that room and it would not have broken. From the walls hung bright silks and enormous tapestries woven with golden thread. Gold cups brimming with wine and plates piled with half-eaten fruits lay discarded among the chaos of colors. The musk smell of women hung thick as fog and mouthwatering, stirring the animal part of me that already was roused to flame by the bloodlust of battle. Here and there braziers crackled and spit, and candles spilled tallow down their sides, and women's robes lay in gaudy crumples where they had been cast off. Svein the Red snatched one up, put it to his nose, and made that deep hum in his throat.

"I'd rather drink mead if this is to be my last drop," Olaf complained, clutching a golden cup and throwing the contents down his throat, "but sometimes a man must take what he is given." He winced and burped and spit the dark, bitter residue across a yellow pillow. I found my own cup and drank, spilling most of the wine into my beard because of the battle shakes in my hand, but it was enough to rinse my tongue of the salt and iron taste of other men's blood.

"We're not finished yet, Uncle," Sigurd said, the two golden ropes of his braided beard hanging stiffly from a face crusted in dark gore so that his eyes shone white as cuckoo spit. Above us the domed ceiling was painted to look like the night sky, a thousand flecks of gold twinkling in the flame light like stars.

"These Greek warriors die easily enough," Sigurd gnarred. "They are not the heroes we have heard about in your tales of the Trojan War, Bardanes. Warming the emperor's feet has made them soft, like hounds kept inside too long."

But Bardanes turned his back on the jarl, his shield and sword raised toward the passage we had come through, because a clamor was building like a wave about to crash onto the shingle. We all tensed as men spewed from the corridor into the chamber, their eyes wild and their shields sprouting shafts.

"We couldn't hold them, Sigurd," Wiglaf panted as Osk and ugly Hedin yelled at the others to hurry so that they could close the door. "There are hundreds of them!"

Sigurd glowered like red-hot iron so that I did not know whether he was angry at Wiglaf and the others for not buying him more time or was raging at the gods for stirring his scheme into bloody chaos.

"That leads to the emperor's private chambers," Bardanes said, pointing toward the gilded middle door of the three in the room's north wall. I had seen the general kill two men, one with a neat sword thrust to the neck and the other with a squall of slashes that carved the man up where he stood, showing that Bardanes had fury to match his skill. "If the traitor is still here, that door will lead us to him," he said, knuckling sweat from his brow.

Among the men pressing in from the passage I saw Gunnar, Halfdan, Ingolf, and Osten. Other sweat-, blood-, and spittle-soaked faces were turned toward

Sigurd, the terror-filled men behind those growling bear masks hoping that their jarl knew a way to jerk us off this hook; Yngvar and Arngrim were among them, and the blauman Völund, who was bare-chested and glistening, his gritted teeth white against his black beard and pitch-dark skin. Many bled from wounds they'd had no time to bind. Others grimaced at unseen hurts.

And then I saw Cynethryth, and my stomach twisted like a warp hung with too light a loom weight. She was sheathed in tough leather, gripped a slender spear, and wore the helmet I had given her, which she had lined with thick felt to make the fit snug. Father Egfrith stood protectively at her shoulder, and even he carried a spear, though what he would do with it I could not imagine. That damned beast Sköll was there too, a rolling snarl coming from its throat, its yellow teeth bared. I reckoned it would do a better job of protecting Cynethryth than Father Egfrith or any of us could, and I noticed that men were keeping their distance, which was wise given that this was no longer the seasick, cringing creature of the last weeks. It was a bristling, golden-eyed, sharp-toothed beast, and Cynethryth seemed to own its soul. She owned mine, too, which made me curse as I hefted my shield, shrugging some life back into my arm, and turned to follow Sigurd.

We tramped across the silks and cushions, making a clatter of the cups and dishes lying among them, and got to the golden door that Bardanes had said led to the emperor's chambers.

"Wait for me!" Aslak shoved his way through the press, his face a sweat-soaked twist of pain because of the shaft lodged in his right calf. Bjarni, too, was limping, though at least Ingolf had managed to cut the blade off the spear that had skewered his leg and together they must have pulled the shaft out. The bright green cloth with which they had bound the hole was blood-drenched, and Bjarni's face had gone the color of cold hearth ash. Yet both he and Aslak wore good brynjas and stone-grim scowls and wanted to finish what we had started.

"This is some fight, hey, little brother!" Svein the Red boomed, slapping Bjarni's back with a *chink* of brynja rings.

"Aye." Bjarni managed a sour smile. "Bjorn would have enjoyed this, I think," he said, which had men nodding somberly. Bothvar was not there, and neither were Beiner or Ogn or several others, but it was too soon to talk about who was gone. Because the Greeks were battering the door. By now every soldier in Miklagard would be coming. Asgot said as much, the old bones snarled up in his braids blood-red and glistening again as though fresh from whatever creatures he had pulled them from.

Sigurd's thought chest must have writhed with twining serpents then, and I would not have liked to be the one to decide what we should do. The Greeks would soon be through that door—ax heads were appearing now among the cracks and flying wood slivers—and so we knew we had a hard fight coming there. That made me think we ought to press on and get to Arsaber now. But if Arsaber *was* through that other, golden door, he most likely would have armed men with him, which would mean we would be starting another fight and so planting ourselves between hammer and anvil.

"Skjaldborg! Shieldwall!" Sigurd yelled in a voice that whipped us all like the lash of an icy wave across the deck in a storm. Men jostled together, kicking silk bolsters away from their feet and hefting mauled and splintered shields. "Tighter, Boe! Raise that shield, Yngvar!" Men encouraged one another and spit disdain toward the door, which was being hacked to ruins so that we could glimpse scale armor and men's faces.

Some of the Danes were growling themselves into a fury. Other men were silent as rocks, white knuckles around sword grips and feet planted, and all of us must have suspected that we had come to the end of our life's thread. The spin of our wyrds had led us to Miklagard, the Great City, and here, far from our homes, we would kill and be killed.

"Floki, Svein, Raven, Penda, to me!" Sigurd hollered, and we four pushed our way through the sweat-stinking press to the front, past comrades who were pleased to see mailed men come between them and the warriors beyond the splintering door. Aslak limped up, too, refusing to stand behind men who were less well armed. "Olaf, take Bjarni and five others and watch the gold door." Uncle nodded and hauled men from the skjaldborg before striding across the fragrant, tapestry-lined room.

"We are sword-brothers from the north," Sigurd roared, beating his sword's hilt against his shield. "We have come to feed the wolf and the raven. Our blades are sharp and thirsty. We will give them blood to drink."

Others took up the chant:

"We are sword-brothers from the north.
We have come to feed the wolf and the raven.
Our blades are sharp and thirsty.
We will give them blood to drink."

We beat out the rhythm as we bawled the words, spit flying and the blood rising like spring sap, hot in our veins. Our voices and the hammering of shields filled the chamber, hard as the marble pillars holding up the roof, the words holding us up and driving away the fear. The Greeks were almost through the wreckage of the door, but they must have feared stepping into that place, for they would find no pleasure among plump bolsters and swaths of colored silk. They would find only agony and despair and death. Some of our men waited on either side of the threshold, blades held ready to chop and maim.

The last part of the door was kicked away, and the Greeks hesitated for a long heartbeat during which my bladder clenched like a fist around a gold coin as we raised our hoarse voices. Then, with a desperate roar they gushed into the chamber, and some were hacked to death before they were fully through the doorway. I heard Cynethryth shrieking at us to kill them all, and then they crashed against our skjaldborg. But we held, our feet like the deep-delving entwined roots of Yggdrasil, thigh muscles bunched and straining. Men grunted and jostled, their blades searching, and the stink of so many fear-filled warriors thickened the air to a reeking fug. We had bent our shieldwall like a strung bow so that the Greeks could not get down our flanks, and from that rampart of limewood we hacked at their shields and spears and sun-browned, black-bearded faces.

"You just hold them, lad, and I'll kill them," Penda gnarred between the hammer blows of his sword among the Greeks. Blood was flying from the blade, but I could not see the damage the Wessexman was doing because I had my head down and my shoulder into my shield and was shoving for all I was worth, leaving the killing to those who were craftsmen at it, men such as Penda, Floki, and Aslak. Svein was pushing too, a great lump of flesh, sinew, and muscle behind his shield, because there was no room for his ax work yet. That would come later, when our shield-wall thinned like a blighted crop and men died.

"Gut the toad-fucking dogs!" Gytha yelled. "Bleed the bastards out!" Eager to get into the heart of the maelstrom, the Wessexman was straining at my left shoulder, jabbing a Greek spear over our skjaldborg so that even in that battle din I could hear his blade ringing against iron helms. Something whomped against the upper half of my shield, smashing the wood into my nose so that I heard the *crunch*. My eyes streamed with the torture of it as the iron tang of my own blood, fresh and untainted by sweat and shit, filled my nose and beard.

"Ódin! Ódin!" screamed someone in a voice as raw as flayed bear meat. What often happens in a shield-wall fight after the first mad shove and hack is that one side begins to move back, and it is usually the side that thinks it should be winning but cannot understand why it is not. It was the Greeks who withdrew now, shields up, chins down, and shoulders bouncing with the force of it.

"Hold!" Sigurd yelled. "Stay where you are, men!" We held, gasping and dragging sweat from our eyes, checking cuts and pains to see if any were serious, for we had all seen men gut speared who thought they had only been winded. There were corpses lying in bloody twists among the silks and cushions, and we should have put our swords through all of them just to make sure. But we were too worried about Greek arrows to leave the relative safety of our skjaldborg, for a good shieldwall will stand as long as the walls of Asgard if it is built of sword—brothers who are further bound by oaths and pride, as we were.

But we should have put swords in those "dead" men.

Sigurd roared at us to step forward, to drive the Greeks back through the doorway while they were still frozen by uncertainty. Svein took the opportunity to step ahead of the rest with his long ax, looping it through the clotted air, a savage grin splitting his beard.

"Carve the maggot-arsed goat humpers up, Svein!" someone yelled.

I saw the "corpse" beneath Svein twitch, and it seemed to happen in a dream in which time slows to a trickle and then runs as fast as sand from a fist. The blood-drenched Greek thrust upward, plunging his hand into the dark beneath Svein's brynja. Svein jerked viciously, then looked down as though he didn't believe what was happening to him. Bright blood bloomed down his breeks, dripping through the wool like heavy rain through old thatch, and then he staggered back and with a roar swung the great ax down, splitting the Greek's head into two gory halves, each with its own staring eye. An arrow thudded into Svein's chest, and I heard him growl a curse as the Greeks cheered and came on again.

"Forward!" Sigurd yelled as the red-bearded giant lurched sideways. But somehow Svein straightened his blood-steeped oak legs and, bellowing like the thunder god, began looping the long ax again in a weave of death so that we had to stop and keep our distance or else be hewn by it. Arrows were tonking off our shields and helms and chinking into Svein's brynja, and then the giant stumbled again, crashing down onto his knees, still gripping the ax.

"Ódin!" Sigurd cried, then ran at the enemy, breaking his own skjaldborg, which was a red-madness thing to do, but Sigurd was my jarl, and so I ran after him, yelling to the war god. Arrows thudded into me, but I kept my feet and hammered my sword against a Greek shield, spitting bloody phlegm into a bearded face as Black Floki thrust his long knife into another man's neck. Then Aslak spun away from the fray, the bottom half of his face lopped off so that his lower jaw and chin dangled in a bloody mess against his chest, held on by a flap of skin. There were no shield-walls now, just a screaming frenzy of butchering, of blades scything and limbs being hacked off. I killed a young man by ramming my shield's rim into his throat so that it crushed his windpipe, and he died gasping like a caught fish. I killed another with my long knife after I had shaken the ruined shield off my arm and fought on two-bladed, sinking that wicked knife under the Greek's armpit and skewering his heart. But the Greeks kept coming, and for every one we killed, two more seemed to take his place. I saw Gap-Toothed Ingolf go down beneath three hacking blades and the

Wessexman Baldred arrow shot through the neck. Olaf was screaming at us to re-form, to make another shieldwall, but he might as well have been trying to put a bridle on the Midgard-Serpent or catch thunder in a pail.

Black Floki was slaughtering men as a fox kills chickens, his black braids dancing as he twisted and turned and cut. Penda was at my side, and we worked together, pushing deeper into a mass of Greeks that was swelling as more pressed into that chamber of death. But we were dying.

Then a peregrine's shriek cut through the grunts like an iced arrow in my guts, for it was Cynethryth. I turned, Penda instinctively stepping in front to shield me, and I saw a brazier crash to the floor, spilling pulsing amber coals in a spray of sparks and flame among the Greeks near the doorway. Men leaped out of the way, and Cynethryth pointed her spear at the Greeks, howling spells at them, her eyes wild and spittle flying from her lips as the silks and bolsters across the floor burst into flame.

In a heartbeat the flames were raging. Black smoke as thick as tar plumed upward toward the bowl of the ceiling, making men gasp and cough and choke, and I crouched, raising my sword as a shield but not swinging it anymore for fear of hitting one of our own. But some of the Danes could not be stopped even by flame and smoke, and those wild men slashed about them like demons so that the Greeks were forced back the way they had come.

"Bring more cushions!" Olaf spluttered, soot-blackened, blood-crusted, and coughing. Those who could summon the sense and get a grip on themselves ran around the room gathering bolsters and women's discarded robes and even yanking the great tapestries from the walls, along with anything else that would burn. They cast it all into the roaring inferno by the door, and the blaze fed savagely so that in no time there was such a wall of flame that not even a bucket's fling of water could have passed through it.

"Shieldwall just here!" Black Floki yelled. "Now, you motherless turds!" And hearing that from Floki, the ragged-arsed, wretched remains of the Wolfpack tramped together and raised their shields, overlapping them and building the skjaldborg again.

I stumbled over to Cynethryth, who was staring into the thundering fire, her bony face sweat-gleaming, the flames reflected in her green eyes and her helmet.

"Are you hurt?" I rasped, which was a stupid question, for I could see that she was not.

Then her eyes flicked to me, and she bared her teeth.

"The emperor," she hissed, pointing across the room toward the gold door. "Get him, you fool."

chapter
TWENTY-SIX

WE LEFT the battered remnants of the Wolfpack in their shieldwall, facing the flames and wreathed in tendrils of black smoke. Men had thrown damaged shields and broken spears into the flames. They'd even stripped corpses and thrown them in, too, but there was not enough to keep that fire raging, and soon the Greeks would come again to kill those on the other side if the smoke did not get them first.

Sigurd was still wild-eyed and bristling like an arrow-shot bear and snarled that he would be first through the gold door to face whatever waited beyond it. Only Floki dared to argue, saying that he would lead the way instead, but the jarl barked that the only way Floki would go first was if he killed Sigurd and became our jarl, at which Floki glowered, hefted his scarred shield, and pushed his dented helmet firmly on. I just stood back and stayed quiet, swallowing blood from my broken nose and breathing through my mouth, which was drier than a mead horn after a Yule feast. That I was still alive at all was lost on me in that red battle fog with my veins still trembling from the madness of it all. But if I had thought about it, I would have smelled our end in the acrid air.

"At least take this, Sigurd, you stubborn son of a she-wolf,"

Olaf grumbled, handing his jarl a shield that was rare in that chamber because it actually looked as though it might stop an arrow or a sword with a bit of muscle behind it. Sigurd nodded, clutching the shield's grip, then stepped up to the gold door.

It was locked, of course, and Sigurd glanced around, perhaps about to call on Svein and his long ax. But Svein was dead, groin cut by a stripling boy with a nothing knife. But Olaf now gripped Svein's ax, and he growled at everyone to stand back, then rammed the eye end of the thick head against the lock over and over, sweaty blood flying from his beard as the golden door quivered under the onslaught. Only the door's skin was gold; beneath it was wood that splintered and cracked, the lock within breaking easily enough so that all it needed was a kick from Sigurd and it was flung wide.

A spear thunked into the door frame a finger's length from Sigurd's face, and the jarl rumbled a curse as he edged into the room behind his shield. Then Floki was in, and I followed him, Olaf, Penda, Bardanes, Hastein, and Yrsa behind me.

"I am wondering if Miklagard would have been better left just a whisper on men's lips," Yrsa Pig-Nose grumbled as we laid eyes on more Greek spearmen. They stood in a line protecting the worm Arsaber, who sat in a throne raised up on a silk-strewn platform. Silk curtains billowed in the breeze blowing through three great wind holes carved in the western wall, and on that breeze rode the clamor of an angry mob outside.

"I am the emperor!" Arsaber shrieked. "The equal of the Apostles! How dare you attack me?" He was swathed in purple robes and stiff gold cloth that lay over both shoulders and wound around his waist, its ends dripping with pearls. His hands glinted with jewels of every color, and his beard was curled and oiled so that any fleas in it would have drowned long ago. His head was bare, though, and there was nothing he could do about that, because the crown of Miklagard's emperors was safely stowed out of his reach in *Fjord-Elk*'s hold.

"You are a traitor and a worm," Sigurd accused him, spitting the words as though they were poison. Two fierce-looking golden beasts crouched on either side of the throne, seeming alive in the flicker of candelabra. "He is the emperor of the Great City," the jarl snarled, pointing at Nikephoros, who was standing bound and bloody at the end of a soldier's spear. There were only six Greeks between us and Arsaber, and they might have been sweat-soaked and twitching like snare-caught hares, but they were scale-armored and helmed and gripped spears and swords. "Tell them to throw down their weapons if they want to live," Sigurd said as the ring of swords and the chaos din of battle swirled up through the wind holes, which I knew must mean that Nikephoros's long shields were fighting for their lives.

Arsaber glared at Sigurd, worrying at his glossy beard and twisting a curl into it.

"What about me?" he asked, maggoting for a way out of the hole he now found himself in.

Sigurd barked a laugh. "You are a dead man," he said. "There's nothing for you but the cold grave."

Arsaber's eyes flared, and he screamed something at his men. They hesitated for a heartbeat and then came for us.

Sigurd knocked a spear blade aside with his shield and swung his sword, shattering scales and biting into a man's ribs. I caught a sword blow on my blade, the clash jarring my arm in its socket, but I lashed out with the long knife, and my enemy leaped back out of reach. At the edges of my vision I saw Penda duck a spear swipe and chop into a man's knee and Floki cross two blades to catch a sword that would have cleaved his head. Yrsa swung a sword at my Greek, but the man was already turning and caught Yrsa's blow on his shield and scythed his blade across Pig-Nose's face in a spatter of blood and skull. I flung myself at the Greek, getting my right arm around his neck and holding on with everything I had, trying to wring the life from him like water from a pelt because I was too close to use a long blade. I unlocked my knees, letting my weight bring him down, and his fear stink clogged my throat as I squeezed him until I heard parts inside him crack like sticks underfoot. I held on, my arms almost bursting with the strain of it, for it is harder than you think to crush a man to death. But the Greek died eventually, piss-soaked and with tears on his cheeks, and I rolled onto the cold stone floor, gasping for breath and cursing because no one had gutted the Greek to spare me the trouble of it all.

My arms and hands were numb, so I flapped them, trying to get the blood back into them, and looked up to see Floki with his long knife at Arsaber's throat.

The soldier who had been guarding Nikephoros threw his spear down and fell to his knees, squawking in Greek, but Bardanes didn't break stride and slashed him to death anyway, which made a mess I would not have wanted to clean up. Then the general carefully pulled the gag from his master's mouth and cut his bonds so that Nikephoros stood there rubbing life back into his hands, and the two of us must have looked like men come inside to a hearth from the freezing cold.

"Fetch the others, Raven," Sigurd said, nodding toward the ruined golden-skinned door and the chamber beyond in which the rest of the Wolfpack waited in their shieldwall for the flames to die and the Greeks to crash against them like an iron wave. Taking a long shield from a dead Greek, I picked my way around corpses, stumbling on legs that suddenly felt dead and as heavy as two sacks of rocks into the huge chamber where so many had died. Gray-black smoke was slung thick as sea fog beneath the great bowl of the roof, and scraps of singed silk floated down like black snow, tainting with bitterness air that was already thick with death's stink. Here and there candelabra still burned, though most of the candles had been thrown into the fire so that the chamber was dim now. Darkness stalked the corners.

"Rolf! Bjarni! We have Arsaber!" I called, vaguely aware that I was standing on the massive picture of a man's face made from thousands of little square stones. It had been hidden before by the bolsters and silks that were now mostly piles of glowing ash before our skjaldborg. Several grim, soot-stained faces turned toward me, the eyes in them the only clean things in all that filth and gore.

"Fall back to the next room and rebuild the shield-wall there," I said to Rolf, whose right eye was a closed, swollen red lump. He nodded, barking orders to the men around him, who grumbled because they knew that by backing off they would be making it easy for the Greeks to flood in. They would have to be quick to get into the emperor's chamber too, for over Rolf's shoulder I saw that the fire had all but gone out. Half-burned corpses crackled and popped, twisted and pulled into grotesque shapes by shrunken tendons and stinking like roasted pigs and molten copper. The Greeks swarmed beyond that threshold, a mass of scaled armor, shields, and bright red helmet plumes below a forest of swaying spears. Perhaps they were awaiting Karbeas's command to attack—if Karbeas was still living—or perhaps despite their hundreds they were reluctant to attack men who had no choice now but to fight to the death. A boar that is surrounded by spears is more likely to rip out a man's guts than is a boar that sees a way out through the thickets, and Bjarni said as much, leaning on a spear, his blood-soaked leg tied above the wound to keep what blood he still had in his body.

"The emperor is safe?" Father Egfrith asked, clutching my shoulder. He reeked of burned hair, and I saw that half of his beard was shriveled and singed.

"Which one?" I asked petulantly, coughing on the putrid sweet scent of burning flesh and looking over at Cynethryth, who was standing behind Asgot and Arnvid. On the blade of her spear was skewered a severed hand, charred so that it looked more like the claw from some nightmare creature. "He's alive," I gnarred at Egfrith. "We've got Arsaber, too. Though I'd wager Floki has cut the bastard's throat by now." The monk's beady eyes blinked with the shock of that, and then he turned and tried to wriggle through the shieldwall, but no one would let him through, and so he ran to the end of the line, spitting Greek across the smoldering dead.

Rolf scowled at me, his swollen, battered eye weeping so that when he rubbed at it, he smeared wet soot across his cheek.

"He's telling those fish-scaled Greek goat humpers that Arsaber is dead and the real emperor is back on his throne," I explained. The Dane hoisted his brows, which I took to mean that he thought there was about as much chance of those plumed warriors believing Egfrith—if they could even understand him—as there was of Bjarni not bleeding to death from that fist-size hole in his leg.

"Back we go then, lads!" Rolf yelled. "Steady now and keep it tight." And with that the skjaldborg edged backward, retreating like the tide and giving up the ground we had fought tooth and nail for.

"Don't be shy, ladies!" Wiglaf taunted the Greeks, whose eyes we could see above their shield rims. "Come and see what we have waiting for you! I am Wiglaf son of Godwine, and I have come to show you how Wessexmen fight!" Those men of Miklagard must have heard the son of Godwine then, because the first of them edged forward into the room, shields raised and heads down as they stepped over dead men—theirs and ours.

"Keep it tight!" Bjarni shouted, dragging his ruined leg across the mosaic floor as the shieldwall moved backward through the dark chamber that had earlier blazed like a sunlit sea, smothered with soft silks and color, but that was now a dingy, stinking, fug-thick place where dead men lay leaking foul juices, reminding the living what lay in store for them.

We were halfway back to the emperor's chamber, our shieldwall bowed to stop the Greeks from getting behind us, by the time there were enough of them through the door to put their shields edge to edge, spears poking through the gaps to make a bristling hedge. Then that hedge parted, and men came forward carrying water skins, which they unstoppered and emptied into the smoldering remains of the fire. Steam hissed up in a thick gray curtain, weaving into the smoke that still swirled below the bowl ceiling and releasing a sweet, putrid smell that made men wince. And because I wasn't locked into the skjaldborg, I turned and loped back into the emperor's chamber, where Sigurd and Floki were hanging Arsaber out of the great wind hole by his feet. Nikephoros was beside them, swathed in purple robes that reached to the floor and hung like a waterfall over his left arm and wearing the stiff gold cloth and the jewels that recently had smothered Arsaber. The emperor was yelling into the warm night, bellowing at the crowds below like a man trying to calm the seething sea.

"Naked as a bairn," Penda said through a grin, which answered the question on my lips as to what Arsaber was left with, for I could only see his bare feet and ankles poking above Sigurd and Floki's two-handed grips, though I could hear him screeching like a snared fox. I moved to one of the other wind holes and looked down, and the hairs bristled on my neck because the vast fountain-strewn, tree-lined courtyard was thronging with Greek soldiers. Flaming torches lit great knots among the thousands, their faces turned up to the Bucoleon and their armor and blades glinting in the dark. The smell of so many men gathered in one place rose on the heated air so that I caught their stink even through the blood and snot crusting in my swollen nose. Leaning farther out, I saw that the armed mass butted right up to the palace's western door, meaning that these men were waiting for their turn to come into the palace and kill us. Our shieldwall beyond the gold-skinned door was like a child's sand wall scraped up on the strand to stop the waves. Penda said our lives were hanging by a cunny hair, but I think a spider's thread was more like it. Yet Nikephoros lived. And he was the emperor of Miklagard.

Like a flea jumping from head to head, the news of the emperor's return spread across the swarming mass, and to Nikephoros's obvious pleasure the Greeks began to cheer. Hearing this, Bardanes nodded to Sigurd, who with Floki hauled the naked traitor back into the room. His body was soft and white and pathetic as a merchant's as he stood there trying to cover his manhood, his oiled beard laced with spittle and his eyes wide with terror. Sigurd shoved him to Bardanes, who grabbed him by his scrawny neck and dragged him stumbling out of that chamber into the massive room beyond. The rest of us hefted shields and followed, joining our sword-brothers in the shieldwall come what might as Bardanes displayed the broken usurper to the imperial soldiers. They were less than three spear lengths from our wall now, which was close enough for us to see the bristles in their horsehair plumes and smell the wine on their breath. Fear sweat dripped from my beard as I gripped my battered sword and waited, listening to Bardanes and hoping that his stream of words would put the flames of this whole thing out.

"Looks to me like some of the bastards know Bardanes," Penda said, eyeballing the enemy wall, a spear gripped and ready to fly. He had lost his helmet in the chaos, and his hair stood up in spikes, which with his blood-smeared face only made the Wessexman look fiercer.

"Then they're bound to want to kill us," I said grimly, for I did not like Bardanes and did not care who knew it.

But it was Nikephoros who put an end to that night's butchery. He strode up behind us, and Sigurd growled at us to split the shieldwall so that the emperor could pass through it, which he did like a sharp knife through tender meat. When the Greeks saw him, there was a gasp and a murmur like the sea. Their eyes bulged, and they dropped to their knees in a great creak and clatter of leather, iron, and steel.

"You'd think they were thralls," Olaf said, shaking his head in disgust. But most of us were grinning, drying blood crumbling from our faces with the stretch of those grins. For the Greeks had their foreheads pressed against the gore-stained stone floor. Curled up like hounds they were, awaiting their master's scourging hand.

And we were alive.

We did not leave the emperor's side for the next few days. Bardanes wanted Nikephoros guarded at all times while he rooted out all those known to have helped Arsaber seize Miklagard's throne, and until he had done that, he would not trust the job to his own people. As Sigurd put it, his mouth tight with sadness, we had proved our loyalty with our blood, and there was no denying that. We had lost so many brothers, men such as Gap-Toothed Ingolf and Yrsa Pig-Nose. Many of the dead were Danes, who for all their ferocity in a fight lacked the skill and discipline of Sigurd's original crew. Big Beiner was among them, his friends having gathered up his gut rope and pushed it back through the gaping slice in his belly so that he could be whole again in Valhöll. Great warriors were gone, and we would never see their faces again. Men such as Bothvar, whose skill with a sword matched his skill with the cook pot, and Aslak, who was one of the best fighters I had ever seen. Men such as Baldred of Wessex, who had once served Ealdorman Ealdred but had become a rider of the waves—a sea wolf. But the brother I would miss the most was Svein the Red, whose loss dragged my soul down like rocks in a fishing net. The giant had been my friend and the bravest man I have ever known. My tears for Svein fell like rain.

With Bram and Svein gone now, the Fellowship felt like a shadow of what it once had been. They had been

with Sigurd from the beginning, and nobody mourned
them more than he. We burned all our dead on heroes'
pyres, though Miklagard was riddled with White
Christ men like a good oak beam squirming with
worms, and those men, priests many of them, came to
sneer and shout and wave their crosses at us, even
braying at Father Egfrith because the monk was standing with the rest of us, staring into the flames. They
dared not come too close, though, for we growled at
them and hurled colorful curses that they believed
were spells, and Asgot threatened them with his sharp
knife. Added to this, Nikephoros had sent us the wood
for the pyres along with imperial soldiers to lug it from
here to there, and so the Jesus men knew not to push
their disapproval too far. To the emperor's credit, he
sent plenty of wood, enough to send the greasy flames
high into the Miklagard night so that our friends'
souls were borne straight to Asgard, for we would not
risk Óðin's Valkyries being unable to find them in that
faraway country.

Those of us who were left were showered with all
manner of things, such as fine cloth, Greek coins, rich
food, and endless jars of red wine, all of which were
like treasure to a Norseman. We stayed in the Bucoleon, which at first put a sour taste in our mouths because of what we had suffered there. But the silks and
finery were all replaced and the blood was scrubbed
from the floors, and by the time the Greeks had finished, it was hard to imagine what had taken place on
those marble stairways and in those vast chambers.
Besides which, all we had to do was peer out of the
south-facing wind holes overlooking the emperor's

harbor and we could see *Serpent*, *Fjord-Elk*, and *Wave-Steed* sitting restfully at anchor on the sparkling blue sea.

But not as restfully as us. We stayed as close to Nikephoros as a scabbard to a sword as he set about gathering the reins of his empire of the east once again. Yet there was no sniff of a threat so far as we could see. Bardanes had seen to that. The general lined the Mese—that wide street running through Miklagard—with more than thirty wooden crosses each twice the height of a man. And on those crosses he nailed those who he thought had been involved with Arsaber's plot to overthrow Nikephoros and his son and coemperor Staurakios. Women were hung up there too, their nakedness for all to see as they wailed and suffered and died, which soured my spit and made me hate Bardanes even more. But it seemed to do the trick, for no one so much as farted in Nikephoros's direction let alone made any move against him, which meant that we spent our days eating and drinking and whoring in the richest city on the face of the earth.

Those days turned into weeks, during which two more men died of wound rot. One of them was Kalf, the Norseman who had survived an arrow in the shoulder in Frankia. This time he was not so lucky, and a gash in his thigh festered in the terrible heat of Miklagard so that he died stinking and sweating and burbling like a stream but making less sense. The other loss was a Dane named Kolfinn who had lost three fingers and half of his left hand where a Greek sword had carved through his shield. Asgot had cleaned and bound the wound, and Kolfinn had not complained, even making a joke about how it could have been worse, for it could have been his drinking hand. But within two weeks his arm was green to the elbow. In three the rot was up to his shoulder, and not even the emperor's physicians with all their skill could save him. So one night he drank enough wine to float a longship, and when he had passed out, his friend Skap cut his throat, and that was that for Kolfinn.

The Greeks saved Bjarni, though, which was worth its own hoard for the joy it gave us all. The Norseman had known the rot would come, especially in that blistering heat, besides which that tourniquet had nearly strangled his leg, as he put it, starving it of blood so that it would be good for nothing anyway other than warning him of impending rain and giving dogs something to sniff at. So Bjarni took the wolf of that by the tail.

"Take it off," he said to Sigurd four days after the fight, sweat gathering on the tight line of his mouth as he lay in the shade of the Bucoleon, watching the imperial dromons come and go. His leg was bound in clean linen, but the flies were buzzing around it. Above us, gulls swirled on the warm breezes, shrieking news of fishing boats casting off from the main harbor.

"I've been waiting for you to ask," Sigurd told him with a hard grin and nod. But Sigurd did not do it; the emperor's physicians did with their wicked-toothed blades and knives sharp enough to cut a fart in half. They burned his ruined leg and gave him a wooden one carved from some dark, glossy wood, and into the thigh of it Bjarni etched some runes that we thought must be some powerful seidr, perhaps commemorating the battle in which he had lost the original limb. So Bjarni lived, stumping around on his new leg and grumbling that it itched like arse worms, though we did not see how it could, being dead wood.

And Emperors Nikephoros and Staurakios made us rich beyond imagining.

When I think of Miklagard, I see gold. My memory chest burns my mind's eye with the blaze of it. Gold roofs, gold statues and doors and tapestries. Gold mosaics and coins and the gold sun glaring down, reflecting off the Marmara Sea and the whitewashed houses and palaces and domes. The emperors rewarded Sigurd, and our jarl rewarded us, and no ring-giver was ever more generous. But Sigurd knew that the oath he had bound us all with had exacted a heavy price. The Fellowship's heart had been ripped out with the deaths of Bjorn, Halldor, Bram Bear, and Bothvar. Of Gap-Toothed Ingolf, Yrsa Pig-Nose, Svein the Red, and Aslak. Men like those could not be carved again from Greek wood, and perhaps Sigurd hoped that the glint of coin would distract us from that hard loss. And yet we had such a story to tell and the gold to pay the skalds to tell it. They would weave the saga of it around the hearth fires of the north, and folk would drink it in, jealous of our fame but eager to hear more. We had come so far along the sea road that men began to say they could no longer remember the faces of their wives and children back home. I was like that with old Ealhstan, who had fostered me. I thought I remembered enough to picture him in my mind until I actually tried, at which point it was like looking at something beneath the surface of the sea. But no one ever found a hoard beneath his own bed, as Olaf put it. We had come far, lost much, gotten rich. And maybe that would have been the end of it if the gods had left us alone to enjoy our hard-won spoils.

The other color that fills my head when I think of the Great City is black. Perhaps because black is the color of blight and decay, of rot and the eventual end of all things. Or maybe it is the blackness of deepest rage, when your mind sinks to the coldest depths and you are no longer in control of yourself.

For the gods had not finished with us yet.

chapter
TWENTY-SEVEN

THAT SUMMER in Miklagard stretched out like one of the bright tapestries lining the feasting hall of the great palace. As long as we gave Nikephoros our word that we would cause no trouble, we were free to roam the city as we pleased, and it soon became clear that some of the men were sinking roots into that hard ground. We were rich and tall and for the most part golden-haired, which made us stand out in Miklagard. Even being viewed by the locals as barbarians only lent a sharp edge to our fame luster, so that often you could not spend your coin even if you wanted to. Greeks would buy us drinks and ply us with food and whatever goods they dealt in, such as leather and soap, spices, fruits, and salted fish, all given freely with thanks for restoring God's regent on earth to his rightful throne. As you can guess, this went down well with men who usually were pulling the oar, being lashed by storms, or standing in the shieldwall, so that in no time at all everyone had employed servants—slaves were not permitted in Miklagard—who saw to our every pleasure so that no Norseman, Dane, or Englishman had to lift a finger if he'd rather sit around on his arse all day drinking wine and farting strange spices.

We spent less time together too. Ten of us always had to remain fully brynja'd and armed, ready to guard Nikephoros or Staurakios when they were about on imperial business, but that duty fell to a different ten each day, so that the rest were always off here or there looking for ways to lighten their sea chests or their balls, spending those pretty gold coins on even prettier women but also on weapons, silly Greek hats, or even bright yellow or red birds that they kept in cages and claimed could talk, though I never heard one say a single word that made sense. Some even began wearing Greek robes, claiming they were better than wool in that heat, which was probably true, but we gave those men such a tongue-lashing when we saw them that most were soon sweating and sulking in breeks and tunics again.

No one talked of going home, for we were caught up in the excited wonder of Miklagard like a dog chasing its own tail.

And all the while a storm was brewing that would soon have me in its maw.

I had barely laid eyes on Cynethryth for weeks, and normally I would have been happy enough about that, for we had grown so far apart that I doubted even Bifröst the Rainbow-Bridge could have spanned the chasm between us. Since Frankia and probably before that, Cynethryth had made it clear that she wanted nothing from me, and at first the twist of that knife had ripped out my guts, leaving me empty. I was past the worst of it by now, though, sometimes even thinking I was better off without the girl, for she was a warped thing these days, moon-mad whispered some, on talking terms with the gods said others. For the most part, then, I could live well enough, and there was nowhere like Miklagard to keep a man's mind off bitter memories.

But this particular day I was drunk. More drunk than usual thanks to a foolish wager between me and Penda over who could drink the most Greek wine and still walk along a spear stave from end to end without his feet touching the ground. I was drunk, and that Cynethryth knife was twisting in my guts again.

I lost the wager, which probably didn't help, though in truth it would not have made a difference. It was time to find Cynethryth, to face that gut-piercing knife, to ask her why she seemed to have forgotten the times we had lain together between *Serpent*'s ribs, giving each other warmth against those cold, bleak, soaking nights. Had she ever loved me? Or was it true, as I suspected, that she had given herself to me on the Frankish shore only so that she would have power over me when she needed it to spare her father, the worm Ealdred. For when a woman like Cynethryth gives herself to you, you are trapped in a web even stronger than an oath to a jarl or sword-brother. For such a woman you will do anything: spit in the gods' eyes, betray your friends, doom yourself.

Later I would blame myself. But after that I would begin to wonder what god had had his hand in the stir of it all, for surely it was too much coincidence that I should choose that day to addle my brain and go to find Cynethryth.

Nikephoros had given Cynethryth her own bedchamber on the east side of the Bucoleon, saying that it was not right and furthermore an offense against God for a woman to live like a man, as he had seen Cynethryth do. Sigurd had reminded the emperor that she no longer appeared to be in thrall to his nailed god, and so why should she care what offended him? The White Christ had let Cynethryth slip through his fingers, he said, to which Olaf had added, grinning, "That's what happens when you have holes in your hands."

But Nikephoros was insistent, claiming that a woman must preserve her modesty if nothing else, and I suspected that he was just as enthralled and intrigued by Cynethryth as he was disgusted by her. For even now, when she was skin and bone and bitter-looking, Cynethryth was still beautiful, the kind of stray that Christians, for better or worse, think they can save.

I did not know where this bedchamber was and must have worn down the soles of my fine leather boots chafing along those endless pillared, sconce-lit passageways before I eventually asked a servant the way. He had been half disappearing down another hallway, cumbered by a pile of clean linens, when I called out, but the greasy toad kept on walking, which got my hackles up, and so I yelled savagely, the noise recalling the madness of the fight that had swirled through that place, taking with it so many friends.

The little Greek stopped and turned, and at first I read his expression as one of fear, though I soon realized it was irritation. Nikephoros loved us. And why shouldn't he? We had put his imperial arse back on his fancy throne. But many of the Greeks, especially the palace hounds and the silk-swathed, floor-kissing courtiers, tolerated us at best. To them we were barbarians, savage outlanders, heathens barely better than beasts. I had no problem with that. To me they were soft, oiled, perfumed nithings, good for nothing, though Bjarni had said he might take one home to Norway to keep in his privy to improve the smell.

Of course this servant could not understand what I was asking him—the wine probably had twisted even my Norse out of shape—but he saw I was a young man and drunk and it was late into the night for me to be prowling the Bucoleon, and so he guessed there must be a woman involved.

He sighed, shook his head, carefully placed the linens on the floor, and walked off. So I followed him.

That place was like a fox's den, full of twists and turns. And foxes. But I knew the Greek had brought me to the right place even before we turned the last corner and saw the door, which was painted with a woman and child I now knew must be the Christ god and his mother. It was the smell that told me we had come to the right place and the same smell that struck me like a kick to the stomach.

"Now go," I said to the Greek, nodding back down the darkened hallway. He shrugged, pursed his lips, and slithered away, leaving me standing before that door like a man who is not sure he wants to know what waits on the other side. Maybe if I had not been full of wine, I would have knocked. Instead I took a breath that was acrid with the herb stink coming from that room and turned the iron ring. The door opened without a sound, and, saying nothing and swallowing the cough that wanted to get out, I walked into a room whose walls were paneled with the same rich dark wood that had made Bjarni's new leg. The air was alive, thick with smoke through which I beat a path with a flat hand, rounding a great swath of shimmering cloth that hung from gold hooks in the white-washed stone ceiling. What I saw then has stayed with me all the years of my life. I could have skewered out my eyes, rinsed them in salt water, and held them over a flame, and still they would be stained with the image.

Cynethryth lay on a bed, naked but for a scattering of storks' wings whose white feathers were still bloody from the dismemberment. She looked to be asleep, dead even, but Asgot was very much alive. The godi was on his knees at the foot of the bed, and his head snapped up to me, hair bones rattling, eyes ablaze with fury. But he did not know true fury.

I flew at him, and he was only half standing when I hit him, throwing him back against the far wall with the force to break bones. He shrieked like some wild creature, and I rammed a fist into his stomach so that he folded like worn cloth, but then his shriek was answered by a low, bowel-melting snarl, and my blood turned to ice as I pivoted to see Sköll crouched, hackles raised and fur bristling, its hate-filled eyes glaring at me. It leaped before I could draw my sword, but I got my right forearm up and the beast clamped its jaws around it so that for a heartbeat that great snarling bulk was hanging from my arm. Then we fell, and I twisted to my right, driving my left shoulder into its belly, punching the wind from it, so that it yelped and released me. But in a blink it slewed out from under me and went for my arm again, biting viciously and shaking its head wildly, and I thought my arm must be ripped off. Half on my knees, I clubbed my fist into its head, missing as often as I struck it because of the shaking, but the beast would not let go, and I felt the skin on my arm burst and its teeth sink into my flesh, so that I screamed with the agony of it. I was aware of Asgot cackling madly and of someone else in the room who was not Cynethryth, but mostly I was blind and deaf with terror and pain, my whole world made of this yellow-eyed stinking beast and its bone-crushing jaws.

I rammed my head against its maw again and again, knocking myself half unconscious because the wolf's skull was granite hard, and Sköll flung me from side to side, and I thought I would die then. But I would not die on my knees, and so I bellowed in pain and fury and clawed at one of those yellow eyes until I felt the wetness of it and then ripped into it, getting two fingers into the bone socket, and the beast growled in pain, so I dug deeper still. Then I pulled my hand free in a spray of gore and went for my long knife, my fingers closing on the familiar grip and snatching it from the sheath. I thumped the blade into Sköll's belly and twisted it so that it came free, and I thrust it again and again, and the beast yelped, its hot blood drenching my hand and arm.

It let go of my arm at last, and its claws skittered across the stone floor as its legs buckled. But I was up again and facing Asgot, who had drawn his own knife, the blade that had killed so many men and beasts over the years. It would not have me.

"I am your godi," he spit. "Touch me and you doom yourself, fool."

"A fair price for killing you," I said, aware of blood running down my right arm beneath the tunic. And that was when I saw Father Egfrith through the smoke cloud. He was up against the wall, arms stretched out like every picture of the nailed god I had seen, but in the place of nails were knives, slender ones, that had been driven through the monk's hands deep into the wood so that he hung there. His legs were bent and to one side, feet up on a bloodstained silk-cushioned footstool so that he could not use those legs to lever himself off the wall, and there he hung, watching, his face smeared with snot and blood. How Asgot had been able to do that to the monk by himself I could not imagine, but Asgot was as dangerous as fire in thatch, and that was why I hesitated for a heartbeat. Then I flew at him, but he was quick, too quick for an old man, and he jumped aside, slashing his knife across my left arm, opening the flesh. I turned, scything my knife at his face but missing, and his blade streaked again, cutting my wrist. He was a wild thing, frothing from a grin as he came at me, lashing madly, and I threw out a hand, somehow catching his bony wrist in my fist, and now I grinned because I was young and strong and burned with hatred for the poisonous old crow. His eyes flared as I squeezed his wrist, crushing it so that the knife fell from his hand. Then I hauled him forward and rammed my forehead into his face, the *crack* of it loud in that smoky place. Ancient blood bubbled from the godi's ruined nose and mouth. Then I brought my blade up into his guts, and the air burst from his mouth so that I smelled its foulness. I smelled Cynethryth on him, too, and I wanted to rip the skin from his flesh for that. Instead I yanked the knife free and grabbed his lank, bone-tied hair, pulling his head back so that he could not help looking into my eyes. His blood was spattering my boots and the stone floor.

"You are a dead man, Asgot," I spit. "I am going to piss on your eyes and shit on your heart."

"You are cursed, boy," he hissed through frothing blood, his face turning white as ash. I felt him trembling from cold as the lifeblood left him.

"I am your death, old man," I said, throwing him back against the wall, down which he slid, grasping at the terrible wound in his belly. He sat slumped for a long moment just staring at me. Then he pointed at me with one bloody clawed hand, and at first I thought he was working some foul seidr on me, but then I realized that was not it. He wanted my blade, for without one he might not enter Ódin's hall of the slain, and that thought was more terrifying than death itself to the godi.

I bared my teeth at him, which was enough of an answer, and he seemed to shudder, his eyes growing heavy. Then I looked at Cynethryth, who was stirring as the effects of the potions Asgot had plied her with began to wear off, and I looked at Egfrith, whose face was a twist of agony. I walked over to the godi, kneeling by him, grimacing against his stink.

"Take it," I said, grabbing his hand and folding the cold fingers around the knife's grip. He might have smiled at that; it was hard to tell. "Wait for me in the All-Father's hall, godi," I said. "I have not finished with you yet." Then I picked up his knife, went back to him, and plunged the blade into his windpipe, leaving it there among blood bubbles as Asgot's last breath escaped in a soft gush.

I felt sick from the smoke and my savaged arm but mostly from the slice Asgot had given my left arm. I could see the bone gleaming in that wound, and I cursed the godi's blade for being so sharp. I'd always healed well and thanked Eir the healing goddess for

it, but this time I feared the wound rot like never before, though I said nothing as I went to Egfrith, hoping he was alive. He was trembling with the red agony
of it, so I ripped a wad of cloth from my cloak and
stuffed it in his mouth for him to bite down on. Then
he glared at me with those pain-filled eyes and, after
several heartbeats, nodded sharply, which was the
sign. But try as I might, I could not lift my right arm,
and I knew that the bone was broken, crushed by
that flea-ridden wolf that now lay in its own piss and
pooling blood. At least I could raise my left arm—
though the agony was blurring my sight—managing
to grip the knife piercing Egfrith's right hand and was
about to pull it free when Cynethryth appeared beside me in an acrid billow of herb stink. She was
naked and did not even look at me as she reached up,
taking hold with both hands of the knife pinning the
monk's other hand.

Together we yanked the knives free, and Egfrith
mewed pitifully as I took his weight on my right
shoulder.

Cynethryth was staring at Asgot's corpse, which
was slumped in the corner, still clutching my long
knife. *Ódin's death maidens must be here soon,* I
thought, scowling at the sight of him.

"I enjoyed killing him," I spit at Cynethryth. She
looked at me, her eyes dull as old ice. Then I left her
standing there naked, her skin white as marble, her
breasts laced with storks' blood above a rib cage
straining against the skin. And I carried Egfrith away.

I found the same Greek servant who had shown me to
Cynethryth's bedchamber, and when he saw Father

Egfrith, he was all arms and gasps and led me to another room, barking at another servant to fetch who knew what. But he wanted the other man to be quick about it, for the Greeks knew that Father Egfrith was a servant of the White Christ and a man of learning, for all that he looked like one of us these days, only scrawnier. The next thing I knew, the room was buzzing with frowning, slick-bearded physicians who pawed over the monk, shaking their heads and mostly ignoring me as I sat bleeding into a plump, ornate couch, the room and everyone in it fading like last night's dream.

The next thing I knew, I was lying in a bed of crisp linen sheets, the sea breeze coming through a small wind hole by my head, bringing the smell of the sea with it. The sheets were bloodstained, at which I managed a grim smile, wondering what the little Greek servant would think about that. Then my guts clenched, and I shoved myself up on one arm and spewed into the pail that suddenly appeared in front of my face. I thought my jaw would break with the force of it.

"That's it, lad; get it all out." I spied Egfrith from the corner of my eye. He was grinning. "The good Lord knows what they've been pouring into you, but it seems to be working."

"Tastes like I've eaten a rotten dog's balls," I gnarred, wiping my mouth with the sheets, which made the monk grimace. It was a small, simple room high up in the Bucoleon with a view of the harbor. My clothes were draped over an old chair at the foot of the bed. They had been washed by the look of them.

"Still," he said, "you're alive."

I sniffed at the dressings, and Egfrith must have

seen the fear in my eyes then, for he said: "There's no decay, which is verging on miraculous, but these Greeks are more skilled than I could have imagined. The wounds look clean, lad. From what I have seen."

I nodded, feeling the sweat bead on my brow. "And you?"

Egfrith held up his hands, the palms of which were linen-bound. Only a small spot of blood stained the middle of the left binding.

"I am, praise be to God, fit and well," he said, "though don't ask me to row any time soon."

"You look ugly as a cat's arse," I told him, at which the monk gingerly raised his exposed finger ends to the scabbed gouges in his face—done by Asgot's fingernails, I supposed.

"Beauty is a hollow chalice, Raven," he said with a chastising look, "from which you will never have to drink." He added that last with a weasel smile. Then he scowled as I waved the bucket away. There's nothing like the smell of vomit to make you vomit. "You could have come along sooner," he said. "I had to watch that heathen devil working his foul spells on Cynethryth. Poor lost soul." He shook his head at the memory. "That was worse than the knives," he said, staring at his swathed hands, and I believed him.

"I only came at all because I was drunk as a rat in a barrel of mead and lost a wager against Penda over who could walk along a spear," I groused, "and look what I got out of it."

He cocked one furry eyebrow and told me that the workings of the Lord truly were curious, which I ignored, instead asking him what the others made of what had happened. I had killed our godi, and that thought lay heavy as rocks in my vomit-racked guts.

He frowned. "That hit them hard as a storm," he said. "And some would not believe Asgot was dead. Not until they saw his corpse with their own eyes, and even then they seemed to be waiting for him to rise again." He scowled. "They burned him like the others. Two days ago."

"A hero's pyre for that rancid old dog!" I spit, thinking I would spew again.

Egfrith leaned closer. "You are in deep water, Raven," he said in a low voice. "Some were for tearing your arms and legs off! They wanted to finish what that beast had started." He shook his head. "Lord, but they're quick to temper. You Northmen are slaves to your own base instincts."

"So what stopped them?" I asked.

"Black Floki," he said, as surprised as I was.

"What about Sigurd?" I muttered. "What does he think?"

"With Sigurd who knows? Though it seemed to me that he is with the rest on it. In their eyes you have done a very dark thing. They talk of curses and spells and all sorts of heathen nonsense." Then he glared at me, his eyes briefly reflecting the terror I had seen in them when he had been riveted to the wall like his nailed god to the cross. "I should not say it, but I will. I am glad you killed that man." He made the sign of the cross over his chest. "He had Satan's wickedness in him. He was twisted."

"It means nothing what you think, monk," I said. "You are not the one who wants to tear off my arms and legs."

I stayed in that room for another three days, letting the Greek physicians feed me, change my dressings, and tip their potions down my throat, for I did not relish the thought of facing the others. I had killed their godi and knew they would not know what to make of that, for the godi spoke to the Aesir for all of us, and without him how would we know how we stood in Óðin's one eye or in Thór's or Njörd's? The men would fear that we were like a ship without its rudder now, drifting where the wind and tides took us, unable to read the threads of our wyrds. But what was done was done, and I would have to face them eventually. I would have to face my jarl.

chapter
TWENTY-EIGHT

IT WAS Bjarni who came for me, stumping in on his rune-carved leg, his face taut as a sailcloth in the wind.

"There's to be a ting," he said, scratching his beard awkwardly. "Sigurd has called it."

"When?" I asked, swallowing drily and reaching for the watered wine on the table by my bed, hoping Bjarni could not see the dread that was rising like sap in my bones.

"Tonight," he said, then shrugged. "There's been a lot of growling."

"Growling about what?" I asked, knowing full well what. Bjarni drew his brows like little bows, which showed what he thought of my question.

"Asgot has been around since Yggdrasil was short enough for you to piss on its top branches," he said. "The old goat's prick was braiding his beard when Thór was getting his arse switched for making the girls cry." Bjarni shook his head. "He was our godi, Raven."

"He was a toad-licking old cunny," I said, looking out of the wind hole at the harbor, which bristled with ships of every kind, and letting a wall of silence build between us.

"How is it?" Bjarni asked eventually. I looked up, and he nodded at my right arm, which was slung across my chest.

"The bone broke," I said, twitching my shoulder because I could not move the forearm at all. "But the Greeks say it will weave itself whole again." I smiled weakly. "That wolf had an appetite like Svein." But those words were poorly chosen in light of Asgot's death now after so many others, and Bjarni managed only a slight twist of the lips. The original Fellowship was as thin as gruel these days.

Then the door creaked open, and the old Greek who tended me most often walked in, frowning when he saw Bjarni so that his face looked like ancient leather. His beard was long and gray, and not a hair of it was out of place as he drifted over to check the dressings on my left shoulder, ignoring Bjarni completely.

"Tonight, then," the Norseman said. "At the ships." I nodded, and he looked around the simple chamber as he lifted the wooden leg with two hands, turning it around to face the door as he had not yet gotten the knack of moving the remaining stump with the wood attached. "You can't hide in here forever," he said. He was right, but I said nothing, waiting until he got to the door before I said his name. He stopped but did not turn around.

"How is your shoulder these days?" I asked. Once— it seemed like a hundred years ago now—I had shot a hunting arrow into Bjarni's shoulder. I had been living in Abbotsend, and he had been my enemy then. Afterward, we had become friends. I did not know what we were now.

"It aches when there's damp in the air," he said. "But wounds are good for reminding a raiding man where he has been. They are good spice for saga-tales, too." I could not see his face, but I heard the smile on it then. "I look forward to hearing you telling graybeards and young'uns of the giant wolf that ate you alive then spit you back out," he said. Then he stumped out of the door and was gone, leaving me with the Greek, who tutted when he saw that I had not eaten any of the sour, face-twisting fruit he had put in a bowl by my bed.

And I felt one less stone in my gut, because Bjarni was still my friend.

It felt good to fill my nose with *Serpent*'s scent again: her seasoned timbers and the pine resin between her strakes, the slick ballast stones in her bilge and the coarse tang of her great woolen sail tightly furled and waiting patiently. But though there was comfort in it, there was no joy, nor would there be until I knew how I stood within the Fellowship. Everyone had gathered, it seemed, apart from Cynethryth, which had been some feat what with men spreading themselves across Miklagard like bees over a great swath of summer meadow. Now they waited on the quayside, some looking out across the harbor, others looking west across Miklagard, watching the sun slip behind the domes and whitewashed houses cluttering the city's hills. All eyes turned to me now, though, and the trickling brook burble of men's voices became a river in spate as I strode into the knot of them, jaw clenched so that my teeth ached.

Men with whom I had stood in the shieldwall stood

as though they were in the skjaldborg now, faces hard as granite cliffs, fists white knots of knuckle and edge. *This does not look good,* I thought, glancing at Egfrith, who nodded to show that at least he was with me. *It has come to something,* I thought, *when I am thankful to have a weasel White Christ slave on my side.*

"I have called this ting because every man here has a right to put what has happened in his scales and weigh it," Sigurd announced. At least all eyes were on him now. "Raven has broken the oath that binds us all." Those words struck me so hard that I could hardly breathe. But I kept my chin high and glared at them all as though daring them to condemn me. "He has killed a brother," Sigurd said, letting the words sink in like blood across dry earth. In my head I heard words from the oath we had all sworn long ago in Frankia. The oath I had broken by killing another who had spoken it. *If I break this oath, I betray my jarl and my Fellowship and I am a pus-filled nithing and may the All-Father riddle my eyes with maggots though I yet live.*

"Oath breaker," someone growled.

"The lad must be moon-mad, killing a godi!" the Dane called Skap said.

Words rose in my throat, but I kept them behind the wall of my clenched teeth. There was nothing I could say to make the thing weigh less heavily on us all. Besides which, I was not going to beg them to understand why I had killed Asgot, why I would do it again given the choice. So I stood there, letting the anchor rope of it play out as it would, come what might, half knowing it would end up around my neck, throttling me.

"Asgot was my father's godi when he raided in Sjæl-land and Lolland and before that," Sigurd said, "when he burned halls in Borre and Oseberg and fought for King Hjorleif Hjorsson." There were chuckles at that because Hjorsson had earned himself more fame for humping his way around Norway's southern coast than he had for winning any hard fights or silver hoards. "I will not stand here and tell you that I had much liking for Asgot," he went on, "for I often found scant honor in his bloodletting. Asgot's love of the old ways blinded him." There were a few nods at this, especially from some of the original Fellowship, men such as Bjarni, Osk, and Gunnar. "But," Sigurd said, raising a ringed finger, "he was a godi. A man closer to the Aesir than other men. To kill such a man, no matter the reasons, is a dark thing."

"Maybe he has doomed us all, not just himself," Osten suggested, not meeting my eye. I could not blame him for fearing that, though, and maybe it was true.

"A blood price must be paid," Arngrim the Dane said, and men listened to him because he was the closest thing we had to a skald, though those words had little skald weave to them. They were as sharp as ship rivets.

As the only White Christ men other than Egfrith left, Penda, Gytha, and Wiglaf stood to one side try-ing to unravel the knot of it all, for there was no one turning the words into English for them.

"A test," Black Floki said. Men turned to him so that I could see him standing there braiding his black hair into one thick rope that hung down the left side of his face as I had seen on Wends in Rome. "Raven is Ódin-favored," he said simply. "You would have to be a witless fool not to know this."

"Wolf slayer!" Bjarni called, not so much proving Floki's point as sharpening it. Though I knew I had been lucky in that fight, for Sköll had been a bag of bones compared with how he was when Cynethryth had tamed him. Unlike men who called themselves sea wolves, it seemed that real wolves did not like being at sea at all.

"So we test him," Black Floki suggested. "If the Aesir demand their blood price for Asgot, then so be it. But if not, let that be an end to it."

This got ayes all around, for though it appeared that no one was about to gut spear me for killing their godi, they all seemed keen that the gods should have their revenge if they wanted it. Better that, they thought, than for all to be ensnared in my feigr, and who could blame them?

So the next day I was taken aboard *Wave-Steed*, and the only good thing about that was that there was a brisk southerly, which meant at least I was not made to row toward my test, which would have been spit in my eye on top of what was coming.

I had heard of *ord vl*, whereby an accused man is made to walk over red-hot plowshares or carry scalding iron nine paces, after which he is judged innocent or guilty depending on how his wounds heal. The Christians did it often, counting on their God to spare the innocent and condemn the guilty, and what the ting had chosen for me was as like the *ord vl* as to put the terror in me.

We sailed to a small island north of Elaea, and there, by a copse of gnarled olive trees, Sigurd himself and Olaf dug a hole in the dry, sunbaked earth. A man-size hole it was, too, which was lucky for them, seeing as I was to go in it. Floki was there and Rolf and some of the others, and they all stood a little way off, grim-faced and watching me the way an owl watches the long grass from atop a post.

Earlier I had told myself that I would keep a hold on my pride and let them do what they must, my head high and my back spear-straight. When it came to it, I fought like a beard frother, even one-armed managing to knock Olaf on his arse and smash out two of Byrnjolf's rotten teeth, which earned me a split lip. But Bragi the Egg and Skap grappled the fight out of me, and among them all they shoved me into that hole and began to pile the earth back in so that I was choking on the dust and filth as I cursed them all in rage and terror.

"We will come back in three days, Raven," Sigurd announced solemnly as a muttering, bloody-mouthed Byrnjolf stamped the earth down around my face, taking altogether too much pleasure in it, so it seemed to me. I could hardly breathe for the earth pressing against my chest. There was only a finger's length between my chin and the scalding sand, and my arms—one of which was broken anyway—were buried somewhere down by my sides and about as useful as tits on a boar.

"This is the silver you give me . . . for feeding . . . the birds with your enemies," I snarled at Sigurd, fighting for the breath to spit insults. "Hounds are

better treated! You are all whoresons! Wait for me in
the afterlife, you pus-filled horse fuckers!"

"I will not doom the Fellowship for one man," he
said, glancing up at the sun, which was in the west
now, beginning its slide toward the world's lip. "Not
even for you, Raven, whom I have treated as a son." He
shook his head sadly. "If our gods are with us here . . .
if they can see so far, they will decide your wyrd."

Olaf worried at his bird's nest beard and scratched
his tanned cheek below the white creases he had gained
around his eyes from squinting against the southern
sun. There were tears of frustration in my eyes as the
men murmured and nodded at their work and made to
leave me there alone on that deserted place beneath the
blazing hot sun.

"Uncle!" I yelled, tasting the sweat on my lips.
"Don't leave me here! Uncle! You arse maggots!" But
they did not even look back and disappeared through
the trees and were gone, and I closed my eyes against
the glare, even then seeing the red threads blooming
bright inside my eyelids.

I was alone, left to whatever fate the gods, who are
spiteful and capricious, chose for me. And yet even if
the gods wanted me alive, because they love to torment
us and I was young enough still to have a hundred
threads of anguish braided into my wyrd, how could
they keep me alive? Four days and three nights in that
heat without a slurp of water, without shade or food
and left to whatever creatures came sniffing by in the
dark. Even a crow could dig the eyes out of my head,
and I could do nothing about it.

Now that the others were gone, the fury was melting

in my chest, turning into ice-cold fear. This was no way to die. I would rather turn green with the wound rot and have Penda cut my throat than be buried and left for the worms and thirsting to death. I was scared enough to piss myself and feel no shame for it.

Because I was a dead man.

chapter
TWENTY-NINE

B LACK-HEADED GULLS came first, a noisy swirl of them trying to work up the courage to land and get their beaks in me. The first to dare sidled up to my face, mistrust and greed swimming in its beady red-rimmed eye as its friends circled above, laughing with the thrill of it all. I yelled, sending the bird shrieking into the purple bruise of dusk, then cursed because I knew that there were other creatures that came out at night and could not be scared off so easily.

For a while I tried to move, hoping that the slight-est shift in the packed earth would enable me to eke out more room to squirm. But the only things I could move were my toes, and that only made it worse be-cause it made every other limb and muscle scream with frustration and resentment. Perhaps it was the weight of earth on my chest and the painfully shall-low breaths that made me drift in and out of sleep, but sometime later I woke as if I had been stabbed, my mind flailing to catch the memory of what had happened to me. The terror was a beast, and my soul was in its jaws, being shaken viciously. Yet my body was as still as a corpse in its coffin.

Night had fallen, and there was no moon. Insects were *chirrup*ing in the breeze-stirred grass, and I could hear the sea lapping at the shore in long, lonely sighs. Something was crawling up my face, and I tried to twist my mouth and blow it off me, but whatever the creature was, it had enough legs to cling on, and so I tried to put it from my mind, knowing that it was the least of my problems.

My ears were straining at every sound: the *snap* of a twig in the olive grove, a *rustle* in the nearby gorse. But it was not my ears that warned me I was no longer alone. Somehow I just knew. It was a prickle in my blood, a cold wind scuttling up the back of my neck. I held my breath, desperate to sift through the night sounds, to discover where this other living thing was. Then my heart thumped in my chest hard enough to hurt, because whatever it was was behind me. Again I fought with every sinew, hoping that by some miracle I could break out of that tomb if not by brute strength then by strength of will. But it was no use, and I blinked the cold sweat from my eyes and waited. Then I smelled it. Wolf. It was pungent and unmistakable, and if anyone should know the smell of a wolf, it was me. I clenched my eyes shut and held my breath, waiting for the teeth to rip into my face, for the beast to chew the flesh from my skull. I would be eaten alive. That was the wyrd those bitches the Norns had spun for me.

But the bite did not come, and slowly I half opened my eyes. Teeth glinted in the dark, but the eyes were not a wolf's eyes. Even by the dim light of the stars I could see that. They were green. Beautiful.

"Cynethryth," I rasped like a sword across a scabbard's throat.

She was crouched, head cocked to one side, and staring at me as though she had never seen a man buried up to his neck in the earth before. Though if anyone should have been staring, it was me, for she had a wolf's pelt draped over her back, the beast's face, jaws and all, resting on her head, its silver hair ruffling in the night breeze. It was Sköll or, rather, what was left of it. Even dead I did not like it being near me.

I noticed Asgot's knife in Cynethryth's hand, and I grimaced at the sight of that blood-hungry thing, because I thought she had come to avenge the godi.

"Better to die by a blade than be pecked to death by gulls," I said through a snarl that matched Sköll's.

"I have not come to kill you, Raven," she said, the tug of a smile at the corner of her mouth. "I have come to make sure you live." She pursed her lips. "If that is what the gods want."

"They do want it," I gnarred, "so get me out of this fucking hole." But Cynethryth shook her head at that.

"You must stay buried," she said, "but I do have food and water for you, and I will come back." Fear flooded through me like the sea through a torn hull.

"Get me out, Cynethryth!" Again she shook her head. "How did you get here?" I asked. I could see no one else, but then again, I couldn't see much of anything.

"A fisherman brought me. He's waiting beyond those trees. Sigurd paid him."

"Sigurd?" My mind was knotting itself like eels in a barrel.

"I cannot stay long," she hissed. "The others will suspect something."

"Fuck the others!" I bawled. "Those whoresons put me in this hole and left me to rot!"

"Listen to me, Raven," she seethed, and there was a cold edge to her voice that made me hold my tongue as still as the rest of me. "Sigurd sent me to help you. He had to do this," she said, pointing the blade at the stamped earth around my head. "For the sake of the Fellowship he had to do something. You killed our godi."

"I remember when you followed the White Christ," I growled, unable to resist. She ignored that.

"Your jarl told me to keep you alive if I could. Olaf was in on it, too. And some of the others, I think."

"Black Floki?" She nodded, plunging Asgot's knife into the earth by my mouth. When she had made a shallow hole, she unslung a water skin from a strap across her shoulder and laid it down in front of my mouth, making a ridge on which she rested the neck.

"Drink," she said. I got my dry lips around the neck and sucked, and the cold water flooded my mouth. "Good," she said. "Now eat." She fed me cheese and cured meat, and I chewed fast, biting off more before I had swallowed because I knew Cynethryth would leave me soon. Then she pulled a ridiculous-looking Greek hat from her belt and put it on my head. "This will keep the sun off you," she said. "I will try to come back tomorrow night. If I can."

"You could dig me out, Cynethryth," I barked through a mouthful of food.

She cocked her head to one side again in a gesture that had too much wolf about it to like.

"How will we know what the gods want, then?" she asked. Then she stood. "I will be back tomorrow night. Stay alive until then, Raven."

"Sigurd sent you?" I asked, desperate to cling to that

floating timber but hardly daring to believe. I did not
want her to go.

"Who else would he send?" she asked. "Who else
can interfere with what the gods are weaving? You
killed his godi," she accused, a finger stabbing blame
at me. There were two black holes where Sköll's eyes
once were. "So tell me, Raven; who else would Sigurd
send but his völva?" she said, which was an arrow
into my thumping heart. That explained the wolf pelt
and rituals, for witches are known to dress in skins
or wear blue, the color of death.

"You are Sigurd's völva?" I almost choked on the
word.

"Stay alive, Raven. Your jarl needs you."

And with that she loped off into the darkness, into
the trees at the edge of my vision. And was gone.

chapter
Thirty

I SLEPT IN that hole, albeit fitfully. What else was there to do? I slept and I dreamed of Cynethryth, but in my dreams she was golden-haired and pale-skinned and still followed the White Christ. Perhaps she loved me in my dreams but perhaps not. It did not matter, though, for in the faint, confused spin of those dreams, we were together and she was not a völva. Dreams are cruel like that. They give you glimpses of how things might have been, filling your soul with a strange and pure joy only to rip it all away too soon. It is like losing a silver hoard you have fought hard for. Only worse.

Much of the night I spent awake and in pain. My right forearm, which Sköll's jaws had broken, had been slung across my chest when they buried me, and now it ached terribly under the weight of all that earth and because there was not enough blood getting into it. But worse was to come. Dawn broke with a damp mist that did not last long enough. The sun climbed above the still-shadowed hills until it was a great golden shield whose blazing fire flooded the sky as far as I could see, filling the world with the heat of a furnace. The wide-brimmed hat that Cynethryth had put on me at least saved my head and face from that searing sun, but the sandy earth around me bounced that heat toward me so that streams of sweat were running through my beard.

I drank sparingly, which I was not used to doing and which was even harder in that heat, careful not to nudge the water skin off the low ridge it rested on because I could not be sure that Cynethryth would return. But she did come back that evening just as she had said she would. The scorching sun had all but boiled the brains in my skull, but the terrible heat was waning when Cynethryth came through the olive trees, appearing like a shadow creature in the half-light, Sköll's forelegs crossed and pinned over her chest.

Again I asked her to dig me out, and again she refused, saying that I deserved to suffer for what I had done to Asgot.

"You would not be our völva if that old sheep's turd was still breathing," I said.

"And you would not be breathing if I did not bring you water," she replied, at which I managed a grim smile. At least we were speaking to each other again.

She cocked one eyebrow beneath Sköll's muzzle. "I had to let Penda in on it," she said. "He drew his sword on Black Floki, demanding to know what had happened to you." She shook her head. "I think the fool would have fought them all, Sigurd included, if I had not whispered the truth of it to him."

Good old Penda, I thought, though I feared what Black Floki would make of being challenged. Floki was not the kind to let a thing like that sail quietly over the horizon.

"Penda gave me this to give to you," she said, putting a skin to my mouth. I drank deeply, and the warm rush of it filled my body so that for a heartbeat I thought I could feel my limbs again, for that skin was bulging with neat wine. "I have brought water too," she said, "but Penda said no man could be expected to stay buried in the ground without a proper drink."

"He's right," I said as Cynethryth began to feed me again. "Bury the crumbs this time," I told her. "I had a beardful of ants all night." She grinned wickedly, stuffing smoked fish and cheese into my mouth, and all too soon she was gone again, leaving me to the night.

Cynethryth came one more time, and when she left, she took with her the skins and my hat—which I had come to love dearly—and left the ground around me looking as it had when they had shoved me into that hole. The next day Sigurd and the others returned to see what had become of me, and some of them seemed surprised to find me alive and said as much, to which I answered that though that might be so, I had rarely felt closer to being dead thanks to them.

Sigurd was all teeth and smile, and Olaf was chuckling, and even Black Floki could not hide the grin in his beard as they swarmed around, looking down at me, which was a humiliation I could have done without.

"Stop grinning, you whoresons, and dig me out!" I snarled, at which Byrnjolf and Skap hoisted brows, clearly amazed that my tongue had not dried up and shriveled like an old man's tarse and balls. "Dig and run, Byrnjolf," I said, "for when I get out, you're going to be on your knees looking for the rest of your stinking fetid teeth."

But even Byrnjolf grinned then because he knew there was no fear of my taking revenge on him. When they had dug the earth away, getting on their hands and knees to pull the last of it away with their hands, I could not climb out. My muscles were cold and dead, so that Sigurd and Olaf had to grab me by the shoulders and drag me out, and then, as I lay helpless as a caught fish, Olaf began to pummel me the way you do to someone who has been caught in a blizzard and is half frozen to death.

"It seems old One Eye does not want to share his mead with you just yet, lad," Olaf said, grinning too much. Not that I could feel the thumps and slaps he was delivering anyway.

"You must be starving, lad," Bragi the Egg said, chewing a hunk of bread but not thinking to offer me any.

"My belly thinks my throat's been cut," I lied. Then Arnvid and Rolf shared a grimace, and together they stepped back, the Dane pinching his nose.

"You stink like a cesspit," Rolf said, which was true enough, for my nose was just about the only part of me that still worked—unfortunately—and I reeked of piss. Shit, too.

"What did you expect, Rolf, you Dane whoreson?" I growled up at him, not even giving them the satisfaction of feeling ashamed for fouling myself. "I've been in that hole for four days. The All-Father whispered to me that he would keep me alive," I said, glancing at Sigurd, "but he flat refused to clean my arse."

Some of them did not know how to take this, and I left that knot for them to pick at, for surely there had been some seidr at work here. How else could I still be alive enough to pay them with insults for sticking me in the ground? A man should die after four days without water. Yet here I was with enough wet in my mouth to call Bragi a bald bairn's backside and Byrnjolf a troll-faced dim-witted stump.

But for all that they seemed glad that I was alive, and as soon as my legs could carry me, I stumbled to the shore and plunged into the surf to wash the filth and the memory of that hole away. Then Black Floki pulled me aboard *Wave-Steed*, and the others rowed her back to the Bucoleon wharf while I sat enjoying the prickling inside my limbs as the blood began to flow again.

"So Cynethryth is our völva now?" I asked Sigurd after those who were around had acknowledged my return with grins and nods and heavy slaps across my back. The sun was high, and we sat in the shade of the palace's south portico, the same one we had stormed those many weeks before, when Svein and Aslak and Bothvar and the rest of them had still been alive.

"The men need someone to tell them the will of the gods," Sigurd said with a shrug.

"And you believe Cynethryth can speak with the gods?" I asked, passing him the wineskin I was drinking from to dull the throbbing pain of my broken arm.

A little way off, Penda was talking with Wiglaf and Gytha, the only Wessexmen besides Egfrith left now. I knew Penda was waiting for me, knew the look on his face too. It was the one he wore when we were in for a long, hard night's drinking.

"The girl has proved to be useful to me," Sigurd

said. "She's been useful to you, too, I think." He almost smiled at that.

"She holds my soul in her hand," I said through a twist of lips. It was a heavy thing to tell my jarl, but somehow it felt better having it out. Like a man being dragged from a hole by his shoulders.

Sigurd nodded. He knew where the winds came from and where they went. He knew me.

"We will have to come up with a scheme, you and I," he said, squinting against the glare of the Marmara Sea, which was, as ever, alive with craft coming and going, filling the emperor's coffers with the gold and silver on which the Great City was built. "The men are getting soft. They are bathing in hot water and wearing Greek clothes." He shook his head. "They don't lift a finger if they can throw a coin at someone else to lift it for them. I am fearful that our wolves will become sheep. Fat ones." He pursed his lips in thought. "We shall let them lighten their sea chests first, though. Men are like ships, Raven; they move more easily when their holds are empty."

"You want to leave Miklagard, lord?" I said, knowing now that he did yet needing to hear it from him. For Miklagard had been the hoard we had sought for so long. He did not answer that, instead smoothing the golden beard at the corners of his mouth as he looked out to sea.

"We are rich, Raven," he said. "Richer than we could have ever hoped to be. We have woven a saga-tale that will warm men's hearts on cold nights for many years to come." He looked at me then, his blue eyes boring into mine like ship's rivets. "Is it enough?" he asked.

And now I did not answer, for I did not need to. I looked at the warrior ring on my arm, the silver ring Sigurd had given me so long ago when I had proved myself in a hard fight. Then I looked out to sea, watching a fat trading vessel wallowing on the merest ripple of wave, her crewmen bellowing at one another like cattle. And I smiled, lips pulling back from my teeth.

It is never enough.

epiLogue

SHALL I go on? I could, you know, for we are still in
the early part of it all. But that seems the proper
place to end it for now, and it has been a long night,
though there is no sign of morning yet. If morning
dares to show its face amid that maelstrom out there.
Are you here, monk? Ah, there you are, skulking in
the gusty corner and filthy reeds, scratching away on
that vellum like a rat worrying an old boot. What are
you writing, anyway? Never mind; I don't want to
know. I couldn't give a fart about it so long as you have
done all I've asked. You'll have the silver I promised,
then you'll go and waste it on prayer books or the
wretched poor who kneel in the filth to your nailed
god. But that's your affair. You must feel like a lamb
out of the fold on a dark night, here in my hall. Yet you
need not fear these men, Father. Most of them would
slice off their own bollocks if you gave them a sword.
Don't you eyeball me, Hallfred, you son of a goat. I've
seen you fall out of a tree and miss the ground! Aye,
monk, they're no Wolfpack, this lot, for all their bristles and growls.

So, where was I? Ah, yes, at the end. Which is also
the beginning really. We few had put the emperor of
the Romans back on his throne. Even to my ears that

sounds like a skald's story stretched too far, and yet that is how I remember it, and I still have some pretty Greek coins to prove it. We were rich. Gods, we were rich. We had a glittering fame hoard too and were known far and wide as hard men. We'd forged a reputation as a war band without equal, but the iron of that reputation had been quenched in the blood of our brothers, whose loss was as keen as a slender blade between the ribs. Bram Bear, Bjorn, Svein the Red, and Aslak, men who had sailed with Sigurd from the beginning, were gone. When the Norns rob you of friends like those, you come to learn the hardest truth of all, a truth that is anchor-heavy and dark as storm clouds. And that is that all the silver and fame you can think of is cold comfort if those who did the most to win it all are not around to boast of it.

If I try, I can still hear Bram now, and Svein too, though their faces are hard to summon and faint as draugar through pelting rain. I hear their laughter. I hear them swearing and chafing and moaning about the food or the mead or the raging sea. And yet they are long gone. They are all gone . . .

Shut the damned door, will you? Before we all get snow in our mead! Ah, boy! Don't just stand there like a post. Come here. Let him through, you drunken whoresons; he's one of my ravens! So what news do you have for me, lad? Here, I won't bite. Closer, so I can hear every word over the fire's roar.

You have done well, boy. You, pass my sword! Arnor, give me my shield. This sword was Sigurd's once and his father's before him. It has never lost its thirst.

So, how many, lad? Ah, that is good. It will take more than one. Even now.

Well, you bloated pig's bladders? Are you going to sit by the fire forever, or would you rather come outside into the freezing dark and watch a wolf kill his prey?

acknowledgments

I FEEL COMPELLED to thank you, dear reader, for coming with me on this incredible journey. While I have been finding my way, yours have been the arms and shoulders pulling the oars. You all have been the best Fellowship an adventurer could hope to sail the sea road with, and it really has been my honor. I always knew I'd write a Viking novel. It's in the blood, literally, and the stories have been weaving themselves in my mind one way or another since I was a young boy. But if you had not climbed aboard for the first tale, *Blood Eye*, there would not have been another saga. Thank you for taking the plunge, not knowing what you would find. That you've stayed with me for the next two journeys I find humbling. I have had so much fun writing these books. It is a joy and a privilege. I like to think they're getting better, too, heading in the right direction, and although the trilogy finishes with *Óðin's Wolves*, I suspect the Norns are spinning still. They have not finished with my crew yet. I sense it like snow in the air, hear it like the rattle of pine trees in a chill north breeze. I hope you come when the war horn sounds.

I'd also like to thank my fellow authors who have accepted me into their brotherhood/sisterhood with such warmth and kindness:

M. C. Scott, Robert Low, Bernard Cornwell, Lesley Downer, Paul Sussman, and Ben Kane. You all inspire me, and I'm glad to know you.

Thanks as ever to my wife, Sally, who is my constant inspiration and who has shared every high and low. To my little Viking girl, Freyja Rose; you are more precious than my poor art can express and have brought untold joy to our lives.

I'd like to thank my publisher, Transworld, for believing in my stories and sharing them with you all. We have a great team behind us, Raven and I, and they know their business like my Vikings know the sea. Thanks to Lynsey for helping get the word out and to my editor, Simon, who took me on with gusto and in whose red pen I now trust. And to Katie Espiner, who began it all for me, what can I say? Thank you feels short measure, but I trust you know what your belief means to me.

So, dear reader, until next we meet. Keep the mails coming; I appreciate every one. We shall journey on together soon enough, though we leave shieldwalls and longships behind. For I hear the distant drum and the clatter of musket balls among a forest of pike staves. It will soon be time to march!